W9-BQI-198

j

Red Velvet Cupcake Murder

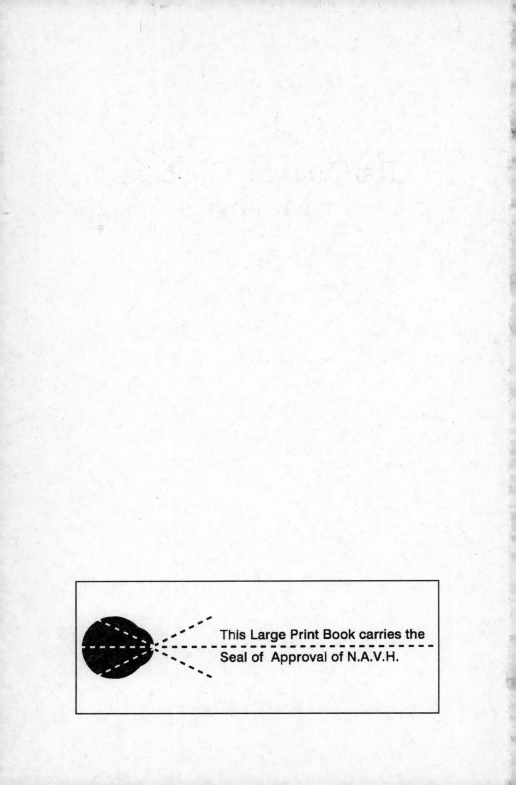

This Large Print Book carries the
Seal of Approval of N.A.V.H.

RED VELVET CUPCAKE MURDER

JOANNE FLUKE

THORNDIKE PRESS
A part of Gale, Cengage Learning

Detroit • New York • San Francisco • New Haven, Conn • Waterville, Maine • London

GALE
CENGAGE Learning®

LIBRARY OF CONGRESS CATALOGING-IN-PUBLICATION DATA

Fluke, Joanne, 1943-
    Red velvet cupcake murder : a Hannah Swensen mystery with recipes / by
Joanne Fluke.
      pages ; cm. — (Thorndike Press large print mystery)
    ISBN-13: 978-1-4104-5604-5 (hardcover)
    ISBN-10: 1-4104-5604-8 (hardcover)
    1. Swensen, Hannah (Fictitious character)—Fiction. 2. Women detectives—
Minnesota—Fiction. 3. Bakers—Fiction. 4. Large type books. I. Title.
PS3556.L685R43 2013
813'.54—dc22   2013000796

Published in 2013 by arrangement with Kensington Books, an imprint
of Kensington Publishing Corp.

Printed in the United States of America
1 2 3 4 5 6 7 17 16 15 14 13

This book is for the Hannah fans who love her almost as much as I do.

ACKNOWLEDGMENTS

Hugs to Ruel and the kids, my chief taste testers. Oodles of love to the grandkids, who think the four food groups are cookies, pies, cakes, and fudge.

Thank you to my friends and neighbors: Mel & Kurt, Lyn & Bill, Lu, Gina, Adrienne, Jay, Bob, Laura Levine & Mark, Danny, Judy Q., Dr. Bob & Sue, Richard & Krista, Mark B., Angelique, Daryl and her staff at Groves Accountancy, Mandy at Faux Library, and everyone at Boston Private Bank.

Thank you to my Minnesota friends: Lois & Neal, Bev & Jim, Lois & Jack, Val, Ruthann, Lowell, Lila & Curt, Dorothy & Sister Sue, Mary & Jim, Tim Hedges, and the waiter at Manny's Steakhouse.

Special thanks to my great Editor-in-Chief

and friend, John Scognamiglio.

Hugs all around to Steve, Laurie, Doug, David, Adam, Peter, Robin, Karen, Vida, Lesleigh, Darla, and all the other folks at Kensington Publishing who keep Hannah sleuthing and baking up a storm.

Thanks to Hiro Kimura, my superb cover artist, who's outdone himself on this cover. Those cupcakes are definitely a work of art!

Thank you to Lou Malcangi at Kensington for designing Hannah's gorgeous covers.

Thanks to John at Placed4Success.com for Hannah's movie and TV spots, and for handling my social media.

Thanks to Kathy Allen for the final testing of Hannah's recipes and taking a bite of banana for the Hannah team.

Hugs to my friend Trudi Nash for going with me on book tours and convincing me that she likes it.

Thank you to JoAnn Hecht for making Hannah's recipes look beautiful and taste yummy at launch parties. Special thanks to Gail DeVri for taking me up to the Seattle Space Needle and pointing out their window-washing cage.

Hugs to Lois Brown, my wonderful food stylist in Phoenix, who bakes almost as much as Hannah does.

Thank you to Dr. Rahhal, Dr. and Cathy Line, Dr. Wallen and Dr. Niemeyer.

Thanks to Jamie Wallace for keeping my Web site, **MurderSheBaked.com** up to date and looking great!

Thank you to Leah and Fern for looking after Hannah on Facebook.

Thanks to the "Double D's" for giving me at least one laugh a day.

Thank you to all the readers who sent family recipes for Hannah to try. Let's hope she doesn't run out of chocolate!

CHAPTER ONE

"You're staring at me again!" Hannah Swensen emerged from the bathroom in a cloud of steam, a towel wrapped around her unruly red curls. She grabbed her favorite robe, shrugged into it quickly, and turned to face the only other occupant of her bedroom. "It's not polite to stare at me when I'm not wearing anything and you're sitting there in your fur coat."

When there was no response to her comment, Hannah sat down on the edge of the bed and picked up the package of panty hose she'd purchased on her way home from The Cookie Jar, her coffee shop and bakery. She wasn't looking forward to putting on her best formal clothing on the hottest, muggiest evening ever recorded in Lake Eden, Minnesota's history. Actually, if she was completely honest, she *never* enjoyed donning formal clothing, even when the weather cooperated. She was much more comfortable in jeans and a billboard T-shirt, or, as a concession to her family, a comfortable pantsuit. She wasn't looking forward to tonight's party either. She'd much rather spend the evening on her living room couch, sipping cold lemonade and watching a movie on television with one of her boyfriends, either Norman Rhodes or Mike Kingston. Unfortunately, her presence tonight was mandatory since The Cookie Jar was catering dessert.

"It's not the heat, it's the humidity," she told her roommate, who was watching her intently. "At least that's what Great-Grandma Elsa always used to say. But she also used to say that nobody in Minnesota needed air-conditioning, that a fan blowing over a block of ice was enough."

This comment was met with widened eyes and what she interpreted as an incredulous look.

"I know," she reassured him. "Great-Grandma Elsa was wrong. Or maybe it was cooler back in her time. I'll turn the air-conditioner on high just as soon as I'm through getting dressed."

Even though the sun would be setting while she was gone, Hannah knew that air-conditioning would be necessary. In some areas of the country, the nights cooled off considerably, but not in central Minnesota. Perhaps the temperature would drop a few degrees as night approached, but that wouldn't provide much relief. The outside walls of her condo had been baking in the sun all day and they would still be warm to the touch long after midnight.

It was hot in her bedroom. She'd opened the window to let in some outside air, but the curtains hung limp and lifeless. There was no breeze and the humidity was still sky high. Hannah could testify to that fact because even though she'd dried off thoroughly after her shower, her skin felt moist and hot again.

"It's not even summer yet," she told him, sighing a bit. "The Summer Solstice isn't until June twentieth this year and today is only the ninth. Technically, it's still spring and this afternoon it was hot enough to fry an egg outside."

It was difficult to tell, but Hannah thought he looked impressed at this news. Earlier in the afternoon, when the mercury had reached its highest peak in the thermometer that hung outside the window in the coffee shop, her customers had decided that it was hot enough to cook an egg on the hood of a car. Hannah's partner, Lisa Herman Beeseman, had volunteered her old black Ford for the test and the egg was duly cracked on the hood. After twelve minutes in the blazing sun, the yolk was still a bit runny, but the white was definitely cooked. Since no one wanted to stand around in the heat any longer to wait for the yolk to solidify, the dozen or so customers who'd trooped out to the parking lot to watch had declared the experiment a success.

Hannah rolled up one leg of the panty hose and glanced over at him again. It seemed to her that he was smiling. "Watch it," she warned. "I don't know if you can laugh or not, but if you even *look* amused, I'll . . . I'll . . ." She paused to choose the most effective threat. "I'll put you on a diet!"

"Rrrowwww!" The twenty-three pound orange and white tomcat, who was perched on top of her dresser, let out a howl.

"That's right. A *diet.* And that means no more salmon-flavored, fish-shaped kitty treats. So if I were you, I'd be very careful!"

Hannah gave a little nod of satisfaction as Moishe turned his head away. She wasn't sure if he'd understood her words, or simply reacted to the tone in her voice, but the desired effect was the same. As she looked down at the rolled sock in her hand, she thought about how much she hated to put on panty hose. The way she saw it, she had two choices. She could stretch out on the bed on her back, raise the panty hose up in the air, and try to thrust both feet into the sock parts at the same time. That required coordination she wasn't sure she possessed. The second method was to sit on the edge of the bed, lean over and place one foot in the sock part, pull the panty hose up part way, and then try to get her other foot in. Either way required perfect balance and the skill of a contortionist.

"Gotta do it," she said, deciding to try the second method. But just as she began to thrust her right foot into the toe of the sock, the doorbell chimed.

There was a ripping noise that sounded very loud to Hannah's ears, and she let out an exasperated expletive that she would never have used around her two nieces. Her toe had poked completely through the sock part and there was no way she could wear these pantyhose now. It was a good thing she'd bought an extra pair.

Hannah reached for her slippers and glanced at the clock on her bedside table. It was only six-fifteen and her sister wasn't due to pick her up until seven. Barring some kind of family emergency or national disaster, there was no way Andrea would be forty-five minutes early.

The doorbell pealed again and Hannah stood up. Salesmen weren't allowed in her condo complex, but sometimes one slipped past the guard at the kiosk. It could also be a neighbor with a problem and now that she was a member of the homeowners' association board, she had a duty to listen. As she hurried down the carpeted hallway with Moishe at her heels, she thought about how interruptions always seemed to come at precisely the wrong time. But was there a right time for interruptions? She really wasn't sure.

Hannah glanced down at her cat as they arrived at the door. She was hoping that Moishe would give her some sort of clue to the identity of the person standing outside the door. "Who is it?" she asked him in a whisper.

If ever a cat could shrug, Moishe did. But there were other signs that told Hannah something about their visitor. His ears weren't back against his head, and he didn't seem agitated in any other way. That meant it couldn't possibly be her mother. Delores Swensen was not Moishe's favorite person and her mother had several pairs of snagged silk stockings to prove it.

"Okay, it's not Mother," she whispered.

"And it can't be Norman. He's my date for the party, but he's working late at the dental clinic and he said he'd meet me there."

Moishe moved closer to the door and the end of his tail began to flick in excitement. It was definitely someone he knew. Hannah was about to unlock the door to see for herself, when she remembered that she should check the peephole.

One glance and Hannah's mouth dropped open. It *was* Andrea! She unlocked the door in a rush and pulled it open. "What's wrong?" she asked the second she saw her sister's worried expression.

"Everything!" Andrea exclaimed, stepping in.

"Bethie's okay, isn't she? And Bill? Tracey?"

"They're all fine. Mother called and told me to get right over here." Andrea shut the door behind her. "I didn't even have time to finish my French braid."

"You can do it in the guest bathroom. The light's good and there's a vanity in there." Hannah stopped speaking as a dire possibility occurred to her. "Mother's all right, isn't she?"

"Mother's fine. She's worried about *you.*"

"Me?"

"Yes. She wanted me to get right over here

and give you the news in person before anyone else told you about it."

"What news?"

"Bad news."

"Is anyone sick? Or injured? Or . . . or dead?" Hannah felt her heart rate soar at the possibility.

"No. Nothing like that. You'd better sit down, Hannah. It's shocking."

"What's shocking?"

"The bad news."

Hannah sat down on the couch. Andrea was so agitated, she wasn't making much sense, but if she sat down it might have a calming effect. "Okay, I'm sitting. Now tell me."

"You've got to promise not to get too upset."

"Why should I get upset? I don't even know what you're talking about yet."

"All right then." Andrea took a deep breath. "*She's* back!"

"Who's back?"

"*Her!* Mother and I just don't know what to do! We never thought we'd see her again, but she's back and she's staying out at the Lake Eden Inn with Roger Dalworth. Sally called to tell Mother. But that's not the worst part of it. Sally told Mother that she's coming to the grand opening with Roger

18

tonight!"

"Sally's coming to the opening with Roger?"

"No! *She's* coming to the opening with Roger. And that's why I had to get right over here to warn you."

"Thanks, but I still don't know who you're talking about." Hannah grabbed her sister's arm and pulled her down on the couch. "Take a deep breath and calm down."

"I can't! Tonight is going to be a nightmare. If I didn't have to go, I wouldn't, but I have to go because I'm selling the condos for Roger. And it'll be even worse for you. I just don't know how we're going to get through it with *her* there!"

"Who's *her*?" Hannah asked, doing her best not to sound exasperated at Andrea's overuse of pronouns.

"Doctor Bev! She's back in town! And Sally thinks she's dead set on revenge!"

CHAPTER TWO

As she stepped inside the beautifully decorated lobby of the recently renovated Albion Hotel, Hannah decided that her struggle to get dressed in her very best outfit might just have been worth it. She'd taken a quick peek at the hotel when it was being remodeled, but she hadn't seen it now that it was finished.

The lobby was absolutely gorgeous. It took up half of the ground floor and it was designed as a recreation and party area for the occupants of the seven luxury condos on the floors above. The old original mahogany floor had been torn up and the best boards saved and refinished. They made up a parquet design around the borders of six massive rose-patterned carpets, each featuring a different variety and color of rose. Wing chairs and couches in matching colors formed five conversational groupings. The sixth carpet held several game tables with matching chairs.

Since she was there early and happened to be the sole occupant of the lobby now that Andrea had gone off to the ladies' room, Hannah walked around to take a look at the lovely rugs. The first rug showcased yellow roses and the rose name, *Midas Touch,* was woven into the border. As she explored the rest of the lobby and read the rose names, Hannah thought about how much fun it must be to name a rose. The purple ones were *Ebb Tide,* the pink were *Tiffany,* the orange blooms were *Tahitian Sunset,* the white were *Polar Star,* and her favorite, the red roses, were called *Sedona.*

As she neared the huge window overlooking the garden on the side of the lobby, she saw that a sizable area had been reserved for special use. Tonight it would be a dance floor with a raised platform that had been set up for a dance band. Chairs, microphones, and a sound system were already in place.

Hannah had just seated herself in a wing chair on the Sedona rose rug to wait for her sister when she saw Lisa beckoning to her from the doorway of the Red Velvet Lounge.

"I need to talk to you, Hannah!" she called out.

"I'll be right there." Hannah got up and

21

walked across the lobby to the bar and grill that occupied the other half of the hotel's ground floor. One glance inside the open doorway and she was suitably impressed. Roger Dalworth, the money man behind converting the old hotel, had done a great job of preserving an early nineteen-hundreds look. The faceted crystal decanters behind the highly polished oak bar glittered in the beams from halogen lights positioned at strategic places in the ceiling. The sepia-tone prints in old-fashioned frames that lined the wood-paneled walls depicted the Albion in its heyday. There were also some scenes of Lake Eden life from that time period, and a player piano complete with a wooden case that held at least three dozen piano rolls. Best of all, the banks of booths that lined the perimeter of the room were upholstered in a shade of red velvet that perfectly matched the color of the red velvet cupcakes that they were serving tonight.

Lisa was arranging cupcakes on the three-tiered revolving display that her husband, Herb, had built for them. When she spotted Hannah, she left her work and rushed over. "I'm glad you're here, Hannah. There's something I've got to tell you!"

"It's okay, Lisa. I know. Andrea told me."

"Thank goodness! I was worried sick you'd run into her before anyone told you. Does Norman know?"

"He should by now. Mother talked to Carrie and Carrie was going to call him."

"This is bad, Hannah. What are you going to *do*?"

"Not a thing until I find out why she's back."

Lisa considered that for a moment. "Okay. I guess that makes sense. But I just know she's going to try to get even with you for exposing the truth about her. There's no other reason for her to come back here. You've got to be careful, Hannah."

"I will be."

"Just don't make the mistake of underestimating her. She might be all sweetness and light tonight, but you can't judge a book by its cover and you know she's bad to the bone. She's dangerous, too. You have to remember that hell hath no fury like a woman scorned."

Hannah gave her first genuine laugh of the evening.

"What's so funny?" Lisa asked.

"You just used three clichés in a row."

Lisa thought about that for a minute. "It's four, unless you didn't count the Shakespeare quote."

23

"It's not a Shakespeare quote."

"It's not?"

"No. It's a misattribution."

"A what?"

"A misquote of something William Congreve wrote in the late seventeenth century. And I did count it."

"Okay, here's another cliché and I don't know who said it first. Leopards don't change their spots overnight."

"I don't know who said it either, but this leopard *did* change her spots. Doctor Bev's got a whole new look. Now she's a blonde. Sally thought she might have had a facelift, too."

"That's drastic."

"That's desperate. I guess she thought she'd better repackage since she was getting so close to the sell-by date."

Lisa's mouth dropped open and then she started to laugh. She laughed long and hard, and then she said, "You've really got a way with words, Hannah. But I'm curious. When did you see Doctor Bev?"

"I didn't. Andrea told me."

"Then Andrea's seen her?"

"No. Sally's the only one who's actually seen her. Doctor Bev's staying out at the Inn with Roger."

"And Sally called to tell you?"

24

"Not exactly. Sally called Mother, and Mother called Andrea, and Andrea told me."

Lisa laughed. "It's good to see that the Lake Eden Gossip Hotline is working. But Doctor Bev didn't actually change her spots, Hannah. All she changed was her appearance. She's still the same scheming, conniving, selfish person inside."

"You can put lipstick on a pig, but it's still a pig?"

"Exactly. It's like you always say, Hannah. The reason they're clichés is that they're true most of the time. And here's another couple for you. Forewarned is forearmed, the best defense is a good offense, and you shouldn't trust her any further than you can throw her."

"I'm ready, Hannah." Andrea stood in the doorway of the Red Velvet Lounge. "I'll show you the condos now, before everybody gets here."

Hannah turned to look at Lisa. "Do you need help arranging the cupcakes?"

Lisa shook her head. "I'm almost through. Don't worry about me, Hannah. Herb's coming back with a couple of chairs and we're going to restock the display when it gets low."

"But I should help you."

25

"No, you shouldn't. Herb has to be here anyway. He's running security here in the lounge."

"Security for what? It's Lake Eden. Nobody's going to steal anything here."

"I know that and you know that, but Roger Dalworth doesn't. He's from Minneapolis and it's different there. Roger hired Herb to cover the whole hotel."

"But how can Herb do that if he's sitting here next to you?"

"He'll be wearing earbuds and he'll be in constant communication with the other members of his security staff. Besides, you said it before. It's Lake Eden. The only thing that might happen is that somebody has one too many glasses of champagne. If that happens, one of Herb's guys will handle the driving and take that person home."

A phrase Lisa had used caught Hannah's attention and she repeated it. *"One of Herb's guys?* How many guys does he have?"

"Six not counting him. They work in pairs. Roger wanted two on the ground floor, two on the second floor, and two outside. The only thing that's not covered is the penthouse and that's because it's not furnished yet."

"Hi, Hannah."

Hannah turned to see Lisa's husband,

26

Herb Beeseman, walking toward them. He was wearing a nice-looking red blazer with the word SECURITY embroidered on the pocket. Below it was some sort of insignia and as Herb came closer, Hannah realized that it was an embroidered cupcake.

"Meet the head of Cupcake Security," Lisa said, smiling at Herb.

Hannah glanced at the cupcake display and then back at Herb's pocket. The embroidery on the pocket was a perfect rendition of the Red Velvet Surprise Cupcakes they'd baked.

"Cupcake Security?" she asked.

"Why not?" Herb gave a little laugh. "It was Lisa's idea. Our motto is, *You gotta be tough with a name like Cupcake.*"

"That's really funny." Hannah laughed. "I'm surprised you didn't use Cream Puff."

"I might have, but it was already taken. Besides, the cupcakes you baked were really pretty and the graphic was more colorful. The guys just love their new blazers."

"Who did you hire?" Hannah asked.

"Four seniors from Jordan High, and two freshmen from the community college. We're also going to run security at football games in the fall. Mayor Bascomb said he might even use us for things like the Winter Carnival and Moonlight Madness later this summer."

"Well . . . good luck with it. I'm sure the boys are glad to get some part-time jobs." Hannah glanced at her sister, who was staring at the display of cupcakes longingly. "What's wrong, Andrea?"

"Nothing's wrong. It's just that your cupcakes look luscious and my stomach's growling. I was so busy distributing fliers for tonight that I didn't have time for lunch."

Lisa plucked a cupcake from the box she'd been using to fill the display and handed it to Andrea. "Taste this and tell us if it's as good as it looks."

"I love red velvet cupcakes!"

"These are Red Velvet *Surprise* Cupcakes," Lisa told her. "Hannah and I put a surprise in the center of every one."

"What kind of surprise?"

Hannah smiled. "If we tell you, it won't be a surprise. Take a big bite. You'll like it, I promise."

Andrea didn't wait for a second invitation. She peeled off the cupcake paper and took a giant bite. "Mmmmm," she said and took another big bite. "Mmmmmm!"

"So what do you think?" Lisa asked her.

Andrea held up her hand for a timeout and popped the rest of the cupcake in her mouth. She chewed, swallowed, and smiled. "It's great! I just love the chocolate and . . . apricot?"

"That's right. They were Hannah's idea. Everybody makes red velvet cupcakes and when we got the order for the party, we wanted to make ours different."

"And better," Andrea added. "I've eaten a lot of red velvet cupcakes and these are the absolute best!"

Hannah glanced down at the price sheet in her hand. The two-bedroom condo she'd just seen was double the money she'd paid for her condo. "Do you really think you can sell these? My complex is a lot cheaper."

"Your complex isn't convenient to downtown Lake Eden. If you lived here, you wouldn't have to drive to work every morning and drive home every night. And your condo doesn't have a view like this." Andrea walked to the windows and pointed. "Every room on this side has a view of the Lutheran church, Granny's Attic, and the Red Owl."

"This is a nice balcony," Hannah said, walking to the sliding glass doors.

"If you lived here, you could see The Cookie Jar from your balcony. I could probably cut you a deal, Hannah. And I know I could sell your place for more than you paid for it. You'd be trading up."

"No thanks," Hannah said quickly. "I like where I live."

"Well . . . just think about it. Your cookie truck is getting old and if you bought this unit, you could walk to work."

"I'll think about it," Hannah said, knowing that she wouldn't, but also knowing that her sister wouldn't stop her sales pitch until every single one of the condos were sold. "Why don't you show me the penthouse?" she suggested, by way of diversion. "I know I could never afford it, but I'd love to see it."

The penthouse had a private elevator that Roger Dalworth had installed. Hannah and Andrea rode down to the lobby and used Andrea's key to activate the private elevator.

"The penthouse takes up the entire top floor," Andrea informed her as they stepped out of the elevator and directly into the penthouse foyer. "The view is spectacular and it has a huge tropical garden with its own Jacuzzi and grotto swimming pool."

"A Jacuzzi and a swimming pool? That's not very practical for Minnesota." It was all Hannah could do not to gasp as she walked into the penthouse living room. There were wall-to-ceiling windows on three sides and

Andrea was right, the view was spectacular. "This is gorgeous, but I'm still thinking about the hot tub and the swimming pool. They'll have to be drained and covered all winter and that means the owner can't use them for six or seven months out of the year."

Andrea shook her head. "There's a climate-controlled dome that fits over the whole rooftop. It was supposed to be here and installed by tonight, but there was a delay and it hasn't arrived yet. That means we can go out in the middle and look, but that's it. Roger's got the rest blocked off with sawhorses because it's not safe."

When they stepped out into the penthouse garden, the June air was balmy and sweet. There was a slight breeze, but not enough to be uncomfortable. They were above the noise of the party, the passing cars on the street, and even more important, the mosquitoes. It was heavenly and Hannah took a deep breath of the perfumed night air.

"Just look at this pool," Andrea said, leading her over to the grotto pool and Jacuzzi area. There was even a thatched roof bar with padded bar stools. Low-level Malibu lights gave the whole area a romantic glow, and the ambiance was intimate and inviting. "Beautiful!" Hannah breathed, feeling a

31

small stab of envy for the lucky people who would live here.

"I shouldn't do this, but I will," Andrea said. "Help me move this sawhorse."

Between the two of them they muscled Roger's barrier to the side, and Andrea led Hannah toward the edge of the roof. "That's far enough," she said, stopping about four feet from the edge. "I want you to see the lake from here."

Hannah peered off into the distance where the lake was shining silver in the moonlight and the surrounding pines were dark sentinels stretching up toward the sky. "Beautiful!" she breathed again.

It didn't take long to go through the rest of the penthouse: multiple bedrooms, each with its own bathroom, a home gym, and a huge gourmet kitchen. There were closets galore, views from windows in abundance, and the total impression was the essence of opulence.

"We'd better go," Andrea said, glancing at her watch. "The guests should be starting to arrive by now and I've got six condos and a penthouse to sell."

Hannah was silent until they were in the elevator on their way down to the lobby. "Do you think anybody in Lake Eden can afford to buy a condo here?" she asked; the question had been bouncing around in her mind since Andrea had opened the first condo door.

"Of course. People almost always buy up."

"Buy up?"

"It's like cars and trading up. They almost always buy something more expensive than what they're selling. The only exception I've had is when I handle a property where the kids leave the nest and they're downsizing. And even then a few people want more luxury than they had. There are people in this town with money, Hannah. And remember, all you really need is the down payment, a good credit rating, and a good job. I'd say nine out of ten people that come here tonight can afford to finance one of these condos. Roger invited two hundred and fifty people and that means over two hundred could afford to buy if I can manage to impress them."

"How about the penthouse? Could nine out of ten afford that?"

"No, definitely not. The penthouse is pricey. But Del Woodley's coming. He could afford the penthouse. And so could Mayor Bascomb if Stephanie would kick in some of her money. As a matter of fact, Mother could probably afford it."

Hannah frowned slightly. She was the only

one who knew the state of her mother's finances. Andrea was right. Their father had been very astute when it came to buying stock and at this stage, Delores could afford it and then some. She thought about saying that, but neither Andrea nor Michelle knew exactly how much money Delores had and Hannah had promised never to divulge the details. "Maybe Mother could afford it, but I'm not sure she'd want to give up her house."

"You're right. That's the house that Dad bought for her and it must have a lot of happy memories for her. She's used to living there and she likes the neighbors. I think the only way that Mother would move is if she got married again. And I really don't think that's going to happen."

The penthouse elevator doors opened, and Andrea and Hannah stepped out. "Hold on a second," Andrea said, turning her elevator key in the lock so that it would remain accessible. "We want people to go up to the penthouse, even if they can't afford to buy it. If they're impressed, they talk about it and they might mention it to somebody who *can* afford to buy it."

"Good thinking," Hannah said. "Are you going to work now?"

"Yes, but Roger wants me in the lounge

for a while. He told me to wait until people had some of the free champagne and free food before I started selling."

"Because then everyone will be in a good mood?"

"That's the theory, and he's right. That's why I always set out cheese and crackers, or some of your cookies when I host an open house. If I get really busy showing the condos, will you do a favor for me?"

"What?" Hannah asked, not about to get trapped by agreeing to something blindly.

"Snag me about six of your Red Velvet Surprise Cupcakes, will you, Hannah? I'd really appreciate it. I'm going to need a couple more to keep up my energy and I want to take some home to the girls and Grandma McCann. That surprise in the middle is a stroke of pure genius!"

RED VELVET SURPRISE CUPCAKES

If you're going to make these cupcakes right away, preheat oven to 350 degrees F., rack in the middle position.

Hannah's Note: To make these cupcakes, you must first make Chocolate Apricot Surprises. Don't worry. They'll only take you 15 minutes at the most. If you'd prefer to make them at night and not bake the cupcakes until morning, preheat the oven at that time.

CHOCOLATE APRICOT SURPRISES

6 ounces semi-sweet chocolate chips (*that's one cup of chips*)
2 Tablespoons apricot jam
2 Tablespoons salted butter

If the apricot jam has big pieces of apricots, cut them into smaller pieces before you measure out the jam. You can also simply pick them out and only use the clear part of the jam.

Place the 3 ingredients in a microwave-safe bowl. (*I used a 2-cup measuring cup.*)

Microwave on HIGH for 1 minute. Take the chocolate mixture out of the microwave and stir the contents smooth.

Tear off a piece of waxed paper and place it on a piece of cardboard or a cookie sheet

36

right next to the chocolate mixture.

Use a quarter-teaspoon measuring spoon to scoop out the chocolate mixture. Scrape it out of the spoon with your impeccably clean finger and drop it onto the waxed paper in little mounds. If it spreads out too much and won't mound, let it cool for a minute or two longer.

Once you start making the chocolate mounds, keep in mind that you will need 24 Chocolate Apricot Surprises for your cupcakes. If you end up with less, pinch a little off the larger mounds and transfer it to the smaller mounds. If you end up with too much chocolate left, either make the existing mounds bigger, or make several mounds on a different piece of wax paper and hide them in a small container in the back of your refrigerator for the times you have a chocolate deficiency.

Refrigerate the Chocolate Apricot Surprises until you're ready to use them in your cupcakes. (**You can make them the night before you make your cupcakes, but only if you live alone. If you have a family, someone is bound to get up in the middle of the night to eat them.**)

RED VELVET CUPCAKES

Preheat the oven to 350 degrees F., rack in the middle position.

1 and 1/2 cups white (**granulated**) sugar

1/2 cup salted butter (**1 stick, 4 ounces, 1/4 pound**) softened to room temperature

1/2 cup vegetable oil

1 teaspoon salt

1 teaspoon baking powder

1 teaspoon baking soda

1 teaspoon cocoa powder

2 teaspoons red food color gel (**if you can't find gel, you can use liquid food coloring, but gel is best — I used Betty Crocker Classic Gel Food Colors**)

1 teaspoon vanilla extract

2 large eggs

2 and 1/2 cups all-purpose flour (**pack it down in the cup when you measure it**)

1 cup buttermilk

1 teaspoon red wine vinegar (**or white vinegar if you can't find red wine vinegar**)

Line 24 cupcake cups with cupcake papers. (**My cupcake pans hold 12 apiece so I used 2 cupcake pans. I also used double cupcake papers in each cup.**)

WARNING ABOUT FOOD COLOR GEL: *Make sure you don't buy red deco-*

rating gel instead of red food color gel. The decorating gel comes in individual tubes and is used to write on the top of cakes in various colors of gel frosting. You need to buy the concentrated food color gel that will color your cupcake batter red. If you can't find food color gel, you can use liquid food coloring, but you'll have to use double the amount.

Place the white sugar in the bowl of an electric mixer. Add the softened, salted butter and vegetable oil. Beat until the resulting mixture is nice and fluffy.

Mix in the salt, baking powder, baking soda, and cocoa powder. Mix it in thoroughly.

Add the 2 teaspoons of red food color gel and the vanilla extract. Beat until the color is mixed in evenly.

Add the eggs, one at a time, beating after each addition.

Add one cup of flour to your bowl and mix it in thoroughly. Then shut off the mixer and scrape down the sides of the bowl with a rubber spatula.

Pour in a half-cup of buttermilk and mix that in thoroughly on LOW speed.

Add a second cup of flour to your bowl. Mix it in thoroughly and then shut off the mixer and scrape down the sides of the bowl again.

Add the rest of the buttermilk (**1/2 cup**) to your bowl. Mix well.

Mix in the rest of the flour (**1/2 cup**) and mix thoroughly.

Mix in the red wine vinegar.

Shut off the mixer, remove the bowl, and give your cupcake batter a final scrape and stir with the rubber spatula. The vinegar may make your batter foam up a bit. That's perfectly all right.

Fill the cupcake papers 1/3 full of batter. (**Lisa and I used a 2-Tablespoon scoop to do this at The Cookie Jar.**)

Take the Chocolate Apricot Surprises you made out of the refrigerator. Peel them off the waxed paper one by one, and put them in the center of each cupcake. Push them down slightly, but be careful not to push them all the way to the bottom of the cupcakes!

Fill the cupcake papers with batter until they're 3/4 full. These cupcakes don't rise very much so you don't have to worry about them overflowing.

Bake the Red Velvet Surprise Cupcakes in a preheated 350 degrees F. oven for 20 to 23 minutes. (**Mine took 21 minutes.**)

Take the cupcake pans out of the oven and let them cool completely on a cold stove burner or a wire rack. Do not remove the cupcakes from the pan until they are completely cool.

Yield: 24 cupcakes

CREAM CHEESE FROSTING FOR RED VELVET SURPRISE CUPCAKES

4 ounces cream cheese (*I used Philadelphia Brand in the rectangular silver package — half a package was 4 ounces*)

1/4 cup salted butter (*1/2 stick, 2 ounces, 1/8 pound*)

1 teaspoon vanilla extract

2 cups powdered sugar (*pack it down in the cup when you measure it*)

Place the cream cheese and the butter in a medium-size microwave-safe bowl. (*I used a quart measuring cup.*) Microwave on HIGH for 30 seconds. Stir. If you can stir the cream cheese and the butter smooth, take the bowl out and put it on the counter. If it's still not soft enough to stir, microwave on HIGH in 20-second intervals until it is.

Add the vanilla extract to your bowl and stir that in.

Add the powdered sugar, a half-cup at a time, stirring after each addition. Continue

41

to add powdered sugar until the frosting is spreadable, not runny.

Work from the center out when you frost your Red Velvet Surprise Cupcakes. Don't go all the way to the edges. Leave a little of the red cupcake showing all the way around.

Yield: This recipe will frost 24 cupcakes. (*If there's any frosting left over, spread it on graham crackers or soda crackers for the kids.*)

When Lisa and I baked these for the grand opening of the Albion Hotel, we sprinkled the top of the Cream Cheese Frosting with red decorating sugar.

CHAPTER THREE

When Hannah and Andrea got back to the Red Velvet Lounge, they found that their mother and Doc Knight had staked out the largest table in the center of the room. "Nice job, Mother," Hannah said, taking a chair. "You got here early."

"So did you. And I must say, Hannah, you look very pretty tonight."

"Thanks, Mother."

"Is that lipstick?"

"Yes."

"And eye makeup."

"Yes, but it's not my fault. Andrea made me do it."

Doc Knight chuckled as he turned to Hannah. "You sound like a kid who's caught with her hand in the cookie jar."

"You're right. She does," Andrea agreed. "But that never could have happened at our house. Mother's cookie jar was always empty unless Hannah came home from school and baked."

Doc laughed again, longer this time. Then he put his hand on Delores's arm. "Lori can burn water, that's for sure. She made me some coffee this morning and I swear it tasted burned."

"Doc!" Delores turned and gave him what Hannah and her sisters had always called *Mother's glare of imminent death.*

"Okay. Maybe I shouldn't have told them that," Doc said by way of apology, but Hannah noticed that his eyes were sparkling with laughter. "Am I forgiven? Or do I have to jump through hoops?"

"You have to jump through hoops," Delores said and then she did something that surprised both Hannah and Andrea. She laughed. "I'll expect you to make the coffee tomorrow and that's a win-win situation for me. I never get a good cup of coffee when I make it."

"Deal," Doc said, slipping his arm around her shoulders and giving her a hug. "By the way, I agree that Hannah looks lovely tonight, but she always looks good, even without any makeup."

Delores nodded. "You're right. Hannah's beautiful, no matter what. I really shouldn't . . ." She stopped and looked thoughtful. "What is that word you use for what I just did?"

"Harangue? Plague? Bully? Criticize?" Doc gave her another little hug to let her know he was teasing. "It's okay, Lori. The girls wouldn't know what to do with you if you didn't criticize them. You've done it all their lives and if you changed now, it just wouldn't be you. They know you love them and want the best for them." Doc turned to Hannah and Andrea. "You do, don't you?"

"Of course we know." Hannah was the first to respond.

Andrea reached over to give her mother a pat on the hand. "Hannah's right. We grew up knowing that."

Delores looked slightly tearful and Hannah began to think that leopards really *could* change their spots overnight. Their mother had just admitted that she was too critical and that had never happened before. There was a moment of silence that was beginning to become just a bit uncomfortable when Doc spoke again.

"We planned to get here earlier, but I wanted to stay at the hospital until Warren Dalworth's visitor left."

"It was someone from Minneapolis with some papers for him to sign," Delores told them. "That didn't take long, but then Roger came in and Doc needed time to talk to him."

"How is Warren doing?" Hannah asked, hoping that there was some good news.

Doc shook his head and sighed. "Not well. He's comfortable, but he knows he's terminal and he can't last much longer. The hardest part was telling Roger."

Hannah shivered slightly. Roger was an only child and his mother had died several years ago. He'd just gotten over one loss in his immediate family and now, today, he'd learned that his father didn't have long to live. "It must be horrible to get news like that," she said.

"It is," Doc told her. "And delivering that news is almost as difficult as getting it. It's one of the hardest parts of being a doctor."

"Is Roger all right?" Andrea asked.

"Yes. He took it well. Of course it wasn't totally unexpected. Warren's been battling cancer for the past four years. There's also the fact that Roger and his father have never been that close, but it's still hard to hear that a parent is dying."

Andrea and Hannah exchanged glances. Hannah didn't want to think about that, and she could tell that Andrea didn't either.

"Did Roger go to see his father?" Andrea asked.

"Yes." This time Delores answered. "And

he told us he'd be staying in Lake Eden indefinitely so that he could see his father every day."

This time there was a three-way glance between mother and daughters, and Doc gave a little nod. "I caught that. You're doing that mother-daughter telepathy thing again. All three of you are worried that if Roger stays in Lake Eden, Doctor Bev will stay, too."

"That's right," Delores said, giving him a fond look. And then, in her best British upper-class accent she exclaimed, "By George! I think he's got it!"

The tension that had settled over them with Doc's news dissolved as all four of them laughed. They were still smiling when Barbara Donnelly walked up to their table.

"Hi, everyone," she said. "I'm sorry I'm late."

"You're not late," Delores told her. "We didn't get here until five minutes ago. Sit down and have some appetizers. They look lovely."

Barbara glanced at the appetizer tray that sat in the center of the table. "Did you do these, Hannah?"

"No. We only catered the cupcakes. Roger hired a catering company from Minneapolis to do the rest of the food."

47

"Sit here, Barbara." Andrea pulled out the chair for her husband's secretary. "But first turn around so that I can see your skirt. It's just beautiful."

"It's more than beautiful, it's gorgeous," Delores corrected her as Barbara turned all the way around. "You look lovely, Barbara."

"Thank you." Barbara smiled as she sat down. "Claire ordered this outfit especially for me. She remembered that I just love monarch butterflies."

"The colors are incredible against the black background," Hannah said, admiring the dozens of embroidered monarch butterflies scattered over the material of the skirt.

"The buttons on the blouse are the perfect touch," Delores told her. "They're monarch butterflies too, aren't they?"

"That's right. And Claire said that each one was hand painted." Barbara looked pleased to receive so many compliments. "The minute Claire showed me this outfit I knew I just had to have it. And it goes so well with my mother's amber beads."

"It's perfect for you," Andrea agreed. "Do you happen to know when Bill and Mike are coming?"

"They left the office right after I did. They said they were going to run home and get dressed, and they should be here any . . ." Barbara stopped talking and pointed to the doorway. "There's our host and hostess."

"What a perfect ad for cosmetic surgery," Delores commented, as Roger and Doctor Bev entered the lounge.

Andrea turned to Delores. "You think Roger had cosmetic surgery?"

"I know Roger did. And she's had some work done on her muffin tops."

"Muffin tops?" Hannah questioned her mother.

"The rolls of fat that protrude from the side and back when you wear a tight skirt or tight pants," Doc Knight explained.

"That's right," Delores said, smiling at him. "Doctor Bev used to have them and now she doesn't. I'm sure she had liposuction. And then there's that little trout pout. Do you see it?"

Hannah turned to Doc Knight. "Translate, please?"

"Her lips have a slight pouty look, most likely from a bit too much Botox."

Delores nodded. "But that doesn't even count the actual surgery. She was beginning to have crow's feet, but they're gone now. You know what crow's feet are, don't you?"

"We know," Barbara said with a sigh. "What else?"

"Her elevens are gone and her parentheses are a lot less deep than they were. And she got rid of her turtleneck."

All three women turned to Doc Knight and he laughed.

"All right. Elevens are slang for the vertical lines that appear between a person's eyebrows when they're frowning. They probably used Botox on those. And parentheses are the classic lines that develop from the sides of the nose down past the corners of the mouth."

"Botox?" Hannah guessed.

"Not usually. They're usually treated with injectable filler like Juvederm. The turtleneck is more difficult to treat and it usually requires a neck lift procedure."

"Surgery," Delores said, "and it's all elective. She left some cash at her doctor's office. Or he did."

"How do you know so much about cosmetic surgery?" Andrea asked, even though Hannah tried to aim a kick at her under the table.

"Well, I . . ."

"Lori was good enough to do some online research for me," Doc Knight said quickly. "I needed to know some of the slang terms so that I could refer my patients who wanted to enhance their appearance to the right cosmetic surgeon."

As Hannah watched, Delores turned to give Doc Knight a luminous smile that clearly said *Thank you for getting me out of a pickle.* Hannah smiled at both of them. There was no doubt in her mind that they were good for each other.

"Whatever," Barbara said, taking a sip of her diet cola. "She really looks good to-night."

"Yes, she does," Hannah said, more chari-table than she felt like being as Roger and Doctor Bev walked to the table for two that had been reserved for them.

"I think she looks at least ten years younger," Delores said. "And ever since Roger got his nose fixed, he's been on the handsome side."

They were silent then, watching Roger and Doctor Bev make their way to the table. Hannah had never seen Doctor Bev looking so pretty, so young, and so beautifully dressed. She was wearing a tight-fitting silver dress that gleamed in the overhead halogen lights. Her makeup was perfect, her hair was perfect, and her smile was perfect. The only note of imperfection was the haughty look on her face.

Then there was Roger, who walked at her side with an assurance that only comes from family money. He'd been raised in luxury and he was used to merely mentioning something only to have someone snap to attention to accomplish it. He was dressed in a black suit that fit so perfectly, Hannah knew it had been tailored especially for him. He had paired it with a lavender dress shirt and a lavender and silver tie. His blond hair was a shade darker than Doctor Bev's blond hair and his eyes were an alert and piercing blue. His teeth were white and gleaming, but one was slightly crooked, giving his smile an endearing quality, and Hannah found herself wondering if that tooth had been specifically capped that way. His skin was a shade of tan that would have been impossible to achieve in a tanning booth or in the short length of time the Minnesota weather had permitted. *Aruba, St. Thomas, St. Croix, or some other tropical vacation spot?* Hannah's mind suggested and she gave a slight nod. Roger was handsome and Bev was stunningly pretty. They were the golden couple.

"Here come Mike and Bill," Barbara said, gesturing toward the doorway. "And Norman's there, too."

Hannah turned to look. Three men were standing in the doorway. One man was her date for the evening, another was the man she also dated and the chief detective at the Winnetka County Sheriff's Department, and the third was her brother-in-law and Andrea's husband, Bill Todd.

Andrea gave a wave and the three men threaded their way across the room toward their table. A few steps and it was apparent that this could take a while. Everyone who saw them wanted to say hello and their progress was slow.

"Did you see the luxury condos?" Barbara asked Andrea.

"Yes. Roger listed them with Stan and I'm handling the sales. I took Hannah up there when we got here."

"I've been hearing all sorts of things about the penthouse. Bill said it's got a grotto pool and a Jacuzzi."

"You should see it, Barbara. It's spectacular."

"Especially the tropical rooftop garden," Hannah added. "It covers half of the roof and the landscaping is already in. Andrea told me they're even going to order a couple of fully grown palm trees."

"Will palm trees grow in Minnesota?" Barbara asked, looking dubious.

"They will if you have a climate-controlled dome that covers the whole area," Andrea was quick to explain.

"I can hardly wait to see it!" Barbara took another sip of her diet drink. "I wonder if I could see my house from up there."

"I know you can, but not tonight. The dome didn't come in time for the party, and Roger's got the perimeter roped off. You can walk around the pool and Jacuzzi area, but you can't go near the edge of the roof."

"I think I'll go up there and look around. And I'll stop and look at the condos on the second floor, too. I know I can't afford one, but it never hurts to dream." Barbara picked up her glass, stood up, and turned to Hannah. "The next time you check on the dessert table, would you bring me one of your cupcakes? I ran into Herb in the parking lot and he said they're incredible."

"Will do," Hannah promised with a smile. It was good to hear praise for their cupcakes. She went off to get one for Barbara and to tell Lisa that people were beginning to say nice things about their cupcakes. By the time she came back and sat down, Norman and Mike were approaching the table.

"Hi, Hannah," Norman said, taking the chair next to her. "You look fantastic."

"Thanks, Norman."

"You're wearing makeup," Mike commented. "You look really good in makeup."

"Hannah looks good with or without

54

makeup," Norman corrected him.

"Right," Mike said, sitting down next to Hannah. "I've got news about the Clayton Wallace case."

Hannah leaned forward expectantly. Clayton Wallace, the band bus driver for the Cinnamon Roll Six, had been the first fatality in the multi-car pileup on the interstate two months ago. Doc Knight had determined that the cause of death was an overdose of heart medication. "It was accidental, wasn't it?"

"No."

"Murder?" Norman asked, drawing the obvious conclusion.

Mike shook his head and Hannah breathed a sigh of relief. Since there had been two fatalities on the same night and one was clearly murder, she'd made a unilateral decision to try to solve the case they knew was murder and to leave the investigation into Clayton Wallace's death to the authorities.

Hannah had never believed that Clayton's death was murder. It just didn't add up. Everyone she'd talked to had believed it was an accident. He'd been the jazz band bus driver since the Cinnamon Roll Six had first begun to tour and everyone connected with the band had liked him.

"If it wasn't an accident and it wasn't murder, what was it?" Andrea asked.

"Suicide."

"Suicide?" Hannah repeated, sounding every bit as shocked as she felt.

"This was his last trip with the band," Mike told them. "Mr. Wallace told the band manager, Lee Campbell, that he was retiring right after they got back to Minneapolis."

"How old was Clayton?" Andrea asked.

"Sixty-two."

"It's not unusual for a person to retire at sixty-two," Hannah pointed out. "Perhaps Clayton was tired of being on the road with the band. I could understand that. Or maybe . . ." She stopped speaking abruptly as another possibility occurred to her. "Did you check with his doctor? Was Clayton ill?"

"The M.P.D. interviewed his doctor. The report's in the case file. The doctor gave him a clean bill of health based on a recent checkup. He was on heart, blood pressure, and cholesterol medications, but everything was under control."

"Did Clayton give a reason why he wanted to quit working?" Andrea asked.

"All he said was that he had some things that he wanted to do. Mr. Campbell told me he mentioned some improvements he wanted to make to his house and a cruise to Alaska he'd booked with a friend."

"That doesn't sound like someone who was contemplating suicide," Norman remarked.

"True," Mike said.

"Then what made the M.P.D. think that it was a suicide?" Hannah asked the important question.

"They said he couldn't have made a mistake like that with his pills, that it must have been deliberate. The three pills he was supposed to take were different shapes and different colors. And he took one of each type every night. The pill box you found in the bus was the type that had one compartment for each day of the week. You remember that, don't you?"

"I remember. When I handed it to you, I noticed that only one compartment was empty. All the rest were full."

"That's right. Clayton had no pill bottles with him, just the pills in the compartments. The M.P.D. concluded that he filled the compartments before he left and they found the bottles in his bathroom medicine cabinet. All three bottles were for a thirty-day supply."

"Let me guess," Hannah said with a sigh. "The bottle with the heart medication was two pills short. And the other two bottles had one pill too many. And that's why the M.P.D. decided that Clayton's death was a suicide."

"That's right."

Andrea began to frown. "I can see their point, but it still doesn't make any sense. Clayton enjoyed driving the band and he liked every one of the boys as much as they liked him. Even if he *had* decided to commit suicide, he never would have done it while he was driving. He would have waited until he got to the Lake Eden Inn and *then* he would have taken the pills."

"Did he leave a suicide note?" Hannah asked.

"No. Or at least the M.P.D. didn't find it when they searched his house. And even if he'd mailed it to someone, it would have surfaced by now."

"Did they find *anything* unusual?" Hannah asked.

"Not really, unless you want to count a gift-wrapped box of Fanny Farmer truffles and an expensive bottle of premium Chianti. The wine was in one of those fancy wine bags."

"He must have been planning to take them to someone when he got home," Norman speculated. "And that means he was planning ahead."

"Right," Hannah picked up on his thought. "And if he was planning ahead, why would he suddenly decide to commit suicide?"

"Maybe he had a date all planned and the woman called him on his cell phone to cancel," Mike suggested.

"And he got so depressed over the cancelled date that he decided to commit suicide right then and there and take all his friends on the band bus with him?" Hannah knew she sounded incredulous, but that's exactly how she felt.

"It was just a suggestion," Mike defended his scenario. "It *could* have happened that way."

Hannah gave a short laugh. "And cows could fly if they just had wings. But you don't really think it happened that way . . . do you?"

"No, I don't. But that's my personal opinion. The official conclusion is that Clayton Wallace committed suicide. It's over, Hannah. I can't reopen another police department's case without good cause. And suspicion without proof isn't good enough. Believe me, we're all just as upset as you are. Bill's just sick about the whole thing, and so are Lonnie and Rick. The worst part is the insurance policy." When Hannah, Norman, and Andrea looked puzzled, Mike went on to explain. "If the official investigation doesn't conclude with natural, accidental, or homicide, the insurance company doesn't pay death benefits. And that means Clayton's son loses out."

"Clayton had a son?" Andrea asked.

"Twenty-two years old, and paralyzed from the waist down. He's living in a group home and doing really well, but there are some medical treatments that might improve his condition. They're expensive. The state of Minnesota pays for part. We're good that way. We take care of our own. But new treatments take time to get approved by the system. Clayton was counting on that insurance money to make his son's life easier."

All four of them were silent for a long moment. Then Hannah spoke up. "I'm sorry I found that pill matrix! And I'm doubly sorry I gave it to you."

Mike reached out to take her hand. "You did the right thing, Hannah. It was evidence and you had an obligation to turn it over to me. That's one of the reasons I'm telling you all this. You played by the rules."

Hannah locked eyes with Mike. He was trying to tell her something, something that he couldn't say. "What do you need to

60

reopen the M.P.D. investigation?" she asked.

"In order to reopen the investigation we need some proof that it wasn't suicide, something concrete. It could be proof that it was murder, or it could be proof that it was an accident. Either one would cause us to reopen the case and conduct our own investigation."

Hannah's eyes narrowed. "Are you saying that you can't get that proof officially, but I can?"

"I didn't say that. You surmised that. And I can't control what you surmise."

Hannah smiled. "Enough said, Mike. And nobody except Andrea and Norman know that we had this conversation?"

"Right." Mike turned to Andrea. "Would you like to dance? Bill could be with the mayor for a while. When I left they were talking about crime rates in Winnetka County, and whether or not they should think about shutting down the Blue Moon Motel."

Hannah exchanged a quick look with Andrea. They'd seen a clandestine photo of Mayor Bascomb and a lady better left unnamed coming out of a room at the Blue Moon Motel. For someone who'd used it as a rendezvous, Mayor Bascomb didn't have much loyalty.

"I'd love to dance with you, Mike," Andrea said, standing up to take Mike's arm.

"How about you, Hannah?" Norman asked when Andrea and Mike had left the table.

"Love to," Hannah said and stood up to follow Andrea and Mike to the dance floor in the lobby. A jazz band had started to play and the music was mellow and perfect for dancing.

"You know about Bev?" Norman asked, taking Hannah into his arms to the strain of an old standard.

"Andrea told me." And then she paused, wondering if she should ask. Did curiosity win out over politeness? Her heart said yes, but her mind said no. Mercifully, she was saved the agony of deciding because Norman went on speaking.

"She hasn't contacted me yet, but there were a couple of messages on the answering machine in my office. I didn't bother to play them. I think Bev and I said all there was to say to each other."

Hannah was glad she hadn't asked, because Norman had volunteered the information. That meant something . . . didn't it? Instead of pondering the question, she moved a little closer to Norman and tried to put Doctor Bev out of her mind. But

Norman's two-time fiancée wouldn't go away. Hannah's eyes widened as she saw Roger Dalworth and Doctor Bev coming out on the dance floor.

"She's here," Norman said, noticing them at almost the same time as Hannah had.

"I saw." Hannah took a deep breath. "Is there anything you want me to do?"

"Just be here for me." Norman pulled her even closer. "I'm not upset. That's not it. I'm just . . . puzzled. I can't figure out why she's back here. And until I know, I'm not going to do anything."

"That's my plan, too. If we're lucky, we won't have to talk to her at all. She's with Roger and it must be serious because she's got a huge diamond ring on her finger. If she's engaged to him now, she might leave us alone."

"Maybe," Norman said, but he didn't sound convinced. "I don't know Roger that well, but he seems like a decent guy. I hope he finds out what a barracuda she is before it's too late."

Hannah, who had a better view of Roger and Doctor Bev, gave a little groan of dismay. "They're coming over this way. I hope she's not going to cause a scene."

"She won't do anything ugly in front of her newest . . ." Norman stopped, obviously at a loss for the right word.

"Conquest," Hannah supplied it.

"Exactly. Would you like to go back to the table?"

Hannah thought about that for a moment. "No. I don't think we should let them drive us away."

"Right." Norman took a quick glance over his shoulder. "Uh-oh. They're coming closer."

"What can they do? Trip us?" Hannah tried for a little humor.

"They can cut in."

Hannah glanced over Norman's shoulder again. "You're right. What should we do?"

"We should let them cut in as if nothing's wrong. It's only one dance. And after that dance, we should both think of some polite way to go back to our table."

"Done," Hannah said as Roger Dalworth tapped Norman on the shoulder. And then she was in Roger's arms, dancing a dance she didn't want to dance, and trying her best not to crane her neck to keep an eye on Doctor Bev and Norman.

It had been an uncomfortable ten minutes, but it was over. Hannah checked her hair in the antique oval mirror that stood on a mahogany stand in the corner of the ladies' room and decided that there wasn't much she could do to it without a curry comb and wire brush. There was nothing she could do except play with the genetic cards she'd been dealt. Delores, at well past fifty, was still beautiful with shining black hair, a svelte figure, and perfectly applied makeup. Andrea had inherited their mother's good looks with the exception of her hair color. She was a natural blonde and she always looked as if she'd just stepped off the cover of a fashion magazine. Hannah's youngest sister, Michelle, was equally beautiful with lovely brown hair. And then there was Hannah, who looked nothing like her beautiful, petite mother and sisters. She was her father's daughter with his shock of unruly red hair, tall, gangly frame, and the same unfortunate tendency to put on extra pounds.

After excusing herself to Roger in order to go to the ladies' room, even asking him where it was to lend credibility to her excuse, she spent five or six minutes sitting on the brocade sofa in the anteroom, staring at her reflection in the mirror, before she ventured out to return to her table.

"Well?" Delores asked before she'd even pulled out her chair.

"She's engaged to him, but that's all I

know. At least he called her his fiancée. I didn't want to ask questions."

Delores turned to Doc. "Sorry. We're doing that mother-to-daughter telepathy thing again. I wanted to know if Hannah found out why *she* was back in town and how long she plans to be here."

"That's what I thought. Maybe Norman will know. He's dancing with her right now."

Delores turned to look. "Norman doesn't look happy."

"Just the opposite," Hannah agreed.

"Shall I rescue him?" Delores asked. "Doc and I can go out there and cut in, just like they did to you. And then maybe Doc can get some information out of her."

Doc gave a little laugh. "Sorry, Lori. I forgot to pack truth serum in my little black bag."

"That's okay," Hannah said, noticing that Norman and Doctor Bev had stopped dancing. "I stopped dancing with Roger to go to the ladies' room and I think she just did the same thing. At least she's heading that way. And Norman's heading this way."

Delores nodded. "I'm going to ask him what's going on. I'm just dying to know if . . ." She stopped speaking as Doc gripped her arm. "What?"

"I heard something."

"What?" Hannah asked.

"It sounded like something crashed above us. I think it came from several stories up, perhaps on the roof of the hotel."

Delores shook her head. "I didn't hear anything. Of course, I was talking."

"You're usually talking," Doc told her and then he turned to Hannah. "Did you hear it?"

"No. I was listening to Mother, just like I always do."

"Right," Delores said, giving a little laugh.

"Wait!" Doc held up his hand. "I think I heard something again."

All three of them were silent for several moments, listening for the sounds that Doc had heard. Other than the noises of the party, the clink of glasses, the clatter of silverware, and the faint strains of music coming from the band in the lobby, they heard nothing amiss. Hannah was about to say that she still hadn't heard any thumps from above when all three of them reacted to what sounded like a faint scream. No more than a heartbeat or two later, something hurtled past the windows.

"What *is* it?" Delores gasped.

"I don't know, but I'm going to find out." Before she had even finished her sentence, Hannah was on her feet racing to the windows to look. The sight that greeted her was strange to say the least.

Butterflies flitted between two bushes in the rose garden. It took a moment of disbelief before Hannah realized that they weren't real butterflies. They were embroidered butterflies on a black background and Hannah swallowed hard.

"What *is* it?" Delores asked again, coming up to the window behind her.

"I'm not sure, but . . . ." Hannah stopped speaking, more certain than she wanted to admit. The butterflies were on a piece of material from a skirt she'd admired only minutes ago. And the broken string of amber beads glittering in the lights from the baby spots trained on the rose garden was equally familiar. The owner of the skirt and the beads was face-down on the ground at the base of one of the rose bushes.

"What *is* it?" Delores asked for the third time. "I can't see past you. Tell me what's going on!"

Hannah moved slightly to the side. Then she drew a deep, steadying breath. "It's Barbara Donnelly. I think she fell off the roof from the edge of the penthouse garden."

"Oh, no!" Delores moved closer to peer past Hannah's shoulder. "Barbara said she wanted to try to spot her house from up there. Can you see her? Is she . . . alive?"

"I don't know," Hannah replied with a heavy heart. "All I know is Barbara is face down right next to a rose bush. And she's not moving at all."

CHAPTER FOUR

They all stood by anxiously as Doc Knight bent over Barbara's still form. They couldn't see exactly what he was doing because Herb had marshaled the six employees of Cupcake Security and they'd formed a circle around Barbara's body. The boys were facing out, holding hands to form a protective barrier, and they looked every bit as anxious as Hannah felt. Herb was standing guard at the entrance to the rose garden to make sure that no one who wasn't a medic or a police officer gained access to the scene.

Delores, who was standing next to Hannah, gave a little shiver. "Do you think Barbara went too close to the edge and fell?"

"I don't know," Andrea answered her. "It seems really unlikely that Barbara would be that foolish. I told her about the barricades and why they were there. I can't believe she'd actually move them."

Delores didn't look convinced. "Maybe

somebody else did. And when Barbara went up there, she simply walked into that area, thinking that it was okay. Maybe she didn't even go all the way to the edge, but the height made her so dizzy, she stumbled and . . ."

"It couldn't have happened that way," Andrea interrupted her mother. "For one thing, Barbara wasn't afraid of heights and they didn't make her dizzy. She was the one who always climbed the ladder to put crepe paper streamers on the ceiling for birthdays at the sheriff's department."

"Then how did she fall?" Delores asked.

Hannah looked just as puzzled as Andrea and Delores. "None of this makes sense," she said. "The only thing we know for sure is that something happened up there in the rooftop garden. And maybe we'll never know what it was if Barbara ends up . . ."

"She's not!" Andrea interrupted her. "I'm sure I just saw her leg move."

Delores drew a relieved breath. "And Doc's still bending over her with his stethoscope. That means he's still checking her vital signs. He wouldn't be doing that if there weren't any."

There was a faint wail of an ambulance siren in the distance and all three women drew breaths of relief. Someone had called for the paramedics and that meant there was hope.

"Where did Bill go?" Andrea asked, noticing that her husband had left the scene.

"Mike's gone, too," Delores noted.

"They're probably up in the penthouse garden, searching for evidence," Hannah guessed. "I can almost guarantee you that they're going to treat the whole penthouse floor as a crime scene unless they learn something that proves it's not."

"They're loading Barbara on a gurney now," Delores pointed out, gazing through the window. "Thank goodness they're not using a backboard. That means her back isn't broken."

"And she's not on oxygen so at least she's breathing all right," Andrea added. "I'm going to see if I can find Lonnie and Rick. I saw them around here a couple of minutes ago. Maybe they'll tell me something."

After the ambulance pulled away carrying Barbara, the party began to break up. Lisa packed the remainder of their cupcakes in a box and brought them to the table where Hannah was sitting with Norman and Delores.

"What shall I do with these?" she asked Hannah.

"Give them to Roger. He paid for them. And if he doesn't want them, take them back to the coffee shop. I think they'll freeze and we can donate them to the next charity event."

"Do you need a ride home?" Norman asked Delores.

"No, but thank you, dear. I drove and I'm going to run out to the hospital to see if I can find out more about Barbara's condition."

"Will you call me and let me know?" Hannah asked her.

"Of course I will." Delores pushed back her chair and stood up. "How late will you be awake?"

"Late. And if I'm asleep the answer phone will get it and I'll play your message in the morning."

"Do you want to wait for Andrea?" Norman asked her after Delores had left.

"Not really. I think I just want to go home and cuddle up with Moishe on the couch."

"How about me?"

Hannah gave him a grin. "Sure. You can cuddle up with Moishe, too."

"That's not exactly what I meant."

"I know," Hannah told him. And then she smiled.

■ ■ ■ ■

Morning came early, much too early to suit
Hannah. When the sky began to lighten
slightly outside her bedroom window, her
eyes fluttered open. It took her a moment,
but then she remembered that it was Sunday, the one day of the week when she
didn't have to go to work. If she wanted,
and she *did* want, she could roll over, pull
the blanket back up, and go back to sleep.
She was in the process of doing just that
when the phone on her bedside table rang.

Out of pure instinct Hannah reached out
to answer it. "Hello," she said groggily.

"Hannah!"

The voice was weak, but Hannah recognized it immediately. She'd heard it only
last night. "Barbara?"

"Yes. Come see me, Hannah. I need you."

For one brief moment, Hannah thought
she'd fallen asleep again and the phone
conversation was a dream. She blinked
several times and sat up in bed, pinching
herself to make sure that she was awake.
"Are you all right, Barbara?"

"He tried to kill me!"

"Who?"

But there was no answer except a soft

click. "Barbara? Are you still there?" Hannah felt a moment's panic. "Talk to me."

But it was too late. The phone line was dead, leaving Hannah wide awake and shaking. Unless someone was playing a very cruel joke, Barbara was alive and she'd just said that someone had tried to murder her!

It didn't take a genius to realize that there would be no further sleep for her this morning. Hannah reached for her slippers and pulled them on. Had the telephone actually rung? Had she actually heard Barbara's voice say that someone had tried to kill her? Or had she only dreamed the whole thing?

"Did the phone ring?" she asked Moishe, who was stretched out on his feather pillow, staring at her. But Moishe was no help as a reality check. His expression remained perfectly neutral.

Hannah glanced over at the phone. It had been centered on her night table when she'd gone to bed, but now it was crooked. She'd reached for it at some point during the night, but had she actually answered it? And had she really talked to Barbara?

As she pondered the question, a dreadful possibility occurred to her. Her Great-Grandma Elsa used to say that people who knew they were going to die and had something important they needed to say, sometimes hung on to life just long enough to say it. Had Barbara called Hannah because she needed to say that it was no accident, that someone had tried to kill her by pushing her off the roof to the garden below? And had she died before she could say who'd pushed her?

Hannah knew that there was only one way to find out. She had to call the hospital. But hospitals didn't give out that kind of information over the phone. She had to figure out a way to trick whoever answered into telling her if Barbara was still alive.

Her mind wasn't working well yet, and Hannah knew it. What she needed was a mug of strong Swedish Plasma. Of course the coffee wasn't ready. She hadn't bothered to set the timer last night since she'd planned on sleeping late.

Uncertain whether she could do something as complicated as making coffee without having coffee first, Hannah padded down the carpeted hallway to the kitchen. When she got there she flicked on the bank of excruciatingly bright fluorescent lights and somehow managed to fill the basket of the coffee maker with coffee, pour in the water, and turn it on manually.

Perhaps she dozed a bit while she sat at the kitchen table waiting for the life-giving brew to be ready. She just wasn't sure, but her neck felt a bit stiff when she glanced up at the clock. Fifteen minutes had passed. A second glance, this one at the coffee pot, confirmed that the green light was on. The world simply did not work right without coffee and now she could have it.

The promise of fresh coffee lured her to her feet and moments later, she was back at the table with a full mug of the magic elixir that transformed her from a zombie into a human being. She took one sip, then another and another, draining half the mug before she reached for the phone to dial the hospital.

She got the nurse at the front desk, someone who identified herself as Margie. Hannah didn't know the night personnel and that was good. At least Margie wouldn't recognize Hannah's voice. "I'm calling to check on Barbara Donnelly," Hannah told her. "She was admitted last night."

"I'm sorry, but we're not allowed to give out any information over the phone unless you're a family member."

Hannah thought fast. "I'm Barbara's sister and I just had a terrible nightmare about her. She didn't . . . *die,* did she?"

"Good heavens, no! Her nurse just walked past here and she said Miss Donnelly was sleeping. I'm sorry you had that dream. It's probably because you're worried about her."

The nurse sounded very sympathetic and Hannah decided to press her luck. "Could you tell me her condition?"

Hannah could hear the nurse typing something in on a keyboard. "She's stable, but guarded. If you'd like more detailed information, just call back when Doctor Knight comes in."

"When will that be?"

"By ten at the latest. Would you like me to leave a note for him to call you?"

Hannah was about to say yes when she realized that then she'd have to give her name. Since she'd lied by claiming to be Barbara's sister, it was best to remain anonymous. "That's all right. I'll call back later. I'd like to come in to see Barbara if she can have visitors."

"Just a moment. I'll check." Hannah heard the nurse type in something else on the keyboard. "Yes, but only two at a time. Our new visiting hours are from two to five in the afternoon, and seven to nine at night. Of course they don't apply to you since you're her sister. Family members are encouraged to visit any time from nine in the morning to ten at night."

"Thank you," Hannah said. "And thanks

for relieving my mind about Barbara." Hannah hung up before the nurse could ask her name. What she'd said was true. She was extremely relieved. So much for Great-Grandma Elsa's theory, at least in Barbara's case!

When she glanced up at the clock Hannah realized that it was only ten to six, much too early to drive out to the hospital, and also too early to call anyone else who might know Barbara's condition. She wished she knew the extent of Barbara's injuries, but there was no one she could ask at this hour of the morning. And now that she'd had her first mug of the coffee that made her world work right, she was wide awake and ready for action.

She needed to bake cookies to take to Barbara. Hannah was up and moving the second she thought of it. If Barbara couldn't have cookies for some reason, the nurses could. She'd mix up some Pink Lemonade Cookies. They were pretty and festive. Not only that, they were absolutely delicious.

Between sips of a second mug of coffee, she managed to gather the ingredients and start to mix up the dough. As she turned on the mixer to beat the butter with the sugar, she thought about Barbara and who might have pushed her to what could have been her death.

Barbara was single. As far as Hannah knew, she'd never been married, but she'd check with her mother about that. She'd also ask if Barbara had been involved in any serious relationships that might have ended badly. Since Delores was a founding member of what Hannah called the Lake Eden Gossip Hotline, she could easily find the answers to any questions Hannah had about her brother-in-law's secretary.

When the butter and sugar mixture was nice and fluffy, Hannah added the baking powder and baking soda to her bowl. After that was incorporated, she added the egg and then the frozen lemonade concentrate that had been thawing on the counter. The rest of the concentrate certainly wouldn't go to waste! She'd add the required amount of water, stir it up in a pitcher, and refrigerate it to have as a special treat while she watched television tonight.

While the stand mixer hummed on low speed and the beaters revolved endlessly, Hannah looked for the red food coloring. Ever since Lisa had discovered that the new red food color gel didn't stain her fingers the way the liquid food coloring did, they'd stocked it in the pantry of The Cookie Jar. Unfortunately, they'd gone through every tube they had making the cupcakes for the party last night. Hannah rummaged through her pantry and found a package of the liquid type she'd had for practically forever, and squirted three drops of red into the dough to color it.

As the color blended in to make a lovely pink, Hannah tossed the bottle of red food coloring into the trash. It was empty, but the other three colors in the package were practically full. Did anyone actually use up another color first?

"It's done," she told the cat, who was waiting to see if she'd spill anything interesting. "I suppose you want a treat for not jumping up on the counter."

Moishe blinked once and then he let out a yowl. If there was one word he knew, it was *treat*.

"Okay then." Hannah struggled for a moment, unlatching the childproof fastener on the cupboard door. All the cupboards had fasteners like that and she really ought to take them off. She'd spent most of a Sunday installing them right after the first time that Moishe had helped himself to his own kitty treats. Moishe had watched her install them and the moment she was through, he'd jumped up on the counter and promptly unfastened one.

She found the can of salmon-flavored, fish-shaped treats and tossed him one. "That's it," she said. "If you're good, you can have another when I put the first cookie sheet into the oven."

Hannah tossed one more salmon-flavored treat into Moishe's bowl and watched him dive in after it. Then she turned back to her cookie dough. The first time they'd tried to bake Pink Lemonade Cookies at The Cookie Jar, they'd discovered that the dough was a bit sticky and they'd simply refrigerated it until the next morning. Now Hannah decided to try another trick she'd learned. She was using a two-teaspoon scooper to scoop up the dough and transfer it to her cookie sheet. She ran a glass of water, placed the scooper in the glass to wet it, shook off the water and then attempted to form the cookies that way. It worked like a charm. Every time the dough began to stick to the scooper, she dipped it in the water again. Once the cookies were in the oven, she sat down at the kitchen table with a fresh cup of coffee to think about Barbara again.

As far as Hannah knew, Barbara had no enemies. Everybody that Hannah knew liked Barbara. She was a popular employee at the sheriff's station, the members of the St. Jude Ladies Society relied on her, and she was a well-liked member of several other Lake Eden clubs. Barbara was helpful, courteous, and sweet. Hannah had never heard her utter a cross word to anyone. She lived modestly in the house she'd inherited from her parents and Hannah was sure that if she asked around, Barbara's neighbors would all say they liked her. Yet someone had a motive for pushing Barbara off the roof. Whoever it was had wanted to kill her. There had to be a reason and Hannah knew she had to discover what that reason was.

Hannah flipped the cover on the brand new shorthand notebook she'd taken out of the drawer and carried it to the table. She stared at the blank page for a full minute and then she took a pen from the container that sat in the center of the table and wrote down a single word followed by a question mark. *Motive?* it read.

TICKLED PINK LEMONADE COOKIES

Preheat oven to 350 degrees F., rack in the middle position.

Hannah's 1st Note: This recipe is from Lisa's Aunt Nancy. It's a real favorite down at The Cookie Jar because the cookies are different, delicious, and very pretty.

1/2 cup salted, softened butter (*1 stick, 4 ounces, 1/4 pound*) (*do not substitute*)

1/2 cup white (*granulated*) sugar

1/2 teaspoon baking powder

1/4 teaspoon baking soda

1 large egg, beaten

1/3 cup frozen pink or regular lemonade concentrate, thawed

3 drops of liquid red food coloring (*I used 1/2 teaspoon of Betty Crocker food color gel*)

1 and 3/4 cups all-purpose flour (*pack it down in the cup when you measure it*)

In the bowl of an electric mixer, beat the softened butter with the sugar until the resulting mixture is light and fluffy.

Mix in the baking powder and baking soda. Beat until they're well-combined.

Mix in the beaten egg and the lemonade

84

concentrate.

Add 3 drops of red food coloring (*or 1/2 teaspoon of the food color gel, if you used that*).

Add the flour, a half-cup or so at a time, beating after each addition. (*You don't have to be exact — just don't put in all the flour at once.*)

If the resulting cookie dough is too sticky to work with, refrigerate it for an hour or so. (*Don't forget to turn off your oven if you do this. You'll have to preheat it again once you're ready to bake.*) Drop the cookies by teaspoonful, 2 inches apart, on an UNGREASED cookie sheet.

Bake the Tickled Pink Lemonade Cookies at 350 degrees F. for 10 to 12 minutes or until the edges are golden brown. (*Mine took 11 minutes.*)

Let the cookies cool on the cookie sheet for 2 minutes. Then use a metal spatula to remove them to a wire rack to cool completely.

FROSTING FOR PINK LEMONADE COOKIES

2 Tablespoons salted butter, softened
2 cups powdered sugar (*no need to sift unless it's got big lumps*)

2 teaspoons frozen pink or regular lemonade concentrate, thawed

3 to 4 teaspoons milk (**water will also work for a less creamy frosting**)

2 drops red food coloring (**or enough red food color gel to turn the frosting pink**)

Beat the butter and the powdered sugar together.

Mix in the lemonade concentrate.

Beat in the milk, a bit at a time, until the frosting is almost thin enough to spread, but not quite.

Mix in the 2 drops of red food coloring. Stir until the color is uniform.

If your frosting is too thin, add a bit more powdered sugar. If your frosting is too thick, add a bit more milk or water.

Frost the completely cooled cookies. When the frosting has hardened, you can store them in layers with waxed paper between the layers to keep them from sticking together.

Yield: Approximately 2 and 1/2 to 3 dozen cookies, depending on cookie size.

Hannah's 2nd Note: When Mother and Carrie tasted these cookies down at The Cookie Jar, they decided that these cookies are as refreshing as a glass of icy cold lemonade on a hot summer

afternoon.

To serve, arrange these cookies on a pretty plate.

Hannah's 3rd Note: I used a sky blue plate when I took these cookies out to Barbara at the hospital. The pink of the cookies and the blue of the plate looked lovely together.

A Note from Lisa's Aunt Nancy: I can see these cookies on a plate with snippets of the candied lemon slices we ate as children on top of the frosting.

CHAPTER FIVE

Barbara's cookies were done. Hannah rinsed out her bowls, spoons, and spatulas and put them in the dishwasher. Once she'd filled the dispenser with detergent and shut the door again, she turned it on. Then she went back to her bedroom to get dressed.

She was just attempting to decide what to wear for a visit to the hospital when the phone rang. She reached out to grab it, hoping against hope that it was Barbara again, but it was Mike.

"Hi, Hannah. I'm not calling too early, am I? I know Sunday's your only day off."

"No, I've been up for a while. Hi, Mike."

"What's wrong? You sounded almost disappointed it was me. Were you expecting another call, maybe from Norman?"

There was a hint of jealousy in his voice and Hannah felt good about that. The two men were friends, but they were also rivals when it came to her. There was nothing like having two men vying for her affections. It kept them both on their toes and it made her feel much younger, much more beautiful, and much thinner than she actually was.

"From Norman?" Mike repeated.

"No, not Norman. What can I do for you, Mike?"

"You can marry me, but I know that's not going to happen anytime soon. In the meantime, how about meeting me for breakfast at the Corner Tavern?"

"Great idea!" Hannah said, and meant it. She needed to talk to Mike anyway to find out if they'd found any evidence at the scene or up on the penthouse rooftop. And, perhaps even more important, she was hungry and she absolutely loved the food at the Corner Tavern.

Once they'd set a time and hung up, Hannah opened her closet to choose an outfit. Since she would be leaving Mike right after breakfast and driving to the hospital, she chose a dark green short-sleeved top with lace at the neckline. It was comfortable, but just a bit dressy, which would be perfect for her visit with Barbara. She was about to take her favorite pair of jeans off the hook and wear those, when she reconsidered. Delores worked at the hospital on Sunday afternoons and Hannah was bound to run into her. The last time she'd seen her mother on a Sunday, Delores had criticized her for wearing jeans. She was used to being criticized by her mother, but there had been a terrible ramification after the criticism. The very next day, Delores had taken Hannah out to the Tri-County Mall to buy her some *appropriate* clothing. Perhaps some daughters would be delighted with a wardrobe purchased by their mothers, but not Hannah. Of course she was grateful that she didn't have to pay for all those tops, slacks, and pantsuits. As she remembered, they had cost her mother a small fortune. But there was nothing Hannah hated more than spending hours at the mall, shopping.

"I'm a hunter, not a shopper," she told Moishe, who'd followed her into the bedroom. "If I have to go out to the mall for something, I find it, buy it, and leave. I don't go looking for a lot of other things. I think that's better than spending hours going from this store to that store."

Moishe closed his eye in a wink and Hannah figured that was response enough. She would have preferred the satisfaction of a yowl or at least a nod, but he looked more interested in the fly that was buzzing outside the screen than in her shopping advice.

"I'd better wear a pair of pants she bought

for me," Hannah said, reaching in the closet for the grey pair. "I don't want another shopping trip with Mother."

"Rrrrrowwww!"

This time the response was both immediate and loud, and Hannah reached out to give him a reassuring pet. "She's not coming here. You'll have the whole place to yourself while I'm gone. I'm just going to meet Mike for breakfast, visit Barbara at the hospital, and come right back here when I'm through."

Moishe started to purr and Hannah wondered if it was a reaction to what she'd told him, or whether the purr was just a coincidence. She decided she'd prefer to think it was a reaction to the news she'd be back soon, and she was smiling as she walked down the hallway to the kitchen.

It didn't take long to pack up the cookies in boxes. Once she'd covered the frosting with wax paper, she closed the lids and carried the boxes out to the Chevy Blazer the neighborhood kids called her "cookie truck." There were other people in town with old Chevy Blazers, but Hannah had made hers distinctive. She'd painted it candy-apple red and there were signs advertising The Cookie Jar on both sides.

The Corner Tavern was only a few miles

from her condo complex and Hannah pulled into the parking lot with five minutes to spare. She found a shady parking spot under the canopy of an elm tree and got out to check the status of the cookies she'd secured in the back. The cookies were fine and she replaced the windshield sunscreen she'd used to cover them, locked her truck, and walked across the parking lot to the entrance.

The air-conditioning was running full blast and she reveled in the cool air that came out to greet her as she opened the door of the restaurant. The interior was rustic with lots of greenery and the air was perfumed with the scent of bacon, sausage, and breakfast steaks on the grill.

"Hi, Hannah," the hostess greeted her. "He's here already. I gave him that table you like in the back."

"Thanks!" Hannah said, even though the hostess had turned away to greet another big party of customers who'd come in behind her. She moved toward the main entrance, but stopped to pet Roscoe, the huge grizzly bear that stood in a fighting stance near the door. Roscoe was old, but he'd been recently rejuvenated by a taxidermy firm in Sauk Centre at considerable expense, but the patrons had taken up a collection to help in the effort. As everyone said who'd dropped a bill or coins in the collection box that had hung on the wall next to the huge grizzly, "This place wouldn't be right without Roscoe."

Hannah gave a wave as she spotted Mike and began to wind her way through the crowded main dining room. The Corner Tavern attracted both young and old. If you didn't like steak, you could get chicken, fresh fish, or even a couple of vegetarian dishes. It wasn't gourmet fare like you could enjoy at Sally and Dick's restaurant in the Lake Eden Inn, but it was well-prepared, totally delicious, and relatively inexpensive. Even better, as far as the Winnetka County sheriff's deputies were concerned, the Corner Tavern was only a stone's throw from the sheriff's station. As a matter of fact, she'd met Andrea and Barbara here for lunch only last week.

Thoughts of Barbara caused worry to cloud her face and Hannah was frowning when she reached Mike's table. "Hi, Mike," she greeted him, forcing a smile.

"What's the problem?" Mike asked as she sat down.

Hannah had expected as much. Mike was a master interrogator. He picked up on every nuance in a subject's voice and even

93

the slightest physical signs of emotion. "I can't decide whether I should have the steak and eggs, or the eggs and steak."

"Very funny." Mike reached out to take her hand. "Seriously, Hannah, what is it?"

Hannah decided to be completely truthful . . . at least to a point. "It's Barbara," she said. "I'm worried sick about her. Did you find any evidence of foul play last night?"

"You know I can't tell you that."

Their waitress came over with orange juice, coffee, and water. "Hi, Mike," she said with a smile aimed more at Mike than at Hannah.

"Hi, Misty. How are you doing this morning?"

"Good. *Very* good. I had a *wonderful* night last night." She gave Mike a kittenish look as she carefully set down his orange juice. Then she set Hannah's down without looking and it would have collided with her water glass if Hannah hadn't grabbed it.

"Excuse me, Misty," Hannah said to get her attention. "This isn't orange juice. It's milk."

"Sorry." By the tone in her voice Hannah could tell she wasn't sorry at all. "I guess I grabbed the wrong glass. You want it anyway?"

"No thanks. I'll take an orange juice, please."

"Okey dokey." Misty reached out to grab the milk and almost knocked it over. "So Mike . . ." She turned back to him. "Do you two need menus this morning?"

"Not me," Mike answered, smiling at her. It was the same sexy smile that always made Hannah's knees feel weak whenever it was directed at her. "I think I know the menu even better than you do."

"I bet you know a *lot* of things even better than I do. Of course I know some things, too. Maybe I even know some things that *you* don't know."

This is incredible, Hannah thought. *She's flirting with him right in front of me. What am I? The invisible woman? Of course Mike probably sees her every day when he drops by for coffee. Or for all I know, he could be dating her!*

Hannah pressed her lips together to keep her thoughts silent. She didn't have an exclusive relationship with Mike . . . or Norman either, for that matter. All three of them were free to date other people. She had no right to complain if Mike dated Misty, no right at all. But that didn't stop the sharp jab of jealousy that ran through her.

It's only because she's ignoring you and she's rude, Hannah's mind said. *That's why you don't like her.*

But Hannah knew it was also because Misty had a Barbie doll figure and Mike obviously enjoyed the way she was flirting with him.

"Back to what we were talking about before Misty," Mike picked up the conversation once Misty had taken their orders and left. "And by the way, she flirts with all of the guys like that. It's kind of cute and it doesn't mean anything."

"Right," Hannah said, although she had her doubts. "I asked you if you'd found anything incriminating at the scene last night in the rose garden or on the penthouse roof."

"And I said I couldn't tell you that." Mike pushed his orange juice over to Hannah. "Take mine. I don't really want it anyway and Misty will forget all about bringing yours. We gave her our orders and she'll put them in, but she can only keep one thing in her mind at a time."

Hannah picked up the orange juice and took a swallow, even though she no longer wanted it. Mike had been nice enough to give it to her and she'd drink it in appreciation. "Let me get this straight. If you found

96

something incriminating at the scene, you couldn't tell me. Is that right?"

"That's right. You know that I can't discuss police business with you."

"I know that," Hannah agreed quickly. "But you just told me that it *is* police business. And that means you found something incriminating."

"I hate it when you do that!" Mike gave her a long-suffering look. "No, it doesn't mean that we found something incriminating. All it means is that we found something that *could* be incriminating and we have to investigate it."

"You're equivocating."

"And you're probing into something that's none of your business."

They glared at each other for a moment and Misty took that exact moment to bring Hannah's orange juice. "Oh, pooh!" she said, her head swiveling from one to the other the way it would if she were watching a tennis match. "Two somebodies here are mad at each other, huh?"

Hannah couldn't help it. She started to laugh. She'd never heard anyone put things in quite that way. A moment later, Mike joined in and they laughed even harder when Misty made a circle by her ear and then tapped her head, in the age-old sign for crazy.

"I'm sorry," Mike said when Misty had left again. "I shouldn't have yelled at you."

"I'm sorry, too. I shouldn't have yelled, either."

"Okay. Let's forget it. It's just that I hate it when you try to trap me with words, especially when I've been up all night and I'm tired."

Hannah reached out to take his hand. "I understand, but I really need to know what's going on."

"Why?"

Hannah hesitated and then she blurted it out. "Because Barbara called me at four this morning and told me that someone tried to kill her. She didn't tell me who and I'm not really sure it was Barbara. I'm going to go visit her at the hospital after breakfast and try to find out more."

"Will you tell me if you do?"

"Yes. Will you tell me what evidence you found last night?"

"Yes, but it's not really evidence. We found a couple of things that didn't look right, but that doesn't necessarily mean anything. They could also be compatible with an accident."

"But you don't think it *was* an accident."

Mike hesitated, and then he shook his

head. "Nope. A couple of the barricades were moved out of the way so that someone could get closer to the edge of the roof. They're heavy and I really don't think Barbara would go to that trouble just to see if she could spot her house from up there."

"Then you know that she wanted to try to see her house from the penthouse garden?"

"Oh, yes. She mentioned it to several people. The idea of seeing her house from above intrigued her."

"Tell me about the barricades that were out of place. Andrea and I moved one earlier so that she could show me the lake. It took both of us to do it because it was heavy. Were the barricades that were out of place too heavy for Barbara to move?"

"No. Barbara's a strong woman. It would have taken a big effort, though."

"What else made you suspicious?"

"The barricades were dirty. They'd obviously been used in the construction and some of them even had grease on them. It doesn't seem likely that Barbara would have moved them in her party clothes."

"That's true."

"There's another thing, too. There was dirt on Barbara's hands, but you'd expect that. She landed in the rose garden. But there wasn't a trace of grease. I had Doc check."

"Is there anything else?"

Mike shook his head. "Not really. We're still waiting for the crime lab to do its thing, but I doubt it'll be very helpful. If someone planned to kill Barbara, they were probably very careful not to leave anything behind."

"If someone did try to kill her and didn't succeed, they might try again," Hannah voiced her concern. "Do you think Barbara is in any danger at the hospital?"

"I don't know. We don't have enough officers to put a round-the-clock guard on her, but I talked to Doc and he's already assigned three shifts of nurses for her. And I really don't think anybody will be brazen enough to try to finish the job while she's in the hospital."

Hannah remembered how much danger Freddy Sawyer had been in when he was confined to a hospital bed.

"Let's not put the cart before the horse. We don't even know, for sure, that somebody *did* try to kill Barbara."

"True," Hannah said, realizing that he was right, but not believing that for a second.

CHAPTER SIX

"You're looking good, Barbara," Hannah said, even though it wasn't true. Barbara's face was puffy and bruised, her left leg was obviously injured in some way because it was elevated in a sling that hung from the ceiling, and both of her arms were heavily bandaged.

Barbara smiled through caked lips, showing several gaps where teeth had been less than twenty-four hours ago. "Thank you. I feel better. Is my father here?"

Hannah exchanged glances with her mother, who'd come along on the visit. Both of them knew that Barbara's father had died years ago when Barbara was still in school.

"Is he here? I have to know!"

Barbara sounded desperate and Hannah wasn't sure what to say. Thankfully, Delores leaned closer to cover Barbara's hands with her own. "Barbara, dear," she said, giving

Barbara's hand a comforting pat. "I'm sorry, Barbara, but your father's not here. He can't come to see you, dear. Don't you remember? He died."

"Oh, no! That's . . . that's awful!" Barbara's words were slurred, something Doc Knight had warned them about. He'd said that when Barbara became upset, her ability to speak deteriorated. He'd also told them that if she asked any questions, they should answer them honestly. And that was precisely what Delores had done.

"Don't think about it now," Delores urged in an effort to calm Barbara, who was clearly agitated. "Thinking about sad things too much won't do any good and it will only upset you."

Barbara was silent for a moment and then she tried to nod. It must have hurt to move her head, because an expression of pain flickered across her face. "You're right," she said. "What was your name again?"

"It's Delores."

"Oh, yes." She turned to look at Hannah. "And you are . . . the daughter."

"Yes, I'm Delores's daughter," Hannah replied, thankful that Doc Knight had mentioned the swelling in Barbara's brain and how it had affected her ability to remember proper names. "My name is Hannah."

"Yes. Hannah. I'll try to remember. It's just so sad about my father. I only got to know him for a little while. And I really wanted to see him again."

She's cuckoo bananas! the outspoken part of Hannah's mind commented.

Be quiet and show a little sympathy! Hannah responded in an internal dialogue. *Barbara has a head injury. Doc Knight warned us that she might say some bizarre things.*

Hannah checked the time on her waterproof watch. She'd ruined several previous watches by forgetting to remove them before rinsing out mixing bowls at The Cookie Jar. They had already been here for three minutes. Doc Knight had placed a five-minute limit on their visit and it was time to ask the important questions before Barbara's nurse came to get them and escort them out.

"Do you remember calling me early this morning?" Hannah asked, getting right to the heart of the matter.

Barbara looked as surprised as anyone with facial swelling, scrapes, and bruises could look. "I called you?"

"You did. You called at a little after four."

"Are you sure?"

103

"It sounded like you on the phone. And when I asked if it was Barbara, you said yes."

"It must have been me then. But I . . ." Barbara stopped and took a quick breath. "I don't remember calling you."

Hannah gave Barbara a moment to compose herself. It was apparent that she was becoming agitated again. While she was waiting, Hannah glanced at the phone sitting on top of the stand sitting next to Barbara's hospital bed. It was definitely within Barbara's reach. Doc Knight had told them that Barbara had trouble remembering things, but that he was hopeful her memory would improve once the swelling in her brain went down.

"Why did I call you? What did I say?"

She sounded much calmer and Hannah knew it was time to ask the question that would upset Barbara the most. "You said that your fall wasn't an accident, that someone tried to kill you."

"Someone tried to kill me," Barbara said, and Hannah wasn't sure if she was simply repeating the accusation in surprise, or whether she was confirming it. "I wonder who it was."

Hannah and Delores exchanged glances again. This conversation was becoming very strange.

"I have to think," Barbara said and then there was a long moment of silence. The only sounds in the room were the hum of Barbara's IV and the soft beeping of the various pieces of electronic monitoring equipment that were arranged around Barbara's bed. Finally, when the waiting had become almost unbearable, Delores cleared her throat.

"*Did* someone try to kill you, Barbara?" she asked.

Barbara hesitated for a moment, as if she was reluctant to say. The pain lines around her mouth whitened and drew taut when she finally dipped her head. "Someone tried to kill me."

This time it was definitely a confirmation. And that meant the most important question had to come next.

"Who was it?" Hannah asked her.

Barbara gave a sigh that sounded so heartbroken that tears formed in Hannah's eyes. But she couldn't stop now. Barbara had admitted that someone had attempted to kill her. "Who tried to kill you, Barbara? I need to know."

"*He* did," Barbara answered in a shaking voice. "I . . . I never thought he'd do something like that. I . . . I wanted him to love me."

105

"I need to know his name," Hannah pressed on, even though Barbara was visibly agitated. "You have to tell me, Barbara."

Barbara took a deep breath that must have been painful because she gave a little moan. "I remember now," she said at last. "My *brother* tried to kill me!"

"Barbara doesn't have a brother," Delores told her as they walked down the hallway toward Doc Knight's office. Today she was wearing her bright yellow blazer and she gleamed like a ray of sunshine against the pale green walls.

"Could he be dead like her father? Barbara said she wanted to see him again and he's dead. Maybe she thought she was dying and she was going to see them in the hereafter."

Delores considered it for a moment. "That might be what she thought when she mentioned her father, but I know for a fact that Barbara's mother had only one child and that child was Barbara. I'm almost sure I heard your grandmother say that there were complications when Barbara was born and Mrs. Donnelly couldn't have any more children."

"Did she have a hysterectomy?" Hannah

mentioned the first thing that occurred to her.

"I have no idea. That was years ago, when I was a child. Adults didn't discuss anything like that in front of children. The only reason I remember as much as I do is that your grandmother shushed my mother and pointed to me. And then she said something about little pitchers."

"Little pitchers have big ears?" Hannah guessed.

"That's it. And since they'd said the same thing when they were discussing Christmas presents, I knew that meant whatever they'd said was important."

"Would Doc Knight know for sure?"

"I think so, dear. When he came to town to take over the practice, all the old charts were stored in a back room. He probably still has them in storage somewhere."

"Could you check on that? I need to make sure that Barbara never had a brother."

"I understand, dear. And of course I can check. I'll ask Doc just as soon as he comes back to his office."

"Thanks, Mother." Hannah waved at Norman's mother, Carrie, who was pushing a cart down the hallway toward them. Carrie, like Delores, was also wearing black pants, but her blazer was bright turquoise.

Hannah's neighbor, Marguerite Hollenbeck, was walking at the side of the cart and her blazer was bright pink. It was part of the Rainbow Ladies' attire. When Delores had agreed to take over as leader of the Grey Ladies, she'd immediately given the volunteer organization a new name and a new cheerful look.

"What's on the cart?" Delores asked as they approached.

"Milk and cookies," Carrie answered her.

"What kind of cookies?" Hannah asked.

"Store-bought chocolate-covered graham crackers," Marguerite told her. "The children just love those. We're taking them down to the family waiting room."

Once they'd passed, Hannah turned to her mother. The fact that there had been cookies on the tray had reminded her of the cookies that were still sitting in the back of her truck.

"I baked some cookies for Barbara, but when I found out she was on a liquid diet, I left them in my truck. Do you think the nurses would like some Tickled Pink Lemonade Cookies?"

Delores gave her a look of pure disbelief. "Of *course* the nurses would like them. Anybody who's ever tasted them likes them. They're very good cookies, dear."

"Great. If I put them on a platter and bring them back here to you, will you pass them around?"

"I'll be glad to as long as I can keep some for Doc." Delores thought about what she had said for a second and then she added, "And for me."

"Of course. That goes without saying. I'll go out and get them right now."

"I'll go with you. That way you don't have to come all the way back inside."

Once the cookies were plated and the platter had been covered with plastic wrap, Hannah told her mother goodbye and climbed into the driver's seat of her cookie truck. She was about to start the engine and back out of her parking space when Norman pulled in next to her. Hannah wasted no time lowering her window and he lowered his at the same time. "Hi, Norman," she greeted him.

"Hello, Hannah. What are you doing here?"

"Visiting Barbara. Is that where you're going?"

"Yes, but it's an official visit. Doc Knight called me in to consult about her broken teeth."

Hannah thought fast. She wanted to learn Norman's assessment of Barbara's condition and it would be easier to ask him questions in person than on the phone. She also wanted to find out whether Doctor Bev had contacted him and that would take a little finesse on her part. But those weren't the only two reasons. The third reason was purely personal and had to do only with the two of them. They'd both been busy in the past few weeks and their time together had been limited by other obligations. Tonight was a free night for her. She had absolutely nothing to do. And since she had enjoyed his company so much last night, she wanted to spend more time with him.

"Would you like to come out to my place for an early dinner?" she asked.

"That sounds good to me. What time?"

"Six o'clock?"

"That should work. Can I bring anything?"

"Yes, bring Cuddles."

Norman smiled when she mentioned his cat. "I'll be glad to bring Cuddles, but I was talking about bringing something for dinner."

"Thanks, but I can't think of anything I need," Hannah said, not bothering to say that she didn't have any idea what she was going to serve.

Once Norman had gone inside, Hannah

backed out of her spot and exited the parking lot. She was so busy trying to think of a meal they'd both enjoy that she almost turned left and took the scenic route around Eden Lake instead of turning right on the shorter route to town.

Before she made the turn, Hannah glanced at her watch. Thanks to Florence's new hours at the Red Owl, she had plenty of time to shop. Florence had announced her new weekend hours in the *Lake Eden Journal* this week. Instead of selling groceries all day on Saturday, she would only be open from noon to six. And although the store had always been closed on Sundays, there would now be a short shopping window from noon to four.

The new hours suited Hannah just fine. She often had company on Sunday nights and she wasn't a very good advance planner. There were staples in her pantry. Every Minnesota cook had them in case of blizzards in the winter, summer rainstorms, or car troubles at any time of year. Hannah had enough stock in the pantry to live on for several weeks, but not everything there was something she'd choose to serve to company. She knew that Norman would be happy to share a can of pork and beans with her, but she wanted to cook something special. When she got to the store, perhaps she'd ask Florence for ideas.

Ten minutes later, Hannah was standing in front of the meat counter facing Florence, who was wearing her butcher whites.

"What'll it be, Hannah?" Florence asked.

"I don't know. I was hoping you could give me some advice. I invited Norman over for dinner tonight and I don't have the foggiest idea what I'm going to serve."

"Chicken Tetrazzini Hotdish."

The response was so immediate, Hannah was surprised. It was almost as if Florence had been hoping she'd ask that very question. "Chicken Tetrazzini Hotdish? I've never heard of it."

"That's because I just made it two nights ago. It's from my cousin, Marci Watts, and she's a really good cook. That hot-dish was so good, I decided to give you the recipe the next time I saw you."

Florence handed her a recipe card and Hannah looked it over. It looked easy and it also looked delicious. "Perfect. It's exactly what I'll make. Do you have any cooked, cubed chicken?"

"Sorry. You'll have to cook and cube it yourself. But I do have some boneless, skinless chicken breasts. Just put salt on them, put them in a greased pan, and cover the pan with foil. Forty-five minutes at three-fifty ought to do it. That's how I cooked mine."

"Great. How many did you use?"

"I used four, but I'll give you five. That way you can bake one for Moishe."

"For Moishe *and* Cuddles. Norman's bringing her over for dinner."

"I'll wrap the chicken while you shop. What else are you going to serve?"

Hannah glanced down at the recipe again. "There aren't really any vegetables in this, so I'll put together a nice garden salad."

"A salad's always good. Throw in some butter lettuce. This batch is better than the iceberg. And get some of those little grape tomatoes. They're tangy and sweet. How about dessert?"

"I'm not sure yet, unless . . ." Hannah stopped and considered the new recipe Delores had asked her to test. Norman wouldn't mind being a recipe tester and she could kill two birds with one stone. "Mother gave me a recipe I need to try. She got it from a nurse at the hospital."

"If it turns out well will you give me a copy?"

"Of course. I like exchanging recipes with you, Florence."

"Just one more thing before you go." Florence leaned over the counter so that she was closer to Hannah. "Did Norman hear from Doctor Bev?"

"Not that I know of. I didn't have time to ask him when I saw him today at the hospital."

"Norman's at the *hospital*?"

"Yes, but he was there to consult with Doc Knight about Barbara's teeth. She broke some when she fell last night."

"I know. One of the nurses told me. Poor Barbara. She's such a good person. I just wish she hadn't gone that close to the edge of the roof."

"Me, too," Hannah said, managing to keep her face perfectly blank as she walked off to do the rest of her shopping. Florence was a charter member of the Lake Eden Gossip Hotline and if she even suspected that Barbara's fall hadn't been an accident, the news would be all over town before Hannah even had time to get up to the checkout stand.

CHICKEN TETRAZZINI HOTDISH

Preheat oven to 350 degrees F., rack in the middle position.

1 and 1/4 cups spaghetti (*I used Ronzoni, half of a one-pound package*)

1 and 1/2 to 2 cups cooked chicken, cut up in cubes

1/4 cup diced, canned pimento (*approximately 1 small jar — you can buy it already diced*)

1/4 of a green bell pepper, diced

1 small onion, diced

Dash of sherry (*optional*)

1 can condensed cream of mushroom soup (*I used Campbell's*)

1/2 cup chicken broth (*I used a bouillon cube dissolved in a half-cup of hot water*)

1/2 teaspoon salt (*I used Lawry's garlic salt since there's no other garlic in the recipe*)

1/8 teaspoon black pepper (*freshly ground is best*)

2 to 3 cups grated cheddar cheese (*or grated Italian cheeses*)

1 clove garlic finely minced (*optional*)

1 small can sliced black olives, drained (*optional*)

1 small can Ortega diced green chilies,

drained (*optional*)

"Slap Ya Mama" hot sauce (*optional, for Mike*)

Hannah's 1st Note: Florence likes things on the bland side and while this hotdish is delicious just the way she made it, I spiced it up a little for Norman by adding a clove of garlic and a small can of diced green chilies. I also added a small can of sliced black olives to add interest. I served this with a bowl of freshly grated parmesan to sprinkle on top of each serving. When Mike unexpectedly joined us for dinner, I put a bottle of "Slap Ya Mama" hot sauce on the table for him.

Break the spaghetti into pieces approximately 4 inches long. Cook the spaghetti in boiling, salted water, according to the package directions. (*Mine cooked for 10 minutes.*) Drain it and rinse it.

Place the cooked spaghetti, cubed chicken, pimento, green pepper, and onion in a large bowl. At this point, add any optional ingredients you decided to add.

Pour the sherry (*if you decided to use it*), the condensed soup, and the chicken broth over the top.

Sprinkle on the salt and the pepper and stir them in.

Add HALF of the grated cheese, and lightly toss everything together with a fork. (*I gave up on the fork and used my impeccably clean fingers instead.*)

Spray a 1 and 1/2 quart casserole dish with Pam or another nonstick cooking spray. Set it on a drip pan, just in case.

Transfer the contents of your mixing bowl to the casserole dish.

Sprinkle the remaining shredded cheese on top.

Bake the Chicken Tetrazzini Hotdish at 350 degrees F., for 45 minutes.

Hannah's 2nd Note: To double this recipe, just double the ingredients and bake it in a larger casserole dish. You don't have to double the baking time, but I'd give it an extra 20 minutes or so.

When I make this for a potluck dinner, I use a disposable, half-size steam table pan. (Use 2 nested together, if the ones you buy are flimsy.) Since it spreads out in the disposable pan, I only give it an extra 15 minutes, bringing the baking time up to one hour. The reason I use a disposable pan is that I don't have to wait around for my pan to be washed at the end of the evening.

Yield: This hotdish serves 4 if you pair it with a nice salad and rolls or garlic bread.

Hannah's 3rd Note: This recipe is so easy I'm going to tell Mother to add it to her repertoire of entrees.

CHAPTER SEVEN

The Chicken Tetrazzini Hotdish had been every bit as easy as Florence had promised. It was a winner recipe. Hannah slipped the casserole dish in the oven, along with the cookie sheet that would act as a drip pan, and set the timer. Norman would be here in thirty minutes and that would give them plenty of time to nibble on the cheese tray she'd prepared as an appetizer and sip coffee or the pink lemonade she'd made from the leftover frozen concentrate.

The next thing Hannah did was read through the recipe her mother had given her for Easy Fruit Pie. She'd picked up a can of peach pie filling because peaches were Norman's favorite fruit.

Since she had a double oven, a feature Hannah gave thanks for every time she baked, she mixed up the crust for the Easy Fruit Pie, spooned on the filling, and slipped it into the lower oven. Then she glanced at the apple-shaped clock on her kitchen wall and set a secondary timer for fifty minutes. Her dessert would be ready and slightly cooled by the time they'd finished their salad and hotdish. At that time, she'd dish it up and couple it with a scoop of the vanilla bean ice cream.

As she went out into the living room to set plates, napkins, and silverware on the coffee table, she thought about what a challenge it was for young cooks to make a meal where everything was ready on time. It took some planning and there were always unexpected delays. When she'd first started to hold dinner parties, she'd always had trouble getting the vegetables to the table on time. She'd coped by serving a lot of one-dish Crock-Pot meals where the meat and vegetable were in the same pot. She'd also learned to prepare the vegetables ahead of time and serve them cold. Her guests had loved sliced tomatoes and red onions with vinegar and oil drizzled over the top, and chilled cooked asparagus with mustard hollandaise. Even today, as a veteran cook, she was careful not to have more than two time-critical items in a meal. She knew that delays invariably happened and company dinners never went like clockwork. The trick was to anticipate and keep it simple.

Hannah had no sooner changed into a comfortable lightweight lounge outfit when the doorbell rang. She opened it without remembering to check the peephole, something both Mike and Norman had warned her against, and smiled as she saw Norman standing there. He was holding a cat carrier and she reached out to take the package in his arms so that his load would be lighter.

"Hi, Norman," she greeted him happily. Norman was the perfect dinner guest. Actually, he was the perfect *everything*. He'd asked her to marry him almost two years ago and she knew she'd never find anyone more loving and faithful. She loved him, she loved his cat. He loved her, he loved her cat. Norman would make a perfect husband. What was she waiting for?

"Rrrrrowww!" Moishe stood outside the cage impatiently when Norman set it down on the rug.

"Okay, big fella. Hold on a second and I'll let her out."

Norman unlatched the crate and Cuddles ran straight to Moishe and batted him with her paw. "And they're off," Norman said as the two cats ran down the hallway with Cuddles in the lead and Moishe chasing her. He held out his arms to give Hannah a hug. "Something smells fantastic," he told her.

"Chicken Tetrazzini Hotdish and Easy Fruit Pie."

"Sounds wonderful." Norman gestured toward the bag she was holding. "Open it. It's for you."

Hannah opened the bag and pulled out a bottle of champagne. But it wasn't just *any* bottle of champagne, and she gripped the bottle even tighter. "Dom Perignon," she breathed, reading the label.

"I thought you might like it."

"Like it? *Like* it? This is Dom Perignon. It's even more expensive than the champagne Mother likes!"

"I know, but this is a split. It wasn't as expensive as a whole bottle and it only holds two glasses."

"Then you're going to have some champagne with me?" The surprise was clear in Hannah's voice. Norman didn't drink and she knew the reason why he didn't. Was tonight some kind of an exception?

"Not for me, thanks. I brought it for you."

Hannah's heart beat a little faster as something occurred to her. "Enough for two glasses, but you don't drink. Are you trying to get me . . ." She paused, trying to come up with the right word, but settled for a euphemism that fell short of what she was intending. "Are you trying to get me *compliant*?"

"Compliant?" Norman gave a short laugh. "That would be a lost cause! There isn't enough champagne in the world to get you *compliant.* Just remember that the more champagne you drink, the sexier I look."

Now it was Hannah's turn to laugh and she did. It was the first good laugh she'd had since she'd visited Barbara at the hospital and it felt good.

"It's good to hear you laugh, Hannah." Norman looked pleased. "But really, suit yourself. Drink it all, or don't drink it all. That's completely up to you. If you don't want the second glass, that's okay with me."

Right. Sure. Hannah's mind went into sarcasm mode. *You brought me a bottle of one of the best champagnes in the world, champagne I've never tasted before and probably won't ever get the chance to taste again. And you actually think I'm going to drink one glass and dump the rest down the garbage disposal?!*

When Hannah looked over at Norman, she saw that he was grinning. Had he guessed she was having an internal dialogue with her mind? "You've got to be kidding about throwing part of this out."

"You bet I am. Let's enjoy the night, Hannah. I know I will. Both of us need to relax and have fun, now that we're about to gear up for two more investigations."

Hannah blinked in surprise. "I know you're talking about Clayton Wallace. We have to prove his death was accidental so we can get that insurance money for his son. But you said *two* investigations."

"Yes. We have to investigate Barbara's fall."

Hannah put two and two together and swallowed hard. "Then Barbara wasn't imagining things when she said someone tried to kill her?"

"Doc and I don't think so."

"Then you believe she has a brother who surfaced for the party and pushed her off the roof?"

"No, I don't believe the brother part of it. She's clearly confused about that. But we do think someone attempted to kill her. Doc and I came up with a possible scenario, and I'll tell you all about it after dinner. Right now I want to open this champagne for you."

Norman took the bottle and opened the champagne while Hannah got an empty champagne glass for her and a tall glass of lemonade for him. She was about to go back into the kitchen for the appetizer tray that she'd prepared when Norman reached out to stop her. "Sit down, Hannah," he invited, patting the couch next to him.

"Just let me get the cheese platter and then I will."

"The cheese platter can wait. Try the champagne first. I want to see if you like it."

"Of course I'll like it," Hannah said with a smile as she sat down beside him and accepted the glass. She took a sip and gave a blissful sigh. The champagne was every bit as good as its publicity. "Lovely," she breathed. "Are you sure you . . ."

"No, thanks," Norman interrupted her. "It's all yours."

Hannah took another sip and then she stood up again. "I'll get that cheese platter now. This champagne will be perfect with the triple-cream Camembert."

Once she'd returned with the appetizer tray and it was sitting between them on the coffee table, she turned to Norman. "Florence told me that the pears were just perfect today, and so were these flame grapes. They don't have seeds. The dark brown crackers are pumpernickel flatbread, and the white ones are salted water crackers. And the cheeses are Danish Stilton with apricots, Wisconsin extra-sharp aged Cheddar, and triple-cream Camembert. . . ."

"Hold it, Hannah!" Norman interrupted her explanation, as he gazed in amazement at the huge appetizer tray. "Are you expecting an army?"

"No. I just got a little carried away when Florence told me about the cheeses. And the leftovers will keep. It's just the two of us for dinner, Norman."

The words had barely left Hannah's lips when the phone rang. Both Hannah and Norman stared at it for a moment, and then their eyes met in total disbelief. "Do you think I should . . . ?" Hannah began.

"Answer it," Norman said with a sigh. "If we're lucky, it's a telemarketer and you can hang up right away."

Hannah reached for the phone as gingerly as if it were resting on the head of a hibernating bear. "Hello?" she asked in a tentative voice.

"Hi, Hannah! It's Mike."

"Hi, Mike." Hannah put her hand over the receiver and whispered, *It's Mike,* to Norman, quite unnecessarily.

"I just pulled into your complex. Is it okay if I come over? I want to find out what happened when you visited Barbara."

Hannah covered the receiver again. *He wants to come over,* she whispered.

Norman didn't say a thing. He just held out his hand for the phone. Hannah handed it over gratefully and listened as the two rivals for her affections conversed.

"It's Norman. Go ahead and come up." He turned to pantomime eating to Hannah and pointed to the phone. When Hannah nodded, he continued. "Hannah just fixed dinner and there's plenty for three."

There was a pause while Mike talked and Hannah assumed he was saying something about not wanting to intrude on their evening. Mike could be polite if he wanted to be.

"That's okay, Mike," Norman said, turning to give Hannah an apologetic look. "I've got something I need to tell you anyway."

This time the response was quicker. Hannah figured that Mike had asked Norman what that was.

"It's about Barbara, but I don't want to discuss it over the phone. Come on up, eat dinner, and then we'll talk about it, okay?"

Hannah frowned. It seemed that whatever information Norman had been planning to give her after dinner was now going to be shared with Mike. So much for exclusivity.

"Sorry," Norman said after the phone was back in the cradle. "I would have had to tell him anyway. I promised Doc I would."

"But you were going to tell me first?"

"That's right. I was."

It was a drop in the bucket, a smidgen, a crumb. But Norman was smiling warmly and for some strange reason, it was enough. Hannah smiled back and that warm-all-over feeling kept her toasty until the doorbell rang to announce Mike's arrival.

Easy Fruit Pie

Preheat oven to 375 degrees F., rack in the middle position.

Note from Delores: I got this recipe from Jenny Hester, a new nurse at Doc Knight's hospital. Jenny just told me that her great-grandmother used to make it whenever the family came over for Sunday dinner. Hannah said it's easy so I might actually try to make it some night for Doc.

1/4 cup salted butter (*1/2 stick, 2 ounces, 1/8 pound*)

1 cup whole milk

1 cup white (*granulated*) sugar

1 cup all-purpose flour (*pack it down in the cup when you measure it*)

1 and 1/2 teaspoons baking powder

1/2 teaspoon salt

1 can fruit pie filling (*approximately 21 ounces by weight — 3 to 3 and 1/2 cups, the kind that makes an 8-inch pie*)

Hannah's 1st Note: This isn't really a pie, and it isn't really a cake even though you make it in a cake pan. It's almost like a cobbler, but not quite. I

have the recipe filed under "Dessert". You can use any canned fruit pie filling you like. I might not bake it for company with blueberry pie filling. It tasted great, but didn't look all that appetizing. If you love blueberry and want to try it, it might work to cover the top with sweetened whipped cream or Cool Whip before you serve it.

I've tried this recipe with raspberry and peach . . . so far. I have the feeling that lemon pie filling would be yummy, but I haven't gotten around to trying it yet. Maybe I'll try it some night when Mike comes over after work. Even if it doesn't turn out that well, he'll eat it.

Place the butter in a 9-inch by 13-inch cake pan and put it in the oven to melt. Meanwhile . . .

Mix the milk, sugar, flour, baking powder and salt together in a medium-size bowl. This batter will be a little lumpy and that's okay. Just like brownie batter, don't over-mix it.

Using oven mitts or potholders, remove the pan with the melted butter from the oven. Pour in the batter and tip the pan around to cover the whole bottom. Then set it on a cold stove burner.

Spoon the pie filling over the stop of the

batter, but DO NOT MIX IN. Just spoon it on as evenly as you can. (*The batter will puff up around it in the oven and look gorgeous!*)

Bake the dessert at 375 degrees F., for 45 minutes to 1 hour, or until it turns golden brown and bubbly on top.

To serve, cool slightly, dish into bowls, and top with sweetened whipped cream or vanilla ice cream. It really is yummy.

Hannah's 2nd Note: The dessert is best when it's baked, cooled slightly, and served right away. Alternatively you can bake it earlier, cut pieces to put in microwave-safe bowls, and reheat it in the microwave before you put on the ice cream or sweetened whipped cream.

Yield: Easy Fruit Pie will serve 6 if you don't invite Mike and Norman for dinner.

Note from Jenny: I've made this by adding 1/4 cup cocoa powder and 1 teaspoon of vanilla to the batter. If I do this, I spoon a can of cherry pie filling over the top.

CHAPTER EIGHT

"What would you like to drink, Mike?" Hannah held her breath as she waited for his answer. She really didn't want to share the exquisite champagne Norman had given her, but she was a good hostess.

"That lemonade Norman has looks good. Do you have any more?"

"I sure do. I'll get you a glass and be right back."

Hannah was smiling as she went off to the kitchen. She felt a slight bit guilty for not telling Mike about the special champagne that Norman had brought, but she told herself that since he hadn't asked for a bottle of his favorite beer when he knew she always had some in her refrigerator, that probably meant he was going back in to work and didn't want to drink anything alcoholic. And *that* meant he would have refused the champagne even if she had offered it.

Rationalization, her mind chided her, but she ignored it as she filled a glass with ice and poured pink lemonade for Mike. She gave the timer a quick glance as she passed by on her way to the living room. Twenty minutes to go before the dessert came out of the oven. It should cool for at least ten minutes, so they would have a full half-hour to enjoy their salad, hotdish, and garlic bread.

"What did you have to tell me?" Mike asked Norman as Hannah set down his lemonade.

"Nothing until after dinner. I'm hungry."

"That's fine with me. I'm hungry and that hotdish smells great."

Mike turned to give Hannah one of his devilishly handsome grins as she set his favorite hot sauce on the table. He'd once told her that her hair was exactly the same color as Slap Ya Mama hot sauce, and she still wasn't sure if that was a compliment or not.

Hannah took a deep breath and did her best not to react to the grin that always made her a bit weak in the knees. She was Norman's date for the evening, not his. But even though her mind was clear on her priorities, she still felt a rush of tingly sensation that ran all the way down to her toes.

She busied herself dishing up the salad in the hope that it would distract her, but she still felt tingly as she ladled out the hotdish, passed the freshly grated parmesan cheese, and made sure both men had a piece of garlic bread.

"It's a feast," Mike said, grinning at her again. Hannah felt a second rush of sensation, but that ended quite abruptly when Mike reached for the bottle of hot sauce and shook it on without even tasting his hotdish first. *Too bad you didn't use jalapenos instead of green chilies,* her mind commented and this time Hannah didn't argue back. No internal dialogue was needed. She agreed perfectly.

Midway through the meal, the timer sounded and Hannah got up to take the Easy Fruit Pie out of the oven. She was just about to return to the living room when she heard Norman respond to something Mike had said.

"No way, Mike." Norman sounded very emphatic. "Remember the time we were discussing a case at the table and how angry Hannah got at us?"

There was a moment of silence. Mike was obviously attempting to remember. "Oh, yeah. I remember now. It was something about how many pounds of pressure it would take to break a tooth. Hannah got pretty hot about that one."

"Which is why we should wait for that kind of discussion until after dinner."

"Right. If we talk about it now, she might not give us dessert. I could use something sweet after this meal. Boy, that hotdish was spicy!"

That's because you used half a bottle of hot sauce on it, Hannah's mind answered him. *Maybe it'll teach you to taste it first to see if it needs more spice.*

Hannah was smiling as she carried in the dessert. Some people added salt without tasting and then complained because it was too salty. Mike did the same thing with hot sauce. Nothing would change him. He'd once told her that his father had done the same thing, and Hannah figured it must be a combination of both environment and genetics.

"Do you want some hot sauce, Mike?" Hannah asked him, smiling wickedly.

"On dessert? Are you kidding?!"

Mike looked shocked and Hannah laughed. "Of course I am. Unless, of course, we're talking about those Jalapeno Brownies I made for you."

"Oh, man! Those were so good!" Mike smacked his lips. "Do you suppose maybe this dessert would . . . ?"

"No!" Hannah cut off the question she knew was coming. "There's no chocolate in here so it wouldn't be the same thing." She paused for a second, glanced down the hallway, and warned, "Feet up!"

Both men were old hands at this game. They plucked their dessert dishes and coffee cups off the table almost simultaneously, and tucked their feet up just as the cats appeared. Hannah was a second late, but she managed to secure the coffee carafe and her own dessert dish in the nick of time.

Two rings around the table and the cats disappeared down the hallway again. Hannah heard a thud followed by a yowl and she knew that Moishe hadn't managed to avoid the laundry hamper in her bedroom. There was a thump and a squeak of springs, and then another thump and a louder squeak of springs, as Cuddles and then Moishe landed on her mattress.

"You need a new innerspring," Norman said.

"I know. I just haven't gotten around to buying one yet. Actually, I need a whole new bed."

"Get one of those airbeds," Mike suggested. "They're supposed to be really comfortable."

Hannah looked at him in disbelief. "An air bed? With a *cat*?"

"Oh. I didn't think about that." Mike set his coffee cup back on the table and lowered his feet. "They're on the bed now. We ought to be safe."

Norman shook his head. "Better give it a minute or two. Cuddles was really wound up. Her eyes had that crazed kitty look."

"But Moishe looked a little tired," Mike said. "He might not want to chase her again."

"That won't stop Cuddles," Hannah explained. "She's an expert at getting him to chase her. I figure we've got about another ten, maybe fifteen seconds before . . . Feet up!"

Mike made a heroic effort and just barely managed to grab his coffee mug and dessert dish. His left foot almost got into a head-on crash with Cuddles, but she missed it, quite literally, by a whisker.

"Whew! That was close!" Mike glanced at the two cats, who were now splayed out on the rug, breathing hard. "I bow to your expertise," he said to Hannah and Norman. "Is that it for this run?"

Norman snapped his fingers and Cuddles looked at him. "That's it," he said. "Her eyes are normal again. Kitty Crazies are over for now."

Hannah glanced at their dessert bowls. Despite the two interruptions, both men had managed to finish their desserts. She dished up another helping for each of them and topped it with scoops from the carton of vanilla ice cream she'd rescued from the table.

For several minutes there was only the sound of spoons clinking against glass dessert bowls and an occasional sigh of contentment. When they were finished and the men had helped Hannah clear the table, they carried a fresh pot of coffee into the living room and Hannah declared that dinner was over.

"Okay," Mike said, turning to Norman. "I know you went to consult with Doc about Barbara's teeth. Tell me what you learned."

To Hannah's eyes, Norman looked sad and she hoped it wasn't bad news. "Five broken teeth, one sheared off at the gum line. Doc and I had to do surgery to extract it."

"Will she be all right?" Hannah was more concerned about Barbara than she was about the teeth.

"She'll recover. The good part is that I took X-rays of Barbara's teeth less than a month ago and that made it simple to extract them. The other good news is that I'll be able to fill in the gaps with bridges just as soon as her gums heal."

Mike looked confused. "I'm glad for Barbara, but why did you need to tell me this?"

"Because Barbara's dental injuries weren't entirely consistent with her fall. When we finished treating Barbara, Doc Knight and I went back to the Albion to examine the area where she landed."

"And you found . . . ?" Hannah held her breath, waiting for Norman's answer.

"We found nothing on the ground where she landed to account for the full extent of her dental injuries. The ground was soft and there was only one rock large enough to break a tooth."

Hannah frowned. "If Barbara didn't break her teeth when she landed, how did they get broken?"

"I know where you're going with this," Mike said. "You and Doc think that Barbara suffered a blow to the face right there on the roof."

"More than one blow, if we're right. Neither one of us believes that the dental trauma could have been accomplished by one blow."

"How many blows?" Hannah asked, and just asking made her feel slightly sick. The thought of someone hitting Barbara in the face was horrible.

"We believe that there were at least three blows. That's consistent with her facial damage and bruising, and also consistent with her dental trauma."

"You mean . . ." Hannah stopped and took a deep breath. "You mean someone attacked Barbara while she was on the roof?"

"That's exactly what we think. Everything stacks up that way. It was a big party and people were all over the hotel. It would have been relatively easy for someone to follow Barbara up to the rooftop garden without being noticed."

"That's true," Mike said. "When we interviewed the guests, only one person remembers seeing Barbara and that was in one of the two-bedroom condos."

"There's only one elevator that goes up to the penthouse," Hannah added. "Did anyone in the lobby see her getting into that?"

Mike shook his head, and then he turned to Norman. "Okay. I'm buying that theory except for one thing. We don't think Barbara fell. We found some scuff marks at the point where she left the roof. But the trajectory of a fall puts her at a different spot than the one where she landed."

"Then the person who attacked her also

pushed her off the roof?" Hannah asked.

"No. That doesn't add up either. The crime scene boys think Barbara jumped off the roof all by herself and now we know the reason why."

CHAPTER NINE

"Hannah. Before you say a word, there's something I have to say to you."

Hannah stood in the open doorway at The Cookie Jar and stared at her partner in surprise. She'd never heard Lisa sound so serious before. There were frown lines on her normally smooth brow, high spots of color dotted her cheeks, and her eyes were blazing with determination. Her glossy brown hair was tousled, as if she'd run her fingers through it in frustration, and her hands were clasped so tightly together that her knuckles were white with the pressure. It was clear that something was horribly wrong, and Hannah drew in her breath sharply as her mind settled on the obvious conclusion. There was only one thing that could catapult her normally calm and cheerful partner into this highly agitated state. "You're not quitting, are you?"

"Quitting?" Lisa looked shocked. "No!"

"What is it then?"

"I absolutely positively will not tell the story of Barbara's fall. I refuse, Hannah! I know it brings in business when I tell the stories of murders, but this isn't murder. Barbara's fall was a horrible, awful accident!"

"Not exactly," Hannah said, and then she wished she hadn't. Lisa's face had gone dangerously pale, and as Hannah watched, she reached out to grab the edge of the counter.

"Don't tell me that Barbara is . . . is . . ."

"No, Barbara's fine. Or at least Barbara's as fine as she can be with her injuries. I saw her yesterday and Doc Knight is almost certain she'll recover."

"Oh, thank goodness! I've been so worried about her I couldn't sleep at all last night. And Herb was gone, helping Mike and Bill at the hotel. Sammy was so scared, he slept with me. And he'd rather sleep in that great bed your mother bought for him."

"Or maybe it was the other way around," Hannah said, taking Lisa's arm and leading her to a stool at the stainless steel work island. "Sit down before you fall down, Lisa."

Lisa sat. And then she looked up at Hannah. "What did you mean, that maybe it was the other way around?"

"I meant, maybe Sammy slept with you because *you* were the one who was scared."

"Oh." Lisa thought about that for a moment. "Maybe. Fox terriers are awfully bright. Dr. Hagaman told me that. But I meant what I said about not telling Barbara's story."

"Good. I don't want you to tell any stories about Barbara. That would be a horrid thing to do."

The kitchen coffee pot was on and Hannah went to pour a bracing cup for both of them. When she came back, Lisa looked calmer, but the frown lines were back. "What else is wrong?" Hannah asked.

"I just remembered something. I said Barbara's fall was a horrible, awful accident. And you said, not exactly. Did you mean it wasn't horrible and awful? Or did you mean it wasn't an accident?"

"I meant it wasn't an accident. And you can't tell the story, okay?"

"I don't want to tell the story. I said that already. What's going on, Hannah?"

"Barbara's confused. She seems to think that her brother tried to kill her."

"Her *brother*?"

"Yes. And Barbara doesn't have a brother. She also asked about her father. And when

144

we told her that he was dead, she was practically inconsolable that she couldn't see him again." Hannah sat down and took a sip of her own coffee. Lisa could keep a secret and she was an expert at the invisible waitress trick. Customers didn't even notice when Lisa came around to refill their coffee cups and they kept right on talking, even if the conversation was personal. It didn't happen every day, or even every week, but once in a while Lisa would pick up some tidbit of information that helped Hannah solve a murder case.

"Two things," Hannah told her. "I'll start with Clayton Wallace."

"The dead bus driver for the band?"

"That's right." And Hannah proceeded to tell Lisa about the M.P.D.'s conclusion and what it meant to Clayton's son.

"Oh, dear!" Lisa said when Hannah was finished. "I'll keep an ear out, but it's pretty unlikely I'll hear anything about someone from Minneapolis, isn't it?"

"Maybe, but stranger things have happened. We do get a few customers who commute to Minneapolis for part of the week. And a lot of folks from Lake Eden have relatives there."

"Okay. How about that second thing you mentioned? It's about Barbara, isn't it?"

145

"Yes." Hannah got up to refill their coffee cups and then she sat down again. "Where were you when Barbara landed in the rose garden?"

"I was serving Doctor Bev and Roger their fourth cupcakes."

"You *served* them when everyone else came over to the display to serve themselves?"

"Yes. Roger came over and asked me to bring the cupcakes to their table. He said they were Doctor Bev's favorites. And since he was paying us for the catering job, I thought . . ."

"You had to do what he wanted," Hannah finished the sentence for her. "The customer is always right."

Lisa gave a little laugh. "Even when they're wrong, they're right. It's the first rule of retail sales."

"You like that night class you're taking, don't you?"

"I adore it. Dr. Schmidt is wonderful! I just have to be careful not to call her Dr. Love."

Hannah laughed. Nancy Schmidt was one of Delores's closest friends, and Hannah had learned early on that Nancy moonlighted as Dr. Love, the Love Guru on KCOW talk radio. No one at the college knew and the few who did were careful to protect her alter-identity.

"She's got such a good sense of humor and the psychology of retail sales is really interesting. I just wish I had her for my stat class."

"Nancy teaches statistics?"

"Yes. It's offered by two departments, psychology and mathematics. I tried to get into Dr. Schmidt's section, but her class was full. I'm stuck with Dr. Lyman from the math department and he's as dry as dust."

"Statistics is pretty boring, no matter who teaches it," Hannah said, remembering her own stat class and how she'd barely managed to stay awake. Of course most of her sleepiness might have been due to the fact that her class had met first thing in the morning and she had been spending most of her nights with Bradford Ramsey.

"Dr. Schmidt's class isn't boring. They meet right next door to Dr. Lyman's class and we can hear them laughing right through the walls. She's a great teacher, Hannah."

"Mother knows a nurse who's taking statistics as part of her psychology degree. She has a great recipe for Easy Fruit Pie. I made it last night."

"What's her name? Maybe I know her."

"Jenny Hester."

"There's a Jenny in my retail psychology class. Does she have dark brown hair with lighter highlights?"

Hannah shrugged. "I really don't know. I haven't met her."

"Do you want me to talk to her on break and ask her if she's the right Jenny? I've got class tonight."

"Sure. And if she is, tell her I tried her Easy Fruit Pie last night and it was a huge success."

"She'll like that. People always like to know that somebody else loves their recipes."

"Okay. So tell me what happened when you delivered the cupcakes to Roger's table," Hannah said, bringing them back to the subject at hand.

"Nothing. They weren't there."

"Neither one of them?"

"No. They weren't out on the dance floor either. I looked around for them. I set the platter with the cupcakes down and I'd just gotten back to the display table when I saw everybody rushing to the windows."

Hannah began to draw a time line in her head, but she wanted to check facts with Lisa. "Did you see me before the rush to

148

the windows?"

"Yes. You and Andrea were sitting at the table with your mother and Doc Knight. I waved, but you didn't see me."

"How about Bill and Mike?"

"I didn't see Mike, but Bill was talking to Lonnie in the doorway. I saw Norman, though."

"Where was he?" Hannah's heart beat faster, waiting for Lisa's answer.

"Norman was crossing the lobby, coming toward the door to the lounge."

Hannah drew a deep breath of relief. She took a moment to glory in the fact that Norman had been entirely truthful to her, and another moment to chide herself for doubting what he'd told her. When she was finished with those conflicting emotions, she asked another question. "Did you hear Barbara scream when she fell?"

"No. The elevator was too loud. I could hear it every time someone went up to the penthouse. There's this screech when it stops at the penthouse floor. Herb heard it too, when you and Andrea went up there. He says he thinks something needs to be oiled and he's going to tell Roger to call Otis."

"Otis Elevator?"

"Yes, they handle maintenance, too. Do

you want to taste the new cookies I made? I got the recipe from my cousin and they're called Coffee and Cream Cookies."

"I'd love to. I'll get more coffee. You get the cookies."

Lisa got up to pluck several cookies off the baker's rack while Hannah refilled their cups. Moments later they were both seated at the work island while Lisa waited for Hannah to take the first bite.

"Wonderful!" Hannah said, taking a second bite. "Great coffee flavor, but there's something else, too. Vanilla?" When Lisa nodded, Hannah went on. "The white chocolate chips are a good contrast. And the miniature marshmallow on top is just perfect."

"So you think we should serve them?"

"Absolutely. Make sure you call Doug Greerson at the bank and tell him you've got a new coffee cookie. Ever since he got that espresso machine for his office, he's turned into a real coffee connoisseur."

"Do you really think he'll like them? He's into Blue Mountain coffee and everything like that."

"He'll like them. And he'll love being asked to taste them. Better call Grandma Knudson, too. The only time her coffee pot isn't full is when she's washing it."

Lisa laughed. "Just wait until I tell my cousin."

"Which cousin is this? You have so many."

"I know. Dad used to say that if we had a dollar for every cousin, we'd be rich. This one is my cousin, Laurie Foster. She's my dad's brother's aunt-in-law's niece. I think she's twice, or maybe it's three times removed."

"Stop!" Hannah held up her hand. "I never can keep your family straight. The next time you talk to Cousin Laurie, tell her I think her recipe is great."

"I will. She'll be thrilled we're going to serve them." Lisa looked down at the traditional thumbprint cookies with miniature marshmallows in the indentations. "I just hope nobody thinks they're too much of a cheat."

"What do you mean?"

"Laurie told me she was going to use marshmallow cream in the thumbprint, so she could call them Coffee and *Cream,* but she found out that marshmallow cream is seasonal in Texas."

"You're kidding!"

"No. She went to five different stores and they all told her that they only carry marshmallow cream around Christmas."

"How about black cow sundaes? Don't

they have them in Texas?"

"I don't know, but I guess they don't make them except during the holiday season." Lisa paused and looked thoughtful. "I wonder if you can make marshmallow cream from scratch."

"I'm sure you can. I know you can make marshmallows from scratch. Great-Grandma Elsa used to do it."

"Were they good?"

"They were fabulous!"

"Do you have her recipe?"

"I'm sure I do. I've got boxes and boxes of family recipes. Do you want me to try to find it?"

"When you have time. It's not a huge priority because Laurie came up with a substitute that looks a little bit like cream. Do you think that's all right?"

"I think that's fine. The white chocolate tastes creamy, too."

"Then you don't think anybody will object to the name?"

"I'm sure they won't. The name's close enough." Hannah took another sip of her coffee. "Tell me more about the penthouse elevator. When I went up there with Andrea, we didn't hear any screech."

"I don't think anyone inside can hear it. The screech is down in the lobby and it happens only when the elevator stops at the penthouse. The only reason Herb and I noticed it is that we were sitting right against the wall."

"And you said the elevator screeches every time it arrives at the penthouse floor?"

"Yes. The reason I know is that Barbara came over to get a cupcake right before she went up to the penthouse. She said, *I'm taking this up there with me just in case I get stuck in that little elevator.* And then she went out and got in the elevator. Herb and I heard the screech when she got up there so we knew she didn't get stuck."

"And you said you heard another screech later, right before everyone went rushing to the windows."

"That's right. Somebody must have called for the elevator and gone up to the penthouse right before Barbara went off the roof. Otherwise the elevator wouldn't have screeched."

COFFEE AND CREAM COOKIES

Preheat oven to 350 degrees F., rack in the middle position.

1 cup white (**granulated**) sugar

1 cup brown sugar (**pack it down when you measure it**)

1 cup salted butter, softened (**2 sticks, 8 ounces, 1/2 pound**)

2 large eggs

1 teaspoon vanilla extract

1/2 cup strong coffee (**room temperature**)

2 teaspoons instant coffee (**I used instant espresso**)

1 teaspoon salt

2 teaspoons baking powder

3 and 1/2 cups all-purpose flour (**pack it down in the cup when you measure it**)

2 cups white chocolate chips (**I used Nestle**)

Approximately 50 to 60 white miniature marshmallows (1 per Cookie)

Spray cookie sheets with Pam or another nonstick cooking spray, or line them with parchment paper and spray that with non-stick cooking spray.

Hannah's Note: This is easier with an electric mixer, but you can do it by hand if you wish.

Place the white sugar and brown sugar in

the bowl of an electric mixer. Beat them together on LOW to combine.

Add the softened butter and mix it in on MEDIUM speed. Beat it until the mixture is light and fluffy.

Mix in the eggs, one at a time, beating after each addition.

Add the vanilla extract and strong coffee. Mix them in.

Mix in the instant coffee, salt and baking powder. Blend well.

Mix in the flour a half-cup at a time, beating after each addition.

Take the bowl out of the mixer and mix in the white chocolate chips by hand.

Drop spoonfuls of dough onto the cookie sheets, 12 mounds of dough to a standard-sized sheet. Use wet fingers to shape the dough mounds.

Press your impeccably clean thumb into the center of each dough mound. Fill the resulting indentation with a white miniature marshmallow. Press it down slightly.

Bake the Coffee and Cream Cookies at 350 degrees F. for 10 to 12 minutes or until nicely browned. (*Mine took 11 minutes.*)

Cool the cookies on the cookie sheets for 2 minutes and then remove them to a wire rack to complete cooling.

Yield: approximately 4 to 5 dozen tasty cookies, depending on cookie size.

CHAPTER TEN

The Coffee and Cream Cookies had been such a huge success, Hannah and Lisa were making them for the third day in a row. Lisa had just finished slipping the last cookie sheet into the industrial oven when the phone in the kitchen rang.

"I'll get it," Hannah said, crossing to the phone that hung on the wall. "This is The Cookie Jar, Hannah speaking."

"Well, Hannah. How nice to talk to you again!" the caller said, causing Hannah to frown deeply. "You know who this is, don't you?"

"Oh, yes." Hannah clamped her lips together, waiting for the caller to continue.

"I have an order for you," the caller said.

"Yes." Hannah motioned to Lisa. There was no way she was going to take this call. "Excuse me, but my oven timer's ringing. I'll put Lisa on to take your order."

Lisa looked puzzled as she took the phone.

"Hello, this is Lisa," she said. And then, after the caller had identified herself, she gave Hannah a sympathetic glance. "Yes, Doctor Bev. We do bar cookies. What type would you like to order?"

Hannah watched as Lisa wrote the order on the pad they kept by the phone. "Yes, we can bake lemon bars. How many pans would you like? Five by two this afternoon? And Mr. Dalworth will pick them up? Certainly. Is there anything else you'd like to order?"

Lisa rolled her eyes in Hannah's direction and gave a little shrug. "I see. Yes, I can get a list and read it to you. I would stay away from chocolate though. It's going to be hot this afternoon. If you'll hold on a moment, I'll get the list."

Lisa hit the hold button on the phone and hurried over to Hannah. "She wants five pans of six different types of bars. That's thirty pans total, and I didn't think you'd want to turn it down."

"You're right," Hannah said, even though she wasn't thrilled about baking for Doctor Bev.

On her way back to the phone, Lisa stopped at the center work island and picked up their book of recipes. She flipped to the bar cookies and picked up the phone again.

"Doctor Bev? I'm back. How about Multiple Choice Bar Cookies with butterscotch chips instead of chocolate?" She listened for a moment and then she jotted it down. "Five pans of those, is that correct?" She listened for another moment and then she said, "We also have Pineapple Right-Side-Up Bar Cookies. They're very popular in the summer."

Hannah watched as Lisa added them to her list. Lisa was a great little saleswoman.

"Apple? Oh, yes. We bake Apple Orchard Bar Cookies. Most people love those." Again, Lisa added a line to her list. "Strawberry? Why, yes. We have Strawberry Shortcake Bar Cookies. They're excellent and they'll hold up in the heat."

Hannah could see the list with its five entries. One to go. As far as she knew, they didn't have any other non-chocolate bar cookies, unless . . . The moment Hannah thought about it she was moving. She grabbed the list and jotted down an entry. She'd never tried those particular bars before, but they ought to work just fine.

Lisa glanced down at the list. She read what Hannah had written and spoke into the receiver again. "I think the only flavor you're really missing out on is raspberry. How about our new Berried Treasure Bar Cookies? They have a thin layer of chocolate on top, but we'll chill them for you." She listened and then she said, "Raspberry is Roger's favorite? Wonderful! He's bound to just love them! They're my very favorite."

Hannah hid a grin. Lisa didn't even know what the bar cookies were, but she was claiming they were her favorite.

"Yes, we'll have them all ready for Mr. Dalworth by two this afternoon. Is there anything else . . . oh! Why . . . yes. We certainly can bake another dozen Red Velvet Surprise Cupcakes. Thank you so much for your order."

The moment Lisa hung up the phone, Hannah asked the important question. "Did she say why she needed so many bar cookies?"

"Yes. The dome for the penthouse garden is coming in at two-thirty this afternoon, and Roger's ordered a tent so that she can serve cold drinks and bar cookies to everyone who wants to watch the giant crane hoist it up and put it in place."

"But . . . how about the crime scene? Doesn't the sheriff's department have it roped off?"

"Not anymore. Herb told me they took

down the tape last night."

"So she's free and clear to play Lady Bountiful."

"Right. How about closing early today and going to watch the spectacle?"

"Might as well. We won't get much business when everybody and their cousin finds out that there's free dessert only a few blocks away."

There was a knock at the kitchen door, but before either one of them could go to answer it, Andrea burst in. "Did you hear?"

"Hear what?" Hannah asked her sister.

"They're delivering the dome for the penthouse garden this afternoon. A gigantic crane is going to lift it up and place it on the roof."

"We heard," Lisa answered her. "Hannah and I were just discussing whether we should close early."

"Close," Andrea advised. "Bill just called to tell me that they're passing out flyers telling everybody to come to the hotel, that there'll be free dessert and drinks."

Hannah exchanged glances with Lisa. "Well, that didn't take long, did it?"

"What?" Andrea looked puzzled.

"The flyers. Lisa just got off the phone with Doctor Bev."

Andrea turned to Lisa. "What did *she* want?"

"Thirty pans of bar cookies at two o'clock this afternoon. Roger's coming in to pick them up."

"At least it's good for your business."

"That's true," Hannah said, "for two reasons. Number one, The Cookie Jar gets paid to bake them. And number two, Doctor Bev can't claim she made them because everyone in town knows she can't bake."

Andrea frowned slightly. "You used to be able to say that same thing about me."

"But not anymore. Those Apple Cinnamon Whippersnappers of yours are super."

"And the Chocolate Whippersnappers you made for the Christmas cookie exchange were incredible," Lisa added. "I brought them home and while I was making dinner, Herb found them. When I went to serve them for dessert, there was one cookie left!"

Andrea laughed, clearly pleased. "The nice thing about whippersnappers is you can make them up out of any cake mix. So far I've used chocolate, spice, and lemon. I wonder what I could do with yellow."

"Pineapple," Lisa said immediately. "Pineapple and coconut. And maybe some kind of nut. Pineapple is Herb's favorite fruit, and he loves coconut, too. If you could make whippersnappers like that, Herb would eat a whole batch!"

"Well . . . I can't think of any reason why it wouldn't work as long as I made sure the pineapple was drained really well. The coconut would help. That's dry. I think I'll experiment a little when I go home tonight."

Hannah began to smile. Andrea was beginning to think like a baker and it was all due to the cake mix whippersnapper recipes. She thought that they were easy, and they were. But Andrea was learning a thing or two about ingredients as she was experimenting.

"As a matter of fact, Barbara loves pineapple," Andrea continued. "If I can get them to turn out really well, I might take some to her."

"Check with Doc Knight," Hannah warned.

"Oh, I will. And that reminds me . . ." Andrea glanced at Lisa. "Lisa knows what's happening, doesn't she?"

"Yes. I told her the morning after Norman and Mike came over for dinner."

"Both of them?" Andrea looked a bit shocked.

"It started out with Norman. I asked him to come over for dinner when I ran into him at the hospital on Sunday. And then Mike called and wanted to come over right before we were about to sit down for dinner. And Norman took the phone and invited Mike."

Andrea rolled her eyes at the ceiling. "Norman's too nice for his own good."

"Sometimes . . . yes," Hannah agreed, wisely deciding not to mention which man had stayed at her condo the latest.

"Mother called me. She managed to find Barbara's mother's medical records. Barbara was her first baby and she couldn't have any more after Barbara was born. She had a hysterectomy."

"So Barbara *couldn't* have a brother," Andrea concluded.

"Not a full brother, but how about a half-brother?" Lisa asked. "That would count as a brother."

"You're a genius!" Hannah said, smiling at her partner. "I never thought of that! Barbara's brother could be her father's child."

"I'll look into it," Andrea promised.

"And I'll ask Dad," Lisa promised. "He has good days and bad days, but on the good days, he remembers a lot. I can ask Marge, too. She might remember."

"Good idea," Hannah said, and then she turned to her sister. "Are you going to see the crane?"

"Yes. Tracey wants to see it and I promised

I would. It's going to be quite a sight, Hannah. How about you? Are you going?"

Hannah made a snap decision. "We're going right after Roger picks up the bar cookies."

"Wonderful!" Lisa began to smile. "I've never seen a crane that big. I'm going to call Marge and tell her so she can bring Dad. I'll ask them to come here first. Then they can take care of the coffee shop while we bake the bars and the cupcakes for Roger."

"Is there anything I can do to help?" Andrea asked.

"As a matter of fact there is." Hannah pulled some money out of her pocket. "Will you run down to the Red Owl and tell Florence that we need eight jars of seedless raspberry jam?"

"Sure. I know she's got raspberry jam. I bought some the other day. But I don't think it was seedless."

"That's okay. We can always melt it and strain it."

"Okay. Anything else?"

"Yes. Six double packages of brownie mix."

Once Andrea had left for the grocery store, Lisa turned to Hannah. "Where's the recipe for the Berried Treasure Bar Cookies? I'll start on them as soon as Andrea comes back with the jam."

"There isn't one."

"No recipe?"

"Nope. I'm just going to wing it. I'll jot down the recipe as I go, and if they turn out, we'll add it to our book."

Lisa stared at her in something very close to awe. "You're going to make up a recipe on the fly?"

"You betcha!"

"But what if the Berried Treasure Bar Cookies don't turn out?"

Hannah gave a little shrug. "That's why I asked Andrea to pick up the brownie mix. I'll just bake six double batches of brownies and glaze the top of the pan with melted raspberry jam. And then I'll frost the top with chocolate frosting."

"Brownies from a mix?"

"Think of it as insurance. I'll use my own brownie recipe unless I run into a time crunch. If that happens, I'll just use the mix."

"Do you think that'll work?"

"Oh, yes. Doctor Bev will never know the difference and we'll have a good laugh at her expense."

BERRIED TREASURE BAR COOKIES
(RASPBERRY BAR COOKIES)

Preheat the oven to 350 degrees F., rack in the middle position.

1 cup cold salted butter (**2 sticks, 8 ounces, 1/2 pound**)
2 cups all-purpose flour (**don't sift — pack it down in the cup when you measure it**)
1/2 cup powdered sugar (**not sifted**)

———————

4 beaten eggs (**just whip them up in a glass with a fork**)
2 cups white (**granulated**) sugar
1/2 cup seedless raspberry jam
1/2 teaspoon salt
1 teaspoon baking powder
1/2 cup all-purpose flour (**don't sift — pack it down when you measure it**)

———————

1/4 cup seedless raspberry jam
1/2 cup (**1 stick, 1/4 pound, 4 ounces**) salted butter
1 cup white (**granulated**) sugar
1/3 cup cream
1/2 cup semi-sweet chocolate chips (**approximately 1/2 of a 6-ounce package — I**

used Nestle)
1 teaspoon vanilla extract

Spray a 9-inch by 13-inch cake pan with Pam or another nonstick cooking spray. Alternatively, you can line the cake pan with heavy duty aluminum foil and spray that with the cooking spray.

The Shortbread Crust: Cut each stick of butter into eight pieces. Zoop them up with the flour and powdered sugar in the food processor, using an on and off motion, with the steel blade until the resulting mixture looks like coarse cornmeal. Spread it out in the bottom of the cake pan. Pat the crumbly mixture down with your freshly-washed hands. This is your shortbread crust.

Hannah's 1st Note: If you don't have a food processor, you can mix up the crust with a piecrust blender or two knives. Don't worry if the crust gets "doughy" instead of crumbly. Once you spread it out in the pan and bake it, the end result will be the same.

Bake the crust at 350 degrees F. for 15 minutes, or until golden around the edges. Remove the pan from the oven, set it on a wire rack or a cold stovetop burner, BUT DON'T SHUT OFF THE OVEN.

While your crust is baking, make the filling so it's ready to pour on top of the crust when it comes out of the oven.

The Raspberry Filling:

Mix the eggs with the white sugar until they're nice and fluffy.

Melt the half-cup seedless raspberry jam in a microwave-safe cup on HIGH in the microwave for 30 seconds. Stir the jam for another 30 seconds to cool it and then beat it into the egg and sugar mixture.

Add the salt and baking powder. Mix them in thoroughly.

Mix in the flour and beat until everything is combined.

Hannah's 2nd Note: This filling will be runny — it's supposed to be.

When the crust comes out of the oven, pour the filling over the top. Stick the pan back in the oven and bake it at 350 degrees F. for another 30 minutes. Take the pan out of the oven and set it on a cold burner. Let it cool for 10 minutes. Then make the Raspberry Glaze.

For the Raspberry Glaze:

Measure out 1/4 cup of seedless raspberry jam and heat it in the microwave for 30 seconds. Stir it until it's smooth. Using a pastry brush, brush the melted jam over the top of the bar cookies. This very thin layer of jam will be the glaze.

Place the pan in the refrigerator so that the jam will cool and solidify. (**Mine took about 30 minutes.**)

For the Chocolate Frosting:

Make the frosting by placing the butter, sugar, and cream into a medium-size saucepan. Bring the mixture to a boil at ME-DIUM HIGH heat, stirring constantly. Then lower the heat to MEDIUM and cook for exactly 2 minutes.

Add the half-cup of chocolate chips, stir them in until melted, and then remove the saucepan from the heat and slide it onto a cold burner.

Stir in the vanilla extract. (**Be careful — it may sputter.**)

Pour the frosting over the cookie bars, grab the cake pan, and tip it so that the frosting covers the whole top.

Stick the pan back into the refrigerator for at least an hour before you attempt to cut and serve your Berried Treasure Cookie Bars.

To serve, cut the cookie bars into brownie-sized pieces and place them on a pretty platter.

Hannah's 3rd Note: Doctor Bev served

these on the day the crane lifted the dome over the penthouse garden on top of the Albion Hotel. Andrea heard her tell several people that she'd baked them, but folks here in Lake Eden know better.

CHAPTER ELEVEN

"I'll go pick up Tracey and meet you on the porch," Andrea said, heading for the kitchen door. But before she got there, she turned to look at the half-pan of Berried Treasure Bar Cookies that were left. "Maybe you could bring those? I mean . . . Tracey hasn't tasted them yet, and . . . well . . . I could use a couple more."

Hannah was amused. Andrea had already eaten three and now she wanted more. The Berried Treasure Bar Cookies had been a complete success. The shortbread crust was tender and crisp, the raspberry filling was redolent with the taste of ripe raspberries, and the red raspberry glaze added a burst of tart flavor that contrasted beautifully with the chocolate frosting on top. Everyone at The Cookie Jar had tasted them and pronounced them a hit, and Marge and Jack had both declared they were the best bar cookie recipe Hannah had ever baked.

"Bring those, too." Andrea gestured toward Hannah's second experiment of the morning, brownies topped with a raspberry glaze that was covered by fudge frosting. "What do you call them? You can't have a recipe without a name."

"Nameless Raspberry Brownies?" Hannah suggested a trifle facetiously.

"Don't be silly. There's got to be a better name than that." Andrea thought for a moment. "Remember that Razzle Dazzle Baked Brie you made for the luncheon at Mother's Cookie Exchange last year?"

"Of course I do."

"Well, why don't we name these bar cookies Razzle Dazzle Brownies?"

"That's perfect, Andrea."

"Thanks." Andrea looked pleased that Hannah liked the name. "I'll leave the screen door to the front porch unlocked. Just let yourself in if you get there before we do. The Petersons left their porch furniture so we'll have a place to sit. And the electricity's still on so I'm going to put soft drinks and bottled water in the refrigerator. Just help yourselves if we're not there yet."

"I'm really glad the Petersons listed their house with you," Hannah told her. "It's got a great view of the hotel."

"And the front porch is screened in," Lisa

added. "We won't be bothered by mosquitoes."

Andrea nodded. "It's a great house. If I
didn't live where I live, I'd consider it. See
you at two-thirty. And please don't forget
those bar cookies!"

Of course there was a complication. There
was always a complication when it came to
large orders. Hannah and Lisa had boxed
all the bar cookies Doctor Bev had ordered
and stacked them on the table by the front
door of The Cookie Jar to wait for Roger's
two o'clock arrival. But two o'clock came
and went and Roger hadn't appeared. It was
now five after two and Lisa and Hannah
were more than ready to lock their front
door and meet Andrea and Tracey at the
Petersons' front porch. Marge and Jack had
already left. Delores had invited them to
watch the crane from the second floor of
Granny's Attic, where an impromptu party
was taking place.

"What now?" Lisa asked Hannah.

"We give him the time for a full professor
and then we take them over to the refreshment tent and dump them in Doctor Bev's
lap."

"Twelve minutes?"

"Yes. That's still the rule, isn't it?"

"It's still the campus legend," Lisa amended it. "I don't think it was ever written down in any rule book. Everybody just knows that you have to wait five minutes for an assistant professor to show up for class, and twelve minutes for a full professor. And if they don't show up by then, you can leave."

"It's good to know things haven't changed that much since I was in college," Hannah said, glancing up at the clock on the wall. "Roger's got four minutes left."

"And here he comes." Lisa pointed to the gleaming black Mercedes that had just pulled up in front of The Cookie Jar.

"Ladies," Roger greeted them with a little salute before he handed Hannah his credit card. "Are you all ready for the big day?"

"We're ready and so are you," Lisa told him. "Your order's on that table. Would you like some help carrying the boxes out to your car?"

"I got it." Roger aimed his remote out the window and the trunk of his car popped open. "Just help me load up."

While Hannah ran the card, Lisa loaded Roger's arms with boxes. When the last one was safely in the trunk, Hannah gave the credit card and the receipt back to Roger.

"Thanks, ladies," Roger said, writing in

the total and signing his name. "See you at the spectacle."

Once Roger had driven away, Lisa went to lock the front door and turn the OPEN sign to CLOSED. Hannah headed for the cash register with the credit card receipt and as she slipped it into the section they used for receipts, she glanced at the total.

"Guess what, Lisa. Roger tipped us twenty dollars."

"Wow!" Lisa exclaimed, looking impressed. "That's more than most people around here tip."

"Well, he can afford it. Are you ready to go?"

"Yes." Lisa gave a final glance around the room as Hannah flicked off the overhead lights. "Uh-oh!"

"What?"

"I forgot to load Roger up with the cupcakes you baked for Doctor Bev. There wasn't room on the table where we stacked the bar cookies and I put them on the table next to it. They're still sitting there."

Hannah shrugged. "That's not the end of the world. Doctor Bev's not going to serve those anyway. We can just drop them off at the refreshment tent."

"Correction. *I* can just drop them off at the refreshment tent. As far as Doctor Bev knows, I have no quarrel with her."

"But you actually *do* have a quarrel with Doctor Bev?"

"Of course I do, but *quarrel* isn't really the right word. *Despise* would be more like it."

Hannah was surprised. Lisa was slow to anger and even slower to hate. Spite was a very strong emotion and Hannah had no idea what Doctor Bev had done to Lisa to deserve being despised. "What did Doctor Bev do to you?"

"Oh, she didn't do much to me except treat me like a hired hand. That's to be expected with people like her. I don't like what she did to you and Norman. She's scum of the earth and she has no conscience. *That's* why I despise her."

The view from the Petersons' porch was perfect and the wicker porch furniture was truly comfortable even though the wicker was made out of plastic and the cushions were weatherproof in case the rain came through the screens in the summer. There was a colorful rug on the porch floor and Hannah smiled as she recognized the braided material. "That rug is made from plastic bags, isn't it, Lisa?"

"Yes. It could be one of my mother's rugs.

She used to make them for rummage sales at St. Jude's church."

"I always liked them. They're practically indestructible."

"That's true. All you have to do is hose them off in the yard if they get dirty and hang them over the clothesline to dry. The only bad thing is that it's a lost art."

"What do you mean? People still make braided rugs, don't they?"

"Sure, but they're talking about banning plastic bags. They're bad for the environment."

"I know. Florence doesn't use them anymore at the Red Owl. It's paper or your own shopping bags that you bring in with you."

"Remember the recycling drives we had at Jordan High to make money for new band uniforms and things like that?"

"I remember."

Lisa looked thoughtful. "Maybe we should have a plastic grocery bag drive before they're all gone. We could store them somewhere for the ladies who still make braided rugs. I think I'll talk to Herb about that."

"Hi, everybody!" Andrea opened the porch door and stepped in. Tracey was right behind her and she hurried over to give Hannah a hug.

"Isn't this exciting?" she asked, hugging

Lisa, too. "We saw Mr. Dalworth and he said the crane is going to be late because they ran into some traffic. The driver called him and said they'd be here at three o'clock."

After soft drinks were dispensed and everyone had pulled chairs into good viewing positions, they sat and watched the cars and the walkers go by. It seemed the whole town of Lake Eden was turning out for what Roger had called the spectacle.

"It's hard to believe, isn't it?" Andrea commented as the red Maserati convertible went past the house for the third time.

"It's Doctor Bev's car," Tracey told them. "I asked and she said Mr. Dalworth gave it to her."

Andrea turned to her eldest daughter. "When did you see Doctor Bev?"

"Remember when you were working in your office and you said I could walk down to Hal and Rose's Café?"

"Yes. I gave you money to get a sandwich."

"I did. I had a grilled cheese. Rose made it for me."

"That's Mrs. McDermott."

"But she told me to call her Rose."

"If she said to, then it's okay."

"I know. Anyway, I was almost done with my sandwich when Uncle Norman came in.

He sat down next to me at the counter and asked if he could buy me dessert."

"That was nice of him," Hannah said with a smile. Norman was really good with kids and Tracey was one of his favorites.

"I said I couldn't have dessert because we were going to go to meet Aunt Hannah and Lisa and have it later."

"But did you thank him for offering?"

"Yes, Mom. That was the first thing I did. I said, *Thanks, but I can't.* And then I told him why. And then Doctor Bev came in."

Andrea and Hannah exchanged glances. Sisterly radar was about to take over. Andrea's look said, *Go ahead and ask her if you want to know more.* And Hannah's return glance answered, *I will, thanks. Don't worry. I won't put her on the spot.*

"You were nice and polite, Tracey," Hannah complimented her. "And we did bring dessert so you won't miss out. Did Doctor Bev have dessert?"

"No. All she did was ask Uncle Norman to come for a ride with her in her new Mister-rati."

"Maserati," Hannah corrected her and then she wished she hadn't because she'd interrupted Tracey's story. "Did Uncle Norman take a ride?" she asked the most important question.

"Not right away. Uncle Norman said he had to get back to the office, but Doctor Bev said no, he didn't, that she'd talked to Doc Bennett and he said he'd stay longer so that Uncle Norman could go for a ride with her."

Uh-oh! She's scheming again! Hannah's mind said and she totally agreed. But what she said out loud was, "So Norman went for a ride with her?"

"Not right then. Doctor Bev sat down on the stool next to me and asked me if I'd like to go for a ride in her brand new car as long as Uncle Norman came too."

That's despicable! Hannah thought, exchanging glances with Andrea. *She was going to get Norman in that car any way she could, even if she had to use my six-year-old niece to do it!*

"What did you say to that?" Andrea asked, looking anxious.

"I was going to say yes until I remembered that I wasn't supposed to go for rides with anyone who wasn't a relative or a friend. You told me that a long time ago."

"So you said no?" Andrea quizzed her.

"Not exactly. That was when I remembered another thing you told me a long time ago, so I said yes."

Andrea looked shocked. "What did I tell you?"

"You said, *Don't worry, Tracey. The dentist is your friend.* And since Doctor Bev is a dentist and so is Uncle Norman, I said yes."

"I guess that came back to bite me," Andrea said under her breath to Hannah and Lisa. And then she turned back to Tracey. "Okay, honey. Tell us what happened on the ride with Doctor Bev."

"Well . . . she wanted Uncle Norman to sit in front, but he said I should sit in front because I could see better up there. So I did and it was fun. We went up by the church and Grandma Knudson's house, and then we went past the old lumber yard at the end of Main Street, and we turned on the street with the hotel to drive by that and the school. Her new car makes noise. It sounds like a roar. People heard us coming and they came out of their houses to see the car go by. They all waved so I waved back and Doctor Bev tooted the horn. It was so much fun!"

"I'm sure it was," Hannah said, wondering whether Norman had gone along on his own volition, or whether he'd decided he should keep an eye on Doctor Bev with Tracey.

"Anyway, Doctor Bev wanted to go drive

around the lake, but I thought you might worry if I was gone too long, so I asked her to drop me off on the corner by the real estate office. And she did."

"And Uncle Norman stayed in the car and went out to the lake with her?" Andrea asked.

Tracey gave a little shrug. "I guess. The last thing I saw, he was climbing into the front seat, and they were driving off."

The next question was Hannah's. "Toward the dental clinic?" she asked.

"No, the other way. That's all I know. Could I have one of your new bar cookies now, Aunt Hannah? Especially since I missed dessert with Uncle Norman?"

RAZZLE DAZZLE BROWNIES

For the Brownies:

Make a double batch of your own favorite brownie recipe in a 9-inch by 13-inch cake pan OR use the shortcut below:

1 family-size box of brownie mix (**enough to make a 9-inch by 13-inch pan of brownies — I used Betty Crocker**) and the rest of the ingredients listed on the box of brownie mix you bought

For the Glaze:

1/2 cup seedless raspberry jam

For the Frosting:

1/2 cup (**1 stick, 1/4 pound, 4 ounces**) salted butter

1 cup white (**granulated**) sugar

1/3 cup cream

1/2 cup chocolate chips (**approximately 1/2 of a 6-ounce package**)

1 teaspoon vanilla extract

Step 1:

Preheat oven to whatever it says on the box of brownie mix you bought.

Step 2:

Spray the bottom of a 9-inch by 13-inch

cake pan with Pam or another nonstick cooking spray. Alternatively, you can line the pan with aluminum foil and spray that.

Step 3:
Mix the brownies according to the package directions.

Step 4:
Bake the brownies 2 minutes longer than it says on the package directions.

Step 5:
After the brownies have baked, let them cool on a cold stovetop burner or on a wire rack for 10 minutes.

Step 6:
After the brownies have cooled for 10 minutes, put the jam in a microwave-safe bowl and heat it on HIGH for 30 to 45 seconds or until it liquefies.

Step 7:
Pour the jam over the top of the brownies and quickly spread it out with a rubber spatula.

Step 8:
Refrigerate the brownies and jam glaze for

at least 30 minutes. An hour is even better. Overnight is fine, too.

Step 9:
Take the pan out of the refrigerator and place it on the counter close to the stovetop.

Step 10:
Make the frosting by placing the butter, sugar, and cream into a medium-size saucepan. Bring the mixture to a boil at ME-DIUM HIGH heat, stirring constantly. Then lower the heat to MEDIUM and cook for 2 minutes.

Step 11:
Add the half-cup chocolate chips, stir them in, and then remove the saucepan from the heat and slide it onto a cold burner.

Step 12:
Stir in the vanilla extract. (***Be careful — it may sputter.***)

Step 13:
Pour the frosting over the glaze, grab the cake pan, and tip it so that the frosting covers the whole top.

Step 14:

Stick the pan back into the refrigerator for at least 30 minutes before you attempt to cut and serve your Razzle Dazzle Brownies.

CHAPTER TWELVE

Hannah was still thinking about Norman riding out to Eden Lake with Doctor Bev when the red Maserati pulled up in front of the Peterson house. A moment later, Doctor Bev got out and walked up the sidewalk to the front porch. "Hannah?" she called out. "Are you in there?"

"I'm here," Hannah replied.

"What happened to my Red Velvet Surprise Cupcakes? You forgot to give them to Roger. And you charged for them. I saw the credit card receipt. If I don't get my cupcakes right now, you owe me a refund."

"It's my fault," Lisa called out. "Sorry about that. When Roger came to pick up the order I forgot to give them to him. I was going to bring them over to you at the refreshment tent, but I saw you driving around in your car and I thought I'd wait until you got back."

"I'm back." Doctor Bev opened the screen

door and stepped in. "Nice little porch. How cozy. I suppose you're here to watch the crane place the dome over my penthouse garden."

"*Your* penthouse garden?" Andrea asked.

"That's right. Roger sent me over here to tell you to take the penthouse off the market because I'm moving in. We picked out all the furniture last night and it'll be delivered tomorrow. He also wants you to meet the delivery truck tomorrow to supervise the placement of the furniture and check to make sure it's in perfect condition. The truck is scheduled to arrive at noon."

Hannah glanced at her sister. It was clear that Andrea didn't like being ordered around by Doctor Bev, but it seemed that Doctor Bev was wearing the pants in the relationship and there was no way Andrea wanted to antagonize an important real estate client like Roger.

"Okay. I'll be there," Andrea agreed.

"I knew you would. I wouldn't want any of my furniture damaged before I even get the chance to use it. And I won't be here. I have to drive back to the Cities to pick up a few necessities."

And I'll just bet one of those necessities isn't your daughter! Hannah thought.

"Is Roger happy about moving back to

Lake Eden?" Lisa asked.

Doctor Bev shook her head. "Roger's not moving back here. His headquarters are in the Cities and he has several projects there. He may move here eventually, but not now. The penthouse is another engagement gift, just like my new car. Roger's so generous."

"So it's just you in the penthouse?" Lisa asked, looking shocked. Hannah knew why. The penthouse had six bedrooms and the idea of one person living there alone was ridiculous.

"I know it's much too large for one person," Doctor Bev seemed to read Lisa's mind, "but I plan on inviting a lot of houseguests. There's entertaining, too. I'll do quite a bit of that. I really have to do something to fill up the place. I put some of my things in the closet this morning and there's so much room left in there. I have to go shopping for more clothing and shoes."

"Won't you be lonely up there all by yourself?" Lisa asked.

"Oh, I won't be there alone. I'll have guests staying with me and I'll be interviewing for staff at the end of the week. Do any of you know a good live-in housekeeper? Or a maid?"

Almost as one, the three women shook their heads.

"I didn't think so. Oh, well." Doctor Bev gave a deep sigh. "I'll just have to go through an agency. I'll need a housekeeper, a maid, a landscaper for the rooftop garden, and a personal assistant. Just think about it. If I can find suitable locals, it could be a real boost to Lake Eden's economy. Isn't that just wonderful?"

There was dead silence for what seemed like an eternity, and then Doctor Bev laughed. "I didn't expect a warm welcome. Norman warned me about that at lunch today."

"Did you and Uncle Norman go back to the café?" Tracey asked her.

"No, sweetie. We went to lunch at the Lake Eden Inn. That's where I'm staying right now, you know."

"I know. Mom told me. She said Aunt Sally called to tell Grandma and then Grandma called to tell Mom, and . . ."

"That's enough, Tracey!" Andrea interrupted her.

"Sorry, Mom. I'll go to the kitchen and get some more lemonade so the adults can talk."

"So precious," Doctor Bev said, smiling sweetly. The phrase, *Butter wouldn't melt in her mouth,* crossed Hannah's mind. "And Tracey's so talkative, too. Between your little Tracey and Norman, I learned everything I needed to know about coming back to Lake Eden to live. Norman's not too happy about it, but I'm very good with men like Norman. He'll come around. I wouldn't be a bit surprised if he spends more time at my penthouse than he does at his dental clinic."

"How about Roger?" Hannah asked, despite her vow to keep silent. "You're still engaged to him, aren't you?"

"Of course I am. I've got Roger right where I want him. I'm very good with men like Roger, too. And Roger can give me so much more than Norman ever could."

Hannah held her breath as Doctor Bev stopped speaking and the silence deepened again. There was no way she was going to ask another question and it was clear that Andrea felt the same way. Lisa, however, didn't share their restraint. "So you're telling us that you're after Norman again?" she asked.

"Why, my goodness! I guess I am! He's such a nice man, who could resist? And I know he'll come around to my way of thinking once he realizes that Roger won't be spending much time with me in Lake Eden. When your lover's away, it's always nice to rely on your other male . . . *friends.*" Doctor Bev stopped speaking and glanced at her watch. "Oh, my! Just look at the time. I really must be going. I promised to let Richard drive my new car and the dome is due to arrive in less than twenty minutes." She gave the most insincerely sweet smile Hannah had ever seen. "I'm also very good with men like Richard, you know. Actually . . . now that I think about it, I'm really very good with all the men." She turned to Hannah and narrowed her eyes. "You really ought to keep an eye on me, Hannah. You might learn a thing or two about how to handle men . . . or perhaps not."

That said, Doctor Bev picked up the box with the cupcakes and left the porch, leaving the screen door open behind her.

"What a witch!" Lisa said, and both Hannah and Andrea knew which word she might have used if Tracey hadn't been close by. She got up to close the screen door, and came back to sit down again. "She said she was going to let Richard drive her car. Who's Richard?"

"Mayor Bascomb," both Hannah and Andrea answered, almost simultaneously.

Lisa looked thoughtful. "Do you think that . . . ?"

"Probably," Andrea said before Lisa could finish her question. "He's been known to play the field. Mother told me that he once had three women on the string, not counting his wife, and not one of them knew about the others."

"Oh, my!" Lisa looked shocked.

"It's true," Hannah told her, starting to grin. "And it seems to me that both Doctor Bev and the mayor have the same talent for multitasking."

Perhaps it was childish and only one of them could qualify as a child, but all four of them had cheered right along with the crowd on the street when the mammoth flatbed truck had arrived with the dome. They'd cheered again when the gigantic crane had lifted the dome, and yet again when it had risen slowly up into the air.

"That crane is really huge," Lisa breathed, watching the dome sway as it ascended higher and higher.

"I'm glad we're watching it from here," Andrea commented. "I'd hate to be out on the street standing under that dome. I wouldn't be able to stop thinking about what would happen if it fell."

"You'd be okay if you were under it and it fell straight down," Tracey pointed out. "It's a dome. It would fit right over you."

"It won't fall," Lisa said. "Herb told me

that it's attached to the crane with steel cables. They're interwoven and even if one strand breaks, the other strands will hold."

Andrea didn't look convinced. "I still wouldn't want to take the chance. Look how it's swaying up there."

Hannah gave a little gasp as the dome rocked from side to side and rose past the second floor of the hotel. "I've never seen anything like this before!"

"Neither have I," Tracey confided. "I wonder if my whole class is here."

"I bet they are," Lisa said. "I think the whole town is here."

"Do you think Mrs. Watson can see it from her studio windows?" Tracey asked, and Hannah wondered if she'd skipped summer dance class to be here.

"I'm almost sure she can see it from there," Lisa answered her. "Danielle's on the second floor over the Red Owl, and the only building that's as tall as the hotel is City Hall."

Hannah looked at Lisa in surprise. "City Hall's only two stories high."

"You're forgetting the cupola on the roof. Herb's watching from there. Rod Metcalf is with him and he's taking pictures for the *Lake Eden Journal.*"

"Can Grandma see it from her shop?"

Tracey asked.

"Yes," Hannah answered. "She can see perfectly from the windows on the second floor. Mrs. Beeseman and Lisa's dad are there and so are some members of the Lake Eden Historical Society. They're having a tea party up there."

"We baked a Double Whammy Lemon Cake for your grandma to serve," Lisa said. "We did a lot of baking this morning!"

"But . . . doesn't it have vodka in it?" Andrea asked.

"The original recipe does," Hannah said.

"So you changed it for Mother and her guests?"

"Yes, and no." It was Lisa's turn to answer. "We made two cakes, one with the vodka and the other with cream. Your mother's guests can choose which cake they want."

"But does the name fit when it's made with cream instead of vodka?" Andrea wanted to know.

Hannah bit back an amused smile. For some reason Andrea was fixating about recipe titles today. "The one with vodka is the Double Whammy Lemon Cake. The one with cream is Lemon Cream Cake."

"Oh. That's okay then." Andrea's eyes widened as the dome rose up even higher than the penthouse. "What are they doing?

It's too high!"

Lisa shook her head. "No it's not. They have to stabilize it over the penthouse garden and then lower it. And they need maneuvering space for that. Herb explained the whole thing to me. They'll bring it straight down and once it stops swaying, the workmen up there will grab the handholds on the inside and guide it down. Once it's in place the crane operator will release the cables and the job is done."

"That sounds like precision work," Andrea said.

"Oh, it is. The people who sold Roger the dome brought their own crew with them to do it."

There was a tense moment as the dome began to lower and the men standing in the penthouse garden reached up for the handholds. For the first time in her life Hannah wished she had a cell phone with a camera instead of the stripped-down model she'd insisted was all she needed.

"They got it!" Lisa exclaimed, pointing up at the dome. "The crane operator just released the cables. The penthouse garden is finished."

"I wish it had been finished on Saturday," Tracey said. "Then Aunt Barbara wouldn't be in the hospital and she'd still be Daddy's

197

secretary."

Hannah didn't say a word. It was readily apparent that Andrea hadn't told Tracey that Barbara had jumped off the roof to get away from someone who was attacking her.

Andrea reached out to give her daughter a hug. "So do I, honey. But Aunt Barbara will be back. Doc Knight says she's getting better every day."

"That's good. Daddy gets crabby when he has a temp. Remember when Aunt Barbara was on vacation and he couldn't find anything in his office? He yelled at everybody."

"That's true," Andrea said with a smile. "He was terribly frustrated. What do you say we watch the crane drive off and then we hurry over to Granny's Attic to see if there's any cake left?"

"Two desserts in one day!" Tracey breathed, smiling as she turned to her mother. "I'd like to see Grandma and I want to taste the Double Whammy Lemon Cake. I bet Bethie has already had some!"

"I hope not," Andrea said and then she turned to Hannah and Lisa to explain. "Bethie is with Grandma watching the crane."

"Why can't Bethie have the cake?" Tracey asked.

"Because the Double Whammy Lemon

Cake is the one with the vodka in it, honey. Grandma wouldn't let her have that."

"I'd better not have any either, otherwise Daddy could arrest me for . . . ," Tracey stopped for a moment and then she started to laugh. "I wouldn't be drinking, so Daddy couldn't arrest me for underage drinking. I guess he'd have to arrest me for underage *eating*!"

DOUBLE WHAMMY LEMON CAKE

Preheat oven to 350 degrees F., rack in the middle position.

Zest from 2 small lemons (*approximately 2 teaspoons*)

1 box white cake mix (*the size that makes a 9-inch by 13-inch cake*)

1 box vanilla instant pudding mix (*NOT sugar-free — the size that makes 4 half-cup servings*)

1/2 cup vegetable oil

1 cup sour cream

1/3 cup vodka (*I used Tito's Handmade Vodka*)

4 large eggs

6-ounce package white chocolate chips (*approximately 1 cup*)

Hannah's 1st Note: When I first made this cake I bought a white cake mix with pudding in the mix. I used it and it was a disaster. The cake browned too fast and stuck to the bottom of the Bundt pan. DO NOT USE A CAKE MIX WITH PUDDING IN IT!

Spray a Bundt pan with Pam or another nonstick cooking spray.

Zest your lemons. They should yield approximately 2 teaspoons of zest. Measure out 1/2 teaspoon of zest and save it for the frosting. The remainder will go in your cake batter.

Place the dry white cake mix and the dry vanilla pudding mix in the bowl of an electric mixer. Beat them together on low speed until they're combined.

Add the vegetable oil, sour cream, vodka, and lemon zest (except for the half-teaspoon you reserved). Beat on low speed until thoroughly mixed.

Mix in the eggs, one at a time on MEDIUM speed, beating after each addition. When you're through, this batter should be nice and fluffy. If it's not, turn the mixer up to HIGH and beat for 2 additional minutes.

Take the bowl out of the mixer, chop the white chocolate chips into smaller pieces so they won't all sink to the bottom of the cake and mix them in by hand. Don't overstir. You want to keep as much air as possible in the batter.

Spoon the batter into the prepared Bundt pan. Smooth the top with a rubber spatula.

Bake the cake at 350 degrees F. for 50 minutes until a cake tester or a thin wooden skewer inserted in the center of the ring comes out clean.

Cool the Double Whammy Lemon Cake

for 20 minutes on a cold burner or a wire rack.

After 20 minutes, loosen the edges of the cake with a knife. Don't forget to run the knife around the tube in the center of the Bundt pan to loosen that, too.

Invert a large plate on top of the Bundt pan, flip it over, and unmold the cake. Let it cool completely on the plate before frosting it with Double Whammy Lemon Frosting.

Hannah's 2nd Note: If you would prefer not to use alcohol in this cake, simply substitute 1/3 cup light cream for the vodka and call it Lemon Cream Cake. It's yummy that way, too.

DOUBLE WHAMMY LEMON FROSTING

1 pound box powdered (*confectioners*) sugar

1/2 cup softened butter (*1 stick, 4 ounces, 1/4 pound*)

1/4 cup vodka (*I used Tito's Handmade Vodka*)

2 teaspoons lemon extract

1/2 teaspoon lemon zest

Reserve a half-cup of the powdered sugar and place the rest in a mixing bowl. Beat in the softened butter.

Continue to beat as you drizzle in the vodka and lemon extract.

Mix in the lemon zest you reserved for this frosting.

If the frosting is too thick, add a little more vodka. If it's too thin, add a little more of the powdered sugar you reserved. When the frosting has reached spreading consistency, frost your Double Whammy Lemon Cake. (*Don't forget to frost the inside of the tunnel in the center of your cake!*)

Hannah's Note: If you would prefer not to use alcohol in this cake, simply substitute 1/4 cup light cream for the vodka and call it Lemon Cream Frosting.

CHAPTER THIRTEEN

"Okay, Mother. I'll come out there right after I feed Moishe," Hannah said, glancing down at the cat who was rubbing up against her ankles. "Is there anything I should bring? I could stop at The Cookie Jar and pick up something."

"No, dear. Barbara can't have solid food yet. Norman said he was going to work on her bridge this afternoon and he told Doc that he'd bring it out to the hospital tomorrow. If her mouth has healed enough, he'll put it in and then she'll be able to eat soft food."

"That's good news," Hannah responded even though she wondered if Norman had gone back to the dental clinic to work on Barbara's bridge after his lunch with Doctor Bev. "I made a double batch of Mom's Bran Muffins yesterday and it made six dozen. Would you like me to bring some out to you and Doc?"

"I don't care for bran, dear, but Doc is always looking for good bran recipes for his senior patients. The only bran muffins I've ever liked were Great-Grandma Elsa's."

"That's what these are."

"But you said they were *Mom's* Bran Muffins."

"That's what it says on the recipe, but Grandma Ingrid must have written it down. The recipe was on the back of a gas bill that's addressed to Grandma and Grandpa Swensen."

"Oh, my goodness! I hope they paid it!" Delores exclaimed.

"They paid it, Mother. It's stamped *Paid in Full.*"

"That's a relief. What time will you be here, dear?"

Hannah glanced up at the apple-shaped clock on her kitchen wall and mentally calculated the time it would take her to feed Moishe, change clothes, and drive out to the hospital. "You can tell Doc Knight I'll be there within the hour. And I'll bring enough muffins for both of you."

Once she'd hung up the phone, Hannah gave a little sigh. She'd been home less than thirty minutes when the phone had rung. Of course she'd thought about not answering, but there was something about a ringing phone that was too compelling to deny. She'd picked up the receiver, said hello, and heard the request from her mother. It seemed that Barbara was extremely agitated today and she wanted to see Hannah.

"Hold on, Moishe. I'll get your food in just a minute," she told the cat, whose rubs against her ankles had turned into head butts that demanded attention. There was still a little kitty kibble in his bowl from his breakfast, but that wouldn't satisfy him for long. Moishe knew from past experience that there would be better, more interesting food coming with dinner.

"Salmon or tuna?" Hannah asked him, taking two cans of gourmet cat food out of the cupboard.

"Rrrrroow!"

"Of course," Hannah said with a smile. "I should have guessed. You had tuna last night so tonight you want salmon. How about a couple of salad shrimp thrown in for good measure?

"Rrrrrrrrow!"

The response was more prolonged this time and Hannah laughed. People claimed that cats didn't understand human language, but she'd swear in a court of law that Moishe knew at least eight words. His tail flicked at the very end whenever she uttered the words *shrimp, chicken, bacon, tuna, salmon,* and the generic *fish.* There were also several non-food-related words that garnered a physical response. *Cuddles* was one. Norman's cat was his favorite friend and his ears perked up every time he heard her name. The other, most evocative non-food word was *Mother.* When Moishe heard Hannah greet her mother on the phone, he bristled and puffed up like a Halloween cat. Hannah could understand that. They'd gotten off on the wrong foot, or perhaps she should say the wrong *leg,* from the very beginning. The first time Hannah's mother had met Moishe, she'd tried to treat him like a cute, cuddly lap cat, and Moishe had taken offense at the baby talk and the attempt to pick him up. Such behavior was an assault to his dignity and Moishe had made that perfectly clear.

To Hannah's relief, the relationship between her mother and her cat was non-violent now. Since those first few meetings with the shredded hose, Moishe and Delores had arrived at an uneasy truce. Whenever Delores arrived at Hannah's condo, she was armed with treats. Moishe would sit next to her on the couch so that she could feed him his favorite fish-shaped, salmon-flavored treats, and he even permitted a pet or two, or a scratch behind the ears. Hannah wasn't sure what would happen if her mother arrived without treats, but she wasn't betting on feline civility without culinary bribery. Every time Delores called to say she was dropping by, Hannah had a treat jar on the chair by the door just in case her mother had forgotten.

Hannah opened the can of kitty gourmet salmon and spooned it into Moishe's bowl, covering the picture of Garfield on the bottom. She took a bag of salad shrimp from her freezer and shook out five before she returned it to the shelf. A few seconds under running water and they had thawed enough to add to the bowl.

"Go ahead and eat, Moishe," she said, as if there were any doubt he'd do just that. "I'm going to take a quick shower and change clothes. I have to drive out to the hospital to see Barbara."

Moishe didn't bother to look up. His face was buried in his food bowl. His tail flicked twice and Hannah figured that was response enough.

Less than twenty minutes later Hannah was in her cookie truck driving out to the hospital. As she zipped along, she considered Doctor Bev's thinly veiled threat about

Norman, and wondered whether Norman would be gullible enough to get involved with his two-time and two-timing fiancée for the third time.

"He knows what she did the last time," Hannah said aloud as she took the turn that led around the lake to the hospital. "He wouldn't fall for that again, would he?" Absolute silence greeted her query. Even though her window was all the way down, the cows grazing along the fence that ran past Frederick Miller's farmland didn't raise their heads to answer.

"Maybe he would," Hannah said out loud, answering her own question. She hoped that wasn't the case, but she wasn't sure, not after the things Doctor Bev had said that afternoon. Hannah had just rounded the tight curve that was marked by the three white crosses that the Sheriff's Department Protective League had put up to signify three speed-related fatalities when she noticed several broken branches hanging from the dogwood that lined the roadway. Someone had taken the curve too fast and mowed through the bushes that hid Miller's Pond from view.

Hannah pulled over to the side of the road. The branches were still hanging from the dogwood and Frederick Miller was known for keeping up his property. If the accident had happened a week, or even several days ago, Frederick would have removed the broken branches. She hadn't heard about any accident at The Cookie Jar and it would have been a topic of conversation. That meant the accident was recent and she could be the first person on the scene!

Hannah turned off the ignition and hurried out of her truck. She pushed aside the branch, stepped past the dogwood, and gazed down at the pond below. What she saw made her gasp in horror. There was a car in the bottom of Miller's Pond!

Miller's Pond was stream-fed and the water was much clearer than a pond without an underwater source. It was deep, at least fifteen feet, and some people might have classified it as a small lake. Even though the car was over ten feet under the water, Hannah was a strong swimmer and she knew she could dive down to it if she had to.

She made a snap decision and scrambled down the steep embankment, slipping and sliding, but luckily, not falling. If someone was still inside the car, she had to try to save them!

As she grew closer, she could see that the car was a convertible, a red convertible. And there, deep in the clear water, she saw a shape behind the wheel.

Hannah didn't hesitate. She slid down the remainder of the embankment as fast as she could, and when she got to the edge of the pond, she kicked off her shoes. A second later, she was wading into the water.

Miller's Pond was a favorite swimming hole for the kids from surrounding farms because it was as shallow as a bathtub for at least twenty-five feet before it deepened. This made it ideal for smaller children as a wading pool, but swimmers had to wade out quite far before the water was deep enough to swim. Hannah waded as fast as she could, splashing out with frantic determination. Finally she reached swimming depth and she swam to the center of the pond as fast as she could.

If someone had been clocking her for the Olympics, Hannah might have made the swim team. When she arrived at a point near the submerged car, she dove down into the water, and saw the car clearly for the first time.

The driver was still behind the wheel, her long blond hair waving in the current from the stream that fed Miller's Pond.

Uh-oh! Hannah's mind shouted out a warning as she shot up to the surface for air. *Are you really sure you want to try to rescue her?* Hannah ignored the inference and dove down again. Yes, it was a red convertible. And yes, there was someone with blond hair behind the wheel. Her imagination had not been playing tricks on her. As she swam around to the side of the car she could see that it was a Maserati convertible and the driver was Doctor Bev!

Hannah worked as fast as she could, locating the seat belt and releasing the latch, but Doctor Bev remained in the white leather driver's seat. Since Hannah couldn't tell if she was dead or alive, she didn't waste time feeling for a pulse. She just shot up to the surface for another big gulp of air and dove back down again.

There was only one thing to do and Hannah did it. She put her arms around Doctor Bev and attempted to pull her from the seat. Even though the water lent buoyancy to her efforts, that was not enough. As Hannah got under Doctor Bev and used her weight to lever her up, she realized what the term *dead weight* meant. She just hoped that it wasn't accurate, as she muscled her rival for Norman's affections out of the seat and pulled her up to the surface.

With one arm clasped around Doctor Bev's chest, Hannah managed to swim with her. She knew if she dropped Doctor Bev, her rival would sink like a stone. Once she got to the shallow part of the pond, she managed to grasp Doctor Bev under both arms and drag her all the way to the shore.

Even though the prospect was almost too much to bear, Hannah immediately began resuscitation. She didn't stop to think. She just followed the procedure she'd learned during the last class she'd taken at the sheriff's station.

Hannah checked her waterproof watch after what seemed like an eternity. Five minutes had passed with no response. Doctor Bev was not showing any signs of breathing on her own. She started the procedure again, but after ten minutes there was no sign of life. Hannah kept at it rhythmically, fruitlessly, until a full twenty minutes had passed. Then she climbed back up the steep embankment to her truck to retrieve her cell phone.

Luckily, her phone was fully charged and she dialed Mike's cell phone. "Mike!" she gasped when he answered his phone. "Come out to Miller's Pond right away. And call for the paramedics. Doctor Bev was in a terrible accident and I think she's dead!"

Chapter Fourteen

"You remembered to bring these after all you've been through?" Delores looked completely amazed as Hannah handed her the box with Mom's Bran Muffins.

For a moment Hannah was confused. Her mind seemed to have slowed to idle speed. It took her a minute to process her mother's words, but then she understood what Delores was saying. "How did you know about it?"

"Doc told me when the call came in for the paramedics."

"Oh." Hannah steadied herself on the edge of Doc Knight's desk. She wanted to sit down, but her clothes were wet and the chairs in front of Doc Knight's desk were upholstered in fabric, not plastic.

"Put these on, dear," Delores held out a package. "You have to get out of those wet clothes. You're shivering."

Hannah accepted the package her mother

handed her. She hadn't realized that she was cold until her mother had mentioned it. Of course maybe it wasn't that she was cold. It could be that she was exhausted from the effort of dragging Doctor Bev out of the water. Whatever the reason, she was shivering and now her teeth were beginning to chatter.

"Go right in there and take a hot shower," Delores ordered, pointing to Doc Knight's bathroom. "It'll make you feel much better. There's shampoo, and towels, and everything you need. And throw your wet clothes in the dryer."

"Okay," Hannah said, not bristling at all, even though her mother was telling her what to do.

"While you're showering, I'll run down to the kitchen and get you a hot cup of coffee. Are you hungry?"

"No," Hannah said even though she wasn't sure she'd eaten recently. For some reason her mind was stalling out and it was difficult to think.

"I'll be right back, dear," Delores said, and then she gave Hannah a gentle shove toward the bathroom. "Go ahead."

Hannah crossed the room even though she wasn't sure she had the energy to take a shower. She'd stood guard over Doctor

Bev's body until Mike and Lonnie had arrived, and then she'd driven the rest of the way to the hospital. As she'd navigated the twists and turns around Eden Lake, she'd felt horribly alone. She couldn't seem to shake the specter of sudden, unexpected death. Doctor Bev had been alive such a short while ago, zipping along the lake road in her fancy new convertible, anticipating the move to her new penthouse condo. Hannah could picture her with her blond hair streaming in the breeze, listening to her favorite music and planning out where to put the new furniture she'd chosen with Roger. She wouldn't have had a clue that only moments later, she'd be at the bottom of Miller's Pond, strapped in her seat, cold and dead, robbed of the riches she'd lied and schemed to get.

Hannah did her best to shake off the dark thoughts. Perhaps Delores was right and a hot shower would help. She opened the bathroom door and blinked in surprise.

The bathroom was actually a suite that consisted of three separate rooms. The first contained what you'd expect in any bathroom. There was a washbowl with a mirror over it, a medicine cabinet, and a commode. The second, much larger room looked like a well-equipped dressing room, and she

216

thought she knew why. Since Doc Knight spent so much time at the hospital, he needed a place to shower and change into whatever clothing was required for his various duties. He would need easy access to operating scrubs, a white coat for rounds, and street clothes for his consultations with families of patients. There was a mirrored closet along one wall and Hannah suspected it was filled with Doc Knight's various choices of clothing. The wall opposite the closet held a gleaming stainless steel washer and dryer. The moment Hannah saw them she stripped out of her wet clothing and threw it into the dryer.

As she stepped into the third room, the room that contained a glass-enclosed shower, she noticed that her mother had set out towels for her to use. That little touch, that proof of caring, made her feel cosseted and loved. The feeling grew as she turned on the shower and stepped under the hot spray. Delores had known exactly what would make her feel better. It was good to have a mother.

Ten minutes later, feeling so much better she could scarcely believe it, Hannah stepped out of the shower. She retrieved the package her mother had given her with dry clothing and opened it. There were green scrubs with *Lake Eden Memorial Hospital* stenciled across the front, and they looked as if they might fit her. Hannah put on the top, stepped into the drawstring pants, and smiled. Everything fit. There was even a pair of hospital socks, the one-size-fits-all with non-skid patches on the bottom. She toweled off her hair, and dried it with the hair dryer that hung on a hook in the dressing room.

"Good enough," Hannah said to her reflection in the mirrored closet doors. The green of the scrubs was actually a good color with her red hair. She was about to walk out of the bathroom when there was a knock on the door.

"Are you all right, dear?"

"I'm fine. I'm ready." Hannah opened the door and stepped out.

"Sit here." Delores pointed to one of the visitor chairs in front of Doc Knight's desk. "I brought black coffee and sweet tea. They say that sweet tea is good for shock, but you choose."

Hannah thought about that for a moment. Normally, she didn't drink tea. This afternoon, for some strange reason, the thought of drinking it was appealing. "I'll take the tea," she said.

"You *are* in shock," Delores informed her.

"You don't like tea."

"I know. It just sounds good."

Delores gave a quick nod. "Shock, just as I thought. It's the only thing that would make you drink tea."

"I'll drink it, but I want a black coffee chaser," Hannah said, feeling a bit better as she sipped the hot beverage. "Of course chocolate would be better, but you don't have any, do you?"

Delores didn't say anything. She just went to the file cabinet next to the window and pulled out the top drawer. She took something out and turned it so that Hannah could see what it was.

"Fanny Farmer?"

"Yes. It's my emergency stash. I think this qualifies as an emergency, don't you?"

"Oh, yes. It's definitely an emergency. Are they soft centers?"

"Of course." Delores set the box between them on the desktop and took off the cover so that Hannah could see what was inside. "You know I like soft centers the best. Doc brought these in for me this morning."

"Are they for a special occasion?" Hannah asked, her fingers hovering over a dark chocolate piece that she hoped was filled with a maple center.

"Not really. It's just a thank you."

"For what?" Hannah reached down and plucked the piece of candy.

"For going out to the mall with him to help him choose two new jackets. Doc has no fashion sense. If it were up to him, he'd still be wearing that awful old tweed blazer. He told me he bought that blazer when his mother was alive and she picked it out for him."

Hannah remembered the tweed jacket. Her mother was right. It was pretty awful. "So the lack of fashion sense runs in the Knight family?"

"It seems so." Delores swallowed the last bite of her pineapple cream dipped in milk chocolate. "Doc always tells me how lucky he is to have me."

Hannah was silent as she reached for what she thought was a coconut cream covered with white chocolate. She wasn't sure exactly what that meant. "Where's Doc Knight?"

"He's still out at the scene, dear. He called me a few minutes ago. He said that you looked a bit glassy-eyed when he saw you out there and that you might be in shock."

"Was it his idea for me to take a hot shower?"

"No, that was mine. The sweet hot tea was his idea."

"Well, it worked. Between the shower, the tea with the coffee chaser, and the box of Fanny Farmer's, I feel much better now."

Delores shoved the box a little closer to Hannah's side of the desk. "Do you think you feel well enough to go and see Barbara?"

"Not quite yet, but soon."

"Then how about telling me what happened at the pond?" Delores asked. And then she paused and looked slightly sorry she'd asked. "But only if you feel up to it, of course," she added.

Hannah took a milk chocolate candy and was pleased to find it had a dark chocolate center. Her mother always asked her to describe the scene of a murder, but this was a car accident. "Okay," she said, and told her mother everything that had happened, beginning with the last time she'd seen Doctor Bev alive and how she'd barged onto the porch of the Peterson house. She told her mother the whole story, the dive into the water to try to save Doctor Bev when she'd spotted the car, her efforts to bring Doctor Bev to shore and revive her, all the way through to when she'd finally given up and called Mike at the sheriff's station.

"Oh, my!" Delores exclaimed, giving a ladylike shiver. "This is a terrible thing to say, but since Doctor Bev was so nasty to you, it almost makes me believe in divine retribution."

Hannah was slightly shocked. She knew that her mother loved her, but when Delores had heard some of the things that Doctor Bev had said to her on the Petersons' front porch, Delores had jumped in to defend her eldest daughter like a mother lion defending her cub.

"This whole thing must have been awful for you dear, especially since you were the one to find her." Delores gave a little sigh and reached out to pat Hannah's hand. "Then again, you usually do."

"True," Hannah acknowledged, "and it's never easy."

"I know, but this must have been worse. I'm sure you wished that you could get rid of Doctor Bev once and for all. As a matter of fact, I heard you say it right before the last time she left Lake Eden. You probably wished her dead on countless occasions. And then you're the one to find her."

Hannah thought about that for a moment. She didn't feel at all guilty. Perhaps her mother was projecting. "I don't think I ever wished that Doctor Bev was dead. I just wished that she would be gone for good."

222

"You're a better woman than I am," Delores said with a sigh. "Have another chocolate, dear. You still look a little pale."

Hannah reached for another piece of candy and realized that there were only three left. She looked up at her mother in total surprise. "Did I eat all those?"

"No. I helped."

"I'll buy you another box the next time I go out to the mall," Hannah promised.

"There's no need. Doc has several right here in the bottom drawer of his desk. He says it makes me more . . ." She paused and gave a little shrug. "I think he used the word *compliant*."

"Oh." Hannah said the most noncommittal thing she could think of. And then she thought, *That's the same word I used when Norman brought me the split of Dom Perignon. Norman said that there wasn't enough champagne in the world to make me compliant. But are there enough boxes of Fanny Farmer to make my mother compliant?*

"Are you ready to visit Barbara now?" Delores asked. "I'll go with you."

"I'm ready," Hannah replied, clamping the cover back on the box so that she wouldn't have to see the evidence of her transgression. And then she stood up and walked out of Doc Knight's office with her mother, making a valiant effort not to think about champagne, chocolate, and compliancy.

Barbara smiled when they entered the room. She was sitting up in a chair by the bed and she looked much better. She was still hooked to monitoring devices and an IV that beeped at irregular intervals, but at least she was out of bed.

"Is that your . . . daughter?" she asked.

"It's me, Barbara. I'm Hannah. And you're right." She gestured toward Delores. "I'm Delores's daughter."

"Hello, Hannah. I didn't know you were a nurse."

"Hannah's not a nurse," Delores said. "But I can see why you thought she was. Hannah got her clothes wet and so she changed into dry clothes from the hospital before we came to see you."

"I see. Green is a good color for you, Hannah."

"Thanks," Hannah said and then she exchanged looks with Delores. Barbara didn't seem as confused today and that was good. Perhaps it was time to ask why she'd been summoned. "Mother said you wanted to see me, Barbara."

"Yes. I was trying to remember the name of your cat and I couldn't remember. I have trouble with names."

"My cat's name is Moishe."

"Yes. Of course it is. I don't know why I couldn't remember. I guess my brain is still swollen. Can your Moishe be a therapy cat?"

"Therapy cat?" Hannah repeated it in the form of a question. She really didn't understand what Barbara was asking. "Do they have therapy cats?"

"If they don't, they should," Barbara replied. "They have therapy dogs. One was here this morning. I don't remember his name. It was nice to see him, but seeing a cat would be better. I miss my cat. Is somebody taking care of him? I tried, but I can't remember the last time I fed him. When I left for school on Tuesday, we were going to have a spelling test and I might have forgotten to give him his food."

"Don't worry, Barbara," Delores jumped in quickly, before Barbara could get upset. "Hannah and I will take care of it."

"Thank you . . . Delores," Barbara said, and both Hannah and her mother realized that it had been an effort for her to remember Delores's name. A moment passed, and then another before Hannah broke the silence.

"Is there anything I can do for you, Barbara?" she asked, still wondering why Barbara had wanted to see her when Delores or Doc Knight could have told her Moishe's name.

"Yes. Bring him to see me."

"Your cat?" Delores asked her.

"Of course not. He died years ago. My mother and I had a funeral for him and he's buried under the rhubarb bushes by the faucet in the back yard. I cried. He was a wonderful cat."

"It's always hard when a beloved pet dies," Delores sympathized.

Hannah gave a sigh of relief. Barbara was back on track again. She'd realized that her childhood cat had died years ago without being reminded that it had happened. Perhaps it was only when it came to her dead father and nonexistent brother that her mind played tricks on her.

"Will you, Hannah? If Doc says it's all right?"

"You remembered Doc's name!" Delores exclaimed, giving Barbara a warm smile. "That's just wonderful!"

Barbara looked thoroughly mystified for a moment and then she shook her head. "It's not that wonderful, De . . . Del . . . Delores. I don't remember Doc's name."

"But you called him Doc!"

"Yes. I did. He's a doctor so I called him Doc."

"Oh." Hannah knew Delores was disappointed, but it didn't show on her face. "You're right, Barbara. It's true that many people call doctors Doc. But you remembered my name and I could tell it was an effort."

"I did, didn't I?" Barbara looked pleased, and then she turned to Hannah. "I think I can remember your name now. When I see you, I remember that you make cookies with bananas and your name sounds like a banana. The only thing that sounds like a banana is Hannah so your name is Hannah. My nurse taught me how to rhyme with names."

"It sounds like you have a wonderful nurse," Hannah said.

"Oh, I do. I just wish I could remember her name. I know it sounds like money, and I called her Honey, but that's not it. It's some other kind of money, I think. But what could it be? Nickel?" Barbara started to laugh. "I'm almost sure her name isn't Pickle!"

Hannah couldn't help it. She laughed. And the moment she did, so did Delores. And then they all had a good laugh together.

"You'll remember her name the next time

you see her," Hannah said, almost sure that was true. This was a good visit with Barbara. She really *was* improving.

"So will you do it, Hannah?" Barbara asked.

Hannah was about to ask what Barbara wanted her to do when the pieces flew into place. "You want me to bring Moishe to the hospital to visit you?"

"Yes. I don't see why I can't have a cat visitor. People around here get dog visitors. There was a little one here last night visiting the man next door. They were training him to be a therapy dog."

Hannah made an instant decision. "If Doc Knight agrees, I'll bring Moishe here tomorrow," she promised.

"Oh, good. He's a nice big cat and I need a big cat."

"Why is that?" Delores asked her.

"For the monster that comes in my room at night. He looks a little like a big white rat. And I think a really big cat like Moishe could chase that monster away."

MOM'S BRAN MUFFINS

DO NOT preheat oven yet — this batter bakes better when it's chilled.

1 cup water
1 cup raisins (*I used golden raisins*)
2 cups bran flakes (*you'll use 4 cups in all*)
1 cup brown sugar (*pack it down when you measure it*)
1/2 cup (*1 stick, 8 ounces, 1/4 pound*) salted butter, softened
3 large eggs
2 teaspoons baking soda
1/2 teaspoon salt
1 teaspoon cinnamon
1 teaspoon vanilla extract
3 and 1/2 cups all-purpose flour (*pack it down when you measure it*)
2 cups buttermilk (*I've used whipping cream when I didn't have buttermilk on hand and it worked just fine.*)
2 cups quick cooking oatmeal (*I used Quaker Quick 1-Minute*)
2 cups bran flakes (*this completes the 4 cup total*)

Measure out the cup of water and bring it to a boil. You can do this in the microwave (*1 minute on HIGH in a microwave-safe container is hot enough for this recipe*), or on the stovetop in a saucepan.

While you're waiting for the water to boil, measure out a cup of raisins and put them in the bottom of a medium-size mixing bowl.

Measure 2 cups of bran flakes and put them on top of the raisins.

When the water has heated, pour it over the bran flakes and raisins in the bowl and stir it around a bit. Try to keep those raisins in the bottom where they'll be covered by the hot water. They need to plump up a bit.

Set the mixture aside on the counter to cool while you mix up the muffin batter.

Hannah's 1st Note: This is so much easier with an electric mixer.

Measure out the cup of brown sugar, packing it down in the cup when you measure it. Place the brown sugar in the bottom of a larger mixing bowl. (*This will be your work bowl.*)

Add the softened butter. (*The butter should be at room temperature unless, of course, you're working in a drafty kitchen in the middle of a cold Minnesota winter. In that case, you'll have to soften it a bit more!*)

Mix the brown sugar and butter together thoroughly.

Add the eggs, one by one, beating after

each addition.

Mix in the baking soda, salt, cinnamon, and vanilla extract.

Feel the sides of the bowl you set aside with the bran flakes and raisin mixture. If it's not so hot it'll cook the eggs, add it to your work bowl now. Mix it in thoroughly.

Measure out the flour, packing it down in the cup when you measure it.

Get out the 2 cups of buttermilk (*or whipping cream if you used that*).

Add about a third of the flour to your bowl and mix it in.

Add about a third of the buttermilk to your bowl and mix that in.

Add half of the flour you have left and mix it in.

Now add about half of the buttermilk you have left and mix that in.

Add the rest of the flour. Mix well.

Add the rest of the buttermilk. Mix well.

Hannah's 2nd Note: You may have to mix in the final 2 ingredients by hand, especially if your bowl is getting too full for your mixer.

Measure the 2 cups of quick-cooking oatmeal and mix that in.

Measure the final 2 cups of bran flakes and mix them in.

Give the bowl a final stir and cover it with

plastic wrap. Refrigerate your batter for at least 2 hours before you bake Mom's Bran Muffins. (*Overnight is fine, too. It's even preferable. Everyone likes a warm muffin for breakfast.*)

When you want to bake, preheat the oven to 375 F. degrees, rack in the middle position.

While your oven is heating to the proper temperature, prepare your muffin pans.

You can either spray your muffin cups with Pam (*or another nonstick cooking spray*) or line them with cupcake papers. Both methods work just fine.

These muffins don't rise very much so fill your muffin cups 3/4 (*three-quarters*) full.

Hannah's 3rd Note: Lisa and I use a 2-Tablespoon scooper to fill our muffin cups down at The Cookie Jar. It's neater than trying to spoon muffin batter into the cups.

Bake your muffins at 375 degrees F. for 20 minutes.

Hannah's 4th Note: You can bake these muffins one pan at a time if you like. As long as you keep the muffin batter tightly covered in the refrigerator, it will be fine for up to 6 weeks (that's right, SIX whole weeks!)

Cool your muffins in the muffin pan for

at least 20 minutes. Just set the whole pan on a wire rack or on a cold stove burner. At the end of that time, you can take them out of the muffin cups and let them cool completely on a wire rack. They're delicious warm, or cold.

Yield: 3 dozen delectable muffins.

Hannah's 5th Note: If you'd rather make jumbo muffins, bake those for 30 minutes at 375 degrees F.

A Word of Caution: Everyone says that bran muffins are good for digestive health. This appears to be true because if you eat too many of these for breakfast, you'll be spending a lot of time in the little room with the porcelain fixtures!

CHAPTER FIFTEEN

When Hannah reached the landing after ascending the covered staircase that led up to her condo, she was exhausted. It had been a terrible afternoon, but thankfully it was over. All she had to do now was make a sandwich for her dinner, and think of something to prepare for Mike when he came over to interview her at nine this evening.

Hannah stood on the bridge that ran between her condo and the condo across the way and wished that she hadn't agreed when Mike had said he'd come by at nine to take her statement. All she really wanted to do was relax and enjoy the slight breeze that blew across the manicured grounds below without commitments for the remainder of the night. The sun had dropped behind the row of tall pines that hid her condo complex from the road, the temperature had lowered a good ten degrees, and the mosquitoes hadn't found her yet.

As she stood there breathing deeply and feeling calmer, she watched the clouds make their majestic progress across the azure of the sky. There was something so comforting about dealing with nature instead of with people, even people she loved. You could watch nature change from one moment to the next and know that you didn't have to attempt to influence it in any way.

There was a high-pitched whine that buzzed past her ear and Hannah knew her nature respite was over. One mosquito had found her and that was enough. Within thirty seconds the first mosquito would ring the dinner bell and bring hundreds of friends and relatives to the buffet table.

Hannah wasted no time thrusting her key in the lock and opening the door. She stepped back, braced herself, and caught the feline who hurtled himself into her arms. "Hi, Moishe. Did you miss me?"

The answer was a purr so loud that she knew he'd been waiting for her at the door. She stepped in, kicked the door shut behind her, dropped her purse in the chair by the door, and carried Moishe to his favorite perch on the back of the living room couch. This wasn't easy. The last time she'd taken him to see his vet, Moishe had tipped the scales at twenty-two pounds. Between dragging Doctor Bev out of Miller's pond, refilling the flour and sugar bins down at The Cookie Jar this morning, and carrying Moishe across the living room, Hannah figured she'd accomplished enough weight-lifting for the week, or perhaps even for the month.

As soon as she'd checked Moishe's water bowl and poured herself something cold to drink, Hannah went back into the living room to see if there'd been any calls. The red light was blinking on her answering machine, and she pressed the button to play her messages.

"Hannah. It's Norman. They just told me."

There was a pause that was just long enough for Hannah to wonder why Norman sounded upset and then to realize that he was referring to Doctor Bev's death.

"I've been so worried. How are *you*?"

Again, it took Hannah a moment to figure out that he was talking about how she'd discovered Doctor Bev's body.

"It must have been horrible for you," his voice went on. "Mike told me you gave her mouth-to-mouth for twenty minutes before anyone arrived."

Hannah thought about that. It hadn't

been awful except in retrospect. When she'd been engaged in the act of attempting to resuscitate Doctor Bev, she hadn't thought about anything except forcing air into her lungs to get her to breathe again.

"You deserve a medal," Norman's voice continued. "I talked to Andrea a couple of minutes ago and she said Doctor Bev was really nasty to you on the Petersons' porch. I'm sorry, Hannah. It's my fault you had to go through all that."

Guilt time, her mind announced. *Norman's been worrying about you for hours and you haven't given him a thought.*

"Anyway, please give me a call when you get home. I want to hear your voice and know that you're all right. And if there's anything I can do for you, please, please let me know. I love you, Hannah."

He loves you more than you love him, her mind accused her. *That's crystal clear. He called you the moment he heard about Doctor Bev. You should have called him from the hospital, but you didn't even think about it.*

"I was a little too busy at the time," Hannah argued out loud. "And you're right. I didn't think about it. I didn't think about anything at the time. I was in shock."

A likely excuse!

"It's no excuse!" Hannah shouted. "It's

the truth!"

"Rrrrrow!"

Hannah looked up to see Moishe regarding her curiously. Or perhaps it was an anxious expression. It was difficult to tell with a cat.

"I'm okay," she told him, and he lowered his head to rest on his paws again. In no time at all his eyes had closed to slits and he was purring softly.

It took a total of five minutes to change her clothes, toss the ones she'd worn when she jumped into Miller's Pond into the washer, and carry her lemonade back out to the living room again. She sat down on the couch, listened to make sure the load in her washer was balanced and not thumping unevenly, and reached for the phone. Her fingertips had just touched the receiver when it rang.

"Hello," she answered, wondering if it was Norman and mental telepathy was at work. But that wasn't the case because it was Andrea.

"Hannah?" Andrea asked a bit tentatively.

"Yes, Andrea."

"I know you probably just got home and you're resting, but . . . can I drive out to see you?"

Hannah didn't hesitate even though she

still had to think of something to make for Mike to eat. "Sure," she said.

"I've got something for you, but I have to stop on the way to pick up some milk for tomorrow. Do you need anything?"

"I'm not sure I . . ." Hannah stopped speaking and began to smile as visions of pancakes swimming in butter and syrup danced through her head. Mike loved breakfast any time of the day or night, so she'd make pancakes and sausage. Mike also loved dessert and she was sure she had some cookies in the freezer. Teamed with the ice cream that she knew was there, they would make a fine dessert.

"Are you there, Hannah?"

"I'm here. I was just thinking about what I needed. Can you pick up breakfast sausage, quick-cooking oatmeal, milk, and maple syrup?"

"Sure. I'm writing a list. Anything else?"

"Where are you going?"

"The Quick Stop. The Red Owl's already closed."

"Do they have any fresh fruit out there?"

"Nothing fancy, but the last time I was there they had oranges and apples."

"That'll do just fine. I'll need an apple."

"Just one?"

Hannah considered that for a moment. If

Andrea hadn't eaten, she'd invite her to stay. And then there was Norman. When she returned his call, he might want to drive out to talk about Doctor Bev's death. That would be dinner for four. And heaven only knew who else would call. She'd better plan for six, just in case.

"Hannah?"

"Sorry. I was trying to plan things. Better bring two apples, just in case. And you'd better bring enough breakfast sausage for six."

"You're expecting company?"

"Not exactly. I'm *anticipating* company. I never know what's going to happen when I start to cook."

"That's because you're such a good cook and everybody wants to come to your place to eat. I'll see you in about forty . . . Hold on. I've got another call coming in." Hannah held on and in less than a minute Andrea was back on the line. "That was Norman. He tried to call you, but your line was busy."

"Of course it was busy. I was talking to you."

"I know. That's what I told him. You really ought to get call-waiting, Hannah."

Hannah wisely said nothing. Her sister had been trying to talk her into getting

240

conference calling, call-waiting, and automatic this and that ever since she'd first moved into her condo.

"I told Norman you'd call him back just as soon as you got off the phone with me. That's okay, isn't it?"

"That's exactly what I was planning to do."

"Good. I thought he sounded a little funny, but maybe we had a bad connection. I'm leaving now and I'll be there in less than forty-five minutes."

Hannah hung up the phone, got herself another glass of lemonade from the huge jug she kept in the bottom of her refrigerator, and returned to the couch. It was time to call Norman.

"Hannah," Norman said, sounding pleased that she'd called. "I tried to call you earlier, but you were talking to Andrea."

"I know. Andrea told me. I got your message, but Andrea called just as I was about to pick up the phone to return your call."

"Are you all right?"

"I'm okay. How about you? That was really a shock."

"Yes, especially since I was in the car with her less than four hours before it happened. She asked Tracey to go for a ride with her, and I didn't think she should go alone, so I went along to chaperone her."

"I know all about it. Tracey told me this afternoon."

"I don't think you know the *whole* story. Once Bev dropped Tracey off at the real estate office, she drove out to the Lake Eden Inn and insisted that I take her to lunch."

"Dentist-napping?"

"That's about what it amounted to. I wouldn't have gotten in the car in the first place if it hadn't been for Tracey."

Norman sounded so sincere, Hannah nodded even though she knew he couldn't see her. "I know that, Norman."

"You know that Bev and I were through, don't you?"

"I know."

"She stopped by the clinic this morning and called me from her cell phone. She asked me to go for a ride and I told her I didn't think it would be appropriate."

Hannah smiled. That sounded like Norman. "What did she say to that?"

"She said it was just a ride and anyone could go along. She just needed someone local to show her the back way to the lake. I said okay, and I sent Doc Bennett out to show her the right road."

"Oh, boy!" Hannah said under her breath. She had no doubt that Doctor Bev had been as mad as a wet hen. And at that moment, something else occurred to her. "You said you went to lunch with her. Tell me about that."

"There's not much to tell. Ask Sally and she can tell you how uncomfortable I was. I didn't want to say anything that could possibly be misconstrued."

"I understand that, but how about lunch? Did Doctor Bev have a lot to drink?"

"Just sparkling water. She said it was too early in the day and Roger had gotten her into the habit of having martinis at five." Norman stopped speaking for a moment and Hannah knew the wheels were spinning in his mind. "You were thinking that she had too much to drink at lunch and that's why she had the accident?"

"Yes."

"Well, that's not it. She didn't have anything alcoholic, at least not at lunch. And she didn't eat either. What puzzles me is Bev was a very good driver. As far as I know, she'd never had an accident before this. It makes me wonder if something went wrong with the car."

"You must be very upset, Norman."

Norman sighed so deeply that she heard it clearly over the phone. "I'm not very upset. And maybe *that* should be upsetting in itself. I don't feel anything for her anymore, Hannah. I wrote Bev off that last night I confronted her in the Cities. When I danced with her at the grand opening of the hotel, she was like a stranger to me. I felt no connection at all. Does that make sense to you?"

"It makes sense. She wounded you in the past so you put on your protective armor. You squelched any feelings you might have and felt nothing."

"That's exactly it. Do you think that's bad?"

Hannah realized that Norman sounded sad and a little anxious. It was clear to her that he needed a friend. "I don't know. Have you eaten yet?"

"Eaten?" Norman gave a little laugh. "Now there's a real non sequitur!" There was a long pause. "You know, I don't remember eating. And all I had was coffee at lunch. I don't think I've eaten since breakfast."

"Well, get in the car and come out here. Andrea's driving out, and Mike's coming over later to take my statement about the accident. I'm going to make pancakes and sausages for everybody."

"Are you sure you'll have enough?"

"I always have enough," Hannah promised. "Come out here, Norman. I really want to see you. And bring Cuddles if you want. She's always welcome."

OATMEAL APPLE PANCAKES

Hannah's 1st Note: This recipe calls for you to mix everything up in a food processor. If you don't have a food processor, you can use a blender. You could also use a food grinder to grind up the oatmeal and then mix everything up by hand. I think you could also substitute instant oatmeal, (*the kind in little packages that you make in the microwave*), for the quick-cook oatmeal and then mix everything up by hand.

1 small apple (*I use Fuji or Gala — if you use Granny Smith or any other tart green apple, you'll have to sprinkle the apple slices with sugar before you add them to the pancakes*)
1 Tablespoon lemon juice

———————

1/2 cup all-purpose flour
1/2 cup quick-cooking oatmeal
2 Tablespoons white (*granulated*) sugar
1 teaspoon baking powder
1/2 teaspoon baking soda
1/2 teaspoon salt
1 teaspoon cinnamon
1/2 teaspoon nutmeg

1 teaspoon vanilla extract
3/4 cup buttermilk or regular whole milk
2 teaspoons vegetable oil
1 large egg

———————

1 teaspoon vegetable oil (*for frying the pan-cakes*)
2 teaspoons salted butter (*for frying the pancakes*)

Hannah's 2nd Note: I've made these with buttermilk and with regular whole milk. Both ways are very good. If you want to try the recipe with buttermilk and you don't have any in your refrigerator, you can easily make a substitute. Just pour 2 teaspoons of lemon juice OR 2 teaspoons of white vinegar into a measuring cup and fill the cup to the three-quarter mark with whole milk. Just let it stand on the counter for 5 minutes and it will be ready to use in this recipe.

Peel and core the apple. Cut it into very thin slices, place them in a bowl, and sprinkle them with the lemon juice. Toss them around a little with your fingers so that all the slices are coated with the lemon juice. (*This will keep the apple slices from*

browning while you make the pancake batter.)

Place flour, oatmeal, sugar, baking powder, baking soda, salt, cinnamon, and nutmeg in a food processor and process with the steel blade for 10 seconds.

Add the vanilla extract, buttermilk, vegetable oil, and egg to the dry mixture in the food processor. Process for 30 seconds or until everything is smooth and well blended.

Heat two teaspoons salted butter and one teaspoon vegetable oil in a frying pan over MEDIUM HIGH heat, or until a small amount of water sizzles and "dances" on the surface of the pan.

Use a quarter-cup measure to scoop out the batter and pour it onto the surface of the pan for each pancake.

Place 5 or 6 slices of apple on the top of each pancake. Push them down slightly into the batter with your fingers, but be very careful not to burn yourself!

When the outside edges of the pancakes show little holes where bubbles have formed and popped, but not filled in with batter again, flip the pancake over and brown the other side. If you can't tell if there are holes on the outside edges, just lift one edge of the pancake with your spatula and peek to see if it's golden brown on the bottom. If it is, flip it over. It it's not, give it a minute or two longer, and then flip it over.

Fry the second side of the pancake until it's golden brown.

Serve the Oatmeal Apple Pancakes hot off the pan with butter and syrup.

Hannah's 3rd Note: If there are any apple slices left over, sprinkle them with sugar, cinnamon, and nutmeg and use another teaspoon of butter to fry them until they're tender. Just put them in a bowl and you can serve them as a side dish with your pancakes.

Lisa's note: I'm going to try these with well-drained crushed pineapple in the batter. I'm also going to try them with banana slices instead of the apple slices. Banana and oatmeal is a wonderful combination!

Yield: approximately 6 quarter-cup pancakes

CHAPTER SIXTEEN

Hannah had just finished transferring her wet clothes from the washer to the dryer when her phone rang again. She took a half-second to set and turn on the dryer and then rushed back to the living room to answer it. "This is Hannah," she said, sinking down on the couch.

"And this is Michelle," Hannah's youngest sister answered. "Can I come and stay with you for a couple of days? I've got a little time off before my work-study program starts, and it's lonely at our house. Everyone else has left on summer break."

"Of course. You know you're always welcome. What day are you coming?"

"I'm here. Mother picked me up at the Quick Stop and Sean said we just missed Andrea. Mother will drive me to your place if that's okay with you."

"It's fine with me. Have you eaten?"

"Not yet, but I've got a couple of energy

bars with me, so you don't have to worry about that."

"It's no worry. I'm already fixing night lunch for Andrea, Norman, and Mike. It's easy to add you and Mother to the mix."

"Oh, good! Mother hasn't eaten either. Can we pick up anything on the way?"

Hannah thought fast. "Some orange juice. That's a natural with breakfast sausage and my Oatmeal Apple Pancakes."

"You got it. How about dessert?"

"I've got cookies and French vanilla ice cream in the freezer."

"That sounds good. I'll pick up some toppings to go on the ice cream. There's no way Mother can eat a whole meal without chocolate so I'll get hot fudge."

"Good thinking." Hannah glanced over at Moishe, who was staring at her intently. "Is Mother wearing silk stockings?"

"Yes. But why did you want to . . ." Michelle stopped speaking and laughed. "I get it! I'll pick up some kitty treats so Mother can placate Moishe. We'll see you in less than an hour."

Hannah hung up the phone and sighed. It didn't do any good to have a cold glass of lemonade if she didn't get the chance to drink it. It was a good thing she made it fairly strong so that all she had to do was pour it in a larger glass and add fresh ice. She had just accomplished that and was on her way back to the couch when the phone rang again.

There were times when she really wanted to answer the phone and times when she really didn't. This was one of those "really didn't" times. In Hannah's case, reluctance bowed to responsibility and took center stage because she reached for the phone. "This is Hannah," she said, trying not to sound as exasperated as she felt.

"Hi, Hannah. It's Mike. I got through early and I would have been out there by now, but Doc Knight's doing the autopsy and I'm waiting for the results. I'm almost sure I can be there by nine, though. Is that all right?"

"That's fine. Are you hungry?"

"As a bear. Do you want me to stop at the Corner Tavern and pick up burgers for us?"

"Thanks, but no. I'm cooking. And just so you know, I'm about to get a houseful."

"Who's coming?"

"Andrea's the first. She should be here fairly soon. And Mother and Michelle are right behind her."

"Great. I haven't seen Michelle in a while. Anyone else?"

"Norman. He hasn't eaten since breakfast

and I invited him to join us. You don't mind, do you?"

"Not at all. I need to talk to him anyway. When I went out to the Inn to interview Sally, she said he had lunch with Bev."

"Had *lunch*?" Hannah was a bit disconcerted. Norman had told her he hadn't eaten lunch.

"Okay, I should have said that Norman was *with* her at lunch. Neither one of them ate. He had coffee and she had sparkling water. Sally also said that Norman looked the opposite of thrilled to be with Bev again. What are you cooking, Hannah? Do you need me to pick up anything on the way?"

"Thanks, but I think I've got it covered. We're having pancakes and sausage with cookies and ice cream for dessert."

"Sounds good! I'll see you as soon as I get those results."

Hannah took time to drink her lemonade and then she went into the kitchen to get out her electric griddle. With six for pancakes, she needed more cooking space than she could get with frying pans on the stovetop. She was just getting out the vegetable oil, butter, flour, and milk when the phone rang again.

"Grand Central," she said as she picked up the wall phone by her kitchen table.

There was a burst of laughter from her caller and Hannah recognized the laugh. "Lisa?" she asked.

"It's me. I just wanted to tell you that Jenny's going to come in tomorrow to meet you."

"Jenny?" Hannah asked, thoroughly puzzled.

"Jenny Hester, the nurse with the Easy Fruit Pie recipe. I talked to her on our break tonight. She just moved here a couple of weeks ago and if she isn't working for Doc Knight at the hospital, she's at the college taking classes. She told me she's been so busy she hasn't had a chance to get to The Cookie Jar yet, but she wants to come in and meet you."

"Great. I'll look forward to meeting her." Hannah paused as she heard a knock on the door. "I'll talk to you tomorrow, Lisa. I've got company coming and I think they're here."

It only took a moment or two to hang up the phone and cross the living room to the door. Hannah opened it without looking through the peephole and chided herself for her negligence. She had to get into the habit of looking before she opened the door.

"You didn't look through the peephole," Andrea accused as she handed Hannah a grocery bag.

"How do you know I didn't?"

"Because I was looking in from outside, and nothing blocked the light behind it."

"Then if I'd looked, all I would have seen was your eye."

"Oh. I guess you're right. But you really ought to look, Hannah. Bill says it's really important."

"I'll try to remember." Hannah glanced inside the grocery bag. "I'm glad you didn't get the really small canister of oatmeal."

"How much do you need for those pancakes?"

"Only half a cup for each batch, but a batch only makes six small pancakes. We'll be six for dinner and I'll need at least four batches, maybe more. I just hope I have enough cookies in the freezer."

Andrea began to smile and it was a very happy smile. "Go put that big bag in the kitchen and then look inside the smaller bag I'm carrying."

"What's in there?" Hannah asked as Andrea followed her to the kitchen.

"Something I hope you'll like. I made them when I got home this afternoon."

The moment the large bag of ingredients was empty, Hannah took a peek at Andrea's smaller bag. "Cookies?" she asked, looking through the almost transparent green plastic lid of the food storage container inside.

"Yes. The kids really liked them and so did Grandma McCann. Of course the kids like almost anything, but Grandma McCann is a really good cook so her opinion counts."

"Yes, it does," Hannah agreed, lifting the lid and removing one of the cookies. If Andrea's nanny and housekeeper thought the cookies were good, they were definitely good.

Hannah took a bite and chewed. And then she took another bite. "Excellent," she said, but only after she'd finished the cookie. "I've never tasted anything quite like them before. You're turning into a very good baker."

"Thanks!" Andrea beamed at the compliment. "Of course Tracey and Bethie deserve some of the credit. Tracey stirred and she reminded me to put the scooping spoon in the freezer so the dough wouldn't stick."

"Good for Tracey." Hannah already knew that her almost-seven-year-old niece was a big help to Andrea, but she wondered what two-year-old Bethie could do to help. "How about Bethie? What did she do?"

"She drank the pineapple juice after I drained the pineapple. And before you say anything, I know that's not really helping, but I told her it was. And she did critique the cookies. She said, *Yummy, Mummy!* And then she asked for another one."

"That's a seal of approval in my book. Are all these cookies for me?"

"Yes. I've got another container at home for Lisa and Herb. I'll bring them by The Cookie Jar in the morning."

"Would you mind if I served your cookies tonight? They'd be really good with vanilla ice cream."

Andrea's face lit up. "I wouldn't mind at all! Who's coming over? You said there were six."

"You, me, Mike, Norman, Mother, and Michelle."

"Then it's a family party except for Bill. He's working late on some paperwork that has to be filed. He says it takes him a lot longer now that he has to explain everything to one of the temporary secretaries. Barbara used to take care of all that." Andrea gave a little sigh. "I wonder if she's ever going to come back to work. It's so sad. And they're still in the dark about exactly what happened and who attacked her. I wonder if she'll ever be able to tell us."

"I think she will. She was rational for longer periods of time when I saw her this afternoon. She said some strange things, but some things made sense, too."

"Let me help you set the table," Andrea offered. "And when we're through, you can tell me all about it."

PINEAPPLE COCONUT
WHIPPERSNAPPER COOKIES

Do not preheat your oven quite yet — your mixing bowl and spoon must chill before mixing this cookie dough.

8-ounce can of crushed pineapple
1 box yellow cake mix (**the kind that makes a 9-inch by 13-inch cake**)
1 large egg, beaten (**just whip it up in a glass with a fork**)
2 cups of original Cool Whip (**not low-fat Cool Whip**)

———————

1 cup (**8 ounces**) sweetened coconut flakes
1/2 cup powdered (**confectioner's**) sugar (**for rolling the cookies**)
15 to 18 maraschino cherries cut in half lengthwise

30 minutes before you're ready to bake, stick a teaspoon from your silverware drawer in a large freezer-safe mixing bowl. Stick the bowl with the spoon in the freezer to chill.

Open the 8-ounce can of crushed pineapple and empty it in a small strainer. Occasionally, use the back of a tablespoon from your spoon drawer to press down on the top of the crushed pineapple in the strainer to speed up the draining time.

After 30 minutes have passed, empty the drained pineapple out onto a couple of paper towels and blot it gently to remove any remaining moisture.

Preheat the oven to 350 degrees F., rack in the middle position.

Either spray a cookie sheet with Pam or another nonstick cooking spray, or line it with parchment paper and then spray that.

Remove the large mixing bowl from the freezer, but leave the spoon in.

Pour approximately half of the yellow cake mix into your bowl.

Add the beaten egg and stir it in.

Add the drained pineapple and mix it in.

Sprinkle the rest of the yellow cake mix on top. Add the Cool Whip and the coconut. Stir everything together until it's well mixed.

Place the half-cup of powdered sugar in a shallow bowl. Then take the spoon out of the freezer.

There are two ways to form dough balls with this sticky cookie dough. One is to scoop out dough with the chilled spoon and place it in the bowl of powdered sugar, rolling it around with your fingers until it forms a small ball. The other, easier way is to dust your hands with powdered sugar, pinch off a small amount of dough, place it in the bowl of powdered sugar and shape it into a ball with your fingers.

Use your favorite method (**you may want to try both to see which one works best for you**) to form 12 dough balls for each cookie sheet.

If you don't have double ovens, place the remaining cookie dough in the refrigerator to wait until you have room to bake a second sheet of cookies. If you forget to do this and leave it on the counter, it will be even stickier!

Place one-half of a maraschino cherry, cut side down, on top of each cookie ball on the sheet. Flatten the balls just a bit by pressing down on the cherry halves.

Bake your Pineapple Coconut Whippersnapper Cookies at 350 degrees F., for 15 minutes.

Remove your cookies from the oven and let them cool for 2 minutes on a cold stovetop burner or a wire rack.

When 2 minutes have passed, remove the cookies from the sheet with a metal spatula and place them on the wire rack to complete cooling. If you used the parchment paper, this is simple. Simply pull the paper off of the cookie sheet and onto the wire rack. The cookies can stay on the paper until they're cool.

Hannah's Note: Pineapple Coconut Whippersnapper Cookies are very pretty. Lisa and I are going to make them for Christmas parties using both red and green cherries since red and green are the traditional colors of Christmas.

Lisa's Note: Herb absolutely adores these cookies. I can't bake them fast enough for him!

Yield: Approximately 2 to 3 dozen very pretty and very yummy cookies.

CHAPTER SEVENTEEN

"I really shouldn't but . . . just one more, Hannah. I really like these pancakes."

Hannah smiled as she passed the pancake platter. Her mother had already eaten two pancakes and this would be her third. As far back as Hannah could remember, her mother had never eaten more than one and a half.

"I like them too, and I don't even like oatmeal," Andrea commented, forking another piece of sausage. "I'd have another, but we want to save some for Mike, don't we?"

Hannah shook her head. "No. I'll make a fresh batch when he gets here. They're best hot off the griddle." She turned to look at the cats, who were rubbing against her legs. "Sorry, guys. You already shared a whole piece of sausage."

"And don't even think about trying that chase ploy again," Norman warned them. "It worked with Lonnie's steak, but it won't work with the sausage. I'm holding the platter and my plate is empty."

Moishe looked as innocent as a cat could look and Michelle laughed. "Look at Moishe. He's pretending he doesn't know what we're talking about."

"I almost forgot." Delores turned to Hannah. "Doc says it's fine if you bring Moishe out to visit Barbara. He thinks it might do her some good to have visible reminders of her current life beyond the isolation of her hospital room. He said reminders of the present could give her a temporal reference."

"So Barbara realizes that some of the people she thought were currently in her life are really in the past?" Michelle asked.

"I think that's what he meant, dear. It does make sense. Andrea and I are going to go over to Barbara's house tomorrow to get some object that's relatively new and one that's from her parents' era. Once she sees the two objects together she may remember that the house is hers now and she's living there alone because her parents are dead."

"That might work as far as her father is concerned, but I don't think it'll have any effect on the monster," Hannah predicted. "Does Doc Knight have any suggestions for that delusion?"

"What monster?" Norman asked, and Hannah realized that he was out of the loop.

"Barbara said a monster comes into her room at night at the hospital. It scares her and she wants Moishe to chase it away."

"Is she dreaming?" Norman asked.

"I don't know and I don't think anyone else does either. Barbara does think she saw a monster though. I could tell that she believed it."

"You're right. She did," Delores confirmed. "Doc told me the monster has him puzzled. Barbara was quite rational all morning, and other than a couple of little slips with us, she was rational during our visit."

Norman looked thoughtful. "Could there really be a monster?" He gave a little laugh as he saw their incredulous looks. "I don't mean a monster like *Frankenstein* or *Beowulf,* but something that Barbara construes as a monster. It could be as simple as a shadow on the wall, or a tree branch that rubs against her window."

"You could be right," Michelle said. "Things look different at night, especially when you first wake up. I remember thinking that my teddy bear turned into a monster at night when I was little."

"*That's* why you always threw a towel over

his face!" Hannah exclaimed.

"That's right. If he couldn't see me, he couldn't eat me."

"It could be something like that with Barbara," Delores suggested. "Doc says it's common for patients on pain pills to have some level of confusion. Barbara could have seen something perfectly ordinary and thought it was a monster."

Hannah wanted to remind her mother that Barbara had described the monster as a giant white rat and shadows weren't white, but she bit her tongue and said nothing. No one wanted to think that Barbara's mind had been badly damaged. They all needed to believe that her condition was temporary and soon she'd return to the happy, productive woman they knew.

Andrea cleared her throat and Hannah looked over at her. There was an expression of anticipation on her face and for a moment Hannah didn't know what her sister wanted. It hit her then, and she gave a slight nod. Moments later she was clearing the table, putting on the coffee, and getting out the dessert bowls Delores had given her for Christmas several years ago. Andrea had been waiting for the meal to be over so that it would be time for dessert. It wasn't that she wanted to eat it, at least not necessarily.

266

What Andrea was anticipating was receiving more compliments on her new whipper-snapper cookies.

At eight-thirty there was a knock on the door and Hannah went to answer it. This time she looked through the peephole because she knew it had to be Mike and he'd be upset with her if she didn't take that precaution. Mike stood there in the light and he wasn't smiling. That made Hannah experience a moment's anxiety, but she managed to shrug it off. He was probably tired from working so hard. And he was probably hungry.

"It's Mike," she said to everyone inside and then she opened the door. "Hi, Mike. Come in."

"Thanks." Mike stepped in, but he still wasn't smiling.

"Are you hungry?" Hannah asked him.

"Yes, but I don't have time to eat." Mike gave a little wave to the group assembled in the living room and then he turned back to Hannah. "I'm sorry, Hannah, but you'll have to come with me."

Hannah was thoroughly puzzled. "But . . . why?"

"I was going to take your statement here, but things have changed. We need to keep this formal. Will you go with me, or not?"

Mike sounded so serious, Hannah knew something was dreadfully wrong. "Of course I'll go with you," she said. "Just tell me what things have changed."

"Doctor Beverly Thorndike's accident was not an accident."

"Murder?" Hannah's voice shook slightly as she asked the question.

"Yes."

There were gasps from the others, but no one spoke. Hannah surmised the reason was that they were every bit as shocked as she was and they didn't know what to say.

"But you've taken my statements in other murder cases right here in the condo. You've never asked me to go down to the station before. Why is it so different this time?"

Mike sighed deeply. He was obviously reluctant to elaborate. He swallowed hard and then he answered in as few words as possible. "Because you're the prime suspect," he said.

CHAPTER EIGHTEEN

"Who baked the Red Velvet Surprise Cupcakes for the victim?"

Hannah glanced over at Howie Levine. He gave a little nod and she knew that it was all right to answer Mike's question. The moment she'd left the condo with Mike, Delores had called Doc Knight on her cell phone to find out the results of the autopsy, and Norman had called Howie Levine, Lake Eden's lawyer, and asked him to meet Hannah when she arrived at the sheriff's station.

"I baked them," Hannah answered.

"Was there anyone else in the kitchen when you baked them?"

Again, Hannah looked over at Howie. She didn't like the idea of getting legal advice on each and every question Mike asked her, but she knew it was the wise thing to do. "Lisa came in a couple of times when they were in the oven, but I was alone when I mixed up the batter."

Howie motioned for Hannah to move closer. Then he spoke in an undertone. "You're being too helpful, Hannah. Just answer the question he asks. Don't volunteer information."

"What should I have said?" Hannah asked, also in an undertone.

"You should have said yes. No more than that. There was someone with you in the kitchen when you baked them. It's up to him to ask who that person was and how long they were there. Don't do his work for him."

Hannah sighed and turned back to Mike again. So far his questions had covered every single thing she'd done from the time she'd gotten up this morning to the time he'd arrived on the scene after she'd discovered Doctor Bev's body in the car and pulled her onto the shore. He'd covered that period of time in minute detail twice, and now he was covering it for the third time.

The door to the interrogation room, the room that Mike had once called *the box,* clicked open, to admit Lonnie. Lonnie didn't say anything. He just motioned to Mike.

"Excuse me." Mike spoke to them politely, and then he stood up and left the room.

Hannah closed her eyes. She'd never been so exhausted in her life. She wondered if every suspect who had gone through the same material multiple times had been as exhausted as she was right now. All she wanted to do was go home and go to bed.

Perhaps she dozed for a brief moment, hoping that all this was simply a very bad dream. When she opened her eyes again, she turned to Howie with a question. "It doesn't usually take this long to give a statement about finding a murder victim, does it?"

"No."

"That's what I thought. They think I put something in those cupcakes to kill Doctor Bev, don't they?"

"It seems that way."

"Do *you* think I killed her?"

"It doesn't matter whether I do or I don't. It's my responsibility to make sure you don't inadvertently incriminate yourself during the interrogation."

"But *do* you think I killed her? I want to know!"

Howie shook his head. "No, of course I don't think you killed her."

Hannah drew a relieved breath. "That makes me feel a lot better. Why don't you think I killed her?"

271

"There were too many mistakes," Howie said. "Using poison or another lethal substance as a murder weapon necessitates planning and premeditation. You have to obtain the substance, you have to devise a way to deliver it to the victim without being detected, and unless you simply don't care about collateral damage, you have to make certain no one except your intended victim consumes it. You didn't do any of those things."

"That's true, but how does that convince you that I'm innocent?"

Howie smiled. "You're smart, Hannah. You would have known all this. And frankly, just between you and me, if you'd set out to kill Doctor Bev, you wouldn't have made any rookie mistakes."

Hannah blinked. She wasn't sure if that was a compliment or not, and she wasn't quite sure how she should respond. But it didn't matter because before she could think of a reply, the door to the interrogation room opened and Mike came back in.

"You're free to go, Hannah," he said.

"But . . ." Hannah began to ask him why he'd suddenly stopped before he finished asking all the questions he'd asked her before when Howie reached out to take her arm.

"Thank you, Detective Kingston," Howie said, and then he turned to Hannah. "Come with me, Hannah. I'll drive you home."

Hannah took the hint that wasn't exactly gentle, and merely nodded. Howie didn't want her to say another word in front of Mike. Mike was all cop and she was all prime murder suspect. This was not a friendly situation and the sooner she put distance between them, the better.

Hannah dove down toward the darkness that gathered at the very bottom of the pond. As she descended into the curious half-light that caused colors to change and fade into some strange hue that went nameless on color charts, she spotted the car. The rippling water made it appear to be moving forward, driving across the bottom of the pond. Even the driver appeared to be moving with her blond hair trailing out in wispy tendrils behind her.

She wanted to leave, to go back up to the surface where it was bright and safe. The driver was dead. She knew that. But as she approached the side of the car, the woman turned her head and stared into Hannah's eyes with her dead wavy eyes. And then she lifted one pale hand and beckoned Hannah closer.

She didn't want to go. She knew she shouldn't go. But some force stronger than the waving water drew her closer to the car. The driver smiled as she approached. Her mouth opened and a rush of bubbles came out. Not dead then. You couldn't make bubbles without air in your lungs.

The woman used one long wavy finger to point to the passenger seat. She wanted Hannah to get into the car and sit next to her. But Hannah didn't want to get in with a dead woman who still had air in her lungs.

There was another burst of bubbles and Hannah heard something. It was barely audible, but it was a word and the word was *closer.*

Despite her revulsion, Hannah felt her body move forward. She seemed to have no control over her muscles as they carried her to the side of the car. And then the woman's arm snaked out to remove the thermos on the passenger seat and to pull Hannah into the seat. Her long wavy fingers clicked the seat belt securely into place, and then she laughed over and over, an insane, cascading laugh like the loons that called across the lake in the dead of night. And then her arms shot out to wrap around Hannah's chest like a band of wet steel that expelled the last breath of air from her body, squeezing, scratching, and kneading her into submission.

And then, as Hannah felt herself sink lower and lower, heading toward the dim recesses of her watery grave, there was another burst of bubbles from the dead woman's mouth that formed words.

Go for a ride, her eerie underwater voice said. *Go for a ride and stay with me forever.*

"Noooooo!" Hannah moaned in terror, pushing back the weight of the dead woman's arms and sitting bolt upright in bed. Almost simultaneously there was an irate yowl from Moishe as he landed on the rug by the side of the bed.

It took a full minute for Hannah to realize that it had all been a dream, a terrible nightmare. She must have made some sounds of distress while she was in the throes of the nightmare and Moishe had jumped up on her chest. She wasn't sure if he'd been trying to protect her from her nightmare or whether he was merely curious, but her sleeping mind had incorporated him into the fabric of the horrible dream.

"I'm sorry if I scared you, Moishe. Come here and I'll scratch you behind the ears. Everything's okay. I'm awake now."

Moishe regarded her with unblinking eyes from the top of her dresser. His tail flicked once and Hannah knew that he was not about to risk a repeat of his unceremonious exit from her bed.

Hannah reached out to turn on the light and stopped in midair. She didn't need the light. Daylight was streaming through her bedroom window. But that was impossible. This was a workday and she always got up in the dark on a workday.

One glance at the clock told her the truth. It was nine-thirty in the morning. She'd slept right through her alarm. Of course that wasn't surprising. When she'd come back to the condo, long after midnight, she'd been utterly exhausted and very grateful to see Michelle waiting up for her. They'd talked about everything that had happened until Hannah could no longer keep her eyes open, and Michelle had insisted that she go to bed. And now she'd slept right through the summons of her extra-loud alarm clock. Or had she?

The button to activate her alarm clock was not pulled out. And she distinctly remembered pulling it out when she'd gone to bed. Someone had come in and turned off her alarm, and since there was no one else here, Michelle must have done it.

Hannah pulled on her slippers, got into her robe, and padded down the hallway to the guest room. All she needed to see was the neatly made bed and she knew that Michelle was up. But Michelle wasn't in the living room and she wasn't in the kitchen either. There was, however, a note propped up next to the coffeemaker.

Coffee's ready to go, the note read. *Just turn it on. No need to hurry. Lisa and I have everything covered at the shop. Jack and Marge are helping. I baked Jamboree Muffins. They're in a basket on the kitchen table. Let me know what you think of them. Mother called. Cancel taking Moishe to see Barbara this afternoon. If you can, Doc Knight wants you to come tonight around six. Mother is bringing Jenny in to meet you at work this afternoon. Hope you got good sleep. Love, Michelle.*

Hannah turned on the coffee machine and sat down in a chair at the Formica-topped kitchen table that was already considered an antique. The basket of muffins sat in the center of the table and there was a stack of paper napkins and a jar of soft butter next to it. There was even a table knife to spread the butter. Michelle had thought of everything.

Unable to resist at least a peek, Hannah lifted the napkin that covered the muffins. There were six nestled inside, their tops puffed and golden. Jamboree Muffins must be one of Michelle's new recipes. Hannah had never tasted a Jamboree Muffin before.

She told herself she should wait for her coffee to be ready, but the aroma of freshly baked muffins was too compelling to deny. Hannah took one out of the basket, broke it open, and began to smile. Jamboree was a perfect name for these muffins since there was a spoonful of strawberry jam in the center.

She ate the first half of the muffin without butter. It was delicious. She spread butter on the second half and that was delicious, too. She wasn't quite sure which way was best so she got up to pour herself a cup of coffee, and decided that in the interests of research, she really ought to run another trial.

It was back to the muffin basket to choose another muffin. There was no way to tell what was inside each muffin so she chose one at random and hoped it would be a strawberry again, or another kind of jam she liked. That brought up the question of whether there was any jam or jelly she didn't like, and Hannah took a moment to think about it. "Mint jelly," she said to Moishe, who'd just come into the kitchen. Andrea had once made peanut butter and jelly sandwiches with mint jelly and they had been simply awful.

Moishe was looking at her expectantly, so she got up and filled his food bowl and gave him fresh water even though Michelle might have fed him earlier. Then she washed her hands and went back to the table to run the second trial.

The second muffin was filled with a spoonful of peach jam. Norman would love muffins with peach jam. She'd remember to get the recipe from Michelle so that she could bake them for him. She probably should have saved this one for him, but she'd already broken it open and it was too late now.

Four cups of coffee and a third trial with another muffin, one with grape jelly inside, and Hannah decided she couldn't decide if the muffins were better with or without butter. She also concluded that she couldn't conclude which jam or jelly she liked best. She had the terrible urge to break the remaining muffins open to see which kind of jam or jelly was inside each one, but she remembered how upset Delores had been with her years ago when Hannah had scraped some chocolate off the bottom of each piece of candy in the box so that she could identify her favorite one. *It's not polite,*

Delores had told a four-year-old Hannah. *You touched them all and now no one else will want to eat them.*

Hannah gave a little laugh at the memory. She hadn't realized it at the time, but her mother had taught her an important lesson that day. If you wanted to eat an entire box of candy and not share it with anyone else, all you had to do was touch each piece. She had the childish urge to touch the remaining three muffins so that they would be hers, all hers, but she told herself that doing so would be childish, and she went off to take her morning shower instead.

JAMBOREE MUFFINS

Preheat oven to 400 degrees F., rack in the middle position.

1 large egg, beaten
3/4 cup whole milk
1/2 cup vegetable oil
1/3 cup white (**granulated**) sugar
2 cups all-purpose flour (**pack it down when you measure it**)
3 teaspoons (**one Tablespoon**) baking powder
1 teaspoon salt
Approximately 1/4 cup jam of your choice

Hannah's 1st Note: ~~This~~ is a great recipe for using up all those jars of jam with little dibs and dabs in the bottom that are taking up too much room on your refrigerator shelf!

Grease or spray the bottoms of 12 muffin cups with Pam or another nonstick cooking spray. Alternatively, you can use paper cupcake liners. Use a muffin pan or a cupcake pan that has cups approximately 2 and 1/2 inches across the top and are 1 and 1/4 inches deep. (**That's a standard size.**)

Hannah's 2nd Note: Don't use an electric mixer to mix up these muffins.

Just stir everything up by hand. The muffin batter should be a little lumpy, like brownie batter, and not over-mixed.

In a medium-sized bowl, beat the egg with the milk until they are well combined.

Stir in the vegetable oil and the white sugar.

Measure out the flour in another bowl. Stir in the baking powder and the salt with a fork.

Add the flour mixture to the egg mixture in half-cup increments, stirring after each increment, but only until the flour is moistened. The resulting muffin batter will be lumpy. That's okay. It's supposed to be.

Fill the muffin cups half-full with batter.

Get out your jam jars. You can use all one kind, or several different kinds of jam. It's totally up to you.

Use a teaspoon measure or a small-sized spoon from your silverware drawer to drop 1 teaspoon of jam into the center of each muffin.

Hannah's 3rd Note: I hope Mother never reads this recipe because I use one of the antique silver collector's spoons she gave me to dish out the jam and drop it into the center of the muffin batter.

Cover the jam with muffin batter until the

282

muffin cups are 3/4 full.

Bake at 400 degrees F. for approximately 20 minutes, or until the muffins are golden brown.

Let the Jamboree Muffins cool in the pan for 10 minutes and then serve them with plenty of butter. They're good warm and they're good cold. They also reheat well in the microwave.

Yield: 12 yummy muffins

CHAPTER NINETEEN

As Hannah prepared to turn in the alley that led to the parking lot behind The Cookie Jar, she noticed that the street ahead was lined with cars. Every single parking spot was taken, even the spot in front of her mother's antique shop, all the way to the end of the block. Perhaps Claire was having a sale at her dress shop, but it was unusual for her to open in the morning. Ever since she'd married Reverend Bob Knudson and moved into the parsonage with Reverend Bob and his grandmother, Claire's hours had been noon to five.

The alley was crowded, too. One whole side was lined with cars. It must be a sale. She'd never seen this many cars on their block before. She pulled into her parking lot and found that it was also crowded. Thankfully, her spot was open. What in the world was going on?

When she opened the back kitchen door

at The Cookie Jar, a buzz of voices floated out to greet her. It sounded like the coffee shop was packed with customers. As she stepped into the kitchen, she saw Jack Herman refilling several of the large display jars they kept behind the counter.

"Hi, Jack," she greeted him.

"Hello, Hannah."

Hannah smiled. It was a good day for Lisa's dad. He'd been diagnosed with Alzheimer's over a year ago, and there were times when he forgot who she was.

"It's noisy out there." Hannah gestured toward the coffee shop and then she turned to hang her purse on one of the hooks by the back door. "Do we have a lot of customers?"

"We do. It's crowded, Hannah. And we're selling lots of cookies. Coffee, too."

"That's good. Is Claire having a sale at her dress shop next door?"

"No, Claire is here. She brought Grandma Knudson down the hill and they're sitting at a table with Ava Schultz and Betty Jackson. Betty ate four cookies already. She loves our new Chocolate-Covered Peanut Cookies."

Hannah felt more than a little uncomfortable. She'd missed less than a halfday's work and she was already out of step with what was going on. "I didn't know we had a new cookie."

"It was Marge's idea when she couldn't find chocolate-covered raisins to make Chocolate-Covered Raisin Cookies. Florence had chocolate-covered peanuts so she changed the recipe a little bit and just used those."

"Very smart," Hannah said, still feeling a little like an intruder in her own cookie shop.

Jack glanced up at the clock on the wall. "Only fifteen minutes to go," he said, picking up the two cookie jars he'd filled and heading for the swinging door that separated the kitchen from the coffee shop. "I'll be right back. I need to talk to you, Hannah."

Hannah was still just as puzzled as she'd been when she walked in the door. Only fifteen minutes to go for what? What in the world was going on today?

"Uh-oh!" she groaned as her mind settled on the obvious conclusion. Lisa was telling the story of how Hannah had found Doctor Bev's body. But how could she tell that story when Hannah hadn't even told her about it? Unless . . .

"Michelle," Hannah said, under her breath. She'd told Michelle everything last night and Michelle could have told Lisa.

But why would Lisa tell the story without running it past her first?

"Hannah!" Lisa came rushing into the kitchen. "Dad said you were out here. Do you want to listen to the story of how you found Doctor Bev's body?"

Hannah shook her head. "Not really. Finding her was bad enough. I don't want to hear all about it again."

Lisa was silent for a moment and then she sighed. "You're upset that I'm talking about it, aren't you?"

"I'm not upset. It's what we always do. But why did you start telling the story before you checked with me?"

"Because Michelle and I thought you might need the money for your defense fund and we decided to make hay while the sun shines. She talked to Howie this morning and Howie said he'd cut his fees in half for you, but it's going to cost an arm and a leg if you're charged and the case goes to trial."

Lisa had just used two clichés in a row, but Hannah didn't call her on it. She was too busy with the two other clichés that were warring in her mind. One was *Don't borrow trouble,* and the other was *Expect the best, but prepare for the worst.*

"We were just trying to help you, Hannah.

But if you want me to stop telling the story, I will."

Hannah thought about that for a moment and then she shook her head. "Don't stop. You go right ahead and tell it. I have nothing to hide and the fact that you're talking about it might convince everyone in town that I had nothing to do with Doctor Bev's death. As a matter of fact . . ." Hannah paused and considered what she'd been about to say. She gave a brief nod and continued. "As a matter fact, let's do a second act tomorrow."

"What's the second act?"

"It's the story of how Mike came out to the condo to take me down to the station. And how Norman called Howie Levine to meet me there. You can even cover the salient parts of the interrogation. I told Michelle all about it last night and you can get all the details from her."

"Great! I'll tease it at the end of the story today and that will bring them in tomorrow." It was Lisa's turn to pause and look thoughtful. "Actually . . . we could even do a third act."

"A third act? What story would *that* be?"

"How the sheriff's department came in here last night to toss the whole place. And how Herb and I spent all night cleaning up when they left. We can also explore what evidence caused Mike to bring you down to the sheriff's office to interrogate you. I know your mother can get me a copy of the autopsy report. She already offered to do it."

"She did?"

"You betcha! She was in here this morning before seven and so was Andrea. Everyone's pulling for you, Hannah. And they'll be pulling for you even more when I tell them what a . . . a witch Doctor Bev was to you on the Petersons' porch. It won't hurt your defense if it comes to that. The sheriff's department tossed the Peterson house, too. And they didn't find any substance that you could have added to the cupcakes to cause Doctor Bev's death."

"That's good to know."

"Yes, it is. Just forget about the business here. Michelle and I are taking care of it, and Marge and Dad are happy to help. Actually, I think it helps Dad a lot to interact with all these people. We'll take care of things here, so you concentrate on proving your innocence."

"I just hope I can do that. It might be easier to prove the killer's guilt than my innocence."

"That could be true, but you know you

can do it. The lady who hates spiders, but captures them in a napkin to take them outside and set them free couldn't possibly kill anyone, even a waste of oxygen like Doctor Bev."

Hannah laughed at Lisa's description of Doctor Bev. "Are you going to use that line tomorrow?"

"I think so. It's a real grabber. As a matter of fact, that'll probably be my last line in tomorrow's story."

"You're a drama queen, Lisa. Just go for it! If I have the stomach later, I'll even listen to one of your performances. And if I manage to prove my innocence while you're doing all that, we'll use the money to go on vacation to someplace where it's warm next winter."

Hannah had just tasted one of Marge's new Chocolate-Covered Peanut Cookies when Jack came back into the kitchen.

"You tried one?" he asked, noticing that a cookie was gone from the six dozen on the baker's rack.

"I did and they're wonderful. Tell Marge I said so, will you?"

"I will. She'll like that." Jack stood there for a moment and then he took a deep breath. "Do you have a minute, Hannah? I need your help."

"Sure, Jack. What is it?"

"I need to . . ." Jack stopped and looked confused. Then he cleared his throat and began again. "I need to pro . . . pro-something. I always forget that word!"

"Say it in a different way," Hannah suggested. It was a tactic she'd learned from Lisa. "What does the word mean, Jack?"

"It means to get married. To . . . *propose*! That's it! I need to propose, Hannah."

"Okay," Hannah said, crossing to the coffee pot to pour two mugs, one for each of them. She gestured toward the stools around the stainless steel work island and said, "Come over here and sit. Have a little coffee and tell me all about it."

Jack smiled as he sat down. "You are good, Hannah. That's why I want to ask you to help. I can't ask Marge and I can't ask Lisa. And Herb's too busy or he'd do it. That boy loves me."

"I know he does. So do Lisa and Marge."

"Yes, they do. But I can't ask them to help me. They're in . . . in something. In the middle of it, you know?"

"Involved."

"Yes. That's the word. They're involved. It has to be a secret until I get it right. Then I'll ask Marge and then I'll tell Lisa. That's

291

the way it should be."

"All right."

"You won't tell, will you?"

"No, Jack. I won't tell."

"I knew you wouldn't. Marge is good, Hannah. And I love her. Did you know that she gave her house to the kids when they got married?"

"Yes, I knew. It was an incredibly generous wedding gift."

"Well, now she doesn't have a house, but I do. And I want my house to be her house. I want us to have it together. That's the way it's supposed to be between a man and a woman. So I want to pro . . . you know . . . ask her."

"You want to propose to Marge."

"Yes. But every time I try to work it out, I can't find the right words. It has to be right, Hannah. She deserves that."

"Of course she does. Did you want me to help you find the right words?"

"Yes! That's exactly what I want. And then, once I know what the words are, I want you to help me re . . . re . . . rehash isn't right. It's a different word. It means to do like actors do."

"Rehearse?"

"That's it! You're so smart, Hannah. I want you to help me rehearse so I can propose to Marge. Will you? Please?"

"Of course I will. When do you want to start?"

"Right now? They said I could take a break. Is right now good for you?"

"It's perfect," Hannah said, even though she had more cookies to bake. Helping Jack rehearse his proposal to Marge was a lot more important than mixing up cookie dough.

CHOCOLATE-COVERED PEANUT COOKIES

Preheat oven to 350 degrees F., rack in the middle position.

Hannah's 1st Note: Mike loves chocolate-covered peanuts and he adores these cookies. <u>For those with peanut allergies, use chocolate-covered something else and another flavor of chips.</u> (I've baked these with M&Ms and white chocolate chips, and they were delicious.)

1 cup salted butter, softened (*2 sticks, 8 ounces, 1/2 pound*)

1 small package (*makes 4 half-cups*) vanilla instant pudding mix (*NOT sugar-free*)

1/2 cup white (*granulated*) sugar

1/2 cup brown sugar (*pack it down in the cup when you measure it*)

1 egg, beaten (*just whip it up in a glass with a fork*)

1 teaspoon vanilla extract

1 teaspoon baking soda

1/4 teaspoon salt

1/2 teaspoon ground cinnamon

1 and 1/2 cups all-purpose flour (*pack it down in the cup when you measure it*)

1 and 1/2 cups quick rolled oats (*I used*

Quaker's Quick 1-minute kind)
1 cup chocolate-covered peanuts (*I used a 12-ounce bag. There was about 1/4 cup left, but not for very long!*)
1 cup peanut butter chips (*a 6-ounce package — I used Reese's*)

Hannah's 2nd Note: You can mix these cookies up by hand, but it's a lot easier with an electric mixer.

Mix the softened butter, dry pudding mix, white sugar, and brown sugar together. Beat them until they're light and fluffy.

Add the egg and the vanilla extract. Mix them in thoroughly.

Add the baking soda, salt, and cinnamon. Mix until everything is incorporated.

Add the flour in half-cup increments, mixing after each addition.

Add the rolled oats in half-cup increments, mixing after each addition.

Remove the bowl from the mixer and stir in the chocolate-covered peanuts and the peanut butter chips by hand.

Drop the cookie dough by rounded teaspoonfuls onto an ungreased cookie sheet, 2 inches apart, no more than 12 cookies to a standard-sized sheet. (*I covered my cookie sheet with parchment paper.*) You can also use a 2-teaspoon size scooper to dish out the cookie dough.

Bake the Chocolate-Covered Peanut Cookies at 350 degrees F. for 10 to 12 minutes or until the edges are golden brown.

Cool the cookies for 2 minutes on the cookie sheets. Then remove them to a wire rack to complete cooling.

Yield: Makes approximately 4 dozen wonderful cookies.

CHAPTER TWENTY

Lisa was between performances when Delores and Jenny came in. She led them back to the kitchen and smiled as she saw that Hannah had baked more cookies. "Thanks, Hannah. We were getting close to running out."

"You won't run out. I've got six pans of bar cookies in the oven right now."

"Great." Lisa turned to the smiling, brown-haired woman standing next to Delores. "Jenny? This is Hannah." And then she turned to Hannah. "I told Jenny and your mother we'd have coffee in the kitchen if you weren't too busy back here."

"I'm not too busy. Nice to meet you, Jenny. Sit down and I'll get our coffee."

"I'll do it," Lisa said quickly. "All I've been doing is telling stories since we opened. With Marge, Dad, and Michelle here, I haven't had to wait on a single table."

"This story was very dramatic," Delores

said, sitting down on a stool at the work island. "Good job, Lisa."

"It was scary too," Jenny added, taking the stool next to Delores, "especially the part about her hair floating in the currents."

Delores gave a slight shiver. "I know. I think I ate two cookies without even knowing I was eating them." She turned to Hannah. "You were very brave to dive down there, dear."

"Brave or foolish, I'm not sure which," Hannah said, accepting a mug of coffee from Lisa.

"Your slaydar makes you do it," Delores said. And when Jenny looked puzzled she explained. "Slaydar is like radar except you don't use it to find speeders. Hannah uses it to find murder victims."

"That's cute," Jenny said, and then she frowned slightly. "Or maybe it's not. It must be frightening to discover murder victims."

"It's not all fun and games," Hannah admitted. "Unfortunately, I can't seem to stop doing it."

"I know. I read about you in the paper, Hannah."

"The *Lake Eden Journal*?" Hannah asked her.

"No, the *Minneapolis Star Tribune*."

"Really?" Delores looked impressed.

"When was that, Jenny?"

"It was when Hannah caught Buddy's killer."

Hannah went on full alert. Jenny hadn't said *When Hannah caught that keyboard player's killer*, or *When Hannah caught that jazz musician's killer*, or even *When Hannah caught Buddy Neiman's killer*. She'd said *When Hannah caught* **Buddy's** *killer*, as if she'd known him. "Did you know Buddy Neiman?" Hannah asked.

"No, but I felt almost like I did. Clay talked about him a lot. He told me he thought there was something very secretive about Buddy. And Clay was right."

"Clay," Hannah repeated. "Are you talking about Clayton Wallace?"

"Yes."

"Then you knew *him*?" Hannah asked, drawing the obvious conclusion.

"Oh, yes. I was his nurse. And we were . . . friends. Good friends. I love to cook and I used to cook dinner for him every once in a while."

Hannah remembered the bottle of premium Chianti, and the gift-wrapped box of truffles that Mike said the Minneapolis police had found in Clayton's house. "Do you like to cook Italian food?" she asked.

"It's my favorite. It was Clay's favorite,

too. He always brought me a bottle . . ."

Hannah held up her hand. "Let me guess. A bottle of premium Chianti and a box of Fanny Farmer truffles?"

Jenny looked mystified as she nodded. "How did *you* know?"

"I knew because the Minneapolis police found those two items in his house. Were you planning on having dinner with him right after his trip to Lake Eden?"

"Yes," Jenny said, and her voice shook slightly. "He was such a nice man and I was hoping that . . ."

Hannah didn't say anything. She just gave Jenny some time to compose herself. A few moments passed and Hannah waited until Jenny was calm again before she asked the next, very critical question. "You said you were Clayton's nurse. Where was that?"

"At the Hennepin Eye Clinic. He was so brave and his sense of humor was wonderful. He knew he was losing his sight, but somehow he managed to cope with it. I think that's why I fell in love with him. And then, after he died, I just couldn't work at the clinic anymore. There were too many memories and I had to go somewhere else."

"Of course you did," Delores said, patting Jenny's hand.

"I have one more question," Hannah told

her. "How bad was Clayton's eyesight when he drove the Cinnamon Roll Six here? It's important."

"Not bad enough to cause an accident," Jenny said, sitting up a little straighter. "I can give you his complete diagnosis and his prognosis, but you probably won't understand it. To put it in layman's terms, his vision was disintegrating from the center out. That means he had just started having trouble seeing small items in the center of his field of vision."

Like pills, Hannah thought, her heart beginning to pound faster. "By small items do you mean things like pills?" she asked.

"That's it exactly. He said he was having trouble putting pills in the proper compartments of his pill box. He said he might need help doing that very soon and I told him to call me any time he needed me."

"When did he say that?"

"The afternoon he left for Lake Eden. He told me he'd managed to do it, but it had been difficult. And I never . . ." Jenny stopped and swallowed hard. "I never heard from him again."

"Would you be willing to tell all this to a detective from the sheriff's department?" Hannah asked her.

"Yes, but . . . I don't understand. Why

301

does the sheriff's department want to know about it?"

"Because the Minneapolis police concluded that Clayton's death was a suicide. And you can prove it wasn't."

Quickly Hannah explained about Clayton's son and how the insurance company wouldn't honor Clayton's policy if the cause of death was suicide. Jenny's eyes flashed with anger.

"Of course I'll help you clear this up!" she promised. "Clay told me all about the provisions he made for his son, and there's no way I'll let the insurance company get away with that!"

Once they'd made some plans and had their coffee and cookies, Jenny and Delores left. Lisa went back to tell her story to the next group of customers, and Hannah was left alone in the kitchen.

"This one just fell in my lap," she said to absolutely no one as she removed the pans of bar cookies from the oven and slid them onto shelves on the baker's rack. "I must have done something right because I really lucked out with Clayton."

Then she poured a fresh cup of coffee, sat down on her stool again, and fervently wished that proving herself innocent in Doctor Bev's death wouldn't be as difficult as she thought it would be.

"Once more from the heart, Jack," Hannah told him. "And remember to keep it simple. All you have to do is tell her you love her and say you want her to be your wife. After that just say, *Will you marry me, Marge?*"

"But what if I forget her name like I did the last time we rehearsed? It won't be good if I forget her name."

"You only forgot because you were nervous."

"I know, but what if I'm nervous again?"

Hannah thought about that for a moment. "You can work around it. Just say, *Will you marry me, my love?*"

"That's good. I can do that. Let's do it again, Hannah."

"Okay." Hannah stood up and Jack got down on one knee. He took her hand and kissed it.

"My dearest," he began, looking up at her. "I love you so much. You're so good, and kind, and . . . and sweet. I want you to be my wife. Please be my wife. Will you marry me, my love?"

Hannah was about to tell him what a wonderful job he'd done when she heard two gasps from the doorway that led into the coffee shop.

"Uh-oh!" Jack said, getting to his feet as fast as he could. "We're busted!"

Hannah swiveled around to see Lisa and Marge standing there with identical expressions of shock and dismay on their faces.

"Jack!" Marge gulped.

"Dad!" Lisa exclaimed, sounding stunned.

If they'd all been acting in a romantic comedy, it would have been hilarious. But this was no comedy and Hannah knew it wouldn't be romantic for very much longer unless she explained things fast.

"It's not what you think," she said. "Jack's not proposing to *me*. I'm just helping him rehearse." She turned to Jack. "Ask her now!"

"Right now?"

"Yes, right now!"

"But we're not through rehearsing."

"Yes, we are. Do it now, Jack!"

As Jack walked over to Marge, Hannah realized that everything was going to be all right. Marge's lips were twitching and she was shaking slightly, as if she was holding back laughter. One look at Lisa further reassured Hannah. Lisa was holding her hand over her mouth and her eyes were bright with suppressed mirth.

"My dearest," Jack said and then he stopped. "Do I have to get down on my knee? This floor is hard and I did it five times already."

"Here, Jack," Marge said, grabbing a towel from the counter and tossing it to him. "Use the towel to cushion your knee."

"Thanks, Marge." Jack positioned the towel, got down on one knee, reached up to take Marge's hand and kissed it. "I love you so much. You're so good, and kind, and sweet. I want you to be my wife. Please be my wife. Will you marry me, my love?"

Marge reached down with her other hand and helped Jack to his feet. Then she smiled and kissed him. "Of course I'll marry you," she said.

"Lisa?" Jack turned to his daughter. "Is it okay with you?"

"It's perfect with me, Dad," Lisa said, going over to give him a hug. "Herb and I were wondering when you'd get around to it."

Hannah had just finished mixing up her last batch of cookies, Oatmeal Raisin Crisps this time, when there was a knock on the back door. She crossed the room and pulled the door open to reveal someone she'd never expected to see.

"Mike!" she exclaimed.

"Hi, Hannah," Mike said, standing there obviously ill at ease. "Is there anyone with

305

you in the kitchen?"

"No." Hannah remembered how hard and cold he'd looked last night when he'd questioned her. He didn't look like that now, but perhaps he was playing good cop today. "You don't have an audience this time around. Should I invite some people so that you can arrest me in front of a crowd?"

Mike looked pained as he shook his head. "Don't be like that, Hannah. I know last night was bad for you, but I was just doing my job."

"I think that's what they said in Nazi Germany!"

"Hannah . . . can you please forget last night for a minute? I'm sorry about what happened. I really am. But I had to follow the rules and do my duty."

"And you're not doing your duty now?"

"No. It's exactly the opposite. I shouldn't be here. I could be fired for being here. It's against every rule in the book. So I'm not here, okay? You can't let anyone know I've been here. I could be brought up on charges if anyone sees me here."

Hannah had the urge to slam the door in his face, but she thought better of it. Mike was here for a reason and unless she was drastically mistaken, it wasn't to try to fool her into incriminating herself.

"Hannah? Please. Can I come in?"

"Okay," Hannah said, relenting. "Come in then. But I'm warning you that you could be seen. Lisa's started telling her story, but Jack, or Marge, or Michelle could come into the kitchen at any time."

Mike stepped in and glanced around the kitchen. "Can we talk in the pantry? We could shut the door. If someone came in they wouldn't see me."

"That's okay, I guess." Hannah led the way, opened the door, and flicked on the light. "Come in."

Mike stepped in and Hannah shut the door behind them. "It's a big pantry," he said.

"I know. Lisa and Herb came down here after your detectives searched it last night. She said it took them a couple of hours to put everything back in place. Were they looking for poison?"

"Not poison. Tranquilizers."

"What?"

"Doc Knight ran more tests and he found traces of a powerful tranquilizer in her system. It was enough to stop her heart."

"Then she didn't drown?"

"No. She was dead when the car hit the water."

307

"So your guys were searching for tranquilizers when they trashed the pantry last night."

"Yeah." Mike looked a little sick. "I'm sorry, Hannah. I wish I could have come down here with them, but I couldn't. I was busy with other things."

"Things like interrogating me."

"Yeah." Mike sighed again, and then he reached out and wrapped his arms around Hannah. "I'm so sorry, Hannah. You have no idea. I didn't sleep at all last night. I felt so bad about questioning you that I couldn't get to sleep. All I kept seeing in my mind was the way you looked at me. Your eyes seemed to say, *You betrayed me.* And that just about killed me."

"It wasn't a whole lot of fun for me, either." Despite herself, Hannah moved a little closer. She wasn't quite ready to forgive Mike, but his arms felt good around her. "I felt like I'd just lost my best friend."

"Me, too," Mike said. "I didn't want to come and get you last night, but I didn't trust anyone else to do it. I knew I had to do everything by the book and I hated it. But when Doc gave us the list of her stomach contents and Mayor Bascomb said she was eating one of your cupcakes when he went for a ride with her, we had to bring you in for questioning."

"Did you pull the car out of the water yet?"

Mike shook his head. "Not yet. Earl's replacing the carburetor on the county tow truck and he's waiting for parts. He thinks it'll be ready by late tomorrow afternoon."

"Then you don't know if there were any cupcakes left in the bakery box," Hannah said.

"We sent a diver down and he found the box. It was in the back seat and it was wedged against the mechanism that raises and lowers the top. It was empty."

"So there's no way to prove that my cupcakes didn't have tranquilizers in them," Hannah said, feeling her hopes diminish.

"I'm afraid not. Either she ate them all or they dissolved in the water. I doubt we'll ever know exactly what happened."

"What else was in her stomach?" Hannah asked, her mind grasping at straws.

"Doc Knight identified coffee, cream, artificial sweetener, and your cupcakes. That's it."

"She didn't get that coffee from me," Hannah said, and her stubborn hopes began to rise again. "Roger didn't order any coffee to go. And since he didn't take any coffee, we didn't give him any cream or packets of sweetener."

"How about when she confronted you on the Petersons' porch?"

"We didn't have any coffee there. All we had was Diet Coke for me, regular Pepsi for Lisa and Andrea, and a couple of cans of lemonade for Tracey. When she came in we didn't offer her anything and she didn't take anything except the box of cupcakes. Doc Knight didn't find any Coke, or Pepsi, or lemonade in her stomach, did he?"

"No, none of those things." Mike reached out to touch her cheek. "I really don't like this, Hannah. It doesn't look good for you. You're the logical suspect and you did bake those cupcakes. There's even a witness who saw her eating one. You have to think of some way to prove you didn't do it."

Hannah caught the nuance and she asked the question. "You think I can prove that I didn't do it?"

"I hope so. I pray so. Concentrate on doing it, Hannah. I'll help you any way I can."

"Then you don't think I did it?"

"I *know* you didn't do it. I know it in my heart."

"Well, I know it in my mind. Somebody else killed Doctor Bev. It wasn't me. It's really not fair that I'm going to have to try to prove my innocence by catching the real killer."

"I agree. It's not right. Our justice system isn't supposed to work that way. But you won't be the only one trying to find out who really killed Doctor Bev. I'll be working on it, too."

"But will they let you do that?"

"Not officially, but that won't stop me. It won't stop anyone else in the department either, but you didn't hear that from me."

"How about Bill? Does he think I did it?"

"Of course not. Bill knows what we're doing . . . unofficially, of course. Everyone's on your side, Hannah. We're just following the rules as far as the paperwork goes, but what we do on our own time is our personal business."

Hannah began to feel much better. The pendulum was still swinging lower and lower over her head, but there were people who believed in her innocence.

"Did Doctor Bev take tranquilizers?" Hannah asked, remembering how Clayton Wallace had taken an accidental overdose of his heart medication.

"No. I'm way ahead of you there. I sent Lonnie and Rick out to her suite at the Inn to check. Roger let them go through everything she had there, and he gave them permission to go through all of his things, too. They didn't find any tranquilizers and Roger said he'd never seen her take anything like that."

"I guess you already know that I don't take them either. And I don't have any in my possession here or at my condo."

"I know that. I'm sorry, but we had to check."

"That's okay if it helps to clear me. How about the tranquilizers themselves? Were they some kind of over-the-counter thing?"

"Doc Knight says no. They were a class A narcotic and they're only available by doctor's prescription."

Hannah looked at him dubiously. "Legally yes, but I'll bet you can buy them on the street."

"I'm sure you can, but not here in Lake Eden. We do have an occasional drug dealer, but it's usually small stuff. This drug was powerful. Doc Knight says it isn't something you'd take to get high. If you tried it for kicks, it would just knock you out. And he also told me that Doctor Bev had enough in her system to stop her heart. There was no water in her lungs, Hannah. She was dead before she hit the water."

"Did you check Doctor Bev's background

to see if she ever had a prescription for the drug?"

"We checked on that the minute Doc Knight told us the name of the drug. No doctor she's ever had wrote a prescription like that for her. We came to the end of the trail on that one, Hannah."

"Okay. Let's talk about the coffee. Is it possible to hide the taste of the drug if it was dissolved in the coffee?"

"We asked Doc Knight that. He said yes. The artificial sweetener she used has a slightly bitter taste. So does the drug. If her coffee tasted bitter, she probably assumed it was from the sweetener."

"Do you know where she got the coffee?"

"Not yet, but we're working on it."

"How about the cup it came in? It might have some residue, or something. Did you recover that?"

"No. Her coffee cup wasn't in the car. And since we didn't find it, there's no way to test it for any residue. Not only that, her car was a convertible and the cup would have been submerged in water. Chances are that even if we'd found it, there wouldn't be any residue left."

Hannah took a moment to mentally add up the facts of the case. Doctor Bev had consumed an overdose of powerful tranquilizers. Doc Knight had identified the drug in her stomach contents, which consisted of coffee, creamer, artificial sweetener, and Hannah's cupcakes. The drug wasn't necessarily baked into the cupcakes. It could have been in the coffee, the cream, or the artificial sweetener. "So the evidence against me is all circumstantial at this point?"

"That's right. But you did have a motive, the means, and the opportunity."

"Not the means," Hannah corrected him. "I didn't have the drug."

"That's difficult to prove."

"Right." Hannah shivered slightly. People had been convicted on circumstantial evidence, but she didn't want to think about that. If she did, she might have another nightmare like the one she'd had last night.

"You shivered," Mike said, holding her tightly. "What's the matter?"

"The thought that I could be convicted for something I didn't do is even more terrifying than finding Doctor Bev. I just hope I don't have a nightmare about *that* tonight. Last night's dream was bad enough!"

"Tell me about it."

"It started when I dove down to the car and Doctor Bev tried to get me to sit in the passenger seat. I wanted to leave, to go back up to the surface, but I couldn't seem to stop myself from moving closer and closer to her. Then she grabbed me and I couldn't get away. She moved some things off the passenger seat and shoved me into it, and then she locked the seat belt. That was when I knew I was going to die down there at the bottom of Miller's Pond with her."

Mike rubbed her back. "I'm sorry I put you through this, Hannah. You really have no idea how guilty I feel. If I could think of some way to wipe last night out of existence, I would. You did a brave thing by trying to rescue Doctor Bev. And you got rewarded by having me haul you in for questioning. Life wasn't very fair to you yesterday."

"True." Hannah's mind kept going back to the dream, back to the point where Doctor Bev had pulled her into the passenger seat. She'd reached out with her wavy arm and pushed the thermos off the seat and . . .

Hannah gave a little gasp and Mike patted her back. "What is it?" he asked.

"The thermos!"

"What thermos?"

"The thermos in my dream. There must have been one on the passenger seat for real or I wouldn't have dreamed it. I'm almost sure there was. I think it was one of those silver ones with a screw-on cap. I might have knocked it off the seat when I unlatched the

315

seat belt and pulled Doctor Bev out of the car."

"I'll send down a diver," Mike said, pulling out his cell phone and dialing the sheriff's station. "If there's a thermos, there may be contents left inside. And if there are contents, Doc Knight can test them."

Hannah listened while Mike made the call. When he hung up, she opened the pantry door. "You'd better go before anyone knows you're here."

"You're right," Mike said, walking across the kitchen with her and opening the back door. "I'll let you know what happens when the diver comes up," he said. "If we're lucky, they'll find the thermos and it'll clear you completely."

"From your lips to God's ears," Hannah said, repeating one of her Great-Grandmother Elsa's favorite expressions. And then she went back to the stainless steel work island with a smile on her face to shape and bake the Oatmeal Raisin Crisps.

CHAPTER TWENTY-ONE

There was a knock at the back door, but before Hannah could cross the kitchen to answer it, Andrea rushed in. "Hannah!" she exclaimed, sinking down on a stool at the work island.

"Hi, Andrea." Hannah pulled the last sheet of cookies out of the oven and slid them onto the baker's rack. "Want coffee?"

"No, thanks. I'm excited enough as it is. Have you got anything chocolate?"

"We're a bakery. Of course I've got something chocolate. You've got a choice between Chocolate Chip Crunch Cookies, Black and Whites, or Triplet Chiplets."

"I'll take the Triplet Chiplets. Then I'll get chocolate three ways. Just wait until I tell you what happened with the furniture!"

"What furniture?" Hannah plucked three Triplet Chiplet cookies off the rack and delivered them in a napkin. "Milk?"

"That would be good. Doctor Bev and

Roger's furniture. They just finished delivering it."

"Of course. I forgot all about it. Roger asked you to meet the delivery truck."

Andrea accepted the glass of milk and took a sip before she nodded. "It's gorgeous, Hannah. Just wait until you see it!"

"The furniture and not the delivery truck?"

"Right. White leather. Can you imagine? It's just incredible against the midnight blue carpet. One piece is a twenty-two-foot curved sectional with four built-in recliners. That's in front of the biggest flat-screen I've ever seen, even bigger than the one Mayor Bascomb bought for the Super Bowl. And the couches they bought to go in front of the fireplace are unbelievable! They're the kind you see in old movies, the ones without arms that you could sleep on if you wanted to. Shrinks use them . . . you know."

"Chaise lounges?"

"Yeah. Just like that. And the bed is up on a pedestal and it looks like something a queen would sleep in. Come with me right now. You've just got to see it! And the dome's in now so we can go out and look at the things they bought for the rooftop garden. Don't say no, Hannah. I need to take some pictures and post them on our website."

Hannah began to frown. "Isn't that a little invasive? It's Roger's furniture and I think you should ask him before you do something like that."

Andrea stared at her in bewilderment for a moment and then she laughed. "Oh, no wonder you thought that! I forgot to tell you. Roger's going to sell the penthouse furnished. He says he doesn't want to live there now that Doctor Bev is gone. He was so sad when they delivered the furniture that he could only stay a minute or two. He's a broken man, Hannah. I think he really loved her."

"Hmmm." Hannah made the most non-committal sound she could think of. It seemed almost inconceivable that Roger hadn't seen the nasty side of Doctor Bev, but she supposed it was possible.

"Come on." Andrea stood up and jammed the one cookie that was left into her pocket. "Let's go!"

Hannah grabbed her purse. "Okay, but that chocolate's going to melt in this heat."

"What chocolate?"

"The chocolate in the cookie you just put in your pocket."

"Oh. You're probably right." Andrea removed the cookie from her pocket and gave a little shrug. "Don't worry about it. I'll eat it on the way to the car."

Since the Albion Hotel was only a block and a half away, it took only a minute or two before Andrea was parking in the reserved area of the parking garage. "Come on, Hannah," she said, getting out of her car and brushing cookie crumbs off her skirt.

Hannah smiled in amusement as she followed her sister into the lobby and across the floor to the private elevator that would take them to the penthouse. "How did you know where to put the furniture if Roger wasn't there?" she asked.

"The delivery guys had a diagram and a man they called an executive account specialist drove in from Minneapolis to help. I really didn't have to do anything except watch and lock up when they were finished."

"So Roger never saw the penthouse with the furniture they chose in place?"

Andrea shook her head. "He said he couldn't bear to see it, and that's when he told me to keep the penthouse on the market and sell it furnished, that it would show better that way."

"I guess that's true." Hannah followed Andrea into the elevator and watched her press the button for the penthouse. "I know it's crazy, but this elevator makes me nervous. It shakes a little."

"I know. I'm not that fond of it, either. But they inspected it and it's perfectly safe."

"What if the power goes out?"

"There's a generator that's supposed to kick in and take over if the main power fails."

"You said it's *supposed* to kick in. Do you have doubts?"

"Yes. The generator is old and Roger's having it replaced with a new one in a couple of days, but for now all we have is the old one."

"How about fire? You're not supposed to use elevators in case of fire, are you?"

"No, but there's a staircase. It's like Sally's old staircase that the servants used when the Inn was a private mansion. This one was for the maids and there's a landing on every floor. The maids used it to carry up the linens when the Albion was first built. It's right off the hallway by the regular elevator."

"There's no hallway on the penthouse floor. Where's the door to the staircase?"

"In the kitchen. You probably didn't notice it, because it looks just like another pantry door."

"Interesting," Hannah said as the elevator

321

doors opened onto the foyer. They stepped into the living room and she gasped at the array of expensive furniture. Doctor Bev hadn't been exaggerating when she'd said they'd spent the entire weekend shopping!

Andrea heard the gasp Hannah gave when she turned toward the living room fireplace. "I forgot to tell you about the grand piano. It's a Steinway."

"Did Doctor Bev play?"

"No, and neither does Roger. It's just decoration."

Hannah was almost speechless. She'd never seen such luxury before. She'd always known that Roger and his father had money, but this was way over the line between sumptuous and conspicuous consumption.

"What do you think so far?" Andrea asked, after Hannah had seen the master bedroom with the furniture fit for royalty, the master bath with an indoor Jacuzzi that could have seated eight, and the gourmet kitchen that contained every piece of culinary equipment that a celebrity chef might desire.

Hannah was silent for a moment, trying to think of the right words. Andrea was obviously impressed with the furnishings and she didn't want to hurt her sister's feelings. "It's a real showplace," she said at last.

"But?"

"How do you know there's a *but*?"

"Because you're my sister and I know you. And you must have a *but* because you had to think before you answered me."

"Guilty as charged," Hannah said, and then she wished she hadn't put it quite that way in light of her recent circumstances. "You're right, Andrea. There's a *but.*"

"What is it?"

"It's a real showplace, but I wouldn't feel comfortable living here."

"Neither would I! Just the thought of raising kids in this living room with the white leather furniture makes me nervous. And that's where the television is. What if the kids wanted a snack while they were watching cartoons? I'd be spending a fortune in leather cleaner. And then there's the Steinway. Tracey takes piano lessons, but she's barely past the 'Chopsticks' phase. And Bethie pounds the keys every chance she gets. They need a practice piano, not a fine musical instrument. That Steinway deserves to belong to a concert pianist."

"Agreed," Hannah said. "It just about killed me when you said Roger and Doctor Bev bought it for decoration."

"And then there's the location of the bedrooms. They're so big and far apart that we'd never hear Bethie or Tracey if they called us at night. Don't get me wrong. It's beautiful, but it's no place to raise a regular family."

"Do you think different furnishings would make it . . ." Hannah paused to think of the right word. ". . . homier?"

"Absolutely. The things Roger and Doctor Bev chose are gorgeous, but they're off-putting. They dictate a certain lifestyle that's just not the norm here in Lake Eden."

"Lifestyles of the rich and famous?"

"Exactly. And that's why I asked the executive account specialist at the furniture store if the furniture could be exchanged for other furniture if the new buyers didn't like it. He said yes, as long as it was an exchange and not a refund."

"But can the new buyer . . ." Again Hannah hesitated. "What's that phrase you used for buying something more expensive than what you were selling?"

"Buy up?"

"That's it. Can the new owners do an exchange down? What I mean is, say the person who buys the penthouse doesn't want the white leather sectional and what they'd like is something smaller in fabric. Can they exchange for something cheaper?"

"Yes, but they won't get a refund. Instead

they'll have a store credit. So if they get something less expensive and smaller, they can also get a recliner for him, a rocker for her, chairs for the kids, and . . . well . . . anything they want. They just can't get money back."

"That's perfect," Hannah said, "especially with the Steinway. You could probably furnish a two-bedroom condo with the money they paid for that."

"I think you're right. I didn't ask how much it was, but I'm willing to bet it was a bundle." Andrea led the way to the staircase leading up to the rooftop garden. "Come and see their patio furniture, Hannah. I don't think anyone will want to exchange that!"

"Oh, my!" Hannah exclaimed as she stepped out onto the rooftop garden and saw the dome. Curved pieces of what looked like glass rose to a height of at least twenty feet above their heads, framing a sparkling panorama of the town and the surrounding area including the blue sky and puffy white clouds above. The lake glittered through the pines in the distance and when a raven flew close to the dome, Hannah actually ducked. "Do birds ever hit it?"

"The manufacturer says no, that the struts between the panes give it structure and the birds know that they can't fly through it."

"That's good. I wouldn't like to be relaxing up here in the lap of luxury and see some poor bird hit the dome. It's so clear it looks like glass, but didn't you say it was some kind of Plexiglas?"

"It's Plexiglas, but it's a special kind that's relatively new on the market. Each section is tinted, double-paned, and argon-filled. If it were just plain glass, it would be really hot up here. We're in direct sunlight and it's hot out today."

"You're right and it's cool here." Hannah held out her arm. "I can't feel the heat of the sun at all."

"That's the argon filling between the panes. It insulates it, but you don't see it."

"Well, it's just amazing. And you can see a full three-sixty except for the area with the staircase and that space right next to it. Why didn't they put windows in that space?"

"Because that's where the window-washing safety cage is docked."

"The what?"

"The window-washing safety cage. I'll show you." Andrea stepped over to the edge of the dome and took what looked like a television remote out of a pocket built into the three-foot-high wall that supported the dome. "Watch this."

Hannah watched as Andrea aimed the remote at the space next to the staircase and pressed a button. Almost immediately something looking vaguely like a cage began to emerge. As it moved closer to the place where Andrea was standing, she unlatched fasteners on one of the struts and pulled the section open.

"That's really clever," Hannah said, watching as the cage stopped directly in front of the open section.

"I know. The first time I saw it, I couldn't believe my eyes. All you have to do if you're a window washer is climb aboard with your equipment and drive it around the track on the outside of the dome. It's got controls inside and you can stop, wash a section, and then move on. It's rated really high for safety because once you're in place, you can't fall off like you could on traditional scaffolding."

Hannah came over for a closer look. "I wouldn't want to climb in there, but I'm impressed."

"I feel exactly the same way. When Roger first showed it to me, he asked me if I wanted to go for a ride."

"Did you?"

"Absolutely not! I told him I'd rather die

than get into something that hung outside the dome above the third floor!" Andrea shut the hinged section, fastened it in place, and pointed the remote at the cage. "There it goes. It fits into an enclosure on the outside of the building where it can't get rained or snowed on."

"Pure genius," Hannah said.

"I think so too. Let's go look at that patio furniture. I'm willing to bet that if you bought this place, you wouldn't replace it."

Hannah grinned as she followed her sister to the pool area. Once a real estate agent, always a real estate agent. It was clear that Andrea hadn't given up on trying to sell her the penthouse. That was ridiculous, but Hannah found herself hoping that she'd know the people who bought it and they'd ask her to visit them often.

CHAPTER TWENTY-TWO

"Ready?" Norman asked, coming in the back door of The Cookie Jar with Moishe.

"I'm ready," Hannah said, bending down to give Moishe a pet. "You brought Moishe in with you."

"Of course I did. I'd never leave a pet in the car. Do you have any idea how hot it can get in a closed car?"

"Yes, and I'd never do it either, even if I thought I'd only be a minute. A minute has a way of stretching into longer than you expect." Hannah picked up the two bakery boxes on the counter. "I'd better not forget these."

"What are they?"

"Monkey Bread for Barbara. Lisa gave me the recipe. It's from her sister, Tony. Do you want to take my truck?"

"No, let's leave it for Michelle."

"That's fine with me. Let's go."

Once they got to the car, Norman opened

the trunk so that she could put the bakery boxes inside and then he opened one of the rear doors and set Moishe on the seat. Then he opened her door and Hannah got in. "Thanks, Norman," she said. "You're a good doorman."

"I'll remember that if I ever give up dentistry. It could be a second career choice for me." Norman slid in behind the wheel. "What's Monkey Bread?" he asked her as he started the car and backed out of the parking space.

"It's like a giant chocolate chip cinnamon roll baked in a Bundt pan. Mother said Barbara was hungry for cinnamon rolls and chocolate so I brought her Monkey Bread. It's made with refrigerated biscuits, the kind you buy in tubes at the store."

"So it's a lot faster to make Monkey Bread than it is to make yeast dough?"

"Right. I didn't really have time to bake my Special Cinnamon Rolls so Lisa suggested Monkey Bread as an alternative. One thing I like about it is that you can slice it like a cake, or pull off chunks and eat it that way."

Norman turned left at the end of Main Street and drove out of town. "Is there any news, Hannah?"

Hannah knew exactly what Norman

meant. When he asked about news, he wasn't referring to Lake Eden gossip or national headlines. Norman knew that Mike had taken her in for questioning. He wanted to know if there were any new developments.

"There's news on a different front," Hannah told him. "We managed to clear up Clayton Wallace's situation this afternoon."

"You can prove it wasn't a suicide?"

"No, I can't *prove* it, but what I learned casts serious doubts that he committed suicide. And that should be enough to get the Minneapolis Police Department to change their findings."

"And then the insurance company will have to pay off?"

"That's it exactly. I'll tell you all about it later, but I do have a little news on that other front."

"The accident that wasn't an accident?"

"Yes," Hannah answered, turning toward him. "At least Mike doesn't think I did it."

"Are you sure? Michelle said he was pretty rough on you down at the sheriff's station last night."

"That's true. He was. But things were different today."

"He hauled you in for questioning again?"

"No, of course not." Hannah took a moment to choose her next words. She didn't want to get Mike in trouble for coming to see her. "I talked to him today. He's on my side, Norman."

"Are you sure?" Norman didn't look convinced. "Remember, Hannah. He's a cop first, and a friend second."

"I haven't forgotten that."

"Good. I'm sure Howie told you to be careful."

"Oh, he did. And I *am* being careful. Actually, I might not have to be careful for too much longer, not if my dream is true."

Norman didn't say anything and for a long moment, there was no sound except for the swoosh of the tires on the asphalt roadway and the hum of the powerful engine. "What dream is that?" Norman finally asked.

Hannah knew exactly what he was thinking. Norman was wondering whether she'd slipped over the edge of sanity from the stress.

"I'm not crazy, Norman," she reassured him. "It's true that I'm under a lot of stress knowing that I'm the prime suspect, and that's probably why I had such a dreadful nightmare last night. But part of the dream came from my memory of diving down to the car in the pond. I won't go into details. It's not important and it was standard nightmare fare. But there was a thermos on the passenger seat in my dream, and it got knocked to the floorboards. I've been trying to remember, and I think there really *was* a thermos in Doctor Bev's car. And since the only time I ever saw the inside of her car was when it was underwater, the memory had to come from that."

"Okay," Norman said, still sounding a bit dubious.

"If there *is* a thermos on the floorboards and the cap is on tight, the contents might prove my innocence."

"Poison in the thermos and not in your cupcakes?" Norman asked, catching on immediately.

"Yes, but not a traditional poison. Doc Knight ran more tests and he identified the cause of death. It was an overdose of a powerful prescription tranquilizer."

"That puts a different spin on it," Norman said. And then, even though he tried not to show any emotion, he shivered slightly. "Tell me she was dead when she went into the water."

"Doc Knight said she was. Mike told me."

"Okay." Norman looked very relieved. "I know dead is dead, and nothing will change that, but the idea of Bev drowning really bothered me."

"Me, too," Hannah said.

They were silent then, each thinking their own thoughts. Norman may have been reliving the good times with Doctor Bev. She knew there must have been some, or they wouldn't have gotten engaged the first time. Perhaps it was rather naïve of her, but she still believed that there was some good in everyone.

Moishe crawled between the bucket seats and settled in her lap. He began to purr and the sound was comforting. Hannah closed her eyes for a moment. When she opened them, she saw that they were approaching Eden Lake and she lowered her window. She loved the damp green smell of the lake with the teeming life beneath its surface.

Life on the shore was equally rich and plentiful. Small animals scurried beneath the trees, insects flitted and buzzed in an effort to claim the air, and birds called from the tall trees that lined both sides of the road, their branches almost meeting overhead.

The lacy green tunnel widened as they approached the hospital. Norman turned into the curving access road that led to the parking lot, and Hannah drew a deep, steadying breath. She reached down to pet Moishe, not entirely to reassure him, but also to reassure herself.

Norman parked in a spot very close to the door, shut off the engine, and turned to her. He reached out and touched her face, caressing her cheek. "Ready?" he asked.

Hannah hesitated for one brief moment, wondering how such a small gesture on Norman's part could be so comforting, and then she smiled. "Ready," she said.

The nurse at the reception desk was a welcome surprise. It was Jenny, and Hannah gave her a big smile. "Hi, Jenny," she said. "Meet Norman Rhodes. He's the town dentist."

"Hello, Norman." Jenny turned to him. "Do you have a card? I need to make an appointment for a cleaning."

Norman produced the card and Jenny tucked it away in the pocket on her uniform. "I don't have any classes tonight, so I'm filling in for the receptionist while she's on break."

"Do you live here?" Hannah teased.

"I ought to. It would certainly save time since I'm almost always here. As a matter of fact, I'm working the night shift tonight."

"Didn't Mother say she was taking you home after I saw you at The Cookie Jar?"

"That was the plan, but Doc Knight called

and needed me for the night shift. When we left you, your mother took me to my place so that I could change to a fresh uniform and then we stopped at her house so that she could change into her dress clothes."

"She must have plans for tonight," Hannah speculated.

"Oh, she does. When Doc Knight finishes up, they're going out to the Lake Eden Inn for dinner." Jenny came out from behind the desk to pet Moishe. "This must be Moishe. Your mother told me all about him."

"Did she tell you *all* about him?"

"Shredded stockings and all." Jenny did a deep knee bend so that she was on Moishe's level. "You're a handsome fellow, aren't you, Moishe?"

Moishe purred, soaking up the attention, and Hannah smiled the proud cat owner's smile. "He likes you, Jenny."

"And I like him. You three can go right down to Miss Donnelly's room. She's expecting you."

Hannah and Norman walked down the hallway with Moishe leading the way. Hannah was surprised at how well he walked on a leash. He seemed quite comfortable in this environment and that was good. She even began to wonder if he could be a

336

therapy cat for some of Doc Knight's other patients.

"Are there any nuts in that Monkey Bread?" Norman asked her.

"No. I decided not to put them in. I wasn't sure if Barbara could chew them."

"She might be able to chew them, but she still has some healing to do. Soft food would be best for a week or so."

"How was she when you saw her?"

"Good. She was really happy to get the bridge even though it's only a temporary. She said she was tired of looking like a bag lady."

"So she was . . . rational?"

"Yes. She didn't say anything strange at all. And she knew who I was and who Doc Knight was. She even called her nurse by name." Norman stopped and frowned slightly. "Of course the nurse was wearing a name tag, so I guess that's not as important as I thought it was."

"It's still a big improvement."

"I know. I told Roger that, and he seemed very relieved. He was really worried about Barbara's condition."

"Roger visited Barbara?"

"No, I ran into him in the lobby. He was out here to visit his father."

Hannah sighed deeply. "Poor Roger!"

337

"I know. First he got the news that his father was terminal, and now his fiancée is dead. He didn't look good, Hannah. I don't think he got any sleep at all last night."

"I can believe that."

"All he could talk about was how much he missed Bev. I think he really loved her."

Hannah didn't reply, mostly because she didn't know what to say. Roger may have loved Doctor Bev, but it was a cinch she hadn't loved him. She'd made it clear to Hannah, Andrea, and Lisa that she regarded Roger as a gourmet meal ticket and no more than that. Roger would have been bitterly disappointed if he'd married Doctor Bev and then found out the truth about her. It would be kinder to leave him with his illusions.

"Why so quiet?" Norman asked.

"Just thinking," Hannah said, not wanting to mention the subject of her thoughts even though she was ninety-nine percent certain that Norman no longer had any illusions about Doctor Bev.

Norman's cell phone rang and he glanced at the display. "It's Mike," he said. "I think I'd better take it."

They were only steps from the small waiting room for expectant fathers and Hannah glanced in to see that it was deserted. "In here," she said, leading the way.

"Hi, Mike," Norman greeted him as he took a chair by the window overlooking the lake. "What's up?" He listened a minute and then he gave a little laugh. "You're right. She's here. Hold on a second and I'll put her on the . . . What was that? You did? Four times?" There was another pause and then Norman laughed. "You're probably right. Just a second and I'll check."

Norman turned to Hannah. "Take out your cell phone, Hannah. Mike says he tried to call you four times and he couldn't even leave a voice mail."

"That's because I don't *have* voice mail," Hannah told him. "But my phone's on." She rummaged around in the bottom of her saddlebag-size purse and drew it out to check. "I don't understand why he couldn't get through to . . . Uh-oh!"

Norman spoke into his own phone again. "Hannah said *Uh-oh.* Do you know what that means?" He listened for Mike's answer and then he chuckled. "You're probably right. Hold on a second and I'll ask her." Norman turned to Hannah with a grin. "Mike seems to think that you probably forgot to charge your phone again."

Hannah sighed. She hated to admit it, but Mike was right. She had forgotten to charge her cell phone at The Cookie Jar even though Andrea had gone to the phone store to get her the right charger and even plugged it into the outlet at the end of the counter.

"Is he right?" Norman asked, looking amused.

"Yes," Hannah said, even though she really didn't want to admit that Mike and Norman were right.

"That's okay. You can talk to him on my phone." Norman handed it over.

"Hi, Mike," she said.

"Hi. So you forgot to charge it?"

"Yes, I forgot to charge it."

"Again?"

"Yes, again. And I've got the charger Andrea bought for me plugged in at The Cookie Jar. I've got one at home too, and I even put up reminder notes by both chargers. At first the notes worked, but they don't seem to work anymore."

"That's because you got used to them. Move them to a new location. You'll notice them then. And when they stop working in the new spots, move them again. When you get used to seeing something, you just take it for granted until it's not there anymore."

What Mike had just said resonated in Hannah's mind. She was always there, either in her condo, or at work. And she always cooked for him. Did Mike take her for granted? Would he appreciate her a little more if suddenly she wasn't there anymore?"

"Hannah?" Mike interrupted her unwelcome thoughts. "Don't you want to know why I called?"

"I do. Of course I do."

"We found the thermos. It was under the passenger seat. You must have seen it yesterday and you just forgot about it with so many other things on your mind."

Like the fact you interrogated me and almost arrested me for murder, her mind said, but Hannah quite wisely didn't repeat it to Mike. After all, he'd recovered the thermos and that was the important thing. "So where is the thermos now?" she asked.

"Doc Knight has it. There was about a cup of liquid left inside and he's running tests on it."

"If he finds tranquilizers in the coffee, does that mean I'm in the clear?"

"It does. I talked to Roger and he says he didn't pick up any coffee from you or from Lisa. It all depends on the lab report. Doc's going to call me the second he gets the results."

"Okay. Thanks for telling me, Mike. I'm

341

really happy that they found it and it wasn't just part of my dream."

"I'm happy too, Hannah. Tell Barbara hello from me, okay? And let her know that everyone out here at the station misses her and wants her to come back soon."

"I'll tell her," Hannah promised and then she handed the phone back to Norman. "Thanks for the phone, Norman."

Just then Jenny came racing up the hallway after them. "Your mother just called," she said to Hannah. "She wants to see you before you go to visit Barbara."

"Okay," Hannah agreed. "Is she in Doc Knight's office?"

"Where else?" Jenny asked with a smile. "Your mother spends most of her time in there. She does a lot of things for Doc Knight."

I wonder exactly what things she does. Hannah's mind asked the question as she relayed the message to Norman, and they continued down the hall to Doc Knight's office.

"Mother," Hannah said, walking in the door. "You wanted to see me?"

"Yes, dear." Delores turned to Norman. "Hello, Norman. Are you going to see Barbara, too?"

"I'd like to find out how she's getting along with her temporary bridge," Norman said.

"She's getting along just fine," Delores said. "She knows she looks better and now she can eat some things she couldn't have before. Pureed everything has to be boring after a while."

There was a yowl from Moishe and Hannah lifted him into her arms. "Say hello to Moishe, Mother."

"My darling Grandcat," Delores crooned, opening the top drawer of Doc's desk. "Come on up here, Moishe. I've got something for you."

Hannah saw the familiar cat treat canister in her mother's hand and immediately placed Moishe on the desktop. "That's very smart of you, Mother," she said.

"That's self-preservation," Delores answered, doling out one of Moishe's favorite fish-shaped treats. "Or perhaps I should say it's *silk*-preservation since I'm wearing hose tonight. What do you have in those boxes, dear? Something for Barbara?"

"Yes. I brought some Monkey Bread for her," Hannah said.

"What's that?"

Hannah took one of the boxes out of Norman's arms and set it on the desktop.

She opened it and let her mother see the contents. "It's a lot like cinnamon rolls and it has chocolate chips between the layers. I didn't have time to make my Special Cinnamon Rolls so I got this recipe from Lisa."

"Very pretty," Delores said. "It smells absolutely fabulous. And that reminds me, have you eaten, dears?"

"Not yet," Hannah answered, turning to Norman. "How about you?"

"Not yet. I was going to ask you if you wanted to go out to eat after we saw Barbara."

"And I was going to ask *both* of you if you wanted to join us for dinner out at the Inn," Delores said, before Hannah could answer Norman. "Doc's running a test on that thermos they found in the car. He just called to tell me he'll have the final results in about an hour, but there's definitely a foreign substance in there."

Without any conscious thought, Hannah crossed her fingers. If the foreign substance turned out to be the tranquilizers that had killed Doctor Bev, she would be cleared!

"I thought we might be celebrating tonight," Delores continued. "Will you join us, dears?"

"Sounds good to me," Norman said.

"Me, too," Hannah agreed. "Tell me what

happened when you took Barbara the things from her house."

"She was perfectly rational," Delores said. "I brought a bowling trophy from the mantle. It had her father's name on it. She recognized it immediately and knew exactly where I'd gotten it. She said, *That's my dad's bowling trophy. He won it the year before he died. I kept it because it used to make my mother laugh. It's so funny, Delores. Just look. They spelled his name wrong.*"

"Did they?" Norman asked her.

"Yes. It was engraved *Patrick Donnelly* and there were three N's in Donnelly."

"The last time Barbara talked about her father, she got very upset and started to cry," Hannah said, remembering how Delores had patted Barbara's hand and told her not to think of sad things.

"Not this time. And she was the one who referred to her father dying the year after he won the trophy. Doc was very pleased when I told him. He's been hoping that her delusions would fade as her physical condition improved."

Hannah nodded. "It sounds reasonable. Let's just hope he's right. What else did you find to bring for Barbara?"

"One of her purses since the strap broke on the one she had with her the night of the party. It's a pretty tan leather shoulder bag with a gold buckle."

Norman looked thoughtful. "I think I remember her carrying that purse last winter. Did she recognize it?"

"Immediately. And she thanked me very nicely for bringing it. She said it was one of her favorite purses. I asked her where she got it and she said Nettie Grant had given it to her for Christmas when Sheriff Grant was still alive."

"It sounds to me as if she's getting better every day," Norman commented.

"I hope so," Delores said, "but Doc warned me not to get too excited. He said that brain injuries were unpredictable and there could be setbacks."

Hannah remembered that Lisa had said the same thing about her father. She'd told Hannah that there were good days and bad days, and there was no way to predict them.

"Is this Monkey Bread for me, dear?" Delores asked, pulling Hannah out of her contemplative mood.

"Yes, Mother. You can share it with Doc Knight and some of the nurses if you want to."

"I will, but only after I have a piece. Or perhaps two pieces. It has chocolate, you said?"

"Lots of chocolate."

"Good. I can hardly wait to taste it!" Delores stopped and looked at Hannah expectantly.

"What?" Hannah asked, not sure what her mother wanted.

"It's like Doc always tells me. Payback is only fair. Aren't you going to say it?"

"Say what, Mother?"

"Say what I used to say to you."

Hannah had no idea what her mother was talking about, but when she saw the large chunk of Monkey Bread that Delores had pulled from the loaf, she began to understand. They were all going out to dinner at the Inn and Delores was eating a large chunk of the sweet bread beforehand. "Don't spoil your dinner, Mother."

Delores laughed. "I won't. And I bet you've waited your whole life to say that."

"You're right." Hannah was smiling as she scooped Moishe up, set him on his feet, and motioned to Norman. It was time to go to see Barbara. As they headed out the door and turned down the hallway, Hannah found herself hoping that Barbara's rational response to the things Delores had brought her would carry over to their visit with her.

Monkey Bread

Preheat oven to 350 degrees F., rack in the middle position.

1 and 1/4 cups white (**granulated**) sugar

1 and 1/2 teaspoons ground cinnamon

4 cans (**7.5 ounce tube**) unbaked refrigerated biscuits (**I used Pillsbury**)

1 cup chopped nuts of your choice (**optional**)

1 cup chocolate chips (**optional**) (**that's a 6-ounce size bag**)

1/2 cup salted butter (**1 stick, 4 ounces, 1/4 pound**)

Hannah's 1st Note: If you prefer, you can use 16.3 ounce tubes of Pillsbury Grands. If you do this, buy only 2 tubes. They are larger — you will use half a tube for each layer.

Tony's Note: If you use chocolate chips and/or nuts, place them between each biscuit layer.

Spray the inside of a Bundt pan with Pam or another nonstick cooking spray. Set your prepared pan on a drip pan just in case the butter overflows. Then you won't have to clean your oven.

Mix the white sugar and cinnamon together in a mixing bowl. (*I used a fork to mix it up so that the cinnamon was evenly distributed.*)

Open 1 can of biscuits at a time and break or cut them into quarters. You want bite-size pieces.

Roll the pieces in the cinnamon and sugar mixture, and place them in the bottom of the Bundt pan.

Sprinkle one-third of the chopped nuts and one-third of the chocolate chips on top of the layer, if you decided to use them.

Open the second can of biscuits, quarter them, roll them in the cinnamon and sugar, and place them on top of the first layer. (*If you used Pillsbury Grands, you'll do this with the remainder of the first tube.*)

Sprinkle on half of the remaining nuts and chocolate chips, if you decided to use them.

Repeat with the third can of biscuits (*or the first half of the second tube of Grands*). Sprinkle on the remainder of the nuts and chocolate chips, if you decided to use them.

Repeat with the fourth can of biscuits (*or the rest of the Grands*) to make a top layer in your Bundt pan.

Melt the butter and the remaining cinnamon and sugar mixture in a microwave safe bowl on HIGH for 45 seconds. Give it a final stir and pour it over the top of your Bundt pan.

Bake your Monkey Bread at 350 degrees F. for 40 to 45 minutes, or until nice and golden on top.

Take the Bundt pan out of the oven and let it cool on a cold burner or a wire rack for 10 minutes while you find a plate that will fit over the top of the Bundt pan.

Using potholders or oven mitts invert the plate over the top of the Bundt pan and turn it upside down to unmold your delicious Monkey Bread.

To serve, you can cut this into slices like Bundt cake, but it's more fun to just let people pull off pieces with their fingers.

Hannah's 2nd Note: If you'd like to make Caramel Monkey Bread, use only 3/4 cup of white sugar. Mix it with the cinnamon the way you'd do if it was the full amount of white sugar. At the very end when you melt the butter with the leftover cinnamon and sugar mixture, add 3/4 cup of brown sugar to the bowl before you put it in the microwave. Pour that hot mixture over the top of your Bundt pan before baking and it will form a luscious caramel topping when you unmold your Monkey Bread.

Hannah's 3rd Note: I don't know why

this is called "Monkey Bread". Norman thinks it has something to do with the old story about the monkey that couldn't get his hand out of the hole in the tree because he wouldn't let go of the nut he was holding in his fist. Mike thinks it's because monkeys eat with their hands and you can pull this bread apart and eat it with your hands. Mother says it's because monkeys are social animals and you can put this bread in the center of the table and everyone can sit around it and eat. Tracey says it's because it's a cute name. Bethie doesn't care. She just wants to eat it.

Chapter Twenty-Three

"Hi, Barbara," Hannah greeted her.

"Look, Hannah." Barbara smiled widely. "My dentist gave me a nice present today. Now I don't look like a bag lady."

"I'm glad you're pleased," Norman said, coming over to kiss Barbara on the cheek. "How does that bridge feel?"

"Good." Barbara turned to Hannah. "Did you bring your cat to see me? Doc said you would."

"Moishe's right here." Hannah lifted him up in her arms to show Barbara.

"You're such a beautiful, big boy!" Barbara said, patting the bed. "Come up here and say hello to Aunt Babs."

Moishe didn't wait for a second invitation. He leaped out of Hannah's arms and joined Barbara on the bed.

"So handsome," Barbara said, stroking his back and then scratching him behind the ears. "Do you like that?"

352

Moishe purred so loudly that Hannah was almost afraid he'd choke. His tongue flicked out to give Barbara a raspy kiss and he rubbed his head against her arm. Hannah was surprised and pleased by his behavior. It usually took Moishe a while to warm up to someone new, but this time no bribery with kitty treats was required. It was perfectly clear that he was wildly taken with Aunt Babs.

"He likes you, Barbara," Norman said.

"I know. I think it's because he recognizes me. Moishe and I are old friends, you know."

"You are?" Hannah asked, frowning slightly. Barbara had never visited her condo and she hoped this wasn't another delusion on Barbara's part.

"Don't you remember, Hannah? You brought Moishe down to your coffee shop when that film crew was in town. I was one of the extras in the movie."

"That's right," Hannah said, even though she didn't remember. It was true that she'd taken Moishe to The Cookie Jar while Ross and his movie crew were in town. He'd used all the shops on Main Street for background, and he'd paid every business owner for the privilege. He'd rented Hannah's business for his exclusive use and since almost everyone in town played some part in the movie, Hannah had done business as usual. The only difference was that for the length of time the movie was filming, The Cookie Jar was classified as a private club and she was allowed to bring Moishe to work with her.

"I was in the coffee shop one day with the other extras in my scene, and Lisa tethered Moishe to our table," Barbara explained. "That's how I met him."

"Of course," Hannah said, even though she didn't remember that particular day. Barbara's explanation was perfectly reasonable.

"I remember that," Norman said, smiling at Barbara. "I was at the next table with Mike. Weren't you the extra with the red umbrella in the rainy afternoon scene?"

"That's right."

Barbara looked delighted that he'd remembered, and Hannah was delighted, too. Barbara's delusions had fled for today, at least. But as her Great-Grandma Elsa used to say, it was time to open a can of worms to see what crawled out. "Mother was telling us that she brought you a bowling trophy?"

"That's right. It was my dad's bowling trophy. He was in a league down at Ali's father's bowling alley. I still remember the shirts. They were aqua blue and they had *Lake Eden Volunteer Fire Department* embroidered on the back. I was in bed, but I heard them laughing when he came home that night. And the next morning my mother showed me that they'd spelled Donnelly wrong on the trophy."

Norman got up to look at the trophy that was sitting on Barbara's nightstand. "You're right," he said. "It says 'Patrick Donnelly.' And 'Donnelly' has three N's. Was Patrick your father's name?"

Barbara shook her head as if to say it wasn't, but then she said, "Patrick was my dad's name."

"What else did Mother bring you?" Hannah asked. Except for the inappropriate head shake, Barbara was batting a thousand tonight.

"A purse. It's over there on the chair. It's one of my favorites. Nettie Grant gave it to me for Christmas one year."

Hannah gave a deep sigh of relief. They'd gotten through the ten minutes Doc Knight had allotted to their visit and Barbara had been perfectly rational the whole time. "I'm leaving this for you, Barbara," she said, placing the bakery box on Barbara's bedside table. "It's Monkey Bread."

"I *love* Monkey Bread. My mother used to bake it. Does it have chocolate?"

"Yes. I got the recipe from Lisa's oldest sister."

"That's wonderful, Hannah. It's the same recipe that my mother used. She made it for a baby shower once and . . . and your partner's sister asked her for the recipe."

"We'd better go, Hannah." Norman glanced out into the hallway. "Here comes Barbara's nurse and she's probably going to tell us our visiting time is up."

"Jenny!" Hannah said, recognizing the nurse as she walked into the room.

"That's it!" Barbara exclaimed. "It's Jenny!" And then she turned to Jenny to explain, "The last time Hannah was here, I told her your name sounded like money. And it does. Jenny sounds like penny. I said that, didn't I, Hannah?"

"Yes, you did." Hannah turned toward Jenny. "You said you were working another shift. Are you Barbara's nurse tonight?"

"Yes. I'm staying with Barbara in her room. They're bringing in a cot in a couple of minutes."

"You're going to sleep in here?" Barbara asked her.

"That's right."

"Oh, good!" Barbara turned to Hannah.

"Jenny can help in case the monster comes back."

Uh-oh! Here we go again! Hannah's mind formed the words that she wasn't about to speak aloud.

"What monster is that?" Norman asked in a normal conversational tone of voice.

"The first time I saw it I thought it looked like a big white rat. That's what I told you, isn't it, Hannah?"

"Yes, that's what you told me."

"Well, I saw it again and this time it looked like a white hunchback seal. The way it moves scares me."

"It won't come in while I'm here," Jenny said.

"I hope not." Barbara turned to Hannah. "Will you bring . . . the big cat back, Hannah?"

"Of course I'll bring Moishe back."

"That makes me feel so much safer. I really don't like that monster."

There was silence for a moment. It seemed that none of them knew exactly the right thing to say.

"Of course my brother is a monster, too," Barbara continued, "even if he doesn't look like one. He's a human monster."

"Your . . . brother?" Hannah managed to ask.

357

Barbara nodded. "I think he still wants to kill me. He probably thought I'd die jumping off the roof, but I didn't. If he comes back when there's nobody here, I'm going to hit him with this!"

Barbara reached out and gripped the bowling trophy tightly. "Dad's bowling trophy ought to take care of him. It's heavy enough. The last time he came into my room, I hit him with the water pitcher. It's too bad it's made out of plastic. I don't think it hurt him at all."

Hannah exchanged glances with Norman. It was time for them to leave. "We'd better go now, Barbara," she said, reaching out to touch Barbara's hand. "Enjoy your Monkey Bread."

"Oh, I will! Goodbye, Hannah. Thank you for baking the Monkey Bread. I'll share it with . . . Jenny." She turned to Norman. "Goodbye, my dentist. Thank you for the new teeth because now I can eat that Monkey Bread."

They could hear Cuddles yowling with excitement as they led Moishe up to Norman's front door. They'd decided that instead of driving back to Hannah's condo to take Moishe home and then retracing their steps to go out to the Lake Eden Inn, they'd simply drop him off at Norman's house so he could play with Cuddles while they dined.

"She knows Moishe's out here," Hannah said, greatly amused by the excited squeals that were coming from inside. "I think you'd better get ready to catch her when you open the door. She could run out."

Norman stuck his key in the lock. "That won't be a problem. Just lead Moishe inside and she'll stay right by him."

Hannah had her doubts, but she did as Norman suggested and Cuddles stuck right by Moishe's side. They walked in tandem down the hallway and when Hannah took Moishe off the leash, Cuddles immediately initiated a game of chase.

"Careful!" Norman warned, pulling Hannah over to the living room couch. "Sit! Quick! And if they jump, lean forward. Cuddles thinks the back of the couch is a speedway."

Hannah sat just in time as the two cats raced into the room. She ducked and leaned forward as Cuddles jumped up and Moishe chased her the length of the couch and then down again.

"The coffee table's next," Norman informed her. "Good thing I put the glass I used last night in the dishwasher."

Norman's coffee table was huge and Hannah watched the two cats skid across its surface. "What's next?" she asked him.

"The reverse. Watch for Cuddles to do a one-eighty against the far wall."

Cuddles did precisely what Norman had described and Hannah laughed. "She pushed off like an Olympic swimmer."

"Lean forward," Norman warned an instant before the two cats skyrocketed along the back of the couch again.

"Is there more?" Hannah asked as the two cats sped out of the living room.

"Yes, in the den. They'll go up and down the staircase at least six times. Then they'll tear straight through here and hit the other staircase to go up to the bedrooms. Unless you'd like something cold to drink, we could leave now while they're occupied."

Hannah glanced at her watch. "Let's leave now and get something to drink at the Inn. I need to talk to Sally anyway."

"Are you planning to get some background information about Doctor Bev and Roger?"

"Yes. It's the scattergun approach. I want to find out all I can about Doctor Bev's daily life while she was staying there. It might not have anything to do with her murder, but you never know what might come to light if you can manage to ask the right questions."

The daylight was beginning to fade as they walked out to Norman's car. The air was filled with the rich perfume of the lilac bushes that grew close to the house, and a few lazy bumblebees droned among the purple, pink, and white blossoms. As night approached, the temperature was beginning to drop a bit, heat lightning flashed against the darkening sky, and the mosquitoes hadn't found her yet. It was the perfect start to a summer evening in Minnesota.

Norman opened her car door and she slid into the passenger seat. "Why don't they bite you?" she asked in her best non-sequitur fashion.

"I don't know. They never have."

Hannah smiled. Norman had known exactly what she was asking. "How about your mother?"

"They bite her."

"Your father?"

"They bit him, too. It's just me. When I was a kid I used to think I was adopted because I was the only one in the family they didn't bother. Then, when I got older, I realized how silly that was."

"That's good."

"Maybe not. That was when I began to

believe that I was from another planet."

Hannah laughed. She'd walked right into that one.

Norman started the car and they drove off. "Do you want the air on?" he asked her.

"No, let's roll down the windows. I love the night air and as long as we're moving, the mosquitoes won't be able to draw a bead on me."

Hannah leaned back and let the night air caress her face as Norman turned on the road that ran around Eden Lake. If she were rich, she wouldn't want an expensive sports car like Doctor Bev. She'd want a luxury sedan and a driver. That way she could lean back and relax as an expert drove her along scenic routes that led only to places she wanted to go. "If I ever get rich, I want a car and a driver," she said, voicing her thoughts aloud.

"You don't have to get rich for that. I've got a car and I drive. And you've got me."

"Yes," Hannah said, smiling softly into the darkness. She had Norman and life was good.

"Hey, you two!" a voice called out from the bar as Sally led Hannah and Norman into the dining room.

"Roger," Sally told them, giving a little

wave in Roger's direction. "He's been drinking here since mid-afternoon. Poor guy. He's really upset and he keeps talking about what a great woman she was. I bit my tongue so many times it got sore, so I excused myself and left him with Dick. Every time he said how much he missed her, I wanted to tell him how lucky he . . ." Sally stopped and made a face. "Sorry, Norman."

"There's nothing to be sorry about, Sally. It's the pure unvarnished truth. Roger's much better off without her. I know I am."

"Norman! Come over here and have a drink!" Roger called out.

"Be right there," Norman replied, and then he turned to Hannah. "You want to talk to Sally, don't you?"

"Well, yes, but . . ."

"Go ahead," Norman interrupted any objection she might make. "Your mother and Doc Knight aren't here yet, and I wanted to talk to Roger anyway."

"Okay," Hannah said, catching on at last. Norman wanted to pump Roger for information and he thought it would be easier done as a guy-to-guy thing.

"How about coming back to my office?" Sally asked. "Dot's the hostess tonight and I'll tell her to buzz me when your mother and Doc Knight come in."

"That's fine with me," Hannah agreed. She loved to go to Sally's office with its picture window overlooking the kitchen.

Once they'd stopped at the hostess station to give Dot instructions, and Hannah had asked about her husband and baby, Jamie, Sally led her down the hallway to her office.

"Sit here," she said, gesturing to the chair opposite her desk. "I want to show you my new dessert. It's called Snappy Turtle Pie and I'm putting it on the menu for the first time tonight."

Hannah watched as Sally picked up the phone and dialed a number. Then she turned toward the window and saw a woman in the kitchen pick up the phone.

"Hi, Mary," Sally greeted the woman. "Could you please find out if anyone's ordered the Snappy Turtle Pie yet?"

Hannah watched as Mary made her way to a man in a chef's toque. A moment later, she was back on the phone again.

"Excellent," Sally said. "And you're on the second pie?" She listened for a moment and then she spoke again. "Ask him if he'll prepare a piece for you to bring in here. And I could use two mugs of black coffee, too. Thank you, Mary."

"What's Snappy Turtle Pie?" Hannah

asked when Sally had hung up the phone. She hoped it wasn't real snapping turtle.

"You'll see. I don't want to spoil the surprise. Norman said you wanted to talk to me. Is it about Doctor Bev?"

"Yes. Mike sent down a diver and they recovered a thermos from her new car. Doc Knight's testing the contents right now to see if they contain the tranquilizers that killed her. I really need to know if anyone here filled that thermos for her before she left yesterday morning."

"Let me check with room service. And if no one delivered coffee to their suite, I'll ask the busboys who were working at breakfast. It's possible one of them filled the thermos."

"Thanks, Sally. It's important. I really need to know."

"Because it could get you off the hook?"

Obviously, the Lake Eden gossip hotline was working. "You're right, but only if the coffee in the thermos tests positive for tranquilizers."

"Let me know as soon as you know. I've been worried about you. I'll find out where that coffee came from. Was it black?"

"No. Doc Knight said she had coffee, cream, sweetener, and my cupcakes in her stomach."

"There was sparkling water too. That's all she had at lunch. I waited on them myself."

"Did Norman look uncomfortable at lunch?"

"Like a sheep about to be shorn. He wanted out in the worst way possible, but you know Norman. He wasn't about to make a scene that might hurt my lunch business."

Hannah knew she was asking questions that had nothing to do with her investigation, but she couldn't seem to stop. "How about Doctor Bev? Did she look happy to be with Norman?"

Sally threw up her hands. "Who could tell with her? All I know is that she kept trying to put her hand over his, and he kept pulling his hand away. I wasn't close enough to hear their conversation, but it was clear that Norman wanted to be almost anywhere but here with her." Sally paused and smiled. "That question wasn't part of your investigation, was it?"

"No, it was personal," Hannah admitted.

There was a knock on the door and Sally shouted for whoever it was to come in. The woman Hannah had seen on the phone in the kitchen entered the room with a tray.

"Here's your coffee, Sally," she said, setting the tray on the table. "And here's the pie."

"Just put the pie in front of Hannah," Sally said, gesturing toward Hannah. "Thanks, Mary. Just leave the tray and I'll carry it in the kitchen when we're through."

Hannah glanced down at the pie and began to smile. "It's darling!" she said, noticing the cookie shaped like a turtle on top. "Where did you get those cookies?"

"We bake them here. It's a recipe from Lisa's Aunt Nancy and she gave it to me. Her aunt sent her three cookie recipes and she said this one was too labor intensive for The Cookie Jar, but it was so cute, she thought I'd like it. It's not too labor intensive for us. Mary loves to fuss with garnishes and things and she really enjoys baking these."

"You're going to spoil my dinner," Hannah said.

"No, I'm not. When your mother called in for the reservation she told me you hadn't eaten for hours."

"That's true." Hannah cut off the tip of the pie and popped it into her mouth. "Mmmmmm!"

Sally smiled. "It's just like a turtle sundae in a chocolate cookie crust. Try the cookie."

Hannah didn't need a second invitation.

She bit into the turtle cookie and smiled with enjoyment. "Tell Mary the cookies are absolutely perfect. This is going to be a huge hit, Sally."

"I think so, too. And since the pie is an ice cream pie, it's great for the summer."

Hannah made short work of both pie and cookie. When she was finished, she laughed.

"What's so funny?" Sally asked.

"I was just thinking of something my Great-Grandma Elsa used to say. It was, *Life is risky. Eat dessert first!*"

SNAPPY TURTLE PIE

1 chocolate cookie crumb pie shell (***chocolate is best, but shortbread or graham cracker will also work just fine***)

1 pint vanilla ice cream

4 ounces (***2/3 of a 6-ounce jar***) caramel ice cream topping (***I used Smucker's***)

1/2 cup salted pecan pieces

4 ounces (***2/3 of an 6-ounce jar***) chocolate fudge ice cream topping (***I used Smucker's***)

1 small container frozen Cool Whip (***original, not low-fat, or real whipped cream***)

Hannah's Note: If you can't find salted pecans, buy plain pecans. Measure out 1/2 cup of pieces, heat them in the microwave or the oven until they're hot and then toss them with 2 Tablespoons of melted, salted butter. Sprinkle on a 1/4 teaspoon of salt, toss again, and you have salted pecan pieces.

Set your cookie crumb pie shell on the counter along with your ice cream carton. Let the ice cream soften for 5 to 10 minutes. You want it approximately the consistency of soft-serve.

Using a rubber spatula, spread out your ice cream in the bottom of the chocolate cookie crumb crust. Smooth the top with the spatula.

Working quickly, pour the caramel topping over the ice cream. You can drizzle it, pour it, whatever. Just try to get it as evenly distributed as you can.

Sprinkle the salted pecan pieces on top of the caramel layer.

Pour or drizzle the chocolate fudge topping over the pecans.

Cover the top of your pie with wax paper (***don't push it down — you don't want it to stick***) and put your Snappy Turtle Pie in the freezer overnight.

Put your container of Cool Whip in the **refrigerator** overnight. Then it'll be spreadable in the morning.

In the morning, remove your pie from the freezer and spread Cool Whip over the top. Cover it with wax paper again and stick it back into the freezer for at least 6 hours.

If you're not planning to serve your pie for dinner that night, wait until the 6 hours are up and then put it into a freezer bag and return it to the freezer for storage. It will be fine for about a month.

Take your Snappy Turtle Pie out of the freezer and place it on the countertop about 15 minutes before you're ready to serve it. When it's time for dessert, cut it into 6 pieces as you would a regular pie, put each piece on a dessert plate, and place one Snappy Turtle Cookie (**recipe follows**) on the center of each piece, the head of the turtle facing the tip of the pie.

Yield: 6 slices of yummy ice cream pie that all of your guests will ooh and ahh over.

SNAPPY TURTLE COOKIES
Preheat oven to 350 degrees F., rack in the middle position.

1/2 cup (**one stick, 4 ounces, 1/4 pound**) salted butter, softened
1/2 cup brown sugar (**pack it down in the cup when you measure it**)
1/4 teaspoon baking soda
1/4 teaspoon salt
1 large egg
1 egg yolk (**keep the white in a small bowl for later**)
1/2 teaspoon vanilla extract
1/4 teaspoon maple flavoring (**optional**)
1 and 1/3 cups all-purpose flour (**pack it down in the cup when you measure it**)
2/3 cup pecan halves cut in half lengthwise

In a large mixing bowl, beat the softened butter and brown sugar until they're nice and fluffy.

371

Mix in the baking soda and the salt.

Add the egg and the egg yolk and mix well.

Mix in the vanilla extract and the maple flavoring (*if you decided to use it*).

Add the flour in increments, approximately a half-cup at a time, mixing well after each addition. (*I know your last increment will be a little short, but don't worry, the flour police will not knock on your door to arrest you!*)

Spray a cookie sheet with non-stick cooking spray.

Arrange the pecan pieces in groups of 5 in a starburst design so that they will resemble the feet and head of a turtle when you put a cookie dough ball in the center.

Shape the dough by rounded teaspoonful into dough balls.

Dip the bottom of the dough balls into the egg white and then set it in the center of your starburst of nuts. Press the dough balls down so that the tips of the nuts will stick out to form the "feet" and "head" when the cookies are baked.

Bake the Snappy Turtle Cookies at 350 degrees F., for 10 to 13 minutes or until the cookies are a golden brown.

Cool on the cookie sheet for 2 minutes and then transfer the cookies to a wire rack to cool completely.

Yield: 2 and 1/2 dozen cookies that will delight children and adults alike.

Hannah's Note: Nancy sometimes frosts her cookies with canned chocolate frosting, but we always make our own frosting at The Cookie Jar. Here's the recipe we like:

EASY CHOCOLATE FROSTING

1/2 cup semi-sweet chocolate chips

1/4 cup whipping cream

1/2 cup butter (*1 stick, 4 ounces, 1/4 pound*)

1 and 1/2 cups powdered (*confectioners*) sugar (*NOT sifted*)

Combine the chips, cream and butter in a saucepan. Melt them together over very low heat, stirring constantly. When everything is melted, turn off the heat and move the pan to a cold burner. Stir everything smooth with a wooden spoon or a heat-resistant spatula. (*Alternatively, you can melt the chocolate chips with the cream and the butter in a microwave-safe bowl for 1 minute on HIGH. Stir to see if everything's melted and if it's not, heat it in 30-second increments until it is.*)

Measure the powdered sugar, packing it down in the cup when you do so. Place it in a bowl large enough to also hold the chocolate mixture.

Give the chocolate mixture in the saucepan a final stir and then pour it over the powdered sugar. Do this fast and all at once. Start stirring immediately and mix until the frosting is smooth. This frosting will look "runny," but don't worry. It'll harden up when the butter solidifies. If it hardens too much as you're frosting the cookies, just heat it very gently over low heat on the stovetop, or, if you made it in the microwave, heat it again on HIGH for 20 seconds or so.

Yield: This frosting should frost 2 to 3 dozen cookies, or a small cake.

Chapter Twenty-Four

"Tranquilizers," Doc said the moment Sally had left. "Three times the normal dosage and that was only in the coffee that was left in the thermos. Whoever did it must have dumped a whole bottle in there."

"I have a question for you," Hannah said. "I know Doctor Bev was drinking sparkling water at lunch yesterday. Why didn't it show up in her stomach contents?"

"Because there's not much to identify in carbonated water. It would merely have diluted the other liquid contents."

"Does Mike know that the tranquilizers were in the thermos?" Hannah asked.

"I called from the hospital to tell him. We invited him to dinner when he stopped by to pick up the report, but he said he was busy and I could give you the good news myself."

I wonder if he's busy with Misty, that waitress out at the Corner Tavern, or whether he's busy with work, Hannah thought to herself. She hoped it was work. But instead of spending time thinking about that, she asked another question. "Was there anything else in Doctor Bev's stomach that . . . uh . . . maybe I shouldn't ask about that now."

"It's all right, dear," Delores said. "This conversation would have bothered me a few months ago, but Doc's been doing his best to desensitize me."

"Is it working?" Doc asked her.

"Somewhat." Delores gave a ladylike little shiver. "But it's not doing much for my appetite." She turned to Hannah. "Could you ask another question, dear? One that doesn't have the words *stomach* or *contents* in it?"

"Actually, there's another important question," Hannah said, remembering what Barbara had said about her water pitcher. "Do you know if Barbara has ever knocked over her water pitcher?"

Delores looked surprised. "I can answer that, dear. Yes, she has and it happened just last night. Her nurse went to get another bag of glucose for her IV drip and when she came back into Barbara's room, the water pitcher was on the floor."

Norman and Hannah exchanged glances. Either Barbara had actually tried to hit someone with her water pitcher, or she'd knocked it over accidentally. Now, after the fact, there was no way of knowing for certain.

"Is it important, dear?" Delores asked when Hannah didn't respond.

"Not really. It's just something she mentioned and I was wondering if it had happened."

"All right then." Delores smiled at Hannah. "Since you're no longer a suspect, I think we should celebrate. I wonder where Sally is with the . . ." Delores peeked out of the curtain they'd pulled for privacy in one of Sally's raised booths. "Here she comes now."

"Knock, knock," Sally said, and then she pulled the curtain open. "Here we are, Delores. I made my special appetizer tray for you."

They all watched in awe as one of the waitresses set a large silver platter in the center of their table. There were small slices of black bread topped with smoked salmon, cream cheese, and capers, several kinds of pâté to spread on toast points, and a round of Brie baked in a pastry crust, surrounded by small bunches of grapes.

"Very impressive," Doc Knight said, smiling at Sally.

"Thank you." Sally smiled back. "I love to

do these appetizer platters."

"Will you join us?" Delores asked, sliding over a bit so that Sally could sit.

"I shouldn't," Sally said, but Hannah noticed she wasn't slow to take a seat. "I understand we have something to celebrate?"

"We do," Doc answered. "Hannah is no longer a suspect in Doctor Bev's murder."

"Well, thank goodness for that!" Sally raised her glass. "Anybody who thought that she was should have their head examined."

"By me," Doc said and everyone laughed.

Sally turned to Hannah. "Would you mind coming with me for a minute? I have that recipe you wanted, but I left it on my desk. And if you don't get it now, I'll probably forget which pile of papers it's in. It'll only take a minute or two."

Hannah wasn't fooled for a second as she followed Sally out of the curtained enclosure. Something was up.

"I've got Josh waiting for you in my office," Sally said, the moment they were out of earshot. "He's one of my newest busboys and he filled Doctor Bev's silver thermos this morning."

"Hannah? This is Josh. He's my newest busboy." Sally turned to smile at the teen-

378

ager, who looked exceedingly uncomfortable. "Tell Miss Swensen what happened when you filled Doctor Bev's thermos."

Josh took a deep breath. "She asked me to fill it with coffee and I did. But first I took it into the kitchen and rinsed it out with scalding hot water the way we're supposed to do with thermoses."

"Very good. What happened next?"

"She told me she wanted a fresh pot of coffee, not the coffee from the carafe we have at the breakfast buffet. She said to put a quarter-cup of real cream in the bottom and then eights packs of artificial sweetener. After that, I should add the coffee and leave enough room so that I could shake it before I brought it up to her room."

"And you took it up to her room?" Hannah asked.

"Yeah. She was on the phone and she told me to leave it on the table by the door. And then, before I could leave, she told me she'd changed her mind and I should take it down and put it on the floor behind the driver's seat of her new car."

"Did you do that?"

"Yeah. It was a beautiful car!"

"Did she give you the keys?"

"She didn't have to. She said it was parked in a no parking zone in the back of the hotel and the top was down."

"Did anybody else see you put the thermos in the car?"

"Sure. There were a couple of other people out there admiring the car. And then, just as I was leaving, Mr. Dalworth came down to drive it up to the front for her."

"Do you know if he saw the thermos?"

Josh shrugged. "I don't know. He didn't see me put it in the car and it was on the floor behind the driver's seat, where she told me to put it. He probably didn't even notice it at all."

Dinner at the Inn had been wonderful, as always, and once Hannah had told them about Sally's new dessert, they'd all had the Snappy Turtle Pie with a Snappy Turtle Cookie on top. Hannah was certain she couldn't eat another bite as she climbed into Norman's car.

"Are you as stuffed as I am?" Norman asked, taking the access road to the highway.

"I'm more than stuffed. I think I'm positively round."

They rode in companionable silence until they reached Hannah's condo complex. They'd already discussed the bus-boy she'd interviewed about the thermos when Hannah had returned to the table. Doc had told them that the fingerprint team hadn't been able to get any clear prints from the outside and they'd all concluded that absolutely anyone at the Inn could have opened the thermos and dropped in the tranquilizers. They'd also talked about Roger and the fact that both Norman and Sally thought he was genuinely heartbroken over Doctor Bev's death. Her murder was still a complete mystery and nothing Hannah had discovered was helping to solve it.

"I can take Moishe up the stairs for you," Norman said as they pulled into Hannah's extra parking space.

"That's okay. I can do it. You look tired."

"I am. It's been a long day and I didn't sleep very well last night." Norman reached over to give her a hug. "If you're sure you don't mind, I'll just drive home and fall into bed."

"I don't mind at all," Hannah told him, picking up the end of Moishe's leash. "Come on, Moishe. Let's go up and get to bed ourselves."

"I'll pull out and make sure you get into your condo okay," Norman promised as Hannah and Moishe got out of his car. "I'll watch from the visitor parking lot."

"Okay," Hannah said, knowing it was

futile to argue. Norman was unfailingly considerate and he'd wait until she got into her condo safely before he drove off.

It didn't take long for Hannah and Moishe to get to the head of the stairs. Both of them were eager to go inside, but they waited until Norman pulled into the visitor parking lot before Hannah opened the door. She gave a wave, Norman gave a polite little beep on his horn, and Moishe led her inside. "Michelle?" she called out.

There was no answer and Hannah glanced at the clock. Her cookie truck had been parked in her spot and that meant Michelle had come back from The Cookie Jar. It was only nine at night. Surely Michelle wasn't sleeping already!

One glance inside the guest room and Hannah could see that it was empty. Perhaps Lonnie had picked up her youngest sister for a date. If Michelle had left, there would be a note in front of the coffee pot or on the kitchen table. Michelle always left a note.

"Go ahead, Moishe," Hannah told him, noticing that he was eyeing the door of her bedroom hopefully. She went in to turn down the bed for him and patted his pillow. "You can go to bed. I'm going to go see if there's a note from Michelle."

As Hannah retraced her steps to the living room, she heard a thump from her bedroom. Moishe had accepted her invitation to go to bed. She flicked on the kitchen light and spotted the note on the table. Michelle was every bit as considerate as Norman was.

Ran into Lorna Kusak when I came back here, the note read. She's having a graduation party for Chris tonight and I said I'd help her with the refreshments. Howie and Esther are there and Lorna said to come over when you get home so you can taste Howie's Guac Ad Hoc. He's bringing a huge batch and everybody loves it.

The last thing Hannah wanted to do was go to a teenage party, but Howie and his wife were there and she wanted to tell him the good news about the thermos and how she'd been cleared as a suspect. Then there was the guacamole. She'd heard that Howie made the best in town and she'd never had the chance to taste it. If she liked it and if she played her cards correctly, she might even be able to talk him into sharing the recipe!

CHAPTER TWENTY-FIVE

Hannah had expected a noisy teenage party, but she heard no music as she approached Lorna's condo. That was odd. Michelle had said it was a graduation party for Chris. She didn't know a single teenager who'd just graduated from high school who would want a party without music. Was the party over this soon?

Light spilled out on the walkway that led to Lorna's front door and Hannah could hear the thumping of dancing feet. The party wasn't over. That much was clear. But how could Chris and his friends dance without music?

Hannah rang the doorbell and a moment later, Lorna opened the door. "Hi, Hannah," she said with a smile. "I'm so glad you could make it! Come into the living room and join the adults. The kids are all dancing on the back patio."

"But I don't hear any music," Hannah

said as she stepped into the quiet living room where Esther and Howie were sitting, along with Lorna's sister and brother-in-law. "How can the kids dance without music?"

"They have music. Come with me and I'll show you."

Lorna led Hannah to the open patio door where they could look out on the party. There were at least ten couples dancing on the patio and every single one was wearing earphones!

"Those earphones are incredible!" Hannah commented, watching them glow in the twinkle lights that Lorna had used to decorate the rafters on the patio. They were made of fluorescent plastic in bold colors and the clear plastic headbands flashed with the beat of the music.

"I know. The kids just love them."

"You bought wireless earphones for everybody?" Hannah asked.

"No, I rented them from a store at the Tri-County Mall. It's a great store, Hannah. It's called Crazy Quiet Parties and they've got all sorts of fun things that don't make very much noise."

"Your neighbors are going to love you," Hannah told her as they walked back into the living room. "Did Howie bring his Guac

Ad Hoc?"

"Three batches," Howie said, overhearing her question. "Help yourself. It's right there on the table. And then come over here and tell me how you like it."

Hannah took a small spoonful of Guac Ad Hoc and surrounded it with salted tortilla chips. She scooped up a little guacamole with a chip and popped it into her mouth. There was an instant explosion of flavors on her palate. She tasted rich buttery avocado, the tang of lemon juice, the fresh hint of oregano, and the smooth coolness of sour cream, all enhanced by just the right amount of garlic and onion. There was a crunch in addition to the tortilla chip and Hannah was amazed to taste bacon. "Wow!" she said, walking back to Howie with another loaded chip in her hand. "This Guac Ad Hoc is fantastic!"

"You like the oregano?"

"I love it. It makes guacamole into something entirely different."

"You can make it with cilantro if you want to. It's just that Florence doesn't always have cilantro and Esther grows oregano in her kitchen window garden. I tasted it, thought it would work, and found an alternative."

"It's a *great* alternative."

"Thanks." Howie looked pleased. "Do you want the recipe?"

"Yes, I'd love to have it."

Howie reached into his pocket, pulled out a recipe card, and handed it to Hannah. "Here you go. I always print these out before I take it to a party." His smile disappeared and he looked very serious. "Are there any new developments, Hannah?"

"There's a big one," Hannah told him. "Mike sent a diver down this afternoon and he recovered a thermos from Doctor Bev's car. The coffee that was left in the thermos was laced with enough tranquilizers to kill her."

"Where did she get the coffee?"

"A busboy named Josh filled it with coffee that morning at the Inn and put it in her car for her. The car wasn't locked and the top was down."

"So anyone out there could have dropped the tranquilizers into the thermos."

"That's right."

"And since you didn't give her the coffee, you're off the official suspect list?"

"Exactly."

Howie looked relieved. "Good! I wasn't looking forward to that trial. I know I could have gotten you off, but that wouldn't remove the cloud of suspicion you'd still have hanging over your head."

"I know. I'll have to figure out who killed her in order to completely clear my name."

"And you're going to do that?"

"I'm going to *try* to do that," Hannah corrected him.

"All I can say is be careful, Hannah! There's someone out there who doesn't care if an innocent person is convicted for the crime he or she committed."

"I know. I'll be careful. Send me a bill and I'll pay you, Howie. I appreciate what you did for me."

Howie waved away that suggestion. "No charge, Hannah. Just bake me some Molasses Crackles every once in a while. I love those cookies."

"That's easy," Hannah said. "We'll deliver them to your office tomorrow."

"Great! I wish every client I've lost this week could bake."

"You lost another client?"

Howie nodded. "A big one. I've got to admit I'm upset about it. Warren Dalworth switched to a lawyer in the Cities."

"Really?" Hannah asked, remembering what her mother had said about the visitor in the three-piece suit who had come to see Warren in the hospital. "How about Roger? He's still with you, isn't he?"

"Yes, but Roger doesn't do much business with me. Almost everything goes through Dalworth Enterprises and Warren controls that . . . at least for now. I no longer know what will happen when Warren dies. And I understand from Roger that his condition is terminal."

Hannah's antenna for trouble went on full alert. "But Warren's wife is dead and Roger is his only son. He'll inherit Dalworth Enterprises, won't he?"

"That's the way Warren set it up with me. I don't know what's changed now that Warren has a new will."

"There's a new will in place?"

"Yes. I never would have known about it, but a guy I knew from law school dropped by to see me at the office the other day. He's working for a big firm in the Cities. I asked him what he was doing here in Lake Eden and he said he drew up a will for somebody and he had to go to the hospital to get it signed. Of course I asked him who his client was and when he said it was Warren Dalworth, you could have knocked me over with a feather."

"Did you try to find out why Warren used someone else?"

"Of course I did. The next morning I went out to the hospital to see Warren and ask

389

him what was going on. Unfortunately, I didn't get the chance to talk to him. He was in I.C.U. and the visitors' list was limited to members of his immediate family. Roger was there, visiting his father."

"Did you get a chance to talk to Roger?"

"Yes. I waited for him to come out and I asked him about the new will. He said that his father had told him about calling in a lawyer from Minneapolis and changing a few things to make it easier for him to take over Dalworth Enterprises when the time came."

Hannah was curious. "Do you have any idea what those changes could be?"

"I don't have a clue unless circumstances have changed over the past month or so. I thought that Warren and I had every contingency covered in the will I drew up for him."

"Did Roger give you any reason why his father called in a lawyer from Minneapolis?"

"Yes. He was reluctant to say it, but Roger thinks his father's mind is slipping. He said Warren probably forgot he had a lawyer right here in town."

"Poor Warren!" Hannah didn't like to think that the man most people regarded as the shrewdest investor and developer in the state could be failing mentally. "And poor Roger, too. It must be awful to see your father failing that way."

"Roger's had a lot of grief lately." He was silent for a moment and then he continued. "Roger was embarrassed. It was clear he didn't want to go into details, but he said that when he asked Warren what was wrong with the will I drew up for him, Warren didn't seem to know who I was and he didn't remember that he even *had* a will."

"That doesn't sound good."

"No, it doesn't. Of course Warren is on some pretty strong pain medication so we have to make allowances for that."

"But do you think he was capable of making out a new will?"

Howie shrugged. "I don't know. I didn't speak to him. But if what Roger says is true, Warren certainly shouldn't have drafted a will without the advice and assistance of someone he knew and trusted."

"Like you?"

"Not necessarily. It could have been someone like Doc Knight, or an old friend he knew in town."

"But Warren did it all by himself."

"That's what I understand. And he did it with a lawyer who'd never met him before and couldn't accurately judge his mental state."

Hannah shivered slightly. "What if there's

something . . . wrong in the will?"

"That's exactly what Roger asked me. He didn't see the new will and all he knows about it is what his father told him. He asked me what he could do if his father had done something crazy, like leave Dalworth Enterprises to a total stranger, or a shelter for homeless earthworms."

"What did you tell Roger?"

"I said that if there was something outrageous like that in Warren's new will, it might go toward proving that Warren was incompetent, or not in his right mind when he instructed his new lawyer and signed the will. The courts have to decide that."

"And if they do, then the new will can be . . ." Hannah stopped, unable to think of the correct legal term. "Revoked?"

"Declared invalid," Howie provided the phrase. "If Warren was not of sound mind when he signed the new will, it doesn't exist."

Forty-five minutes was long enough to stay at a teenage party even if the teenagers were dancing to music the adults couldn't hear. Hannah and Michelle got back to Hannah's condo at five minutes to ten.

"Do you want to catch Moishe, or shall

I?" Michelle asked as Hannah drew out her keys.

"I'll do it, but I don't think he'll be jumping into anyone's arms tonight. He was so tired, he was snoring on my pillow when I left."

"Cuddles?" Michelle asked.

"Cuddles," Hannah confirmed it. "They were playing chase when we left for dinner."

Hannah held out her arms, but no orange and white twenty-two-pound cat landed anywhere in the vicinity. They walked in, shut the door, and listened to the faint snoring coming from Hannah's bedroom.

"Your guard cat is sleeping," Michelle commented.

"I know. How about you? Are you tired?"

"Not really. Maybe we should bake. That always gets me relaxed enough to go right to sleep."

"Sounds good to me," Hannah said, heading for the kitchen to switch on the lights. "What do you want to bake?"

"Something we can use tomorrow at The Cookie Jar. You decide."

Hannah thought about that for a moment, but before she could decide, the phone rang. She reached up to grab the wall phone that hung near the kitchen table. "Hello?"

"Thank goodness you're home, dear!"

"Mother?" Hannah was surprised. She'd seen her mother less than an hour and a half ago. Surely nothing drastic had happened in that short length of time.

"You weren't in bed, were you?"

"No, Mother. Michelle and I were about to bake. Where are you?"

"At the hospital. We're having some trouble with Barbara tonight."

"What kind of trouble? She's not worse, is she?"

"Not physically. This is very silly, but Jenny's talked to her, Doc's talked to her, and I've talked to her. We just can't make her understand that you're not bringing Moishe back tonight. She insists you said you were."

"Uh-oh!" Hannah sighed deeply as she thought back to her parting words. "Barbara asked me if I'd bring Moishe back and I said I would. I had no idea she wanted me to bring him back after dinner *tonight*."

"That's what we all told her, but she said you promised. And she claims she can't go to sleep until you get here with Moishe. She's very agitated, dear. Doc says he can give her an injection that will put her to sleep, but he hates to do that when she's doing so much better in every other way."

"Tell Doc Knight to hold off. I'll be there

in . . ." Hannah glanced at the clock. "Less than twenty minutes. Better warn her though. Moishe's tired from playing with Cuddles while we were at dinner and he'll probably just fall asleep on her bed."

"I think that's what she wants, dear. She's hoping that Moishe can stay overnight. We can rig up a litter box in Barbara's bathroom. That's no problem. And I can take the rest of Jenny's shift and sleep on her cot in the room."

Hannah made a quick decision. "No, Mother. I'll take Jenny's cot and stay with Barbara and Moishe."

GUAC AD HOC

Hannah's 1st Note: This is Howie Le-vine's guacamole recipe. He's Lake Eden's most popular lawyer.

2 ounces cream cheese

4 ripe avocados (*I used Haas avocados*)

2 Tablespoons lemon juice (*freshly squeezed is best*)

1 clove garlic, finely minced (*you can squeeze it in a garlic press if you have one*)

1/8 cup finely chopped fresh oregano leaves

1 Italian (*or plum*) tomato, peeled, seeded, and chopped

4 green onions, peeled and thinly sliced (*you can use up to 2 inches of the green stem*)

1/2 teaspoon salt

10 grinds of freshly ground pepper (*or 1/8 teaspoon*)

1/2 cup sour cream to spread on top

Bacon bits to sprinkle on top of the sour cream

Tortilla chips as dippers

Howie's Note: I use chopped oregano because Florence doesn't always carry cilantro at the Lake Eden Red Owl. This

guacamole is equally good with either one.

Heat the cream cheese in a medium-sized microwave-safe bowl for 15 seconds on HIGH, or until it's spreadable.

Peel and seed the avocados. Put them in the bowl with the cream cheese and mix everything up with a fork. Mix just slightly short of smooth. You want the mixture to have a few lumps of avocado.

Add the lemon juice and mix it in. It'll keep your Guac Ad Hoc from browning.

Add the minced garlic, chopped oregano leaves, tomato, sliced green onion, salt, and pepper. Mix everything together.

Put your Guac Ad Hoc in a pretty bowl, and cover it with the sour cream. Sprinkle on the bacon bits. If you're NOT going to serve it immediately, spread on the sour cream, but don't use the bacon bits. Cover the bowl with plastic wrap and refrigerate it until time to serve. Then sprinkle on the bacon bits. (*My bacon bits got a little tough when I added them to the bowl and refrigerated it. They were best when I sprinkled them on at the last moment.*)

Hannah's 2nd Note: Mike and Norman like this best if I serve it with sliced, pickled Jalapenos on top. Mother won't touch it that way.

Yield: This amount of Guac Ad Hoc serves 4 unless you're making it for a Super Bowl game. Then you'd better double the recipe.

CHAPTER TWENTY-SIX

"Thank you for coming, Hannah," Barbara said, reaching out for Hannah's hand once Moishe was settled comfortably on her bed. "You don't know how much this means to me." She turned to Jenny. "You can leave now, Jenny. You must be tired. Delores said you worked two shifts today."

"I can stay if you need me," Jenny offered.

"No, but thank you," Hannah said. "You should go home and sleep in your own bed. I'll stay here with Barbara and Moishe."

"A moment, Hannah?" Jenny asked, gesturing toward the hallway outside Barbara's door.

"I'll be right back, Barbara," Hannah said, getting up from the chair to follow Jenny out.

"That's all right. I've got my nice big Moishe to protect me." Barbara stroked Moishe's fur and he purred. "Take your time, Hannah. I'll be fine with Moishe here."

Jenny led Hannah a few steps down the hallway before she spoke. "It's amazing how calm she is now," Jenny said in a hushed voice. "We were all terribly worried about her. Doc Knight took her blood pressure and it was through the roof. Then, the moment we told her that you were on your way with Moishe, she calmed right down. I took her vitals right before you came and everything was perfectly normal."

"Has she mentioned her brother or the white monster again?"

"No, and Doc Knight took her down to radiology when he got back here from dinner. The swelling's almost gone. We're all hoping that's why she hasn't mentioned her brother or the white monster again."

"Me, too. Are there any instructions for me? Anything I should or shouldn't do?"

"Nothing. A nurse will come in to check on her every hour or so. She's off most of her pain meds and those are delivered by the IV drip anyway."

"So nobody will be replacing any bags of medication or anything while I'm here?"

"Not until six in the morning. That's when her day nurse comes on. Do you want me to leave instructions for her to wake you?"

"Yes. That'll give me time to drive home, catch a quick shower, and go to work."

"*If* you can sleep on that cot. It's not the most comfortable bed in the world."

"If I don't, I'll give Michelle my truck and sleep when I get home. I'll be fine, Jenny. Don't waste time worrying about me. I do have a question, though. What do I do if Barbara can't sleep?"

"If you can't sleep either, you can play the name game with her. She loves to play that."

"What is it?"

"It's a game Dr. Schmidt taught me. She's testing it with patients who have brain injuries and also with Alzheimer's patients. The object is to alleviate the anxiety of attempting to remember and simply have fun with silly rhymes and amusing mental pictures."

"And this game is Dr. Love's . . . uh . . ." Hannah stopped speaking and mentally kicked herself for using Dr. Schmidt's radio name. It wasn't public knowledge that Dr. Schmidt, head of the psychology department at the community college, was the voice behind the Dr. Love advice to the lovelorn show on KCOW radio.

"That's all right, Hannah. I know she's Dr. Love. She's my college advisor and she told me."

"That's a relief! I knew I was going to slip up sometime, and I'm glad it happened with

401

someone who already knew. What I meant to ask you was whether Dr. Schmidt's name game is a kind of mnemonic device."

"Yes. That's exactly what it is. And it's certainly worked well with Barbara. She remembers your name by rhyming it with your banana cookies. When I say, *What is the Cookie Lady's name?* She pictures you with a plate of your banana cookies and says, *Banana Hannah.*"

"How about my mother? Does she remember that her name is Delores?"

"Yes, and we had a terrible time thinking of a rhyme or a mental picture for her. Barbara came up with it herself. She imagines your mother singing with a *chorus* and says *Delores.*"

Hannah laughed. "I'm willing to bet that Barbara's never heard my mother sing! What does she do for her dad?"

"His name is Patrick, but that was a little too difficult. I found out from your mother that all his friends called him Paddy. Barbara takes that literally and imagines him eating *a patty* melt at the café. *Patty* sounds like *Paddy* and she remembers that his full name was *Patrick.* That seems to be her most difficult name. Sometimes she remembers it, but at other times she tells me she can't remember her father's name. There seems to be some sort of mental block. I haven't figured out what it is yet."

"Are there any other names I can ask?"

"Yes. Her mother's name, the sheriff's name, the detective's name, and her dentist's name."

"She doesn't call Norman *my dentist* any longer?"

Jenny shook her head. "She calls him *Norman* or *Dr. Rhodes.* She has an image for both names."

"Hannah? Are you coming back?"

It was Barbara's voice and Hannah realized she'd been gone long enough to make Barbara nervous. "I'd better go. I'll let you know how everything goes if we play the name game."

When Hannah walked into the room, Barbara's face lit up in a huge smile. "You're back!" she said. "I'm glad, Hannah. Moishe and I were getting worried."

"You didn't have to worry," Hannah told her. "Jenny was just teaching me how to play the name game with you."

"Can we play it now? I think Moishe is asleep. He's snoring."

Hannah listened for a moment and then she laughed. "He certainly is! He sounds like a buzz saw. Do you remember your dentist's name?"

"I see him with an umbrella in a rain-storm! Storm! That's it! *Stormin' Norman!*"

"Very good!"

"I just learned that one today. Why did you want to talk about Norman?"

"Because he has a cat named Cuddles."

"That's a cute name. Does Moishe know Cuddles?"

"Moishe went to play with Cuddles while Norman and I went out to dinner with Doc Knight and my mother."

"You mother is in a *chorus.* That means your mother is *Delores*!"

"That's right. Norman and I left Moishe at his house with Cuddles. They played chase."

"Moishe chases Cuddles? Or Cuddles chases Moishe?"

"Cuddles always initiates the chase, but it goes both ways. It's a good thing Norman has a big house. They get a lot of exercise."

"And that's why Moishe is so tired." Barbara reached out to stroke Moishe's back as if in sympathy. "Cuddles is younger, isn't she?"

"Yes, quite a bit younger."

"It must be difficult to chase a younger female," Barbara said, laughing a little. "Those are words to live by, Hannah . . . especially if you're our mayor."

Hannah laughed and so did Barbara, but Barbara sobered quickly. "Do you think Moishe will wake up if the monster comes?"

Hannah felt her heart sink down to her toes. It was obvious that Barbara still had one of her delusions. "I'm sure he'll wake up," she said.

"That's a relief. I just know he's coming tonight. There's a moon. There's always a moon when the monster comes. That's how I know he's white." Barbara stopped speaking and frowned. "What is it called when you're white but you shouldn't be? Everyone else around you is colored. It's . . . something to do with lack of pig . . . pig . . . pig-something."

It took Hannah a moment, but then she caught on. "Pigment," she said. "A person or an animal lacking pigmentation is called *albino.*"

"That's it! Albino! My mother said they had an albino hired hand on the farm when she was growing up. He had to wear dark glasses all the time because he had trouble with his eyes. Thank you, Hannah. I'm not sure I would have remembered that word without you."

"You're welcome, Barbara. You mentioned your mother. What was your mother's name?"

"There she is at the kitchen table, eating a big bowl of strawberries. Berries. *Berry.* My mother's name was *Terry.* That's short for *Theresa.* My mother's name was Theresa."

"Wonderful! How about your dad? What was his name?"

"There's Dad at Hal and Rose's Café, eating a patty melt. *Paddy.* That's short for *Patrick.* My dad's name is Patrick."

"What was the former sheriff's name?"

"He's in his office watering a *plant.* It's . . . Sheriff *Grant*!"

"Very good. Now, what was your father's name?"

Barbara was silent for a long moment and then she shook her head. "I don't like that one, Hannah. I don't remember. I'm tired now and I think I want to go to sleep. Is that all right with you?"

"That's fine with me, Barbara. I'm tired, too. I'll sleep right here on the cot."

"All right, Hannah. Sweet dreams."

"And sweet dreams to you, Barbara."

The cot was uncomfortable, but she was tired. Even though she tried to stay awake for a while, Hannah felt herself dozing off. She dreamed of a white monster and she felt her eyes fly open. And there it was! Right there on the wall! It was a shadow, a grotesque shadow that looked like a combination between a rat and a humpback seal. The monster was gliding along the floor.

She must be dreaming. She *had* to be dreaming. The shadow was at least four feet tall and the monster was as long as Barbara's hospital bed. It was stealthy and silent as it traveled around the room, and Hannah didn't seem capable of moving, or calling for help, or doing anything except stare at the monster.

And then there was a thud as something heavy hit the floor. And a screech, followed by a yowl that split the night air.

Moishe was a blur of movement as he hissed, and puffed up to twice his normal size, and confronted something on the floor at the foot of Barbara's bed.

"Moishe!" Hannah sat bolt upright on the cot as something white, a creature much smaller than the menacing shadow, raced toward the window and leaped out through the screen.

Hannah moved faster than she'd ever moved before in her life, jumping off the cot to catch Moishe in mid-air as he was about to leap out of the window in hot pursuit.

"It was the monster!" Barbara exclaimed. "I told you there was a monster! Nobody believed me when I said it was real."

"They'll believe you now," Hannah promised, shutting the window, but not before she saw the torn screen. Then she took Moishe back to Barbara's bed and put him down so that Barbara could pet him.

"My big brave Moishe!" Barbara murmured, petting and soothing him. "What a wonderful brave kitty you are! You saved me, Moishe. I knew you would." And then she turned to Hannah. "The monster was real, wasn't it, Hannah?"

"Yes, it was," Hannah answered, shivering slightly. Perhaps, in the daylight, she might not have been so startled, but the shadow had been truly frightening.

"What was it?" Barbara asked her. "Was it some kind of animal?"

"It was a weasel. Some people call them stoats. I saw a couple of them when I stayed overnight with my grandparents on the farm. The weasels used to try to get into my grandmother's hen house to steal the eggs, but I've never seen any that large before. You were right, Barbara. It was an albino weasel."

"I've never seen a weasel." Barbara's voice was shaking. "No wonder I didn't know what it was! Will it come in here again?"

"Never," Hannah promised her. "The window's shut now so it can't get in. Your screen was torn at the bottom and that's how it got in. I'll find Freddy in the morning and ask him to replace it for you."

CHAPTER TWENTY-SEVEN

"A weasel!" Michelle exclaimed. "No wonder Barbara was scared. They're ugly."

"That's true and its shadow was huge. It was enough to scare me when I saw it."

"And you'd seen weasels before," Delores pointed out.

Lisa gave a little shiver. "I'm glad I wasn't there. I've never seen a weasel and I don't think I want to."

"At least it's all taken care of now," Delores said. "Doc said Freddy replaced that screen at seven this morning. Barbara won't have to worry about monsters anymore."

Just the two-legged kind, Hannah thought, remembering what Barbara had said about her brother.

"I'd better start the coffee in the coffee shop," Lisa said, carrying her coffee cup to the sink.

Michelle was right behind her. "I'll get

the tables ready," she said.

"And I'd better go over to Granny's Attic and get to work. Luanne brought in some items from an estate. I have to price them and put them out on the floor."

Hannah sat there for a moment, wondering what she should be doing. Michelle and Lisa were taking care of the coffee shop, the baking was done, and the industrial dishwasher was washing all the bowls and utensils they'd used. There really wasn't anything for her to do.

"Except to solve Doctor Bev's murder case," Hannah said aloud. "And figure out who attacked Barbara in the penthouse garden."

"Hannah?" Lisa came through the swinging restaurant-type door that led to the coffee shop. "Oh! I thought your mother was still here."

"No, she left right after you went out to the coffee shop."

"But . . . I thought I heard you talking to someone."

"It was no one important," Hannah said with a laugh. "I was just talking to myself."

"I do that all the time. But I've got Sammy so I can always use the excuse that I was talking to the dog."

"Too bad he's not here. I could have used

that excuse." Hannah pointed to the small padded envelope that Lisa was carrying. "What's that?"

"I don't know, but it's for you. I stopped by the post office before I went home yesterday, and this was in our box." Lisa handed it over. "What smells like chocolate?"

"Brownie mix cookies. I decided to use up the brownie mix that Andrea bought for me and I just threw them together as an experiment."

"Can I have one?"

"Sure. Get it from the bottom rack. Those are the Fruit and Nut Brownie Cookies."

Lisa went to get a cookie and Hannah looked at the address on the envelope. It was written in green ink and it read, *Hannah Swensen, The Cookie Jar, Lake Eden, Minnesota.* "No street address," she said.

"I noticed that. There's no zip code either." Lisa took a bite of her cookie and smiled. "These are really good cookies, Hannah."

"Thanks." Hannah looked down at the envelope again. "Our box number's not on here, either. It's a good thing we live in Lake Eden and they know who we are at the post office. I wonder who sent it."

"Maybe you should open it and see what's

inside. There could be a note or something."

"Good idea." Hannah pulled the tear strip on the padded envelope and peered into the envelope. "It doesn't look like there's anything inside." She held the envelope open, turned it upside down, and shook it out on the counter.

There was a clink as something hit the countertop. Both Hannah and Lisa stared at it for a moment and then Lisa asked, "What is it?"

"It's a button. And it's shaped like a . . ." Hannah stopped speaking and grabbed Lisa's hand as she reached for it. "Don't touch it!"

Lisa pulled back quickly. "Why?"

"It's a button from the blouse Barbara wore the night she jumped from the penthouse garden. There could be fingerprints on it. Do we have any paper bags?"

"Sure." Lisa ran to the pantry to get out one of the wax-lined paper bags they used when someone bought one or two cookies to go. "Here."

Hannah considered the bag for a moment and then she shrugged. It was lined with wax, but it would have to do. If she left the button out on the counter, someone would be sure to pick it up and destroy any potential fingerprints.

"Okay," she said, grabbing a paper napkin and pushing the button into the bag. "I'd better call Mike."

"I'll do it," Lisa said, heading back into the coffee shop to use the phone there.

A few seconds later, there was a knock on the back door and Hannah went to answer it. It couldn't be Mike. Lisa had barely had time to pick up the phone and punch in the number for the sheriff's station.

"Norman!" Hannah was pleased when she saw him standing there. "Come in and have coffee. I've got a lot to tell you."

"What did Bev send you?" Norman asked, noticing the envelope on the countertop.

"Doctor Bev?"

"Yes. That's her handwriting." He pointed to the padded envelope on the counter. "And she always used green ink, even years ago when we were in dental school."

Hannah felt her knees turn weak and she leaned heavily against the counter. It was a package from a dead woman, a woman who had been murdered.

"What is it?" Norman hurried over and put his arms around her to steady her. "Take a deep breath, Hannah. You look like you're about to keel over."

"I'm okay now," Hannah said, even though she wasn't entirely sure she was. "It was just a shock, that's all."

"You still look kind of shaky. Do you want some water, or something?"

"Water would be good, but chocolate would be better."

"Where is it?"

Hannah pointed to the baker's rack where her experimental brownie cookies were cooling.

"I figured that around here chocolate would be easy," Norman said, heading over to the baker's rack and picking up a cookie. He carried it over to her and put it in her hand. "Eat this."

Hannah took a huge bite and her eyes began to water. "Where was this cookie? Which rack?" she managed to gasp out.

Norman shrugged. "I think it was the top rack. Do you want me to check?"

"No, but water would be good now. Water would be very, very good! Second thought? Milk! Just bring me the carton. And please hurry!"

Norman was back in very short order with a carton of milk in one hand and a glass in the other. "Here you go," he said, trying to hand her the glass. But Hannah waved the glass away and grabbed the carton. A second later, she was glugging down milk straight out of the carton, something she'd never been allowed to do when she was a child.

"Is there something wrong with this cookie?" Norman asked her, bending down to pick up the rest of the cookie that Hannah had dropped on the floor.

"No. It's perfect. Mike's going to love them when he gets here. Better dump the rest of that cookie in the garbage and wash your hands before you touch your face or rub your eyes."

Norman examined the pieces of cookie he held in his hand, and started to laugh. "Chopped Jalapenos," he said.

"Right. I made three batches of brownie cookies. One has raisins, chocolate chips, and walnuts. They're called Fruit and Nut Brownie Cookies. The second batch has chopped green chilies. They're called Hot Stuff Brownie Cookies. And the third batch has chopped jalapenos. I'm calling those Four Alarm Brownie Cookies."

"And I gave you a cookie from the four alarm batch?"

"Right. And guess what?"

"What?"

"I don't feel at all shaky any longer. I just feel like drinking more milk."

By the time Norman left, Hannah felt much better. She'd told him all about Moishe's encounter with the weasel and he'd shared her excitement over the fact that one of Barbara's delusions hadn't turned out to be a delusion after all. But Norman hadn't been able to offer any reasonable explanation for the button that Doctor Bev had sent to Hannah. They'd gone through the possibilities and had come up with only one scenario that worked. The crime scene team had missed the button when they'd searched the penthouse and Doctor Bev had come across it when she'd moved some of her things to the penthouse on the morning of her death.

The oven timer rang and Hannah took the final batch of cookies from the oven. The Cookie Jar was crowded again today and she'd mixed up a batch of Old-Fashioned Sugar Cookies just in case the dozens and dozens of cookies they'd already baked weren't enough. Once the cookie sheets were on the racks and cooling, Hannah sat down with a cup of fresh coffee and thought about the package that Doctor Bev had sent her.

There were so many unanswered questions. Why hadn't Doctor Bev written her name anywhere on the envelope? Was it because she had wanted to remain anonymous? Or had Doctor Bev simply dropped the envelope in a handy mailbox, intending to tell Hannah where she'd found it before it came in the mail? There was another possibility, a darker possibility that neither Norman nor Hannah had mentioned. Was Doctor Bev the person who had attacked Barbara? She hadn't been a large woman, but neither was Barbara and Doctor Bev was younger and stronger. But then why had Barbara told them that her *brother* had attacked her? If Barbara was unable to remember Doctor Bev's name, wouldn't she have said her *sister* instead of her *brother*?

Hannah gave a sigh of pure frustration. She simply couldn't explain why Doctor Bev had sent the button to her. That was the trouble with trying to devise a likely scenario when you were missing key pieces of the puzzle. There was only one person who could have filled in the gaps and that person, Doctor Bev, had been murdered before she could explain anything to anybody.

"Lisa called the station and said you needed me," Mike said, walking into the kitchen from the coffee shop. "What's up, Hannah?"

Hannah pointed to the padded envelope on the counter. "This," she said. "It came in yesterday's mail and I opened it this

418

morning. The only thing inside the envelope was a button from the blouse Barbara was wearing the night she was attacked."

"Did you touch the button?"

"No. I used a paper napkin to push it in here." Hannah handed him the small paper bag.

Mike opened the bag and glanced inside. "It's pretty small and it's got a rough surface, but maybe they can recover some partials. You touched the envelope when you opened it, didn't you?"

"Yes, and so did Lisa. She got it out of our box at the post office and she carried it in here to me."

"I think we can forget about fingerprints on the envelope. It went through the mail and it must have been handled by several people including Lisa and you." Mike walked over and picked up the envelope to examine it. "There's nothing distinctive about the envelope. You can buy them at any stationary store. No return address?"

"None, but I know who it's from."

Mike looked surprised. "You do?"

"Yes. Norman recognized the handwriting. And the fact that it was addressed in green ink convinced him that it was from Doctor Bev."

Mike's eyes narrowed. "And you're sure

the button is from Barbara's blouse? Maybe somebody else had the same outfit."

"No. We noticed the buttons the night of the party. Barbara told us her outfit was a designer original from Beau Monde Fashions. Claire would never sell two outfits that were exactly the same." When Mike looked perfectly clueless, Hannah laughed. "Never mind. It's something a guy would never understand. Let's just say that I'm almost positive no other woman in town has a button like that."

Mike stared at the button for a moment and then he looked up at Hannah. "So what do you think? Was Doctor Bev trying to tell you that *she* attacked Barbara?"

Hannah shook her head. "I don't think so. That would mean that she felt guilty and wanted to confess. And I don't think she ever felt guilty in her life."

"You're probably right about that."

"There's another reason I don't believe she attacked Barbara. What possible motive could she have? She barely knew Barbara."

"So you have any idea why she sent the button to you?"

"None whatsoever. Norman and I talked about it. It could be something as simple as the crime scene techs missed the button when they searched the penthouse and she found it later."

Mike shook his head. "I'm almost sure that didn't happen. I was there and I saw them go over every inch of the place."

"How about the penthouse garden?"

"They raked all the dirt and vacuumed everything else. If that button was there, they would have found it."

"How about outside in the rose garden where Barbara landed?"

"They raked that, too. I don't believe Doctor Bev found that button in or around the hotel. I think she came across it somewhere else."

"Okay, but why did she send it to me?"

"Because she knew you were Barbara's friend and you'd visited her in the hospital."

"How would she know that?"

"Roger may have mentioned seeing you there."

"Why didn't she just hand it to me on the Petersons' front porch?"

"She might have mailed it already."

Hannah was silent for a moment and then she shook her head. "Time for truth, Mike. You know and I know that none of this makes any sense. Agreed?"

Mike didn't look happy, but he nodded. "Agreed."

"Doctor Bev sends me a button from the

blouse Barbara was wearing when she was almost killed, and then, right after she mails it, Doctor Bev is murdered. What does that tell you?"

"What does it tell *you*?"

"It tells me that Doctor Bev knew who tried to kill Barbara. And that person murdered Doctor Bev before she could tell anyone about it."

Mike was silent for a long moment. "You could be right," he finally said.

"I *know* I'm right. But that doesn't get us any closer to identifying the killer, does it?"

"Not really. Did you find out anything new, Hannah? I know you've been working on this."

"A few things, but I'm not sure where they fit. How about you?"

"Same here. I've got a bunch of unrelated facts that don't seem to form any sort of a pattern."

Hannah sighed and then she looked him straight in the eyes. "I'll tell you if you'll tell me."

"Deal," Mike said. "But if you tell anyone we shared information, I'll deny it."

"I'll never tell. How about you?"

"I won't tell either." Mike reached out to take her hand and squeeze it. "Our secret?"

"Our secret," Hannah agreed, squeezing

back. "How about coffee, cookies, and clues in that order? I've got some Four Alarm Brownie Cookies you might like. They've got chopped jalapenos in them."

"Sounds good to me," Mike said. "I'll pour the coffee."

"And I'll get the cookies." Hannah headed to the baker's rack to dish up the cookies. When she came back, Mike had already set their mugs of coffee on the stainless steel work island and he was taking his notebook out of his pocket.

Hannah set the plate of cookies in front of him, but she kept the shorthand notebook she called her murder book in her hand. "So we're really going to do this?"

Mike opened his notebook and shoved it over to her. "Here you go. Get ready to read."

"And here's mine," Hannah said, opening hers to the first page and handing it over.

THREE-WAY BROWNIE COOKIES

1. Fruit And Nut Brownie Cookies
2. Hot Stuff Brownie Cookies
3. Four Alarm Brownie Cookies

Preheat oven to 350 degrees F., rack in the middle position, for all three types of brownie cookies.

1. To make **Fruit and Nut Brownie Cookies,** follow the recipe below:
2. To make **Hot Stuff Brownie Cookies,** leave out the cinnamon, raisins, and chopped nuts. Add one small can of chopped green chilies, well drained and patted dry with paper towels.
3. To make **Four Alarm Brownie Cookies,** leave out the cinnamon, raisins, and nuts. Add one small can chopped jalapenos, well drained and patted dry with paper towels. (*If you can find a can already chopped, use those. If you can't, you'll have to chop your jalapeno peppers by hand.*)

1 box brownie mix (*the kind that makes an 8-inch square pan*)

3 Tablespoons all-purpose flour
1/2 teaspoon cinnamon
1/2 cup chopped nuts (**your choice — I used walnuts**)
1/3 cup vegetable oil
2 large eggs
1/2 cup chocolate chips
1/2 cup raisins

Spray cookie sheets with Pam or another nonstick cooking spray, or line them with parchment paper and spray that.

Pour the dry brownie mix into a mixing bowl. Add the 3 Tablespoons of flour and the cinnamon. Mix thoroughly. (**I used a fork to do this.**)

Add the chopped nuts and mix them with the dry ingredients to coat them.

In a separate bowl, whisk the oil and the eggs together.

Pour the egg mixture into the bowl with the brownie mix. Stir until everything is combined, but DO NOT OVERSTIR.

Stir in the chocolate chips and the raisins.

Drop the cookies by rounded teaspoonfuls onto the cookie sheet, 12 cookies to a standard-sized sheet.

Hannah's 1st Note: If you wet your fingers, you can shape these cookies into rounded mounds.

Bake these cookies at 350 degrees F. for 8 to 10 minutes. (*Mine took the full 10 minutes.*) To test for doneness, lightly touch the top of a cookie. If it feels firm to the touch, they're done.

Cool on the cookie sheet for 2 minutes and then remove the cookies to a wire rack to cool completely.

Hannah's 2nd Note: This recipe is so easy, I gave it to Andrea. It's a first cousin to her "whippersnapper" cookie recipes. The only difference is that her recipes use cake mix, and this recipe uses brownie mix. My youngest niece, Bethie, adores these cookies. Her favorites are the Hot Stuff Brownie Cookies variation. She says they tickle her tongue and she calls them "Hot Chockitts".

CHAPTER TWENTY-EIGHT

It hadn't done a particle of good and Hannah was depressed when Mike left. She'd told him she knew about Barbara's attempted murder and Doctor Bev's actual murder. Mike had been equally forthcoming, but they still hadn't been able to narrow the suspect list. Actually, neither one of them even *had* a suspect list. The best they'd been able to come up with was that the attack on Barbara had been a random act of violence perpetrated by an unknown suspect. They had agreed that the attack against Barbara and Doctor Bev's murder could be connected somehow, but they were unable to identify exactly what that connection was.

Hannah was still trying to fit the new information she'd learned from Mike into what she'd already discovered when her cell phone rang. She jumped up from her stool and hurried to the counter, where her cell phone was plugged into the charger. She unhooked it and answered, "Hello?"

"Hannah. This is Jenny from the hospital. Your mother gave me your cell phone number."

"Hi, Jenny," Hannah said, wondering why Jenny had called. "Barbara's all right, isn't she?"

"Barbara's fine, now that Moishe chased away the monster and Freddy fixed her screen."

"It's good to know that Barbara was right about the monster. And it's entirely understandable that she didn't know what to call it since she'd never seen a weasel before. It makes me wonder about her other delusions, and whether there's some sort of reasonable explanation for those, too."

"I hope there is. Barbara and I have been working on her delusion about her father and we've had an interesting development. Do you remember when I told you about the name game and Barbara's block about her father's name?"

"I remember."

"We just tried it again and we had the same block. She remembers that her dad's name is Patrick, but she blocked when I asked her about her father's name. That was when it suddenly occurred to me that perhaps the word *father* means another person to her, a person that isn't her dad."

"Like who?" Hannah asked.

"Like her priest. Barbara's records show she's Catholic. And many Catholic families refer to their priest as *Father*. That's why I called you. Your mother said the Catholic priest's name is Father Coultas. I tried that with Barbara and she knew who he was, but she still blocked when I asked her for her father's name. I called you to see if you had any suggestions."

Hannah thought about that for a moment. "Yes. We call the Lutheran minister Reverend Bob. Maybe Barbara's parents called the Catholic priest by his first name."

"Do you know what it is?"

"Yes, it's Paul. Does she get any mental images when you ask her about her father?"

"I'll find out. If it rhymes with Paul, we are on to something. I'll call you as soon as I find out."

After she hung up the phone, Hannah paged through her murder book again. There was something she was forgetting. She turned to the notes she'd made about their confrontation with Doctor Bev on the front porch of the Peterson house and one line jumped out at her. *Said she's already taken some things up to the penthouse.*

Mike's detective team had already searched through Doctor Bev's personal possessions at the Lake Eden Inn, but they hadn't searched the things she'd taken up to the penthouse at the hotel. The baking was done for the day. She could leave now, if she chose. Hannah was about to call Andrea to see if her sister would let her into the penthouse to search when her cell phone rang again.

"Hello," Hannah said, after she'd switched it on.

"Hi, Hannah. It's Jenny again. I tried *Paul* as her father's name, and Barbara said that wasn't right. Then I asked her if she had a mental picture of her father and she told me that he was sitting underground in a cave or a cavern. Does that mean anything to you?"

"Not really, unless you can think of something that rhymes with *spelunker.*"

Jenny laughed. "Somehow I don't think that's it."

"Neither do I. Any other ideas?"

"Not at the moment. I'll think about it though."

"How about Barbara's brother? Does she have any mental pictures for him?"

"No. She says it's just a blank in her mind."

"Call me back if Barbara comes up with anything new. I'll have my cell phone with me."

"I really hate to bother you like this, Hannah."

"You're not bothering me. Barbara's my friend and I want to help in any way I can."

Once she'd ended the call, Hannah sat down on her stool again. Barbara pictured her father in a cave or a cavern. That was a new development and at least she had a mental image now. Perhaps it would become clearer as the swelling in her brain abated and then the mystery would be solved.

"Thanks, Andrea," Hannah said as they parked in the reserved section for the penthouse. "I really appreciate this."

"That's okay. I'm curious, too. I want to find out what things Doctor Bev moved."

Hannah got out of Andrea's Volvo just as huge drops of rain began to fall. They hit the dusty pavement sending up little puffs of dust as she followed her sister into the lobby of the hotel. "Why do you want to see what Doctor Bev moved?" Hannah asked.

"Because the last time I moved, I took the most important things first. I'm just curious to see if she did the same thing."

Hannah thought about that as they walked

through the beautiful lobby to the penthouse elevator. "I'll bet she did. I know I did. When I moved from Mother's house to my condo, I brought my books and my boxes of recipes first."

"Oh." Andrea gave a little sigh.

"What's the matter?"

"I'm embarrassed."

"Why?"

"Because the first things I moved were my nail polish collection and my makeup. Do you think I'm terrible?"

"No, I think you're Andrea. Don't ever change. I love you just the way you are."

Andrea smiled the most beautiful smile Hannah had ever seen. "Thank you, Hannah. I hope you never change either."

As the two sisters approached the elevator, there was a loud crack of thunder that made both of them jump, and the lights flickered several times. A bright flash of lightning lit the lobby with an almost iridescent white light, and Hannah blinked several times in response to the brightness. When she could see normally again, she noticed that the lights had dimmed to pale amber. A moment later they were back to full luminescence.

"Uh-oh," Andrea said, pulling Hannah back from the elevator doors. "No way we're taking the elevator. The power might go out."

Hannah agreed wholeheartedly. The last thing she wanted to do was get stuck in the penthouse elevator while an electrical storm raged overhead. "I guess we'll have to wait until tomorrow," she said.

"Wrong. Follow me." Andrea led Hannah to a door several feet from the elevator. "We'll take the stairs." She unlocked the door, switched on the lights, and beckoned Hannah inside. "Don't worry. I've got the flashlight on my phone if the lights go out and the emergency generator doesn't work."

"They installed the new one?" Hannah asked, remembering that Andrea had mentioned replacing the old generator.

"Yes. Roger told me they put it in yesterday, but I'm not sure it's hooked up yet. And I don't want to go down there to look because it's scary down there."

"How is it scary?"

"It's a full basement, but you have to know which hallway to take to get where you want to go. They're really narrow hallways, almost like tunnels, and I'm always afraid I'll get lost and I'll never be able to find the stairway to get out. You almost have to leave a trail of breadcrumbs like Hansel and Gretel, you know?"

"I understand. I'm not fond of old basements myself."

"It's just that it smells damp and musty, and you know that you're under the ground. Every time you come around a corner, you expect to see a mole, or a rabbit, or a groundhog." Andrea reached out for the railing. "Come on, Hannah. Let's go. This staircase goes up to the third floor."

Up to the third floor? Hannah repeated her sister's words in her mind and added a question mark. Perhaps climbing up to the third floor would be easy for Andrea, but she wasn't looking forward to the climb. "Is this the servant's staircase you told me about?"

"Yes. It was really a single-person staircase when it was built, but Roger had the contractors widen it and it's a lot better now. Now it's big enough for two to climb up together."

"Two what?" Hannah asked, dropping behind her sister after the first few steps. "Two anorexic toddlers?"

Andrea laughed. "I know it's not very wide even now, but you should have seen it before the contractors enlarged it. Remember Barbara's mother?"

"Theresa Donnelly? Yes, of course I do."

"When she worked at the Albion in her

senior year at Jordan High, she must have been a whole lot thinner than she was when we knew her. I saw a photo of her on the third floor landing and there was barely enough room for her to carry up a breakfast tray."

Hannah didn't say anything. She was too busy trying to breathe as they crossed the second floor landing. Andrea was like a gazelle leading the way, and she felt like an elephant lumbering up the stairs.

"Almost there," Andrea said, taking the last five steps in staccato rhythm and crossing the third floor landing to the door at the top of the stairs. "Just wait a second and I'll unlock it."

Just wait a second? Hannah might have laughed if she'd had the breath for it. Of course she'd wait a second. She wasn't going to move until she stopped panting.

Luckily, Andrea had trouble with the key and it took at least a minute before the tumblers rolled back and the door opened. "Here we are, Hannah," she announced.

"Great," Hannah said, finding her voice for one word at least.

Andrea stepped in and flicked on the lights. "Where do you want to start?" she asked.

"Let's look around and see if we can spot

the things that Doctor Bev moved in."

"I know there's nothing of hers in here," Andrea said, glancing around the kitchen. "It was perfectly bare when they delivered the furniture. There was nothing in the living room either. I would have noticed. Let's try the master bedroom. She might have put something in one of the closets."

"That sounds . . ." Hannah's comment was interrupted by another boom of thunder and a near-blinding flash of lightning. "Does this place have lightning rods?" she asked.

"You don't need them on the roof anymore. They have built-ins now. Come on, Hannah. Let's go check the closets."

Hannah followed her sister into the master bedroom. The master closet had double doors and Andrea opened them. "I thought so!" she said, spying several matching suitcases on the floor. "This wasn't here the night of the party. I showed several people the closets."

Andrea carried the suitcase to the bed and opened it as Hannah watched. The clothes inside were clearly new. Their tags were still attached.

"Wow!" Andrea said, pulling out a pair of white leather pants and a matching vest. "I'd kill for something like this."

Maybe someone did, Hannah thought, not

eliminating jealousy as a motive. *Did Roger have any serious girlfriends in Minneapolis who might be inclined to get rid of his new fiancée so that they could try to take her place?*

"Jewelry," Andrea breathed, opening a cleverly constructed velvet folder that contained pockets and slots for rings, necklaces and bracelets. "Oh, Hannah! Just look at this one!"

Hannah looked and knew just enough about jewelry to echo Andrea's gasp. The necklace Andrea was regarding with an emotion bordering on reverence glittered with diamonds and rubies. "Is it real?" she asked, hardly daring to believe that it was.

"Oh, yes. And it's probably worth twice the price of this expensive penthouse."

"Enough," Hannah said, reaching out to close the velvet jewelry folder. "Let's see what else is here."

Five minutes passed as they went through the contents of a second suitcase, and another five or six minutes were taken up with a third. They were about to open the fourth matching leather suitcase when Andrea's cell phone rang.

"Hello?" she answered. As Hannah watched, worry lines furrowed her forehead. "But I thought Mrs. Dunwright was coming to pick you up from dance class."

That was enough to tell Hannah that her niece Tracey was calling. She waited as Andrea gripped the phone a bit tighter.

"Of course I will," Andrea said. "Don't worry about a thing, Tracey. Just tell Florence I'm on my way. There's lightning outside, so stay inside the Red Owl with Karen until I get there."

"Sorry, Hannah," Andrea said, as she ended the call. "Tracey and Karen Dunwright are stuck at the Red Owl and I have to go pick them up. I'll take them to the house and be back here in ten minutes, okay?"

"That's fine," Hannah said. "I'll go through the fourth suitcase and look around for anything else."

It didn't take long to go through the fourth suitcase. When she was finished, Hannah put it back in the walk-in closet and shut the door. As she went back into the living room, she heard her cell phone ringing in her purse.

"Coming!" she called out, even though there was no one to hear her. And for once she was lucky, locating her cell phone almost immediately and answering it before the caller hung up. "Hello?" she said quickly.

"Thank goodness you answered!" Jenny said, sounding relieved. "Barbara asked me to call you. She remembered something else about her father. She said he was underground in a cave or a cavern and there were lots of rabbits down there with him. What's that, Barbara?" There was a pause and then Jenny came back on the line. "Barbara says it's not a silly rhyme like Stormin' Norman, or Berry and Terry. It's just where he is."

"Okay," Hannah said, already going through the possibilities. "Tell Barbara thank you. And please call me if she thinks of anything else."

"I'm only here for another ten minutes or so. Then another nurse comes on."

"Okay. Ask Barbara to call me if she thinks of anything else. Write down my cell phone number for her before you leave."

"All right, but I'm not sure. . . ."

Jenny's voice trailed off and Hannah knew she didn't want to express any doubts about Barbara's ability to call while Barbara was listening to their conversation. "I understand," Hannah said, "but it's worth a shot. She called me before and she might be able to call me again."

"I'll give Barbara your cell phone number before I leave," Jenny promised. "Have a good night, Hannah."

"I will if Andrea ever comes back here," Hannah said, watching as rain began to pepper the penthouse windows.

"Where are you?"

"At the penthouse in the hotel."

"The penthouse? What are you doing up there?"

"Andrea and I needed to check something out, but she got called away."

"You must be investigating."

"You're right, but it didn't work out the way I hoped. Have a nice night, Jenny. I'll talk to you soon. And don't forget to give Barbara my number."

As Hannah hung up, another flash of lightning streaked across the sky. Almost immediately, rain began to hit the windows, harder and harder until it formed sheets of water. The lights flickered again, and Hannah fervently wished that Andrea would hurry so that she could go home to her familiar condo and Moishe. And just as she wished it, the lights flickered one more time and went out.

"Oh, great!" Hannah groaned, hoping against hope that the emergency generator would kick in. She waited a full minute, but nothing happened. It was apparent that the new generator in the bowels of the basement wasn't yet operational.

Hannah stuffed her cell phone into the pocket of her summer-weight jacket and sat down on one of the expensive leather couches that Doctor Bev and Roger had ordered. The power was out and there was nothing to do but watch the summer storm rage outside the windows.

Think about something else, her mind told her and Hannah did. She thought about Barbara's father, underground in a cave or cavern, surrounded by rabbits. Andrea had mentioned something about rabbits when she was describing the basement. Accompanied by the booming of thunder, the startling flashes of lightning, and the drumming of rain against the windows, Hannah thought back to what her sister had said. *Every time you come around a corner, you expect to see a mole, or a rabbit, or a groundhog.*

Hannah let her mind roam freely. *Hallways like narrow tunnels. Interconnected. Moles. Groundhogs. Rabbits.* Barbara had said that her father was surrounded by rabbits in a . . .

"Warren!" Hannah shouted, startling herself. "It was a rabbit warren! Her father's name is Warren!"

How many men named Warren did she know? Hannah thought about that for a moment. There was Warren Strandberg, the minister of the Bible Church in Lake Eden, but he'd only been here for ten years or so. She wasn't sure where he'd lived before he came to Lake Eden, but unless he was from one of the neighboring towns, it was unlikely that he could be Barbara's father.

There was Warren Frank, the son of the man who owned the bait shop at Eden Lake. He was in his mid-thirties and couldn't possibly be Barbara's father.

Warren Drevlow was a possibility. He was the right age. But Hannah wasn't sure how long he'd been in . . .

Her cell phone rang, interrupting her train of thought. She retrieved it and answered, "Hello?"

"Hannah! It's Barbara!"

"Hi, Barbara." Hannah was pleasantly surprised. Barbara had managed to punch in the correct numbers for her cell phone. "Is Jenny still there?"

"No, she left. I'm all alone and my brother tried to kill me again!"

"What?!"

"You've got to believe me, Hannah. This time I've got proof. He put something in my bag."

"Your bag," Hannah repeated and then

she gasped. "Do you mean your IV drip bag?"

"That's right, but don't worry. I pretended I was sleeping and I had my arms under the sheet. The minute he touched the bag I pinched off the tube."

"That was quick thinking!"

"Thank you. I knew what he was going to do because he said, *Say goodbye, Sis. Now I'll be rid of you for good.* And then he put something in the bag. And then, when he left, I pulled out the needle."

Hannah swallowed hard. What she'd just heard was truly frightening. "Ring for the nurse, Barbara. And if there's an emergency button, hit it! Don't let anyone hook you back up to that IV drip."

"Don't worry. I won't. And I won't let them throw out the bag, either. I want Doc to test it to see what my monster brother put in there."

"That's smart, Barbara." Hannah was impressed with Barbara's presence of mind. "Did you see your brother's face? Can you describe it for me?"

"I can't describe him, Hannah. I only had my eyes open a tiny bit. And I can't remember his name, but I remembered my silly picture for him."

"What is it?" Hannah asked, feeling her

heart begin to race in excitement.

"He's standing at home plate with a bat. He's in the World Series and he's wearing a blue and white uniform. I know it's a silly rhyme, but I can't remember the names of the teams."

Hannah thought fast. It had to be a pro team that wore blue and white uniforms. "The Toronto Blue Jays."

There was a pause while Barbara considered it. "No, not them."

"How about the Kansas City Royals?"

"No. I don't think that's it, either."

"I wish I could think of more teams, but . . . wait! How about the Dodgers?"

"That's it. He's *Roger* the *Dodger.* Do you believe me, Hannah?"

All the pieces of information in her head rose up into a whirlwind and snapped into place. Barbara was Warren Dalworth's daughter. And Roger was her half-brother. And unless she was way off base, Warren had called in a lawyer to change his will to include Barbara. He'd done the decent thing by telling Roger about it and Roger had decided to kill his half-sister so that he could have Dalworth Enterprises and its millions all to himself.

"Do you believe me?" Barbara asked again.

"Yes, I believe you," Hannah told her. "I know you're right, Barbara."

"Then you have to believe this. I think Roger was standing outside my room when Jenny called you and told you about the rabbits. And he knows where you are because he must have heard Jenny ask you if you were in the penthouse investigating. You have to get out of there, Hannah! I think he's going to come looking for you next!"

"Barbara. Listen to me!" Hannah went into near-panic mode. "Ring for the nurse, hit the emergency button, and then call Mike at the sheriff's station. Tell him I'm up in the penthouse and Roger is coming here to kill me like he killed Doctor Bev. I'll give you the number of the sheriff's station. It's . . ."

"Stop," Barbara interrupted. "I worked there almost all of my life, Hannah. I know the number. I'll call Mike's cell, too. Just get out of the penthouse. And if you can't get out fast enough, find a good place to hide until Mike gets there."

CHAPTER TWENTY-NINE

Hannah grabbed her purse and slung it over her shoulder. Then she punched in Andrea's number on her cell phone. "Andrea?" she said when her sister answered. "Don't come back to the penthouse. Roger killed Doctor Bev and he just tried to kill Barbara again. Call Mike and tell him to hurry. Roger could be here any minute."

"Roger's there, Hannah. I'm just driving past the garage and his car's parked in the penthouse section."

"Is he still in his car?"

"No. Get out of there, Hannah! Hurry! I'll call Mike!"

There was a click and Andrea was gone. As she slipped her cell phone back into her pocket, Hannah had the feeling of being abandoned, of losing her sole connection to normal life. Somehow she managed to shake off the feeling. It could stop her from thinking clearly and she needed to keep her wits about her.

Leave now, every instinct told her. *You can get down to the second floor before he can get up here. Leave your purse here so he thinks you're hiding here. Make him take the time to look for you up here. That'll give you time to go the rest of the way down to street level. And once you're there, you can run for your life.*

Acting almost instantaneously, Hannah tossed her purse on a chair and made a beeline for the stairwell door. She was halfway down to the landing when she realized that she didn't have the key to open the door to the second floor. There was nowhere to go but back up.

She turned, grabbed the rail and hurried up. She was on the second step from the top when she heard the door at the bottom of the stairwell bang open.

Heavy footfalls began to ascend the stairs, but Hannah didn't stick around to see if it was Roger. She took the final two steps at a leap and went through the door to the penthouse, slamming the deadbolt home behind her. It wouldn't stop him for long, but it could buy her time enough to find a good hiding place.

A second later, she'd retrieved her purse from the chair and was hurrying to a second staircase, this one leading to the penthouse garden. With energy born of fear, she climbed those stairs faster than she'd ever climbed stairs before, and she emerged under the see-through dome at a run.

Where should she hide? Hannah hesitated for a split second before her mind provided the answer. She'd hide where he'd never expect her to hide, *outside* the dome in the rain.

The moment she thought of it, Hannah raced across the expanse of the rooftop garden and picked up the remote that controlled the window-washing safety cage. She aimed the remote at the area Andrea had shown her and pressed the button. Slowly, much too slowly to suit Hannah, the cage came out of its sheltered dock and began to move toward the hinged window.

For someone who didn't enjoy heights, thinking about swaying out there in the wind and the rain wasn't pleasant. As a matter of fact, it was downright terrifying. She reminded herself that getting killed by the man who'd murdered Doctor Bev and had tried to kill Barbara twice was even more terrifying. Given the choice, she would much prefer braving the elements at a dizzying height, even in a thunderstorm.

At last, after seeming to take forever, the

cage reached the entrance point. Hannah shut off the remote, opened the hinged window panel and sent up a quick prayer for Mike to hurry as she stepped into the cage. As she closed the hinged panel behind her, a bolt of lightning so bright it almost blinded her zigzagged down from the sky to the earth. It was followed by a clap of thunder so loud it shook the cage.

Hannah blinked several times and shielded her eyes from the pouring rain so that she could see the internal controls. They were clearly marked with arrows that she could see, even in the rain. All she had to do was push the control left to go left, return it to the center to stop, and right to go right. As she set the cage into motion, she noticed that there was a large red button marked *Emergency Stop*. She didn't really want to consider what type of situation would necessitate an emergency stop, at least not right now. Roger could come through the stairwell door any moment and the cage seemed to take forever to reach its docking point.

The wind whipped her hair against her eyes and Hannah used the sleeve of her jacket to wipe them again. Another bolt of lightning sliced across the sky and again, it was almost immediately followed by a deafening clap of thunder. If the lightning kept flashing and Roger reached the rooftop garden before the cage docked, he'd see her!

Hannah dropped to the floor of the cage and huddled in a corner, trying to shield herself from the elements. Of course that didn't do much good. The cage was formed of heavy metal mesh and the rain came through from what seemed to be every direction. She shielded the top of her head from the rain with a rag that someone had left on the cage floor. It smelled vaguely of some acidic substance, probably ammonia, and as the lightning flashed again, Hannah noticed a squirt bottle of eco-friendly window washing fluid in a pouch attached to the side of the cage.

Time seemed to slow and almost stop as the cage journeyed slowly toward its enclosure. She huddled there, wet and shivering, hoping that the cage would dock before Roger realized that she must be up here. She was only inches from safety when the door to the stairwell burst open and Roger ran through. She caught one glimpse of his enraged and desperate face as the cage disappeared behind the wall and slid into its dock.

"Hurry, Mike!" Hannah whispered as she reached down to retrieve her purse to search the contents for any type of weapon. Unless several ballpoint pens and an old stick of soothing balm for chapped lips could somehow aid in her defense, she was out of luck. There was something else on the floor and Hannah picked it up. It was the remote. She'd taken it with her. Would Roger notice that it was missing from the pocket on the wall? Should she have returned it to the pocket before she'd climbed into the safety cage? Hannah thought about that for a moment and decided that it was six of one, half-dozen of the other. If she'd returned the remote to the pocket, it wouldn't be missing, but Roger could use the electronic device to activate the mechanism and bring her place of hiding back to him as smoothly as a metal duck gliding by in a shooting gallery.

Hannah wasn't sure which was worse, hiding out of sight and not being able to watch what was happening, or being able to see Roger search for her. The tension of waiting in the dark in the small enclosure was so high it was physically painful. Her breath caught in her throat and she thought she'd never be able to breathe again. And then, right when she was beginning to panic, her body forced her to take the next shuddering, gasping breath to start the cycle all over again. Every muscle in her body cramped, leaving her in agony and unable to do more than shake from the cold and her fear. And then she heard it. The access pane, the one she'd shut so carefully after she'd stepped into the cage, crashed open and Roger's voice boomed over the noise of the thunder, and the wind, and the rain.

"I know where you are, Hannah. Come back!"

Not on a bet! Hannah's mind answered, but she said nothing. Instead she waited, her finger poised over the emergency stop button. If Roger had another remote and he tried to bring the cage back to him, she'd hit the button and hope that it would override any other commands.

Nothing, absolutely nothing happened. Long moments passed as Hannah waited in fear and in dread. Roger was completely insane if he thought she might move the cage to the entrance point simply because he'd asked her to do it. Or was this some type of trick? Was he lulling her into a false sense of security so that he could get to her another way?

"Come to me, Hannah!" Roger called out again. "Come to me, or I'll come to get you. And it'll be much worse for you if I have to do that!"

Hannah ignored the implication. If she

moved the cage to him, he'd kill her. That was a foregone conclusion. He wanted her to think that he could come to the docking station to get her, but he couldn't. There was no way he could come to get her unless he stepped out onto the track outside of the dome and inched his way around to the docking station. Surely he wouldn't do that . . . would he? Was he crazy and desperate enough to do that?

Delay, her mind said and she agreed. She was almost positive that Barbara would call Mike. And she knew that Andrea would. Help could be here any moment and all she had to do was keep Roger talking until they came to arrest him.

It was counterintuitive to get closer to the man who wanted to kill her, but Hannah did it anyway. She was almost certain he didn't have a gun or he would have leaned out the window to shoot her by now. It was hand-to-hand and Roger was strong. He would win, but she wouldn't let him get that close. She had no intention of bringing the cage close enough to the opening so that he could grab her. Or stab her. Or bludgeon her. Or whatever. She would stay at more than arm's length away at all times. And she would keep him talking until help came through the door.

"Okay," she called out in a voice so steady that it surprised her. "I'm coming. Just tell me why you tried to kill Barbara."

There was a loud rumble of thunder and then he answered. "The first time? Or the time I actually killed her?" he asked.

And then he gave a laugh that chilled Hannah to the bone. It was clear that Roger had slipped over the edge. He was crazed, insane, homicidal, dangerous, maniacal, psychotic . . . but she didn't have time to think of all the words that applied to Roger now. She had to keep him talking until Mike arrived.

"I want to know about the first time," Hannah yelled out between claps of thunder. "How did you get her up here alone?"

"That was easy. She was already here. I just moved a barricade and told her that since she was with me, she was perfectly safe and I'd show her the view."

Hannah waited until the rumble of thunder had faded away. "The view of her house?"

"Of course."

"But why did you try to kill her?"

"I'm surprised you haven't figured it out by now, Hannah. Everyone says you're smart. It's because she's my half-sister and she was going to get part of my inheritance.

I couldn't let that happen."

"So you attacked her?"

"Yes, with a hammer. Move closer, Hannah," Roger said, noticing that she'd stopped the forward motion of the cage. "You're delaying."

"It's just because I want the whole story. Did your father actually write a will that gave Barbara half?"

"Of course not. He gave her a fourth. He knew how hard I'd been working for him and he knew I deserved the lion's share."

"Of course you did," Hannah appeased him. "But why kill Barbara when you got so much more than she did?"

"Because she didn't deserve anything!" Roger howled above the sound of the wind and the rain. "She'd done nothing! I gave my life for Dalworth Enterprises!"

"Really?" Hannah asked, knowing full-well she had nothing to lose. "I thought you made a good living from your father's corporation."

"Oh, I did, but not good enough. I'm worth much more. I'm worth more than a hundred percent and Barbara was cutting into my share."

"I see," Hannah said, hoping that the door would crash open and Mike would arrive.

"Come closer, Hannah. And then I'll tell

you more. I know you want to know everything."

"I do want to know," Hannah said, sliding
the control knob to forward. The cage
moved slowly a few feet toward Roger and
then she stopped it. "Why did you need so
much money?"

"Because I had debts! It's not easy running Dalworth Enterprises. You have to pay
off everybody to get the permits you need.
My father never understood that, so I had
to play some games with the books. Everybody does it. And then there were expenses.
You have to look like you have money when
you're playing with the big boys."

He cooked the books, Hannah's mind said,
*and I'll bet most of those mythical payoffs
were for him.* But Hannah didn't say that.
Instead, she tried to sound very sympathetic. "I understand," she said.

"Good." Roger sounded pleased that she
understood. "Come here, Hannah. I don't
think there's anything more you need to
know."

"Oh, but there is!" Hannah said, moving
another foot or two closer. "I have to know
why you killed Doctor Bev."

"She was a leech! And she was a cheat!
She was blackmailing me once she found
out I tried to kill Barbara. She came up in

the elevator and she saw me hit Barbara. And then she saw Barbara jump off the roof."

Suddenly the fact that Lisa had heard the penthouse elevator squeal shortly before Barbara jumped made sense. Doctor Bev had gone up there. She'd sent Barbara's button to Hannah as insurance, intending to explain it if Roger failed to give her what she wanted. But Roger had killed her before she could explain and Hannah had been left with a mystery.

"She was smarter than you are," Roger said. "She figured it all out and she demanded millions from me."

"And of course you didn't want to give her those millions."

"Why would I? I could have anyone I wanted, not a rundown forty-year-old broad who thought she was hot stuff."

Hannah felt a moment's pity for Doctor Bev. She'd picked the wrong guy. "But you lost your Maserati when you killed her."

"It was insured and there's plenty more where that came from. And now I'm tired of talking. You've got time for one more question before I come out there and haul you in."

"Where did you get the tranquilizers you used to kill Doctor Bev?"

457

Roger laughed so loud that it boomed in her ears almost louder than the thunder that was rumbling overhead. "I know where to go and I've got connections. I can get anything for a price. Are you going to come closer, Hannah? Or do I have to come out there and kill you?"

"You have to come out here," Hannah said, sounding a lot more confident than she felt. Where was Mike? Where was Bill? Where were Lonnie and Rick? Had she been left to deal with a homicidal maniac all by herself?!

And then Roger smiled the most terrible smile she'd ever seen. It was a smile born of monsters, just the way Barbara had described him. He stepped out of the hinged pane and onto the track that led to her cage, and he moved like an acrobat toward her.

Hannah acted by pure instinct. She grabbed the bottle of window washing fluid and when he was close enough, she sprayed it directly into his eyes.

Roger bellowed and Hannah watched in disbelief as he reached up to rub his eyes. He staggered on the track and lost his balance, reaching out to brace himself against the dome, but the panes were slick with rain and he lost his balance. He screamed as he toppled from the track and his voice faded into the distance as he fell three stories into the parking lot.

Hannah didn't look. She couldn't. She just huddled in the bottom of the cage and trembled as Mike and three deputies came through the door and rushed to the open window.

"Hannah!" Mike yelled. "Bring the cage here."

"I . . . I . . . okay," Hannah managed to say, pushing the lever.

"Shut it off," Mike instructed, and Hannah wondered how he knew that she might very well have kept going. "Give me your hand."

Hannah reached out and Mike grabbed her hands to help her out of the cage. She might have lost her balance and collapsed to the floor in shock if he hadn't gathered her into his arms and held her.

"Good job, Hannah," he said. "We got his confession on tape."

"You mean . . . you were here all along?" Hannah managed to ask, beginning to gather her wits about her.

"Yes, but we had you covered. The minute he tried to get in the cage with you, we would have grabbed him."

Hannah drew back and slapped him hard. "I was terrified that you wouldn't make it here in time. Don't ever do anything like that to me again!"

"What are you talking about? You were perfectly safe."

"But I didn't know that!" Hannah began to tremble with anger and then she started to cry. "You're awful! And I hate you!"

Mike gathered her back into his arms and held her. "No, you don't. You were just scared. And if there were some way we could have let you know we were there, we would have."

"Is he . . . dead?" Hannah asked, feeling slightly appeased.

"The boys are down there now, but it looks bad from up here. He landed in the parking lot with nothing to break his fall."

"Then I . . . I killed him?"

"Not you. Circumstances killed him and it's what he deserves. He almost murdered the best secretary we ever had at the sheriff's station. We all love Barbara. And even worse, he was about to kill the woman I love. I do love you, Hannah. You know that, don't you? I know I don't always act like it, but I do."

Just then the stairwell door burst open and Lonnie ran in. "He's dead," he announced. "His head hit the parking lot like a ripe . . ." He glanced at Hannah and stopped speaking. "Never mind."

"Good," Mike said. "That'll save the taxpayers the expense of a trial."

"Andrea and Norman are down in the penthouse. Is it okay if they come up?"

"Sure. They can take Hannah home. We've got work to do here." Mike gave Hannah another hug and then released her. And when Lonnie left he said very quietly, "I'm glad we talked this afternoon, Hannah. I went to see Warren and I was already on my way back to you when Barbara and Andrea called."

"You were?" Hannah was confused. "What took you so long?"

"It wasn't very long. I got the call from Barbara and I'd just hung up when Andrea called. It took me another ten minutes to get here, but that's all."

Hannah stared at him in shock. "Really? It seemed like much longer than that!"

Mike hugged her again. "Have you heard that time flies when you're having fun?"

"Yes," Hannah said.

"Well, I guess it must be just the opposite when you're not having fun."

CHAPTER THIRTY

One week had passed since Hannah's harrowing experience in the window washing safety cage and she was smiling as she arrived at the Lake Eden Inn with Norman.

"I think it's nice that your mother always gives these congratulatory dinners for you," he said as they made their way to the dining room.

"I do, too. I wonder if she'd invite us to a consolation dinner if I didn't catch the killer." Norman gave her a shocked look and she laughed. "Just kidding. Come on. Let's see if we're the first ones here."

As they approached the table they saw that there were four early arrivals sitting at the table. "Too late to switch Mother's place cards," Hannah said under her breath. "I'll bet I'm the bologna again."

"The what?"

"The bologna in a Norman and Mike sandwich. Mother always seats me between the two of you. Sometimes I feel like roast beef, or peanut butter, or even tuna salad. Tonight I feel like bologna."

Norman was laughing as he greeted Michelle and Lonnie. Seated opposite them were Lisa and Herb, and Hannah went over to greet them. "Hi, guys," she said. "Where's your Cupcake Security blazer, Herb?"

"I'm off tonight, but I've got my best three guys working at the mall."

From the way Lisa was grinning, Hannah sensed breaking news. "What are they doing at the mall?"

"Protecting Stephanie Bascomb. She's out there picking up a few things at the jewelry store. Lisa and I think it might have something to do with that ride the mayor took in a certain expensive convertible."

"I see." Hannah exchanged amused glances with Lisa. "And will they make sure that Mrs. Mayor gets home safely?"

"Yes, but not right away," Lisa told her. "Claire's opening Beau Monde Fashions at seven, just for her. And after Mrs. Bascomb selects a few things she desperately needs, Herb's boys will bring her out here to meet the mayor for dinner."

"Your staff has nice duty tonight," Hannah said, nodding at Herb.

"The guys think so," he said. "They get to"

eat an expensive dinner on the mayor's tab."

Andrea and Bill walked in and when everyone had greeted them, Hannah turned to Bill. "Mother said that Barbara was back at work. How is she doing?"

"Great. She works mornings and spends the afternoons with her real father at the hospital. She told us they're making up for lost time."

"That's wonderful," Lisa said. "I'm so glad to hear she's doing all right."

"Barbara's a lot better than all right," Mike told her. "She's already found everything the temporary secretary misfiled."

"That's right," Andrea said. "Best of all, she even found Bill's umbrella and that's been missing since last fall."

As they chatted and found their places, the rest of their party arrived. Soon everyone was seated, including Hannah, who was the bologna just as she'd expected. Sally had opened champagne and sparkling white grape juice for the table and everyone was in a celebratory mood.

"I've got a question for you," Andrea said, turning to Hannah. "How did you ever have the courage to get into that window-washing cage?"

"Remember when you said you'd rather die than step into something that hung outside the dome above the third floor?"

"I remember."

"Well, that was my choice. So I got in."

Delores shivered a little. "You were very brave, dear." Then she raised her glass. "Let's have a toast to Hannah and everyone here who helped to catch another killer."

Their glasses were filled and presented to them by Sally and two of her best waitresses. Everyone raised their glasses and took a sip.

"Hear, hear!" Doc Knight said, smiling at Delores. "And now I think that Lori has an announcement to make." He gave her a little nudge. "Come on, Lori. It's time for your speech."

Delores stood up, rather reluctantly Hannah thought, and cleared her throat. "There's a second reason I asked all of you to join us here tonight. I need to announce . . . I mean, I *want* to announce that . . . well . . ." She stopped speaking and cleared her throat again.

"Just tell them, Lori," Doc encouraged her. "Everyone here loves you. They'll understand."

"I hope so. Anyway . . . the second reason we asked all of you to join us here is because . . ." She faltered again and turned to Doc. "I just can't do it. The girls loved their father."

"So did you, Lori, but time has passed, and you don't look all that good in black."

Delores turned to look at him. "Thank you . . . I think." Then she turned to address them all again. "Doc and I are getting married."

Doc got up to put his arm around her. "Well done!" Then he turned to them. "The thing is, Lori and I need your help. We don't want a lot of hoopla or anything like that, but my patients and Lori's friends are going to feel cheated if they don't get to come to the wedding. And that's where you come in, if you approve, that is."

"Of course we approve," Bill said.

Mike nodded. "You bet we do."

"Tell them what we need, Lori." Doc gave her another hug.

Delores took a deep breath. "If you girls don't mind, I really need you to plan the wedding for us. We'll help you with the guest list, but whatever else you decide is fine with us. Will you help us?"

"I will," Lisa said quickly, "and I'm not even your daughter."

"Thank you, Lisa." Delores beamed at her.

"I'll help you, Mother," Michelle said. "I'm really glad you're marrying Doc. He's perfect for you."

"And I'll help," Andrea offered. "I think

it's just wonderful!"

Delores turned to the only daughter who hadn't spoken, the one who had been old enough to grow up with her father and love him the most. "Hannah?"

Hannah winked at her mother to show she was kidding and then she gave a shrug. "I don't know, Mother. On one hand, I like the idea of getting our flu shots for free."

There was a burst of laughter around the table and the tension dissipated. Hannah waited until everyone was silent again, and then she continued. "On the other hand, Doc's going to be our stepfather and we don't even know his first name. You call him *Doc.* Everybody calls him *Doc.* That's like calling the president of a company *Prez.* I don't know if I can help you with the wedding plans if I don't know the groom's first name."

Delores exchanged an amused glance with Doc. "I told you before, dear. His name is Doc."

"I know that's what everybody calls him, but what's his *real* first name?"

"Doc!" Delores said again, dissolving into a cascade of laughter. "It was Murdoch, but he shortened it to Doc. I'm going to marry Doctor Doc!"

RED VELVET CUPCAKE
MURDER RECIPE INDEX

BAKING CONVERSION CHART

These conversions are approximate, but they'll work just fine for Hannah Swensen's recipes.

VOLUME:

U.S.	Metric
1/2 teaspoon	2 milliliters
1 teaspoon	5 milliliters
1 tablespoon	15 milliliters
1/4 cup	50 milliliters
1/3 cup	75 milliliters
1/2 cup	125 milliliters
3/4 cup	175 milliliters
1 cup	1/4 liter

WEIGHT:

U.S.	Metric
1 ounce	28 grams
1 pound	454 grams

Oven Temperature:

Degrees Fahrenheit	Degrees Centigrade	British (Regulo) Gas Mark
325 degrees F.	165 degrees C.	3
350 degrees F.	175 degrees C.	4
375 degrees F.	190 degrees C.	5

Note: Hannah's rectangular sheet cake pan, 9 inches by 13 inches, is approximately 23 centimeters by 32.5 centimeters.

ABOUT THE AUTHOR

Like Hannah Swensen, **Joanne Fluke** was born and raised in a small town in rural Minnesota, but now lives in sunny Southern California. She is currently working on her next Hannah Swensen mystery and readers are welcome to contact her at Gr8Clues@aol.com, or by visiting her website, murdershebaked.com.